The Bold and the Dominant

The Doms of Her Life, Book 3

Shayla Black, Jenna Jacob, and Isabella LaPearl

The Bold and the Dominant
The Doms of Her Life, Book 3
Shayla Black, Jenna Jacob, and Isabella LaPearl

Published by Shayla Black, Jenna Jacob and Isabella LaPearl

Edited by: Shayla Black, Riane Holt, and Amy Knupp of Blue Otter

ISBN: 978-1936596348

Authors' Note

The DOMS OF HER LIFE is a serialized succession of novels best read in order:
One Dom To Love
The Young and The Submissive
The Bold and The Dominant
The Edge Of Dominance (Coming Soon)

We hope you enjoy reading these stories as much as we did writing them.

Happy Reading!

Shayla Black
Jenna Jacob
Isabella LaPearl

Dedication

This story is dedicated to all the survivors. Those amazing souls among us who have triumphed over evil, conquered their demons, and bravely put one foot in front of the other each and every day. You inspire us.

For our husbands, who give constant support and understanding.

Thank you to the readers who joined us on this wild ride. Keep hanging on. It might be a little bumpy for a bit—but in a good way.

Acknowledgements

A special thanks to Nurse Melissa, Rachel, Charity, Riane, Amy, Liz, Chloe, and Fedora for your insight, guidance, and help.

And finally a toast to each other for the endless hours of laughter, bloopers, and church ladies. The friendship shared is priceless.

Thank You

Shayla Black, Jenna Jacob, Isabella LaPearl

Chapter One

December 5, four a.m. — Liam's lodge

"Hammer. Wake up," a familiar voice whispered in his ear. "There's a problem."

Macen "Hammer" Hammerman jackknifed up, the fog of sleep dissipating. Liam O'Neill stood above him, leaning over the bed.

Why the hell was his best friend waking him up in the middle of the night?

With a frown, Hammer rose on one elbow. "What?"

Liam's stare fell on Raine Kendall in the rumpled bed they'd all shared last night. Hammer glanced at the woman they both loved. Images of her moaning, melting, and writhing between them flashed through Hammer's brain like a sensual strobe. Thankfully, she was still asleep, her inky lashes fanning over her rosy cheeks.

But Liam's face tightened, the man's tense expression giving him pause. "Tell me."

"She's exhausted. Let's not wake her." He jerked his head at the open door. "Bathroom."

Hammer scowled. Had something happened after he'd crashed? Had Liam and Raine fought? No, he wouldn't have slept through that. Whether she was upset or in the throes of passion, she never held back.

What if Liam had reconsidered their arrangement and refused to share her anymore? That idea whacked Macen with fury. After years of denying himself her touch, he couldn't wait to have her again. If his Irish pal thought she still belonged exclusively to him simply because she'd once worn his collar, he'd lost his fucking mind. Hammer had rescued the scared runaway from an alley and taken care of her for six years. That damn well counted for something.

Besides, Raine needed them both. She'd only begun to lower those towering walls around her heart in the past two days, when they'd finally started working together. Sharing her might be a new arrangement, but he and Liam had been down this path before, though not with her…and not with success. Still, Raine made them better men—and partners. Hammer knew Liam had sensed the same perfection when they'd held her. Would he really want to mess with that?

Before Hammer could say a word, Liam grabbed his trousers, donned them, and stomped to the bathroom.

Hammer brushed his lips over Raine's forehead. "I won't let anything or anyone come between us, precious. I promise."

Feeling a twinge of pain in his jaw where Liam had punched him the night before, Hammer stood and worked it from side to side. Their fight had been inevitable. Jealousy and resentment had brewed for the past month, ever since Liam had taken an interest in Raine. Hopefully, the brawl had finally cleared the air between them.

Sighing, Hammer yanked his pants up and joined Liam, shutting the door behind them. In the light, Macen noticed his friend's nose was slightly swollen, but neither of them looked too worse for wear.

"I'm listening. What's the problem?"

Liam sighed. "Gwyneth just called me."

What did Liam's ex-wife want? The British beauty looked like every man's wet dream, but under the pretty exterior, she was his worst nightmare. "You keep in touch with that bitch?"

"Hell no." Liam reared back. "You know I changed my number after the divorce. I did it so she couldn't call me."

"How did she find you, then?"

"No bloody idea." But he didn't look thrilled.

"So…she called you. Why is that a problem?"

Liam hesitated. "She's at Shadows."

"*What?*" That declaration jolted away the vestiges of sleep. He raked a hand through his mussed hair. "I thought Gwyneth lived in London. Why did she drag her skanky ass across the pond and park it in my club?"

"She said she needs to see me." He rolled his eyes.

If his ex-wife simply wanted to shoot the shit—or even ask for more money—she wouldn't have flown over five thousand miles to do it. Foreboding gonged through Hammer's gut.

"Any idea why?"

"She says it's life or death." Liam sent him a dry stare. "She bawled it, actually."

If Gwyneth meant *her* death, it wouldn't be a huge tragedy.

Hammer crossed his arms over his chest. "And that concerns you how?"

"She wouldn't explain, just said she needs to see me right away."

In other words, Gwyneth was staging more theatrics. Hammer scoffed. "Surely you're not thinking of meeting her."

"I'd rather not, but I doubt she'll leave of her own accord, and I can't think you want to leave her in your club."

"Not for five minutes. I'll call Pike and have him kick her out."

Liam gritted his teeth. "Fine by me. She's the last person Raine ever needs to meet."

"Absolutely." Gwyneth had a razor blade for a tongue. No way would he let the bitch slice Raine open.

Hammer reached into his pocket and pulled out his phone to call the Dungeon Monitor he'd left in charge. He hoped this would fix their problem, but he knew Gwyneth. She wouldn't be there if she didn't intend to stir the shit pot. No one had a bigger spoon.

Gwyneth despised him, so if she'd come to his club and was willing to deal with him to see Liam, she wanted something badly.

"If she's after more money, she's got a lot of nerve hitting you up. She cheated, and you still gave her a generous settlement." Hammer glanced at his phone. Sixteen missed calls and three text messages. "Shit."

Liam leaned over to read his screen. "Bloody hell. Here we go."

Pike: Call me ASAP.

Pike: Liam's wife is here. Help!

Pike: What a cunt! BFP.

"BFP?" Liam asked.

"Big fucking problem," he explained. "Obviously, he hasn't thrown her out because he thinks she's still your wife. I'll set him straight."

Pike answered on the first ring. "Thank fuck it's you, Hammer. What am I supposed to do with this…woman?"

"Show her the door. Gwyneth is Liam's *ex*-wife. She's got no business at my club."

"I've tried to get her to leave, but she's not budging."

"Call the cops. She's trespassing."

The Dungeon Monitor hesitated. "If I do that, what happens to the baby?"

Hammer froze. "The what?"

He couldn't possibly have heard that right.

"What is it?" Liam frowned.

He thrust a hand in his friend's face and focused on Pike. "Say that again."

"A baby. She's got a fucking baby. I assumed it was Liam's, so I put them in your office."

Oh, holy shit. No. That was impossible…right?

Hammer eyed his friend, his brain whirling like a cyclone. Liam, a father? That would be news to everyone—especially to Liam.

"I'll call you right back," Hammer barked and hung up. Then he turned to Liam and pointed to the toilet. "You should probably sit down."

Liam scowled. "Why? What's going on?"

Hammer hoped he'd jumped to conclusions. Pike had only assumed. Liam and Gwyneth had separated over two years ago, so it shouldn't even be possible. In theory.

He pinned Liam with a heavy stare. There was no delicate

way to ask this question. "When was the last time you fucked your ex-wife?"

He gaped at Hammer as if he'd lost his mind. "Why the hell would you ask me that?"

"Because Gwyneth arrived at Shadows with a *baby*. Please tell me there's no chance that's your kid."

Liam paused for a long moment, then turned white as a ghost and stumbled back, sliding onto the toilet seat as if all the air had escaped his body. "Oh, fuck me…"

Hammer gnashed his teeth. "Apparently, she already did."

* * *

If this kid was his, Hammer was right; Gwyneth had fucked him but good.

Liam rubbed a hand over his face, his thoughts whirling. *A baby?*

"I last saw her at a benefit about a week after our divorce was final. Because I helped a local children's hospital with fundraising, I received a community award. Gwyneth walked in, and I couldn't leave. So I got shitfaced. Next thing I know, it's morning. I'm naked in her hotel room, and she's going on about how we'd shared the fuck of the century."

Hammer cringed. "Did you?"

"No." He paused, trying to stay calm and logical. "At least I don't think so."

"You don't *think* so? Either you put your dick in her or you didn't."

"I was bloody drunk. I don't remember."

"But you don't know for sure?" When he shook his head, Hammer looked as if he wanted to hit something. "Fuck. Fuck, fuck, fuck."

Liam broke out in a cold sweat.

"Exactly how long ago was the benefit?"

He wished he could forget. "A year ago this past October."

Mentally, Liam counted out the months and watched Hammer do the same on his fingers.

"That would make this baby…what, five or six months old?" Hammer shook his head. "Hang on. Your ex isn't the kind of woman to endure nine months of pregnancy and a minute of single motherhood in silence."

"You're right," Liam agreed, grateful for Hammer's common sense.

"If this baby is yours, why did she wait until now to say something?"

"That's a fine question. Did Pike happen to mention how old the baby was?"

"I was too shocked to ask."

Liam shook his head. "I won't believe the kid is mine until Gwyneth proves it because she's too crafty to have come all this way with some half-baked notion. She'll have spun a tight timeline, like a fucking spider determined to trap me in her web." He swallowed the ball of unease lodged in his throat. "Christ, I need a drink."

"Sounds like you also need a paternity test and a damn good lawyer. But you know…maybe she's not here to claim this kid is yours. Maybe she's here for something else." Hammer didn't sound like he believed that.

Neither did Liam.

If the child was his, he'd be a good and loving father. Whatever his beefs with its mother, the baby shouldn't suffer. But if this was another of Gwyneth's manipulations, she might not survive his wrath.

Hammer clapped him on the back. "Let's move this downstairs before Raine wakes up and overhears us. We'll talk in the kitchen. And get you that drink."

With a nod, Liam staggered to his feet and exited the bathroom, pausing to stare at Raine. She looked beautiful in sleep. Peaceful. She'd had so little of that in her life, and he refused to let Gwyneth destroy it.

Last night, he and Hammer had gotten Raine between them for the first time. He'd never felt such pleasure as he had sharing the woman he loved with his best friend. Finally, they'd managed to open her heart, and she'd unfurled so passionately between them. That nagging jealousy had plagued him again afterward, but he'd shoved it down. He and Macen balanced one another to be exactly what she needed. If they could just drown in Raine's soft body again, love and protect her, he'd work through that issue.

But his ex-wife's sudden appearance—only hours after they'd committed to Raine—put all that on hold. *Bloody terrible timing…* Liam wanted to howl at the injustice.

"Come on, man," Hammer urged.

With a reluctant nod, Liam turned and followed him downstairs. Once they reached the kitchen, he sat at the table, trying to force a calm he didn't feel.

Hammer prowled through the liquor cabinet in the adjacent living room, then held up a bottle. "Scotch?"

He'd love some liquid oblivion, but hadn't that gotten him into trouble in the first place? "I'd better not. I need to keep my wits about me."

"Especially if you're going to tangle with that snake." Hammer stashed the bottle and wandered back into the kitchen, pacing.

"Agreed." Encroaching rage and panic threatened to overtake him, but he couldn't succumb. "I'll head down the mountain and handle this mess Gwyneth is trying to lay in my lap. I'll be back by nightfall."

"Are you crazy? If you leave to see your ex now, Raine will be devastated."

"Why?" Liam reared back. "She knows that Gwyneth cheated on me and that I don't love her."

"In her head, yeah. But in her heart?" Hammer shook his head.

"If this baby is mine, it was conceived well before I met Raine. It's not as though I strayed."

"The baby won't upset her. You leaving now to see Gwyneth will. Remember, you uncollared her five days ago. You did it for the right reasons, but it cut her to the bone. If Raine wakes up and you're gone, what do you imagine she'll think?"

Liam groaned. "That I mean to dump her again, this time for my ex and our ready-made family."

"Yep, and all of her abandonment issues will resurface. Besides, I'd rather not leave you to deal with that bitch alone. I may have kept my distance these last few years, but we're in this together. I won't fail you again."

Liam gave a little sigh of relief that Macen had his back

once more. "That means a lot to me, but I don't need you to hold my hand. Gwyneth is my ex-wife. My mess. I'll clean it up. I don't want it touching you or Raine."

"There must be another solution besides you leaving. After we pried her open physically and emotionally last night, she'll be vulnerable for days. Despite the shit ton of progress we made last night, a few hours of bliss isn't enough for her to change the way she thinks. She'll shut down. God knows how hard it will be to open her again."

Bloody hell, Hammer was right.

He pinched the bridge of his nose to quell the developing ache behind his eyes. "I need to find out if that's my kid."

Macen scowled, looking downright ruthless. "Let *me* go to the club. I'll sort Gwyneth out and get you an answer."

"I don't think that will work any better. If you leave now, what will Raine think of that?"

Hammer paused, then cursed. "That the conquest is over, and I've moved on to find another. Damn it."

"Precisely. That's why I want to sit her down and explain. I'll reassure her that I mean to be back by tonight."

"Explain what? We don't have any facts except that your ex-wife is in town, she's brought a kid, and she wants to see you."

Liam rubbed a palm against his aching forehead. "We have to tell Raine something. Keeping her in the dark is asking for trouble. After two days of drilling the importance of honesty and communication into her head, we promised her the same. Surely you haven't forgotten how she just handed us our balls because we weren't walking the walk."

"How could I?" He snorted. "I don't want to be dishonest, but it's our duty as her Doms to protect her. Gwyneth's sudden appearance will incite Raine's worst insecurities."

"You're right. I want to give her more credit. And give *us* some. But after only one night together—most of it having sex or sleeping—we haven't established a solid foundation of trust yet."

"Exactly. And I'll be honest. If Gwyneth finds out about Raine, I'm worried your ex will do something devious. We know she's capable."

Was she ever... "If Gwyneth came to make a mess of my life, I wish she'd done it a month from now. Hell, even a week from now. By then, our relationship with Raine would be stronger. But Gwyneth has already lit the fuse on this bomb."

"I don't like it."

"I'm determined to keep Raine safe, just as you are, but Juliet's suicide rattled you. It makes you a mite overprotective at times."

"Don't psychoanalyze me," Macen grumbled. "You used to be easy to deal with. When we shared in the past, you let me make the decisions."

For eight years, Hammer alone had carried the burden of failing Juliet. Now that Liam knew the circumstances, he realized he'd failed the woman just as much.

"I was barely more than a kid then, and I let you decide with Juliet because she was *your* wife." And Liam hadn't loved her the way he loved Raine. "But her death taught me that if we're both involved, we should both be responsible."

Hammer nodded. "You're right. And that was the hardest fucking lesson to learn."

Liam stood and stuck out his hand. "I know. I almost lost my best friend because of it."

Hammer brought him in for a shoulder bump and a manly hug. "Like you could get rid of me that easily."

With a little smile, he sat back in his chair. "How do we prepare Raine so she isn't blindsided?"

"I can't believe you two are finished with that pretty girl already." Seth Cooper sauntered down the stairs and entered the kitchen. "Pussies. I have more staying power than you both combined."

"They look like they left Raine alone to start in on each other," Beck, aka Dr. Kenneth Beckman, said with a smirk, waltzing in behind Seth, surprisingly showered and dressed.

"Piss off, you wanker," Liam grumbled as he sat once more. "Go back to bed."

"But before you do, make some coffee," Macen groused.

With a shake of his head, Beck crossed the room and began brewing a pot of liquid caffeine. "Still haven't figured out how to work complicated machinery, huh?"

Hammer eyed the coffeemaker gratefully. "We're a little preoccupied at the moment, trying to sort out a clusterfuck."

"What mess did you two make this time?" Beck asked.

"Did Raine pack her bags and leave you again?" Seth looked at them as if they were idiots.

"No," Liam shot back. "She's upstairs sleeping. My ex-wife is the problem."

"Newsflash: She's always been a problem."

Hammer agreed, then filled the men in on Gwyneth's unexpected visit and the extra bundle of joy she'd brought with her.

"Holy shit! Is it yours? Did you have ex sex with Gwyneth?" Seth looked as if he might puke at the thought.

"I don't know." Liam sounded every bit as miserable as he felt.

"Or maybe you nailed your ex because your palm had a date with some other cock." Beck chuckled.

Liam flipped him off.

"Is she hot at least?" Beck wagged his brows.

Hammer rolled his eyes. "Oh, she's hot, all right. A hot mess of toxic waste."

"I can do toxic." Beck shrugged. "Does she like pain?"

Liam shook his head. "She's much better at dishing it out than taking it."

Seth just laughed. "It's always a goddamn soap opera with you two."

"If you're not going to help, get the fuck out," Hammer growled.

"Hey! I dropped my life in New York and braved the San Andreas Fault to help," Seth defended with a scowl, then turned a concerned gaze on Liam. "Do you remember *anything*?"

"I do. Waking up next to Gwyneth in horror. I leapt out of bed, hit the loo, then got the hell out."

"Crap." Seth looked stunned. "How old is this kid?"

"We need to find out." Hammer scowled and plucked his cell phone from his pocket. He dialed Pike, then engaged the speakerphone.

"That was a little bit longer than 'right back.' Just saying," Pike grumbled.

"What's happening there?"

"Nothing. Mom and baby are in your office," Pike

answered.

"Who else besides you has seen them?" Liam asked anxiously.

"No one. Since a kid at a BDSM club is bad for business, I stashed them out of sight quickly. Most folks were gone by then, anyway."

Liam let out a breath of relief. The less anyone knew about Gwyneth, the better chance gossip wouldn't reach Raine before he'd had a chance to tell her himself.

"Good," Hammer replied. "But I don't want her in my office. When we hang up, stash them in one of the rooms we've just remodeled. The farther back, the better."

"You got it."

"Thanks. Now, how old is this baby?" Hammer demanded.

"Um…" Pike went silent. "I don't know."

"Take a wild guess."

"It's small."

"*How* small?" Hammer exhaled heavily.

"It's a baby-sized baby. It's… I don't know, wearing little clothes and shit."

"All babies wear little clothes." Hammer gnashed his teeth. "Is it a boy or a girl?"

"I haven't volunteered to change its diaper, but I'm guessing it's a boy because she calls it Kyle and swears he looks like his daddy."

Liam's heart froze. "Does it fucking look like me?"

"How the hell would I know? All babies look the same—drooling, squalling, smelly little monsters," Pike grumbled.

Hammer muted his phone. "Why did Master Donald and his wife, Vivian, have to be out of town right now?"

Good question. They were getting nowhere with Pike. "When are they due back?"

"Later today, but we need to take action before then."

"Hammer," Pike shouted. "Hammer!"

He unmuted the phone. "What?"

"When are you coming back to deal with this? I'm not getting hazard pay here, and I've got to tell you, O'Neill, your wife is—"

"Ex-wife," Liam barked.

"We're working on it," Hammer insisted. "But we need to know how old the kid is. Just give me your gut feeling, Pike. Is it a month? A year?"

"I have no goddamn clue," he screeched. "It's small and it screams. I'm trying to be helpful, but…shit."

"God, you two are morons," Beck cut in, all business now. "Pike, can the kid walk?"

"I don't know. She held him a lot, but now he's sitting in a little cage thing, drooling."

"It's called a playpen," Beck snorted. "Tell me how she held him. Was it in her arms or on her hip?"

"Mostly on her hip, but when she fed him, she, like, cradled him."

"Breast or bottle?"

"Bottle, damn it," Pike groused. "But I would have liked to have seen her tits. Gorgeous woman. Nice rack."

Hammer rolled his eyes.

Liam banged his head on the table, wishing he could just get an answer. Or disappear altogether.

"Did he reach up and grab the bottle when he ate?" Beck continued.

"Yeah," Pike answered.

Liam was damn glad Beck knew what questions to ask. He didn't have a clue.

Beck nodded. "Okay. Does he have teeth?"

"I saw two on the bottom when he screamed earlier. That kid has a healthy set of lungs."

"Hang on, Pike." Hammer darted an expectant glance at Beck. "What do you think?"

The doctor shrugged. "Based on what I've heard, my best guess is somewhere between five and seven months."

That fit perfectly with Gwyneth's silken-spun timeline. Dread sank into Liam's belly like a boulder.

"Fuck," Hammer breathed.

"God, did I really knock her up that night?" Liam groaned, slapping a hand down his face.

"I think we've got a better idea now, Pike," Hammer said. "Thanks. We'll be in touch."

"Wait! When the hell are you coming back?" Pike sounded

antsy.

Liam and Hammer shared a gaze of silent communication. The answer to that was something they still had to work out.

"Not sure yet. I'll keep you posted." Hammer ended the call.

Liam's head pounded as if a drum line practiced on his skull. "We have to tell Raine something when she gets up."

The coffee finished brewing, and Hammer pounced on it, nearly shoving Beck aside to pour a steaming mug. He took a sip with a long, satisfied sigh. "Until we're sure that kid is yours, I think our responsibility is to shield her from Gwyneth."

"Withholding the truth isn't the answer," Liam interjected. "Besides, Raine is clever. She'll figure it out."

"She will." Beck nodded knowingly. "She's proven herself pretty capable at handling whatever life throws at her, even you two bozos. You just need to sit Raine down and tell her about Gwyneth's unexpected visit the right way."

"There is no right way," Hammer asserted. "Not without facts."

"I agree," Seth piped up. "If you tell Raine that Gwyneth is here to pin paternity on you, then it turns out your ex is here for a totally different reason, you've upset her for nothing."

Liam blinked in disbelief. "You'd withhold the truth? Guess that explains why you've never managed to keep a sub for much more than a night."

"Never wanted one for longer than that," Seth shot back. "I'm not saying lie to the girl."

"Neither am I," Hammer insisted.

"If you go mute, Raine will figure out long before you fess up that something's wrong," Beck chided. "You want to protect her, Hammer, but how is she supposed to feel secure if she knows you're not being honest?"

"Exactly." Liam nodded.

"I'm worried. We're asking Raine for a lot of trust. I don't think we've given her enough of a foundation yet." Hammer sent him a sour glare.

"Well, as entertaining as it is to watch you two ladies smack each other with your purses, I don't have time." Beck glanced at his watch. "I got a call from the hospital, and I have to get back and assist in an emergency surgery this afternoon. So Liam, I can take that spanking new Escalade of yours and leave, but I won't be back for at least five or six days."

Liam blanched. "That long?"

"Transplant patients are high maintenance."

"We can't leave Gwyneth and that baby at my club," Hammer pointed out. "She needs to find a hotel. Or better yet, go back to London."

Liam's phone buzzed in his pocket. He glanced at the screen, swore, and shoved it in his pants again. "Damn it, she won't stop calling. And I don't want this hanging over my head for days. I'd rather find out what she wants and put it behind me." Liam stood. "What if I ride down with Beck and hear what Gwyneth is bleating on about, then bring the car back by nightfall?"

"We already talked about this," Hammer reminded him.

"Not only that, you'll be giving her exactly what she wants," Seth pointed out. "You. Alone. Split apart from everyone who could support you, especially Hammer and Raine."

Liam paused. He hadn't considered that. Since Gwyneth was at Shadows, she already knew he was with Hammer, whose lifestyle she abhorred. Likely, she suspected Liam was involved in kink again as well. But she also knew they'd shared Juliet and might assume the two of them had found some sub to fill that role once more. Knowing Gwyneth's spiteful nature, if she'd come for him, she intended to wreak havoc—and would gleefully spread that to others in his life. She would start by dividing and conquering.

To hell with her. Whatever damage Gwyneth thought to incite, it only served to solidify his commitment to Hammer and Raine.

"Over my dead body," Hammer returned immediately. "I say we all go back. We'll tell Raine that Beck has an emergency. It's not a lie."

Liam shook his head. "It's also not the whole truth."

"Well, unless you're staying here, you need to be ready to pull out in thirty minutes," Beck said. "If you're going, you better figure out what to tell Raine as you pack up."

"Can I just say you two make me glad I lead a boring life?" Seth jabbed.

"Fuck you," Liam and Hammer shot back in tandem.

After Liam filled a mug of coffee, he followed Hammer upstairs again. Anxiety still gnawed at him. They had to reach some quick decisions. What would they tell Raine about their sudden departure? How would she react?

"Even if we agreed that we should tell her about Gwyneth, Beck's emergency doesn't give us long enough to explain everything and reassure her," Hammer said over his shoulder. "She'll have more than thirty minutes' worth of questions. We'll never get out the door in time."

As much as he hated it, Liam couldn't disagree. "And I can't see telling Raine in the car."

"With Beck and Seth there? No. She'd be embarrassed if they see her upset, and I'd rather not have them witness her slicing our nuts off with the sharp edge of her tongue."

"I don't like it," Liam rejoined. "As soon as we reach Shadows, we sit Raine down and tell her everything."

As they approached the bedroom, Hammer turned back with a scowl. "When we reach Shadows, we figure out our next move."

Before Liam could argue, Hammer pushed the door open and stepped inside. The soft moonlight reflecting off the snow spilled through the curtains. The scent of their shared passion lingered in the room, and Liam slid his gaze over the sheets draping her curves. His cock swelled instantly behind his zipper.

Hammer charged across the room and flipped on the bathroom light, then began tossing clothes into their suitcase. Liam gathered their condoms and personal items from the nightstand and shoved them in a duffel bag. Once he'd finished, he sat on the mattress beside Raine and skated his knuckles over her bare shoulder. Her skin felt like warm velvet.

Visions of all the ways she'd seamlessly taken them both last night, shattering time and again around them, filled his brain. How long would it be until they could lose themselves in that nirvana again? He had to hope that Gwyneth wouldn't try to drive a wedge between them.

The chances of that… Liam grimaced. Not good.

Macen zipped the luggage shut, then sat down beside him. Liam switched on the bedside lamp. Raine recoiled and frowned.

Her eyes flickered open, big pools of blue, before she slammed them shut again, then grabbed the edge of the pillow and folded it over her face. “It’s too early.”

“I know, love,” Liam crooned.

She sighed, then rolled to her back, the pillow falling away. She wore an adorable pout as she brushed her dark hair from her face.

“What time is it?” Raine asked hoarsely.

“Before sunrise.” Hammer dragged the covers down, exposing her to the morning air.

Goose bumps broke out all over her body. Neither could resist touching her. Liam brushed a hand over her cheek. Hammer stroked a soft hand up her calf, fingertips gliding along the back of her knee, before dipping down to her graceful feet.

Her nipples hardened. Her pale skin flushed. Liam bit back the need to strip off and bury himself inside her, to forget everything else. He held back, instead cupping her head and caressing his thumb over her temple. “It’s time to rise and shine.”

She stretched, her back arching, her nipples thrusting up in invitation. Her legs parted slightly. Beside him, Hammer tensed, his gaze fixed on that bare, slick paradise they both wanted again. Oblivious, Raine groaned and reached up, letting out a happy sigh as she melted into the mattress.

When she opened her eyes once more, the come-hither enticement on her face nearly made him decide that Beck’s timetable must have some flexibility.

Unable to stop himself, Liam brushed his palm down her shoulder, lingered on her breast, then splayed over her abdomen. Hammer’s fingertips reached up her thigh. She shivered.

“Can’t we stay in bed?” she breathed.

“No.” Liam wished they could as he cradled her hip. “Get that saucy, wee ass moving.”

She propped herself up on her elbows to glance at them. Her gaze landed just beyond Hammer, on the suitcase all packed by the balcony doors. She zipped her stare over to the empty nightstand. Her pout became a frown, disappointment and confusion crossing her brow. “We’re leaving?”

Hammer sent her a sharp nod. “Unfortunately, we have to

head back to the club."

Raine blinked. "Already? I thought we were going to stay here for a few days."

"Beck got called into surgery this afternoon," Liam explained.

"Then let him take the car and go. I'm sure the three of us could find *something* to do while he's gone." She batted her lashes.

"Trust me, precious," Macen growled. "There's nothing we'd rather do than come back to bed and make you scream, but Beck won't be back for days, maybe a week. We can't stay here that long, no matter how badly we'd like to."

"And we would." Liam stroked a hand through her silky mane. "Now up with you. Here. Take a sip of coffee and get dressed."

As she sat up, Liam handed her the mug. She wrinkled her nose at the scent. "That sucks, but I suppose that's the life of a surgeon."

"We'll make it up to you," Hammer promised with a sly grin.

"Deal." She took a sip of the dark brew, then winced and handed the coffee back.

Liam took the mug. "Now stop driving us to distraction. Up with you. We've got to get on the road."

She frowned at them as she climbed out of bed. "Let me brush my teeth and use the bathroom."

"Ten minutes." Hammer rose and retrieved the suitcase.

Liam grabbed the duffel. "We'll be downstairs. Don't keep us waiting."

Chapter Two

Raine blinked as she watched them leave the bedroom. "Seriously?"

Last night, she'd finally been granted her dream come true when Liam and Hammer had taken her together. Never before had she felt so treasured, surrounded, and safe. After all the sensual touches and words of love they'd exchanged, this morning they'd hustled her back to real life without a single kiss. Or even a hug. No, she hadn't expected rainbows or carriage rides—or marriage proposals. But they'd behaved as if nothing particularly special had happened. In fact, she'd sensed a strange vibe humming around them.

With a sigh, she padded into the bathroom. Maybe Beck's need to head down the mountain had thrown the guys for a loop. Someone's life hung in the balance, and it wasn't as if she wanted Beck's patient to die so she could have a leisurely morning in bed with Liam and Hammer. But yeah, she'd expected more.

After emptying her bladder and searching around for her toiletries, she realized they'd left her one zippered pouch with her toothbrush. A comb lay next to it. She frowned. No skin care, makeup, or deodorant. She wanted to poke her head down the stairs and point out their oversight…except she bet it wasn't.

Raine huffed. She could do a bit more in ten minutes. After years of having her under his roof, Hammer especially should know that.

Instead, they couldn't shove her out of the lodge—where everything wonderful had happened—fast enough. Simply because of Beck's tight timeline…or did they want to put last night behind them?

Frowning, she completed the parts of her morning routine she could and tried to figure out what the heck was going on. Nothing added up. She hadn't thought they'd lose interest already, but she wasn't sure what other conclusion to reach. Disquiet wound through her.

As Raine headed out of the bathroom with her few items in hand, she noticed the pile of neatly folded clothing on the overstuffed chair in the corner. When she shook out the garments, she realized they were the same ones she'd worn to the lodge a few short days ago. Those two hadn't packed her many clothes. Did that mean they had intended to spend most of their time with her in bed…or that they hadn't planned to stay here for long?

Scowling now, she pulled on the little black skirt, her tank, cardigan, and kitten heels. No undergarments. At the moment, she wasn't sure whether that delighted her or just pissed her off.

Feeling unsettled, she grabbed her toiletries again and made her way downstairs. Liam rushed from the kitchen and shoved a travel mug in her hand. "I made some of that tea you like."

Raine softened a little that he'd remembered. "Thank you."

He dipped his head, and she settled against his warmth. But when she parted her lips to kiss him, he merely planted a peck on her cheek, then pulled away. "Everyone is waiting in the car."

Before she could reply, he ushered her out to the chilly winter morning, helping her through the snow and into the backseat of the warming SUV. She scooted into the middle, against Hammer's big body, as Liam dashed back to the porch to lock the door of the lodge. Neither Beck nor Seth turned his head from the front seat as Liam slid into the vehicle, sandwiching her in.

From the window, she watched the lodge as they pulled away, feeling bereft at leaving this place—and the magical night they'd shared—behind.

As Seth stared at his phone, Beck raised an impatient gaze from the rearview mirror. "Settled?"

"Good morning to you, too," Raine quipped.

"Morning. Sorry to rush you, princess." Beck's tone lacked remorse.

"I totally understand why you have to get back," Raine replied, then sipped her tea and sent Liam and Hammer a forced smile. "They've promised to make it up to me."

"We will." Hammer arched a brow at her. "Did you not get enough sleep?"

When he dropped a hand to her knee, she remembered every single reason she'd gone virtually without rest. Her breath hitched after just one touch. "Not so much."

"You didn't seem to mind it last night, now did you, love?" Liam questioned.

She slanted a seeking gaze his way. The knowing look in his dark eyes made her flare hot and squirm. The memories rushed back until her nipples peaked under the soft cotton of her shirt. Her skin almost felt too tight as she recalled being enveloped between Liam and Hammer while they'd both filled her, coaxing her from one orgasm to the next.

He knew damn well she hadn't minded. The question was, had he? Liam had struggled with jealousy in the past, some part of him resenting that she loved Hammer, too. Did that have anything to do with this morning's mood?

Raine shook her head softly. "No."

As much as the men had mended their rift to work together to help her overcome her insecurities, everything about the morning had stirred them up again. Raine hated to admit how much she still needed reassurance, but barely a month ago, Hammer had been nailing every free sub in the dungeon. And just a handful of days ago, Liam had severed their exclusive but admittedly dysfunctional relationship. Believing now they both loved her forever wasn't easy.

She crossed her arms over her unbound breasts feeling somehow naked, stripped, sitting between them and wearing so little…and wondering if they still wanted her—together—in their future.

"I didn't think so." As if sensing her anxiety, Liam clasped her hand, his warmth reassuring. "Besides being tired, how are you feeling this morning? Sore?"

Raine was terribly aware of every sweet ache in her well-used body, especially the blissful burn lingering between her legs. She could happily grow accustomed to that discomfort.

Would she ever feel it again? Or just more of this confused yearning for the seeming devotion they'd given her last night?

"A bit, but I'm fine," she murmured.

"Are you sure?" Hammer asked to her right.

She turned and nodded, knowing emotion swam in her eyes. Hammer had finally made love to her, baring everything in his heart—a revelation after years of her unrequited love. He wouldn't shut her out and turn her away again, right? But if he didn't, could Liam handle it?

"It was the best night of my life." The words slipped out. Maybe they were too honest for the setting, for the mood in the vehicle. But Raine couldn't have stopped them.

He flashed her a wicked smile, and a shiver rippled up her spine. She turned to take in Liam's reaction but found him gazing out the window, his attention elsewhere.

Doubt became anxiety and seized Raine's belly. She gnawed on her lip. What if he did regret last night? But…they'd woken her together with tender affection. That should have allayed her worries. But the fear just wouldn't let up. What was going on? Had he and Hammer fought? Or decided they couldn't bear repeating last night?

With a frown, she tugged on Liam's hand. "Are you all right?"

He jolted ever so slightly and turned to her with a questioning gaze. "I'm fine. Forgive me. I'm a bit preoccupied with things I shouldn't be when I've got a beautiful lass by my side."

"Is anything wrong?" Raine smoothed her thumb over his knuckles.

He squeezed her hand. "I'm just away with the fairies, is all."

Yes, Liam wasn't always a talker, but he usually indulged and coaxed her. Something definitely troubled him now. Maybe he needed a bit of time to work through everything that had happened. After all, they'd changed their dynamic from a couple to a threesome overnight.

"If there's anything you want to talk about, I'm here." She cupped his cheek and tried to comfort him.

He just sent her a faint smile and kissed her forehead, then directed his attention out the window once more, dismissing her. Mentally, he'd left her again.

Alarm clanging through her, she turned to Hammer, her expression silently asking what was wrong.

He laid a finger over his lips for silence, then snaked his fist into her hair. He tugged, tipping her head back slightly before crushing her lips under his own. A rush of desire thundered through her, sizzling her even more when he swiped his tongue over the seam of her lips, demanding entry. Raine opened for him, and Macen delved deep, sweeping inside for a thorough, sweltering kiss.

But what if Macen's affection upset Liam even more?

With a soft whimper, Raine pulled back and blinked at Hammer, searching for answers.

He skimmed his lips up her neck, across her jaw, and worked toward her ear. "Everything is fine, precious."

"He's upset," she whispered with a shake of her head.

"None of us got much sleep last night," he murmured in hushed tones. "Not every bad mood means we're pushing you away. Give him a little time."

What Hammer said made sense. Sometimes her moods weren't stellar, and that was no reflection of her feelings for Hammer or Liam. He was a man, so not every thought was about her, the three of them, or the future. Hell, he might simply be cranky because he hadn't had a hot breakfast yet. Though Liam had seemed fine when they'd awakened her, she had to trust that Hammer wouldn't lie, especially if Liam had doubts about them.

For the next ninety minutes, the miles slipped past. Once Raine finished her tea in the uncomfortable silence, she set the empty cup in the holder attached to the back of the console, then reclined her head and tried to nod off as the droning tires hummed along the road.

To her frustration, she couldn't sleep. The silence grated.

She didn't expect everyone to be chipper before seven a.m. But this morning's hush was nothing like the teasing, bawdy conversation they'd had on the way up the mountain. Instead, Seth had his head tipped back as if he was catching some *Z*'s. Beck probably had work on his mind since it had called him away. Hammer didn't usually have much to say in the morning. All true…but the utter void of sound, along with Liam's odd demeanor, kept her worries bubbling.

Hoping for a distraction, she leaned forward and cocked her head in Beck's direction. "So, what kind of surgery is your emergency?"

"A heart transplant," Beck offered. "My patient's been waiting over a year for the right match to come along. He's lucky. Too many die before they make it to the top of the donor list."

"I bet he's grateful but he must be scared."

"Sure. But I've talked with him more than once about how the procedure works. He and his family knew if a donor heart became available, we'd have to move fast." Beck shot a glance at her through the rearview mirror. "The donor will be taken off life support about noon Eastern. We're expecting the organ to arrive a few hours later."

Raine nodded. No wonder everyone had been in such a rush to head back. "It's a complicated surgery, right?"

"It is, but I've had plenty of experience with transplants. This patient needs it bad. His heart looks like a liver."

She frowned. "How long will it take?"

"That all depends. Each one is different, but the norm is around four hours, barring any complications. I won't know until I slice open his chest and slide in the spreader—"

"Are you taking your play to work now?" she teased, then sobered. Beck might actually be perverse enough to take an implement intended to keep a sub's thighs parted and use it on someone needing a new ticker.

"Funny. I meant the kind of spreader that pries open the rib cage."

She knew, but it was fun to yank his chain. "I'm shocked people actually trust you to fix them once the anesthesia has kicked in. There they are, all helpless and at Dr. Sadist's mercy."

"Don't be a smartass, or are you eager to have another 'chat' with my rubber paddle?"

Raine flinched. "No. Not even a whisper."

Beck laughed. "Once I have the patient open, I can really get busy. After I've secured the bypass and cut the aorta, I need to get a good cross-clamp going. But once in a while, you get a spurter. That's always messy. Blood everywhere."

The mental picture his words painted turned Raine's empty stomach. "I'm glad you can fix him, but please don't say any more."

"What? You don't want to assist me in the OR?" he teased.

Raine sent him a sour expression, pressed a palm to her stomach, and slumped back between Hammer and Liam. "Not unless you want me vomiting *in* the patient's chest."

"Stop, man. She can't even watch an episode of *The Walking Dead*." Hammer chuckled and slung his arm around her shoulders, drawing her close. "You've always been a squeamish little thing."

She wrinkled her nose. "I can't help it. I hope you don't kid about the surgery like that with patients and family, Beck."

"Nope. I put on my responsible doctor mask."

"I'll bet that explanation is still too graphic for me." She winced. "I feel sick."

"If you're going to toss your tea, let me know. I'll hold your hair back," Hammer offered.

She huffed at him. "You'll pull my hair, you mean."

"Every chance I get," Hammer growled softly in her ear.

"Hold off on barfing all over the backseat," Beck quipped. "I'm stopping in a couple of miles for gas."

"Good. I need to hit the restroom." Raine crossed her legs. The tea had gone right through her.

Seth jerked awake and scrubbed a hand over his face. "Huh?"

"We're stopping," Beck explained again.

A few minutes later, the doctor whipped into the parking lot of a convenience store. After pulling alongside a gas pump, Beck killed the engine.

"Can you let me out?" she asked Hammer.

Before he could reply, Liam's cell phone buzzed. Beside

her, he tensed as he dug the device out of his pocket and scanned the screen. A terrible anger crossed his face.

Suddenly, Macen scrambled out of the car and tugged on Raine's arm.

"Hang on," she insisted. "You don't have to yank me out."

Hammer didn't let up. "You said you had to go."

As soon as she stepped out of the car, Raine snatched her arm back with a scowl. Liam wasn't the only one acting weird today. "I'm not a toddler. I can hold it until I get inside. Geez…"

Hammer darted a glance behind her. Raine peeked over her shoulder to see Liam climb out the other side of the vehicle, cell phone pressed to his ear as he marched away in agitation. Raine frowned.

"I'm just trying to be helpful." Hammer took her arm once more. "I'll walk you to the bathroom."

Walk her? "I can find it by myself. The place isn't that big."

Hammer narrowed his eyes and he hauled her toward the mini-mart. "Then get your sexy little ass inside and take care of business."

Raine turned to leave. She totally understood the urgency of Beck's situation. But Hammer furiously watching whatever tense exchange Liam had? *That* worried the hell out of her.

"Who is Liam talking to?" she asked.

Hammer tugged his wallet from his back pocket. "I don't know. When you're done in the restroom, grab some bottles of water for us."

"I hate it when you do that."

"Do what?"

"Ignore my questions. Obviously, something is upsetting Liam."

"If there was something you needed to know, I'd tell you."

"Would you?" Raine bristled. "I don't think you're giving me the whole story. Wasn't it just…oh, last night that you two promised me honesty and communication?"

"Tuck your insecurities away, precious." He pushed the twenty-dollar bill into her hand. "Go to the bathroom. Get the water. I'll meet you at the car. Everything is fine."

Everything wasn't fine. Something had upset Liam, and Hammer didn't want her to know what. They'd sworn that if they all communicated their thoughts and feelings, the three of them could have a great future. What they meant was, if she opened up and ripped her guts out for them, they would appreciate that, but they didn't see the need to reciprocate.

Hurt scalded her. Supposedly, she was important enough for them to share what was in their hearts. Why wasn't she important enough for the truth?

Without another word, Raine hurried into the store. Just inside, she paused behind a rack of greeting cards and spied out the large plate glass window. Beck filled the gas tank. Seth stood outside the passenger side of the car, stretching his arms high above his head as he yawned. And Liam… He still had the phone pressed to his ear as he paced the parking lot with long, deliberate strides, back ramrod straight.

"Sure. Everything is just peachy," she muttered. "Assholes."

Liam had been this sort of distant before he'd uncollared her. Though the situations weren't the same, for whatever reason, Liam wasn't letting her in. Even worse, she suspected everyone in the car knew why…except her.

Her faith and trust began to slip.

Raine nearly knee-jerked and considered packing a bag as soon as she reached Shadows. But they'd been through too much these past few days, worked through so many issues—at least she'd thought so. They'd told her they loved her. God knew she loved them.

Through so many of her half truths and uncertainties, they'd stuck it out and kept chipping away at her walls until they'd uncovered her heart. Didn't she owe them the same? Maybe they were being secretive for a good reason.

Outside, Hammer tossed a glance over his shoulder, looking toward the store. Raine slouched lower, ignoring the confused clerk's stare from behind the counter.

A moment later, Macen jogged over to Liam, who ended his call. They exchanged words.

She couldn't read lips and would never be able to hear anything from inside. Damn it, she really did need to use the bathroom.

Quickly, she dashed toward the ladies' room. Business done and hands scrubbed, Raine made a beeline for the chiller fridge in the back of the store and gathered up five bottles of agua.

She didn't know what was going on, but she was determined to get some answers, whether Liam and Hammer wanted to give them to her or not.

* * *

Macen thundered toward Liam, who had stopped midstride, waving his free hand in a clipped swipe. Hammer couldn't hear his friend's angry words over the stirring wind. As he crossed the lot, Liam stabbed his finger to the screen and terminated the call, then shoved his cell back into his pants.

He blew out a breath and stood with his hands on his hips. "Fucking hell."

"What did she want?" Hammer clapped Liam's tense shoulder. "Did you two talk about the baby?"

"I didn't get a chance to ask. She's been up to mischief. I thought you had Pike watching her."

"I do. What happened?"

"Evidently, Gwyneth has decided we're still married and wanted to move her things into my room. She snooped around the club until she found it."

"What?" Hammer felt his blood pressure soar.

"Oh, it gets better, mate. Inside, she found Raine's clothes, jewelry, toiletries—the works. Gwyneth knows I'm with someone. She doesn't know who yet, but how long do you think it will take her to find out?"

"Son of a…" Hammer growled, feeling murderous. "That fucking bitch. What gives her the right to go prowling around your room? Around my club? Where the hell was Pike?"

"Good question. He should have locked her up."

Hammer jerked his phone from his pants and called the DM.

"Yes. She's still here," Pike announced, not even bothering to say hello.

"I know, since she's snooping around," Hammer hissed. "Lock her up until we get back."

"She's what?" Pike sounded dumbfounded. "When?"

"I don't know. Have you let her out of your sight?"

"Well, I had to take a piss. Afterward, I found her making a bottle in the kitchen."

You mean Raine's kitchen. "No more bottles. No more freedom. No more…" Hammer felt like a keg of dynamite, lit and ready to erupt. "*Don't* let her out of your sight again. We're over halfway back. Give us another hour or so."

Hammer ended the call and sucked in several deep breaths. "Tell me what Gwyneth said."

"I had trouble hearing it all. She'd turned on the bloody waterworks again. She was bleating on about how our marriage must have meant nothing to me and she didn't understand how I could be involved with someone again so quickly, as if she'd never existed, and all that tripe."

Gwyneth's call had clearly added weight to his friend's worry, and it pissed Macen off even more. He'd spent the last several hours trying to wrap his brain around different reasons for Gwyneth's sudden visit—besides the baby. He hadn't come up with a single, plausible scenario, only managed to give himself a headache.

"You split up more than two fucking years ago," Hammer pointed out.

"We've got to tell Raine what's going on," Liam insisted. "She's already suspicious. After I uncollared her, we traveled a bumpy road to reach this point. I don't want her doubting my commitment and feeling insecure again. But my head's not all here just now, and I don't think we'll be able to keep Gwyneth and the baby under wraps much longer."

Hammer shook his head. "We already agreed not to tell Raine in the car. Or without all the facts. Until then, pull your head out of your ass and start paying attention to her."

"It's not that simple. I'm in a foul mood, Macen. I've had no sleep. Maybe telling her now isn't the best way to handle it, but it would sure as hell be a load off my mind if we did."

"That's not fair to her," Hammer shot back.

"What if Gwyneth and her serpent tongue are waiting at Shadows to confront Raine? What if we're leading our girl into a fucking ambush?" Liam roared. "It'll be too late to confess anything to Raine then, much less protect her."

"We'll protect her," Hammer insisted. "But nothing's changed. If we tell her, and it turns out the baby isn't yours, the only thing we've accomplished is to shake her up good. We stay on course. It's our best choice."

"If Raine finds out Gwyneth is at Shadows before we can tell her, there will be hell to pay," Liam thundered.

"So, we'll keep that from happ—"

"Hey," Seth called out, drawing Hammer's attention.

Over Liam's shoulder, he spied Raine pushing her way outside the store. She'd seen them fighting, no doubt. Her tight expression hit him like a blow to the gut.

"Raine's coming," Hammer warned in a low whisper.

Liam turned and stiffened, obviously seeing her unhappy expression.

Raine strode toward them with purpose. "What's going on? What are you two fighting about?"

Hammer shot Liam a knowing glance, then quickly forced himself to relax. "We weren't fighting, precious."

"Oh, really?" She arched a brow in disbelief.

"No, we were just having a little discussion," Macen assured.

"About?"

Liam shook his head, gripped her arm, and led her toward the car. "Hammer is just being a mite pig-headed."

Oh, that was smooth. Macen closed his eyes briefly and gnashed his teeth. Liam couldn't see the forest for the trees. If he wanted to keep Raine from asking questions… Oh, that's right; he didn't. Liam wanted to spill the whole fucking story, minus a few key facts, and send her into a tailspin.

Raine shrugged from Liam's grip. Turning the tables, she wrapped her fingers around his arm. "About what?"

Liam stared down at her, considering. "Love, I didn't want to worry you, but I think you should—"

"Beck's going to take off without us. We need to hustle up." Hammer pulled Raine to his side and pinned Liam with a pointed stare.

"Is everyone pissed, packed, and ready to roll?" Beck asked.

Seth smiled. "Damn. And it was just getting interesting."

"No one asked you," Hammer growled.

The undercurrent of tension swirled between him and Liam. Hammer knew Raine felt it, too. She'd grown totally suspicious, and the situation would soon spiral out of control if he didn't do something—fast.

Liam muttered a curse under his breath as he stomped to the rear driver's side door and opened it. "Let's go."

"Wait. What is it I should…do? Know?" Raine anchored her hands on her hips. "What's going on?"

Shit. "Nothing. At least nothing more important than this." Hammer pulled her into his arms and slanted his lips over hers, pinning her against the door. The air rushed from her lungs as he deepened the kiss. Taking total possession, he swept a hand to her nape and filtered his fingers through her hair, pressing every inch of his hard body to hers.

Any second, he expected Raine to bite his lip like a hellcat. Damn it, he wanted to redirect her attention, but kissing her in broad daylight with a honking trucker speeding past just wasn't his style, and Raine knew it. Even inside the club, with members' eyes constantly watching, he kept his personal life separate. But in private, he didn't hold back. Even if Raine believed his sudden rush of affection, she'd be quizzing Liam again before they reached the highway.

She gave him a little shove and a suspicious glare. "What was that for?"

"I can't stop thinking about last night," he answered in a husky, hungry voice.

"And you couldn't wait?"

"I've waited for years. I won't wait anymore." He opened the back door and nodded her way. "Get in."

Leaning down as Raine bent to enter the backseat, he watched Liam extend his hand to help her.

Before he could distract Raine again, she focused on Liam. "What were you going to say? What is it you didn't want me to worry about?"

She had one knee poised on the buttery seat, her ass arched in the air. Hammer slid his hands up her thighs and settled them on her backside, squeezing her soft, bare flesh.

Raine reached back and swatted his hand. "Stop that. I'm not going to let you take me here at the gas pump."

"If I want to, I will." Hammer landed a sharp slap across her ass.

With a little yelp, she crawled closer to Liam and tossed a piqued glance over her shoulder. Macen eased in next to her and shut the door.

"Talk to me, Liam." Raine cupped a slender hand to his face. "What's upset you?"

Hammer sent his friend a look of warning, then clenched his jaw. "Nothing you need to worry about."

Raine glared back at him. "You keep answering for him. What are you up to?"

"About eight inches."

Liam scowled as Beck barked out a laugh and pulled the car onto the highway. Raine tsked at Hammer, shaking her head, before she turned back to Liam. Macen did the same. And damn it, he knew that look. Liam was waging a fierce internal battle. Thankfully, the man's cell phone rang again, diverting his attention.

Gritting his teeth, Liam yanked it from his pocket and punched a finger at the screen to decline the call.

Liam rarely showed his anger to Raine. A Dom should always be in control of his emotions, but now fury rolled off his friend in churning waves.

Turning off the phone entirely, Liam shoved the device back in his pocket.

"Who on earth was that?" When Liam didn't answer, Raine pleaded, "Talk to me."

"Just some things I need to deal with later." Liam sounded tightly wound.

"What kind of things?" Her voice trembled.

Hammer heard the worry in her tone. *Oh, hell…*

Liam paused and stared at Raine with both warmth and resignation. "Love…"

Fuck, his friend was going to cave.

"He's having some issues with his company, precious." Hammer interrupted. "That's all."

* * *

Macen, you son of a bitch. What the fuck do you think you're doing? Despite their audience, he'd been ready to tell Raine everything and let the chips fall. But Hammer had wrested control of the situation—again—forcing Liam to either refute him in front of Raine or join the subterfuge.

Liam felt the noose tightening.

If Hammer managed to fuck up their relationship beyond repair… Liam's hands curled into fists. The prick would have to die.

Swallowing back the curse scalding the tip of his tongue, Liam ignored the guilty apology skewed over Hammer's face and focused on Raine. She looked somewhere between concerned and relieved.

"Why didn't you tell me that?" Compassion filled her voice. "I worried that—"

"I know what you worried about. Trust me when I say it's not you. Never you, love." He cupped her chin and gently kissed her. All the tension left her body as she melted beneath his lips. "I didn't want anything to spoil this time between us, especially after all we've been through. I'm sorry if I worried you."

Wrapping her in a tight embrace, Liam tossed Hammer a glare that promised retribution. Macen might have embroiled him in this deceit, but Liam would be damned if he'd spoon-feed Raine lies of his own.

"I understand," she said softly, pulling back to cup his cheek. "I want to help."

Wasn't that just like Raine? The submission in her heart sparked to life, big, bold, and beautiful. It was her nature to want to fix this for him, take on his worries, and keep the waters calm. He loved her all the more for it.

"Just be patient with me while I sort out this mess. Like I've said, this is something I need to deal with. But I promise, I'll rush through it as quickly as I can. Nothing is more important than you."

"Nothing in the world," Hammer echoed, drawing a knuckle down Raine's cheek. "We're here for you, precious."

Cupping her face, Macen drew her attention away from him. In a way, Liam was grateful. Raine was sure to ask more questions, and there wasn't enough room in the car for him to tap-dance around the details. On the other hand, talking to her had felt good, eased something in his chest.

"I need your lips again," Macen cut in, coaxing her in a raspy voice.

Liam saw her hesitate. Clearly, she wanted to make sure he was all right. His attitude softened, and he nodded her way. If Hammer could soothe their girl with a kiss, he shouldn't mind. In fact, he should be happy.

Raine smiled, the gesture finally reaching her blue eyes, before she turned and faced Macen.

Liam watched the other man brush his lips over Raine's, making her melt and sigh. Then Macen dipped his head again, covering her mouth, going deeper. Taking control.

As he funneled his hands in Raine's hair and began to devour her, Liam stared. Hammer was doing exactly to Raine what they'd forbidden her to do: distract with sex. Cheeky bastard.

The soft kitten moans she made as Macen claimed her mouth echoed in Liam's ears. The sounds filled his head and crawled up his back. Hammer knew he had a fair bit on his mind. Liam hadn't objected to a peck or two, but he wished the man hadn't elected to stick his tongue down her throat and bloody climb all over her.

He shot them an annoyed glance. Neither noticed. Hammer caressed his way down her lush body with covetous, possessive strokes. A tic spasmed in Liam's jaw. The shit piled on his plate already overflowed, and Hammer appeared to have forgotten that Raine was their girl, not just his when his hand fell between her soft thighs, nudging them apart. And he didn't look as if he intended to stop at a feel. Did Hammer really mean to fuck her in the car?

Liam's blood boiled.

Macen stroked her pussy with one hand, then began to cup her heavy breasts with the other. Raine continued to whimper, oblivious. A shudder rippled through her body as the other man's thumb brushed one of her turgid peaks. After all the ways they'd consumed her the night before, her body still responded in perfect, total surrender—at least for Hammer.

Because she'd always loved him. Misery wound through Liam. Where did that leave him?

I don't need your love, lass, just your trust.

Liam slid a hand down his face. He'd uttered those words to Raine a month ago, before he'd even kissed her once. At the time, they'd been true. Now he wished he'd never said that at all. Maybe she would never feel for him all she felt for Hammer.

Raine's thighs parted farther, welcoming Macen's busy fingers. Resentment seared Liam as Macen tugged at her tank top and her plump breast spilled into the man's palm as if it belonged there.

"You need to feel this," Hammer coaxed Liam. "She's so hot…like liquid velvet. Just as incredible as last night."

Yes, Liam remembered her wet, silky warmth surrounding him, sucking at him. She'd taken him to paradise repeatedly. But his anger over Gwyneth's scheme, the fear he might be a father, and now Hammer laying his hands all over Raine obliterated those magical moments. They were both so lost in pleasure.

No, you go right ahead. Neither of you need me when you've got one another.

Beck darted a glance in the rearview mirror, straightening up slightly and lifting his chin, focused on Hammer's strumming fingers. Seth suddenly tensed as if he'd zeroed in on the sexual air swirling in the car.

Shifting in his seat, the big blond man looked over his shoulder, his gaze settling on Raine's splayed thighs barely covered by the skirt. "Damn. That's pretty. Smells good."

Liam wanted to punch his friend in the mouth.

"It's not yours," Hammer growled.

Liam's gut twisted. Who the fuck was Macen talking to? Just Seth? It didn't seem that way. At the moment, Raine didn't feel like his at all.

Clenching his teeth, he turned away to stare out the window. His body hummed with frustration and suppressed fury. Every little catch of her breath stabbed him deep. At the scent of her hot, feminine arousal, jealousy burned like acid.

"Spread wider for me," Hammer muttered thickly.

"Liam," Raine moaned in a breathy whisper.

He turned and watched her squirm in her seat, wanton and desperate, uninhibited. Raine had opened herself utterly to Macen, so Liam didn't answer. What could he say? She didn't need him. And he didn't need her pity.

Hammer grunted in approval as he kissed her and swallowed her moan. Liam watched as Macen planted his fingers deeper in her pussy. Raine reached out to clasp Liam's hand and lift it to her breast as if pleading for his touch. Desire snaked through his veins. No denying she had beautiful breasts, and he'd like nothing more than to work his way deep inside her again. But he'd be damned if he'd be a third wheel. An afterthought.

Liam let his hand slide back to his lap and shifted his body, separating himself even farther from the lovers. He focused out the window once more.

"Are you ready to fly for me, Raine?" Hammer teased.

Not for us, *asshole. Just for you.* Liam gritted his teeth.

"Yes. I need…" she panted out, struggling to catch her breath.

Clearly, she would have no trouble orgasming without him.

"Beg sweetly, and I'll give it to you," Hammer promised.

"Please. But I… Liam?" she called to him again.

He flinched, pretending not to hear. Why were they bothering now?

"Shh, he's fine. Straddle my lap, precious," Hammer muttered, his voice thick with lust.

"Wait, Macen." Raine gasped, rustled. "Just…stop. Don't!"

"What?" Hammer sounded like he struggled to catch his breath.

"Liam?" she called to him again. "What's wrong?"

Oh, so it finally matters to you two that I'm here?

"I'm not in the mood." He tried not to snarl the words.

Hammer sighed heavily. "For fuck's sake…"

Liam heard the whisper of fabric, as if Raine readjusted her clothing. Still, he didn't turn to look at them; he couldn't. Scraped raw, he tried to breathe, grab a hold of his temper. No such luck. It continued to pulse, white, hot, and unrelenting.

So they hadn't actually fucked in the car. Small bloody comfort. How much longer before he could get out of this rolling torture chamber and put some distance between them? The road signs told him it would be longer than he'd like.

Holding in a curse, he glanced over his shoulder to find Hammer staring at him with something that resembled fury. Liam opened his mouth to let his rage fly, when Macen zipped his stare down to Raine. Liam followed suit.

The rejection in her posture—the way she hunched her shoulders protectively, head down, arms wrapped tightly around her middle—ripped at his heart. The sweltering resentment bubbling in his veins evaporated instantly. He'd turned her away, and now she tried to hide in her own skin and shield herself from the pain.

Bloody fucking hell. Liam felt as if someone had hit him in the chest with a battering ram.

He'd done this to her. And why? Where had all this ugly envy come from? It wasn't as if Raine cheated on him with Hammer. Yet he wallowed in betrayal, like the night he'd collared her…and she'd left him to spend it in Hammer's bed. The only difference was that now Hammer intended to screw Raine in front of him instead of behind his back.

He knew what sharing a sub meant, and Raine was the epitome of everything he'd ever wanted. So why had he needed to exercise all his self-control not to beat Hammer to a pulp and rail at her? Had he really thought they didn't give a shit about him? Christ, he had enough to deal with. He didn't need to add more torment to the list, especially self-inflicted.

All he wanted in that moment was to hug Raine close, feel the warmth and comfort of her soft and sure in his arms. With his pride so wounded, he didn't know how reach out to her. And after hurting her, did he even deserve to?

Hammer cleared his throat. Liam met his friend's gaze. Understanding flickered before Macen arched his brows and nodded toward her. The message was clear: Fix the damage he'd done to their girl's fragile heart.

Seeing her so completely withdrawn gutted him. He couldn't indulge in this pity party. He wasn't the only one with feelings, troubles, and worries. As her Dom, his job was to give Raine what she needed. Right now, that was reassurance. Liam loved her too much to let her believe he didn't want her.

Groaning, he gathered Raine into his arms. She held herself stiffly as he cradled her against his chest. Then she blinked up at him with an ache that nearly destroyed him.

"I'm sorry for being an ass, love," he murmured.

With a cry, she threw herself against him, wrapping her

arms around his neck. She clung. Little sobs shook her.

Combing his fingers through her hair, Liam held her tighter, rubbing her back and kissing her face. “I’m so sorry. Can you forgive me?”

Raine sniffled and nodded, gripping him as if she feared he would disappear—or leave her. Remorse stabbed him again.

Beck weaved the SUV through the congested Southern California traffic as Raine drifted off in his arms. Without her cries, the car went completely silent. Liam felt waves of disapproval coming from every direction. He closed his eyes, knowing he’d earned it. What the devil had gotten into him?

When Shadows finally came into view, the sight filled him with dread. He didn’t want to let Raine go. He didn’t want to face his ex-wife.

He didn’t have a choice.

Beck killed the engine. “Welcome home.”

Chapter Three

Let the games begin.

Hammer glanced down at Raine. Thankfully, she still lay sleeping peacefully in Liam's arms. He really wanted to slam his pal against the nearest hard surface. Evidently, Liam hadn't purged his jealousy via his fists last night. Instead, he'd let his cheating ex crawl up his ass and flip his switch again. Hammer didn't want to disturb Raine until Beck and Seth were ready to lead her safely inside. Then…all bets were off.

"Hold tight. I'll be right back. Then we'll wake her together." He tamped down his anger to whisper to Liam before tapping Beck and Seth on the shoulder. Jerking his head, Hammer motioned the other two to join him outside the car.

They each opened their doors and exited, shutting them softly, then clustered behind the vehicle.

Hammer turned to Beck. "Do you have time to bring us a DNA kit before your surgery?"

"Yeah. I can swing it. It should only take an hour or so. Once the lab has the swab, I'll have it rushed through so you've got results in less than twenty-four hours."

"That would be great. I owe you. Thanks." Hammer kept his voice low, hoping that by this time tomorrow, they would have concrete answers.

So they would know whether their future was fucked.

Sighing, he glanced at Seth. "While we were en route, Gwyneth spied and found Liam's room—and Raine's things inside."

"It would be my pleasure to hurt her," Beck volunteered with cheer.

Hammer smiled, appreciating a little comic relief. "I'd enjoy watching. Hell, I might even help. Sadly, there's no time for fun. Liam is going to remove the bitch from my club, so I plan on taking Raine out for a while until the coast is clear." He faced Seth again. "For now, I need you to escort her to Liam's room so she can shower. In the meantime, he and I will talk to Pike and get the scoop."

"No problem," Seth assured. "While you two are gone, I'll make some calls and see if I can dig up any info on Gwyneth's recent activities, try to find out who else might have fathered that baby and what she's been up to."

Seth's skills as a private investigator would be an asset, and Macen was in favor of anything that would make her go the fuck away.

"Much appreciated." Hammer nodded. "Before we bring Raine inside, would you go in first and make sure the she-beast is contained? We don't want her springing any nasty surprises on Raine."

Seth chuckled. "No problem. I'm not sure anyone can hold Gwyneth back with a whip and a chair, but I'll try. Oh, maybe I could use a tranq gun instead?"

"If I had one, Pike would have already emptied that bad boy in her," Hammer drawled. "Let's get the car unloaded and get this nightmare over with."

Beck hauled out the luggage as Seth ducked inside the club, then emerged a minute later and gave Macen a thumbs-up.

With a little sigh of relief, Hammer opened the passenger door. Liam greeted him with a grim look of determination before he gently roused Raine. She rubbed her eyes as she eased off of Liam's lap. Hammer helped her from the car.

"Why don't you go inside and take a long, hot shower?" he suggested, ushering her across the parking lot. "I'll take you to breakfast."

"That sounds heavenly," she moaned, then glanced back at Liam, who followed them. She looked like she wanted to say something more, but Beck sauntered up with a suitcase.

Seth grabbed his own duffel and followed close behind. "Come on, little one. We've got your things. Let's get them to your room."

Liam held the door to the club open. She reached out to touch him, sending a hopeful gaze his way. "Are you coming to breakfast, too?"

"I'd love to join you, lass. But I'm afraid I need to tend to some matters."

Disappointment weighed in the heavy fall of her shoulders. The anger Hammer had been shoving down at Gwyneth's untimely return sparked to life again.

"I'll square everything away as quickly as I can so I can spend time with you." Liam smiled, as if his earlier burst of jealousy had never occurred. "I promise."

"I hope it doesn't take too long." Raine stared at him, so raw and yearning.

God, Hammer wanted nothing more than to drag the two of them away, find a place where they could block out the rest of the world, and solidify their future.

He felt it slipping through his fingers.

"Me, too. I love you, Raine," Liam murmured.

Hammer joined in, brushing a strand of windswept hair from her lips. "We both love you, precious."

"I love you both, too." She smiled tremulously.

"Go get ready," Hammer instructed with a caress to her back. "I'll come find you in a few."

Beck nudged her toward the portal. Raine peered back over her shoulder, almost reluctant to leave.

"We've got her," Seth assured before he swaggered by, and the wooden door closed behind him.

As soon as they disappeared inside, Hammer spun around to glower at Liam. "What the hell happened in the car?"

Liam threw his hands in the air. "I have a lot on my mind. Then you lied to her, which I can't say I'm happy about. And when you started mauling her…I lost it."

Mauling? "At the time, I thought I was saving our asses."

"By almost fucking her in the car?" Liam sneered. "Please… I was all but invisible to you."

"Invisible?" Hammer gaped. "We both asked you to get involved. Raine herself asked you *three* times, and you tuned her out. Did you want her to beg?"

Liam's face closed up. "You two were doing fine on your own."

The green-eyed monster still choked him, nice and tight.

"I thought we worked through this shit last night." Wasn't that why he and Liam had pounded the crap out of each other in the snow? If it hadn't worked, he'd ruined a great pair of Vuitton loafers and sported several bruises for nothing. "Remember how right it felt to get Raine between us? In the car, I tried to remind you of that—and everything we've worked so hard for. You wouldn't have a thing to do with us."

"Sex wasn't foremost on my mind."

"You couldn't have touched her? Kissed her? Let her know you cared a little?" he shot back. "You saw the complete rejection on her face."

"I didn't mean to hurt her. But there was a bit of a crowd in the car, mate."

"Beck and Seth?" Hammer resisted the urge to remind the man that he'd fucked Raine's ass with a watching crowd—including him—not terribly long ago, but that argument served no purpose except to prolong this fight. Instead, he clenched his teeth, reaching for the last thread of his patience.

In the span of a few hours, they'd eroded too much of Raine's progress. Gwyneth now breathed down their necks. Liam might be a father. And Hammer realized that his friend's jealousy ran far deeper than he'd imagined. Goddamn it, they were supposed to be working together. They couldn't afford to let rancor fester between them.

"I'm not blaming you," Hammer promised.

"Good. You've got some responsibility in this, too," Liam said. "When she figures out you've lied, it will blow up in our faces. What do you plan to tell her then?"

"That I did it to protect her," he shot back. "I'll take full responsibility for *my* lie. But you have to own up to yours as well."

"What the hell are you talking about? I'm not the one who told her I was stressed out because of my business," Liam spat.

"It wasn't that long ago you turned on that Irish charm and played Raine so you could trick me into claiming her. If she finds out, she'll be heartbroken."

"That's ancient history. Besides, I just meant to help you." Liam stabbed a finger in his chest. "She needed some confidence and affection. Where would all of us be if I hadn't put my plan in motion? You'd still be fucking Marlie with your eyes closed, pretending she was Raine."

Hammer shuddered. Liam was probably right. "Would it make you feel better if I said I was grateful?"

Liam sent him an exasperated glare. "I didn't seduce Raine to hurt her. Besides, I wasn't in love with her then."

"That won't make a damn bit of difference to her."

Liam bristled. "I meant well."

"So did I. Look, I didn't see how else to avoid the truth," Hammer returned. "You're my fucking best friend."

He sighed. "You're mine, too."

"Then get it through your thick skull that I'm trying to share a girl with you, not stab you in the back. I have absolutely no intention of taking Raine away. If you thought that earlier…" He sighed, rubbed at the back of his neck. "I-I'm sorry."

Surprised flickered across his face. "Say that again."

Apologies didn't come easy to him, and everyone knew it. "Fuck you."

Liam cracked a smile, then sobered. "I'm sorry, too, mate."

Before the moment could turn totally awkward and bromancy, a surprisingly frazzled Pike rushed out the door. "What took you so long? Holy shit…"

Macen extended his hand. "Thanks for holding down the fort and handling our little problem."

"Little?" The Dungeon Monitor scoffed.

"I appreciate all you've done," Liam offered. "If I'd known Gwyneth had plans to show up, I never would have left. Thank you for keeping this situation under wraps."

"Don't ask me to deal with her again unless I get to shove a ball gag in her mouth." Pike smiled grimly, then turned to Hammer. "Before I forget, you had a visitor last night, too."

Hammer frowned. He hadn't been expecting anyone. "Who?"

"Some old wino-looking guy. Said his name was Bill and that you owed him money."

Hammer's heart stuttered, and he clenched his fists. "Big guy? Beer belly? White hair?"

"Yeah, that's him." Pike nodded.

Raine's father. He and Liam shared a seething glance. For years, Bill had known where to find her, and Hammer had paid the asshole to stay away. The moment he'd stopped paying, Bill had darkened his door.

"Fucking hell." His friend looked ready to punch his fist in the door. "Bill knows he's not welcome here. We don't need this shit, too."

Pike looked confused. "I told him you'd be back soon. Sorry, man. I didn't know he was trouble."

"He is, but nothing we can't handle," Hammer assured. "Go home and get some sleep."

With a nod, Pike dug his keys from his pocket before sauntering to his motorcycle. They watched in silence until he rode away.

"Why would Bill think you'd give him more money?" Liam asked. Hammer noticed a new line of worry creasing his friend's face. "You told him you were done."

"I'll remind him of that shortly. But the way Raine retreated into herself in the car is exactly what I feared would happen if we told her about Gwyneth."

"Don't be daft. She was upset because she thought I'd rejected her."

"That's part of it, but she also knows we're keeping something from her. It's crushing her, and I can't stand to see it anymore. So I've changed my mind. We need to tell her what's going on. You were right."

"I think you'd better repeat that." Liam arched a brow. "I'm not quite sure I heard you."

"Get your ears checked, prick," Hammer grumbled. "You were right. There. I said it. Gloat all you want. But it doesn't matter if we have all the facts, we owe her the truth about Gwyneth, the baby, her dad sniffing around…everything."

"We do," Liam agreed, then glanced at his watch. "I'd love to tell her now, but I don't dare keep Gwyneth waiting anymore. She might go back to my room and find Raine in the shower."

"Then I'd have to bury the bitch," Hammer agreed. "And I promised to feed Raine. I could explain the situation to her at breakfast, but it's something I think we should do together."

Liam nodded. "Yes. Gwyneth is my ex-wife."

"And the lie about your business woes is mine, so I need to apologize for that."

Liam frowned. "When you take Raine out, she'll ask more questions. Try to be honest."

"I'll do my best." But Hammer didn't expect that to be easy. "Before we go, I need to deal with Bill. That's something we can't afford to put off."

"You're right. My first priority needs to be keeping Gwyneth away from Raine long enough to get that baby swabbed and the sample dropped off at the hospital."

"Fuck yes. Do you think that baby is yours? Really?"

Liam grimaced. "I'm afraid to find out."

Hammer was, too. "You also need to get Gwyneth out of Shadows and moved…somewhere. A hotel, the local Y, a freeway underpass—I don't care. As long as she isn't under my roof and near Raine."

"I can't just dump her off anywhere. The kid might be my son." Liam sighed.

"I know."

"We'll keep in touch via text. When we get everything squared away, we'll explain this mess to our lass."

"Maybe we'll take her to a nice, romantic dinner. Make sure she knows she's important."

"I think she'd like that," Liam agreed. "Once we come home, we sit her down and explain, let her ask questions."

"Then we'll make sure she knows she's loved," Hammer vowed.

Liam smiled. "That we will."

They'd made a plan. The time to execute had come. Now Hammer just hoped everything fell in line.

* * *

Why couldn't she, Liam, and Hammer just be happy for five freaking minutes?

Raine made her way down the hall inside Shadows and headed toward the room she'd been sharing with Liam, wishing she could just enjoy a bright new future with the men she loved. Instead, something had gone terribly wrong.

If Liam had business issues, why the hell had Hammer been trying to feel her up in the car, almost flaunting her at Liam? If he'd meant it as a distraction, the ploy had failed miserably. Her gorgeous Irishman almost never turned down the opportunity to touch her. This morning, he hadn't seemed interested in the least.

Was the fact that he and Hammer had shared her last night troubling Liam now? Or had something else entirely upset him? She hated not having any answers.

Since Liam and Hammer had spent days with her to open up communication, promote trust, and focus on honesty, she'd really hoped they wouldn't lie. But she suspected they were.

At her side, Seth held her elbow, guiding her down the hall.

Aching to be alone, she tried to shrug out of his hold. "I can find my way."

"Please prove to me you learned *something* at the lodge." It wasn't exactly a request, as evidenced by the bite in his voice.

Just behind him, Beck carried her suitcase and barked out a laugh. "That's the thing about the princess. Her temper sometimes overrides her good sense."

Over her shoulder, she shot Beck a dirty look. "Since when is being factual a problem?"

"It's all in your tone," the doctor said, his voice full of soft warning. "If Hammer and Liam haven't pointed that out yet, I'll make sure they do."

Seth tightened his grip on her elbow, scanning the halls tensely, as if he expected a ghost to jump out at him. What was up with all these men this morning? Whatever it was, they had no intention of telling her. She couldn't blame Beck or Seth. They were simply following Hammer and Liam's lead.

Raine sighed. "Sorry I'm cranky. I'll feel better after some food."

"Hammer will take care of that," Beck said. "Shower up. He's got to handle a few things with Pike, then he'll get cleaned up and take you to breakfast."

And what would Liam be doing? She couldn't stand not knowing. She already missed him and had no idea when—or if—he'd be back. Yes, he'd told her that he loved her, that no one was more important. Why did she have so much trouble believing it?

Raine really hated being whiny and insecure.

"Is Liam leaving me?" Tension knotted her belly. "I'm a big girl. If he's packing his bags, just give it to me straight. I can handle it."

Some of the stiffness melted from Seth's face. He shifted his arm around her waist. "No. I've known Liam almost ten years. I stood up with him the day he got married. I've never seen him love a woman as completely as he loves you."

Those words should have made her feel better. She wanted them to.

Though Liam had sworn his mood this morning had nothing to do with her, she couldn't forget that he'd removed his collar less than a week ago. Yes, he'd done it to foster her growth. But after being abandoned by her mother, her siblings—everyone important to her except Hammer—believing that Liam really meant to stay simply wasn't easy.

Raine knew Seth meant what he said. "Thank you."

Beck touched the small of her back. "Trust me, no one could pry those two away from you with a crowbar. Liam is just working through some stuff, princess."

"Is it *all* business?" Because he seemed affected pretty personally by a strictly professional problem.

The doctor shrugged his beefy shoulders. "I've got a major surgery to prep for, so I didn't ask too many questions."

Raine turned to quiz Seth, who just shrugged and continued leading her to the bedroom. "I'm not usually up at such an ungodly hour. Mentally, I'm still asleep."

These guys stuck together. They knew something and weren't about to tell her.

Beck gave her a reassuring smile. "I'd warn you if they intended to pull the rug out from under you."

The dungeon's resident sadist could be a big, ol' teddy bear. Funny that she used to fear him. In a few weeks, he'd become an essential friend.

"Thanks."

"I have to head to the hospital. You're in good hands," Beck promised, nodding Seth's way as he handed off the suitcase.

Raine moved into Beck's personal space, opening her arms to him. He enfolded her against his chest, like the warm embrace of a protective older brother. "I wouldn't have survived these last few days without you."

"I'll let you talk me up next time I find a new sub I'd like to scene with." He winked.

She gave him a little laugh. "You got it."

As Beck backed out of the room with a wave, Seth shut the door behind them and nudged her toward the bathroom. "Shower up."

His posture made it clear he wasn't leaving.

"Liam and Hammer asked you to babysit me?"

He shrugged. "They don't want you alone when you're upset."

"I'm not going to run off again." She'd been completely miserable those few days without them. As long as they had any chance of building a future together, she'd put her all into it.

"Good to hear. Quit stalling."

She sighed and made her way into the bathroom, shutting the door behind her. Seth had seen every bare inch of her at the lodge, and she wasn't embarrassed by her nudity. But she wanted a moment alone to try to piece together what was going on.

A good shampoo, a deep conditioner for her hair, and a razor across any stubbly skin later, Raine didn't have any new theories.

When she emerged from the shower, she grabbed Liam's robe from the back of the door, inhaling his deeply familiar scent. She closed her eyes, and a slew of memories assailed her.

The night Hammer had introduced them over beer and seafood—and she'd felt a surprising zing of attraction. The morning she'd made a fool of herself over Hammer after his fling with Marlie, and Liam had comforted and—for the first time—kissed her. Meeting Liam's gaze in the mirror when he'd claimed her in the dungeon in the midst of a roomful of people…then minutes later when he'd made love to her again privately. The day he'd collared her in a beautiful ceremony. The terrible morning he'd uncollared her for failing to trust in him, communicate with him, or be honest about her fears. The way he and Hammer had worked together these past few days to build a new foundation for their future. And the amazing moments last night when they'd solidified everything in their hearts.

Raine felt as if she and Liam had loved a decade in that short month, and the idea that he might be pulling away now crushed her.

Belting the robe around her waist, she determined to be ready when Hammer came. He might not tell her everything happening, but surely she deserved to know something more than a vague platitude about Liam's business. Raine meant to convince him. Somehow.

She moisturized her face and put on a little lip gloss, then towel dried her hair and searched for her comb. When she didn't find it in her drawer, she automatically opened Liam's, wondering if he'd borrowed it. She cursed when she remembered it was probably in her suitcase, out with Seth in the bedroom.

But just as she made to close the drawer, something caught her attention, and she pulled the handle again.

Yep, there sat a pacifier. Blue with little holes surrounding the rubbery mouthpiece. The flat front said *MUTE BUTTON* in a childish font.

Raine picked it up with a puzzled frown. Why would this be in the bathroom she shared with Liam?

Chapter Four

Once Seth and Beck escorted Raine to her room, Hammer stormed into his office and slammed the door. Could this day get any fucking worse? First Gwyneth and her baby, then Liam's meltdown, Raine's withdrawal, and now Bill Kendall.

"What next?" Hammer spat.

Hopefully, he'd reached his shit quotient for the day.

After grabbing his phone, he punched in Bill's number. Raine's pitiful excuse of a father answered on the third ring.

"About time you got back to me, Master Pervert."

So the asshole had caller ID. What shocked Hammer was that Kendall's voice lacked the usual slur. Macen glanced at his watch. Not quite eight a.m. He'd thought it was always cocktail hour at the Kendall household.

"What the fuck do you think you're doing, coming to my club?"

No need for subtleties. In fact, Hammer cursed himself for not beating some fear into the lowlife piece of shit years ago. Instead, he'd paid Raine's father a monthly stipend to steer clear of her. And continued to pay it long after she'd turned eighteen. But providing her a safe haven had been worth every penny. He'd have spent everything he owned to keep her out of Bill Kendall's abusive hands.

"You're late with your payment," the old man complained. "I want my money."

"I won't give you another cent," Hammer grated out. "I made that clear during my visit last week."

"Do you have any idea what I can do to you?" Bill lashed back, his voice ugly.

"I know you *think* you have power over me. You've got nothing, Bill. Fuck off."

"If you don't pay up, I'll tell the police you kidnapped my minor daughter and raped her."

"Say anything you want." Hammer called his bluff. "You've got no proof, and Raine will insist you're lying."

Even if the man made those ludicrous allegations and actually found someone willing to listen, Hammer felt sure he and Liam could keep Raine safe.

Besides, he had some insurance of his own.

"Do you honestly think I need proof?" Bill scoffed. "You run a den of iniquity. To the community, you're Satan himself. Tying up women, beating and raping them, and god knows what else. They'll line up ten deep to watch you fry. And I'll just laugh."

Hammer gritted his teeth. "You're forgetting one very important fact. I've got a witness who heard you confess that you tried to rape your own *underage* daughter."

A murderous, blood-red rage filled Hammer every time he thought of Raine struggling against her repugnant father.

"Liam will be more than happy to testify under oath exactly what you said," Hammer added.

Bill scoffed. "The word of another known pervert doesn't mean anything."

"I've also got the medical doctor who examined her the night I found her all beaten and bruised to back me up."

"I'll tell the judge and jury that you gave them both a piece of my underage daughter's ass to persuade them to fall in line."

Hammer gripped the phone tightly. He fought the urge to drive to Bill Kendall's house and beat him with a crowbar until the man's brains littered his filthy, threadbare carpet.

"I still have the photos cataloging everything you did to her, you miserable piece of shit," Macen reminded. "You fuck with me, and all your neighbors will know what kind of monster you were to Raine as a girl. They'll see every bruise and laceration your daughter suffered beneath the hands of their pedophile neighbor."

"I'll sue you for slander, you self-righteous bastard," Bill screamed. "Give me my money or you'll be sorry."

"Don't threaten me, old man. You come around Shadows again, and I'll put a bullet through your head. That's a promise."

With fury buzzing in his ears, Hammer hung up and let out a deep sigh, trying to bring his temper under control. A breath didn't do it. Another only helped marginally. He needed to go check on Raine, but he couldn't until he dialed back his urge to kill her father. One look at Hammer's face and he knew she'd see rage—and start asking more questions.

Slamming a fist on his desk, Hammer cursed long and low, then fired off a text about Bill to Liam, who was probably still occupied with the viper. Not that his friend needed something else to fucking worry about.

Text sent, Hammer closed his eyes and sucked in a breath.

"Was that Raine's father? It didn't sound as if the chat went well."

Hammer snapped his head up and stared at Seth, hovering in the doorway. "God knows the only time a chat with Bill Kendall will go well is when he's six feet under. I wish I'd recorded that conversation, damn it. How is Raine?"

"In the shower. She's quiet—for now. You know that's subject to change once she decides she's pissed off about the way you two are behaving."

Seth hadn't known Raine long, but he was catching on fast.

Macen nodded. "I expect her to blow past her hurt soon and throw a righteous little fit."

"Yeah. She's earned it. You two promised her honesty and communication so she could trust you. Neither of you is delivering. I'll talk to Liam about why he's licking his wounds. But you're lying to her worse than a used car salesman. Are you two just trying to see how fast you can fuck this up?"

Seth wasn't far off the mark.

"Thank you for your opinion, Dr. Phil, but Liam and I have already worked this out. We have a plan."

Seth rolled his eyes. "Because those always work out so well for you two."

Hammer glared. "Did you come here for a reason? If not, I'd appreciate it if you kept an eye on Raine. I'll be there in a minute."

As soon as he got his worry for her safety and his need to strangle Bill under control.

"I did come here for a reason." Seth sighed. "Go easy on Liam. He's under a lot of strain. Problems are coming at him so quickly he's juggling chainsaws."

"We both are. Bill is no picnic."

"I've gathered. But Liam wasn't in good shape when I sent him to Los Angeles to visit you, so this is extra strain he doesn't need."

"What do you mean? He just came here to avoid winter. And maybe some of the places in New York that reminded him of his marriage to Gwyneth, but—"

"Is that what he told you?" Seth snorted.

"Yeah." Hammer shook his head. "Wait. Back up. You *sent* him to me? For what?"

With a droll grin, Seth shrugged. "At the time, we were both under the impression that you had your shit together. I thought you could help fix him."

Hammer paused. Seth's words did a flyby in his brain, buzzing around, but he couldn't quite catch them. "Fix what? He said he'd done his soul searching after his divorce and was fine."

"Unless he searched for his soul by bleeding masochists with a single tail, then no."

He blinked at Seth, feeling his jaw hit the floor. "Liam? He's not a sadist."

"He sure played one back home for a few months. He was scary convincing, too."

Hammer groped around for his chair and sank into it. That wasn't like Liam at all. "What the fuck? Did Gwyneth twist him up that badly?"

"After he caught her cheating, he seemed so damn angry all the time. Controlled, of course. Maybe too much. But under that, he just seethed."

The puzzle pieces started falling into place. Liam had been

so furious with Beck for spanking Raine with a rubber paddle the night he'd collared her because he'd once inflicted that sort of pain himself on subs far more willing. His fury when Hammer's inner beast had come out also made sense. *Takes one to know one.*

"Why? He didn't love Gwyneth," Hammer pointed out.

"No, but she sure as fuck wounded his pride."

Yes, and scarred his ability to trust. Damn it, why hadn't Liam even hinted that he'd had a problem in New York? "I can't imagine him having a sadistic side. I haven't seen it, not here. What made him stop?"

"If I had to guess? You."

Of all the things Seth could have said, that shocked him the most. "Me?"

"Yeah, once he got here, he realized you were in love with Raine and wouldn't let yourself touch her. He—"

"Focused on my problems, not his own." Hammer pinched the bridge of his nose.

"Bingo."

Hammer knew Liam well. That was the kind of thing his friend would do, sacrifice himself to help a brother. "Shit."

"So you see why I'm a little concerned about two 'blind' men showing Raine the way."

"Point taken."

"Good." Seth nodded. "Liam is better since he came here. I think Raine makes him want to be better in a way Gwyneth never did. In a way Juliet never could."

Hammer closed his eyes. God, almost everything had changed since he and Liam had shared Juliet a decade ago—except Macen's craving for a relationship that looked a lot like their past few days at the lodge. Together, they had drilled to the heart of Raine's issues and rewarded her progress with pleasure. Liam had been the right partner all those years ago, but Juliet could never have been their right woman. Not only had she lacked Raine's warmth and soft heart, she hadn't taken control of her life. She'd never communicated that they made her feel like a "fuck doll" until she'd learned she was pregnant and spoken out with a bottle of pills. By contrast, if he and Liam did something that made Raine feel less than loved, she would squeeze their balls until they changed course. She chose to surrender her power; she didn't give it over because fighting was too much effort.

Hammer knew he was still dealing with the aftermath of Juliet's suicide, but he'd had no idea Liam was still so impacted by Gwyneth's betrayal. Now that he did, he had to get smart about Liam's hot buttons.

"Thanks for sticking your neck out for him. You've given me a lot of information I need."

Seth shrugged. "He and I are tight, but you two have a bond that's…beyond. I couldn't help him anymore. I think you can. I know Raine can—if you manage to keep it all together."

Hammer felt himself getting a bit choked. "We will. I'll do whatever it takes."

* * *

Outside in the bright sunlight, Macen shoved on his sunglasses as he helped Raine into the passenger seat of his Audi. After jogging around the vehicle, he slid behind the wheel and eased through the parking lot. He glanced in the rearview mirror, hoping to catch a glimpse of Liam escorting the ice queen and the kid away. No such luck. Hammer wouldn't breathe easy until Liam's ex was out of his club—and out of their lives.

The idea of his friend fathering a child on that bitch made Macen more than a little ill. Liam didn't lack the capacity to love the kid or provide for him. Hell, he'd be a model father. The idea that he'd have to deal with his ex-wife for the next eighteen years ate at Hammer. If the baby did prove to be Liam's, the strain of that was bound to spill over to Raine. Hammer could only wonder what would happen then.

Blending two lives happily was difficult enough, let alone three. Adding Gwyneth into the mix? A nightmare. He'd do whatever necessary to help Liam and Raine deal, though, if he could spend the rest of his life in the bliss he'd felt last night.

Raine turned on the radio and nibbled on a nail as she listened to a mournful ballad. Yeah, she knew something was wrong. It was all over her face.

"I know you said Liam has a business issue. If that's the

case, when we were in the car, why wasn't he on the phone trying to fix it?" she asked. "That seems unlike him. I'm worried."

Sometimes, the girl was too clever. Though he'd expected her to ask more questions, he'd also promised not to lie. "Liam is having a meeting now to find out the scope of the issue. He should know more after that."

"But he seemed angry. Did someone betray him? Screw up?"

More than you know… "He suspects someone is trying to dupe him. But he's smart, so he'll get it all worked out. If he needs us, he'll let us know."

Raine sent him a slow nod. She didn't look happy, but Macen hoped that was the end of her interrogation. Though he was more accustomed to shielding her from ugly truths, he and Liam had to come clean. He was nervous as hell about telling her everything tonight, but he refused to lose her when a few words might keep her near. Hammer tried not to think that those same words might also push her away.

Swallowing the tight lump lodged in his throat, he prayed that before breakfast was through, Liam would have Gwyneth confessing the truth and this whole shit storm sorted out.

They pulled into a local diner, and Hammer helped Raine from the car. Once seated in a booth, he chugged his coffee and fixated on the adorable little line that appeared between her brows as she sipped juice and studied the menu. "What sounds good, precious?"

"It's all tasty." She shrugged. Tipping the edge of the menu down, she gazed at him with pensive blue eyes. "But it would have been my pleasure to cook for you. Why didn't you let me? Liam needs food, too."

Guilt sludged through his veins. A confession sat on the tip of his tongue, but he and Liam had agreed to tell her together. Raine would need reassurances from them both.

He took another swig of coffee and tried to smooth out his expression. "I know. I love that you want to cook for us. But you're tired."

"I'm fine."

The waiter arrived with a pad and a pen before he could say

anything else. Raine ordered next to nothing. With a scowl, Hammer asked for his favorite dish, along with a few hearty sides to share in case he could coax Raine into eating more.

"Christmas is in less than three weeks," he began. "I'm sure you'll want to start decorating and planning the annual holiday gift exchange for the members."

Hopefully, that project would take her mind off everything else, at least until tonight.

Raine frowned. "How long have you known Liam?"

No such luck. He sighed and rubbed at the back of his neck. "Almost a decade. He's fine. Everything is going to be fine."

"Has he ever been into adult-baby play?"

Hammer had braced himself for a question about Liam's mood, his troubles, his lack of honesty—anything except his fetishes. "What?"

She blushed. For all that Raine had finished growing up in a BDSM club, she'd never participated until the last few weeks. Some things she understood purely from observation. "You know, 'daddy' play. Diapers, bottles, rocking, and powdering butts. Is he into that?"

Her question made it clear she didn't like the idea at all.

Hammer didn't think he had to lie about that…but he also hadn't known that Liam had spent any time as a sadist. "He's never expressed even a remote interest. Why do you ask?"

Raine let out a little sigh, but that line of confusion still wrinkled her brow. "I found this just after my shower."

She reached into the pocket of her jacket and slammed something on the table between them. It sounded plastic as it hit the faux wooden surface, but nothing could have surprised him more than to see a pacifier sitting between them.

Instantly, he knew Gwyneth had left it behind for Liam—or Raine—to find. Even before they'd returned to Shadows, that bitch had been planting what she hoped were seeds of destruction.

He gritted his teeth and swallowed back rage. His goddamn blood pressure must have shot up fifty points. Macen felt like a pressure cooker ready to explode.

"That's definitely odd," he finally choked out.

"You don't know anything about it?"

He shrugged, trying really hard to keep his promise to Liam and not lie to Raine. "Maybe it belongs to one of the other club members who used it in their play. Maybe it got caught up in the laundry and—"

"I found it in the bathroom, in one of Liam's drawers with his toiletries."

Oh, that bitch. Hammer really wished he could just kill Gwyneth. He'd be doing the world a big favor. "I don't know for sure. Let's talk to Liam about it tonight. I doubt he's interested in making you his baby girl, not in that way."

"Good." She shoved it back in her pocket. "After my terrible relationship with my own father, I can't imagine taking pleasure in playing with a man pretending to assume that role."

That didn't surprise Hammer at all. "We may be perverts, but I've never had any interest in little girls, pretend or otherwise. I wouldn't touch you for how many years? I can't imagine Liam feeling any differently." At her halfhearted nod, he tapped a finger under her chin. "Smile."

Raine tried, but her confusion bled through. Hammer wished he could say more to soothe her.

The waiter returned, setting down numerous plates teeming with pancakes, bacon, eggs, hash browns, and toast. Hammer's empty stomach demanded attention. He'd never realized how many calories sex consumed, and they'd had a lot of it in the past twelve hours.

The forty-something guy darted back with a fresh glass of orange juice for Raine. When Macen stopped eating to thank him, he noticed that she'd barely picked at her food. Concern gripped Hammer again.

"Eat up," he encouraged. He would have ordered her if he'd thought it would do any good.

A painful fifteen minutes later, she'd barely consumed an egg and a piece of toast. Hammer had devoured most of his, but they still had a mountain of leftovers.

As the waiter cleared everything away, he excused himself and headed to the men's room. When the door closed behind him, he dug out his phone and fired off a text to Liam.

Hammer: What's your status? We're heading back to the club. That ok? BTW, Raine found a pacifier. Guess who left that…

Pacing, he waited for a reply. Seconds passed to minutes. Growing more anxious and pissed off, Hammer clenched his teeth and texted Liam again.

Hammer: If you haven't taken out the trash, keep the bag contained. I'll tell Raine to nap. I'll text you when she's asleep. We'll meet at bar.

"Fuck!" Hammer growled. He despised not knowing what was going on.

Shoving his phone away, he sucked in a couple of deep breaths. He had to keep his shit wired tight until Liam was ready to sit Raine down and talk.

Pasting on a smile, he returned to the table. Raine slouched in the booth, leaning her head against the wall.

"You're exhausted," Hammer murmured as he held out a hand to her. "We're going back to the club, and I'm going to tuck you into bed."

"I won't argue with you," she answered sleepily as she crawled out.

"There's a first."

She stood and glared. "Ha. Ha. Very funny."

One of her acid smiles was better than no smile at all. "Come on. Let's get you home."

"Will you nap with me?" she asked as they headed to the car.

He tangled his fingers with hers. "For a bit. But I still have a club to run."

The sunlight shining on her face made her glow. Hammer couldn't resist trailing a knuckle down her soft cheek or pressing his lips to hers.

"Mmm," Raine purred as he pulled back. "I like you like this."

"Like what?"

"Affectionate. Loving. Soft."

"Trust me, precious. I'm not soft at the moment," he teased as he glanced at the erection straining against his zipper.

"If we can stay awake long enough, maybe we should fix that." She winked.

As many times as he'd turned Raine away in the past,

Hammer didn't think he could ever do it again. His days of denying how much he loved her were over. He just hoped that Gwyneth and her machinations didn't turn Raine against him and Liam in the end.

Chapter Five

Liam strode down the corridor toward the remodeled rooms—and Gwyneth. He'd spent the last four hours dodging her calls while trying to figure out if Kyle was his son. A babe with Gwyneth… Oh, god. Though the boy couldn't choose who his mother was, Liam didn't relish dealing with that bitch for the next eighteen years, especially while he tried to cement his precarious threesome with Raine and Hammer.

This morning in the car, he'd taken his frustration out on the wee lass. The unreasonable jealousy had twisted his thoughts, clouded his judgment. Why else would he have rejected her? The way she'd withdrawn to ward off the pain he'd inflicted still soured his gut with raw guilt and shame.

And despite knowing how badly he'd screwed up, Liam wondered right now what his best friend was doing to the woman they loved.

Fuck. He tried to shake the vision free and concentrate on the coming battle with Gwyneth. But the news of Bill's threat waited there to gnaw at his composure, too.

God, the day was already a catastrophe. Hammer's lie to Raine only added to the shit. And Liam didn't dare ask what else could go wrong. Nor could he let his ex-wife see him rattled. He needed to put himself on lockdown—fast.

As he reached the end of the hall, Liam donned a mask of indifference, then opened the door Pike had stashed Gwyneth behind.

From the portal, he surveyed the room. In a playpen sat the boy with a smattering of dark curls atop his round head and big, dark eyes. They had that much in common. He jerked a little blue rattle in his tiny fist and cried loudly. Tears soaked his bright red cheeks.

Where is your mother?

Liam heard the hum of a blow dryer behind the closed bathroom door. The baby was upset, and Gwyneth thought it was a fine time to do her hair?

With a sigh, he glanced back to the tyke. Now was as good a time as any to see if he could find more than a hint of resemblance.

Carefully, he lifted the baby and brought him closer. Ten fingers. Ten toes. Fat cheeks, a roly-poly belly, and a tiny little mouth. Could this be his son? If so, shouldn't he recognize his own progeny on some level? He frowned.

"She named you Kyle, did she?"

At the sound of his voice, the boy calmed, those big eyes following Liam as his lower lip pouted and quivered between occasional hiccups. Liam repressed a smile. Then he felt something wet on his thigh and realized the babe's nappy was drenched.

Seeing a half-opened bag of diapers and a box of wipes beside it, he scooped up one of each. Holding the baby away from his shirt, he laid the child on the bed. Kyle immediately began crying again, but Liam softly shushed him as he examined the diaper, wondering exactly how it fit together. A tab at each hip appeared to keep it secure.

When Liam removed the wet diaper, a miracle occurred. Kyle—most definitely a boy—quit crying. Liam's ears stopped ringing. A minute or two later, he'd wiped the baby down and swaddled him in a new nappy. Not bad for a first attempt.

Liam brought Kyle against his chest. He and the boy examined one another.

This could be my son.

And maybe not. After all, while they'd been married,

Gwyneth had been fucking her personal trainer.

Those little lips trembled again, and Liam gave him a teasing scowl. "Shh. There's no bawling in a BDSM club. You'll scare the members away."

A little frown fell between those bright brown eyes—a startling resemblance to his own—then a chubby fist made its way to the mouth, and Kyle began sucking.

"Are you hungry, then? You look like you could use a decent steak."

"He'll have to make do with formula and strained vegetables," said a familiar voice.

Liam turned to find Gwyneth standing in the door to the bathroom, a little smile hovering on her face.

His ex-wife looked markedly different since he'd seen her last. Her long platinum hair still hung sleek and straight, but her face was mostly naked. She wore a shapeless black sweater and a pair of faded blue jeans, sans shoes. Liam frowned. He couldn't recall Gwyneth ever looking so casual. Hell, he didn't remember her even owning a pair of jeans when they'd been married. In fact, without Prada, Vuitton, and camera-ready makeup, he almost didn't recognize her. The cool, elegant wife he remembered had been replaced by a seemingly normal, if tired, new mother simply trying to cope.

He almost felt sorry for her…but not quite.

Before today, he'd seen her exactly once since their divorce. For him, that had been one time too many. As far as he was concerned, he had moved on and found true love. Gwyneth being here could only fuck that up.

With a tentative smile, she approached, presenting her cheek for him to kiss.

Liam handed her the baby and backed away. "Gwyneth."

She took the boy, the welcome in her face faltering. "It's good to see you. Isn't it, Kyle?"

"Why are you here?"

The child opened his little mouth, and his face scrunched up in displeasure. His lungs expanded, and an ear-piercing wail tore from his throat.

Wincing, Gwyneth shot Liam a pained expression. The squalling babe grabbed at her pale hair as she anxiously patted his back. "The travel has been hard on him. He's off his sleep schedule."

As she pulled a tissue from her pocket and cleaned the boy's cheeks and nose, Liam continued to scan the little face.

Once the lad had calmed, he pinned his ex with a curious gaze. "Whose child is that?"

She drew in a deep breath, collecting herself, before stepping toward him. "Please sit down, Liam. I—we—have come a long way because there's something important I must tell you. I realize this is sudden, but I hope you'll hear me out."

Liam tensed as she sat on the edge of the bed and juggled the baby in her lap, waiting for him to take a seat in the nearby chair.

He didn't. "You're lucky I took your call at all, much less came to see you. Answer my question. Whose baby is that?"

She took a deep breath. "This is Kyle. He's our son."

Actually hearing his worst fear spoken aloud sent icy dread sliding down his spine. The gravity of the situation hit him full force. He darted a glance between Gwyneth and the boy. Was it possible? He wished like hell he could remember the night of the benefit.

Liam crossed his arms over his chest, trying to read her expression. He saw nothing except an anxious, slightly doe-eyed stare he didn't quite believe.

But why would she be here if he hadn't fathered her son? Gwyneth didn't need money. Not only had he given her half of his fortune in the divorce, she was the youngest daughter of a very wealthy, doting father. She didn't need a husband to raise a baby; she could just hire a nanny. When this child had been conceived, they'd already been divorced, so it wasn't as if she needed to dupe her trusting spouse into believing another man's seed was his own. And if she'd waited all this time to inform him that he'd become a father, she didn't need a last name for the birth certificate.

So what did she want? And why had she come to him?

"Is he now?" Liam asked.

She looked a little crestfallen. "Yes. I know I've shocked you. But…" Gwyneth sent him a pleading stare. "I couldn't keep you apart from your son any longer, darling."

Gwyneth expected him to believe that his feelings suddenly mattered? That didn't sound like the woman he remembered.

Liam gave her a contemptuous snort. "Christ, woman. Let's get one thing straight before you say another word. I'm not your darling, your dearest, your husband, or anything else anymore."

She had the good grace to look contrite.

"Why did it take you six months to reach the conclusion that I need to know my supposed son?"

"Five and a half, actually," she hedged.

Because those two weeks make a huge difference.

"Why didn't you bother telling me you were bloody pregnant in the first place? You had nine months to reach out then."

Liam was quickly losing his patience. He glanced at the lone chair in the room near her—and remained standing.

"Well, that night, after the benefit, in my hotel room…it was like old times. You were charming and loving. It was glorious."

"Oh, for fuck's sake. I was drunk."

Her shoulders stiffened. "Our lovemaking was magical. I was thrilled you wanted me again. I thought it was a new beginning for us, Liam."

Nausea turned his stomach. Was it possible he'd been soused enough to fuck her? If he had, he doubted he'd thought of anything as practical as birth control.

"But when you woke, you were surly and couldn't leave fast enough. I'd just realized I was still in love with you, so I was devastated." She teared up. "Yes, I'd made terrible mistakes during our marriage—"

"That doesn't matter now. Why didn't you tell me you were pregnant?"

"Well, I moved to London to lick my wounds. Then my father fell terminally ill." She stopped as if anticipating sympathy. When he gave none, she continued. "Between caretaking and settling into my new flat, I didn't realize I was pregnant. Once the doctor confirmed it, I tried to reach you. But you'd changed your number. I knew you no longer wanted me, and I was hurt. I grieved. I became determined to raise your baby on my own to make up for the wrongs I'd done to you."

"Or rather, you decided that because I wasn't your prince

charming, you'd punish me by withholding my son."

She swallowed. "No. You left me no way to contact you."

"Please. I might have changed my mobile number, but you knew where I lived up until a few months ago. You could have written me a letter, e-mailed, or called my work."

"I didn't think the post or an electronic message was the proper way to tell you that you'd soon be a father. I didn't contact your business because you're often traveling, and your secretary reads everything first." Gwyneth gave him a delicate grimace. "I realize now it was very wrong of me. I'm sorry."

Wasn't that just like her, sweeping the unforgivable under the carpet at every turn? Before the divorce, Liam had found it difficult to absolve her of cheating. He'd tried but fallen short. Forgiving her for keeping his son—if Kyle was his—from him? Impossible.

Inwardly counting to ten, Liam bit back his anger. "I'm not buying into this story without a paternity test."

"I brought proof. Look." Moving to the dresser, she grabbed a stack of documents, then handed them to Liam. "See? Here's his birth certificate, his immunization records. I even have ultrasounds of my pregnancy."

Reluctantly, he shuffled through the papers in his hand. Details jumped out at him, like the child's surname. *O'Neill.* Almost choking, he noted the boy's birthdate and weight, scanned the ultrasound pictures, which looked like little more than a strange blur of shapes and shadows.

Liam wasn't moved. Sure, she had documents to support her claims, but until he had undeniable proof that he'd fathered the boy, he was skeptical. "Kyle may be your son, but none of this proves he's mine. I want a paternity test."

"I haven't been with anyone but you since we separated," she pleaded with big green eyes.

If, by some miracle, she was telling the truth, that would make him Kyle's father. But Gwyneth abstaining would be akin to a miracle. "I don't care."

"Liam, what kind of awful parents would we be if we subjected our son to such humiliation?"

"Don't be ridiculous. The lad isn't old enough to know what's happening. It won't hurt him. We don't even have to draw blood. I merely have to swab the inside of his cheek."

She swiveled away, drawing the baby closer to her body as if shielding him. "That's unnecessary. I know I hurt you before, but I wouldn't lie about something as important as this."

He arched a sharp brow. "I found you fucking two men while you wore my wedding ring. I think you'd lie about anything if it suited you."

"Don't use that language in front of the baby." She covered one little ear.

Liam rolled his eyes. "He can't even talk."

"But he's beginning to form his linguistic abilities. That's not the sort of speech he should hear. I've been reading—"

"I'll take his DNA sample this morning. Until the lab results come back, we've nothing more to discuss."

"But he *is* our son," she beseeched.

"We'll see. I'll be back with a swab shortly. Wait here."

As he turned to leave, she clutched his arm. "Don't go. I've brought Kyle here so you two could bond." She paused and sent a tender glance into the boy's face, then stared at Liam again. "He *needs* his father."

"If he's mine, then I *will* be a part of his life."

"If? Look at him. You can't deny that face."

"I can until I have proof."

"Please don't take your anger for my mistakes out on Kyle. I'm sorry I've ruined everything." Tears welled. "Had I not been so impulsive, had I realized I was throwing away a loving husband…" She paused, her chin quivering. "Being a mother has forced me to grow up. I'm not the same woman you married. I hurt you deeply, and you'll never know how sorry I am."

She sounded remorseful, but he wondered if she was actually capable of giving a shit about anyone else, much less feeling regret.

Liam pursed his lips. "I'm not buying it, Gwyneth. It's unlike you not to hound me for more—more money, a bigger house, child support, a bigger fucking wardrobe. Why haven't you?"

"I…" She seemed to shrink before his eyes. "I was ashamed."

"I beg your pardon?"

"Are you really going to make me explain? I was ashamed by my actions, Liam." An aching sadness spread across her face. "I know the trust we once shared is long gone, even if my feelings for you remain. I understand if you're too wounded to find it in your heart to forgive me now. But don't turn your back on our son."

Liam frowned at the sleepy-eyed tyke. "I've told you, I'll be a father to the child, if he's mine."

She laid a trembling hand on his arm. "You were always such a wonderful husband. I know you'll be an amazing father. He'll need that, especially now…"

The babe gave a huge yawn, looking as if he were bored.

"Meaning?"

She sniffled, taking a long moment to pull herself together.

"For pity's sake, woman." Liam shook his head. *Open your mouth as easily as you open your legs.* "What are you trying to say?"

"Kyle is suffering from some…issues you should know about."

A little knot of worry formed in his gut. "Is he sick?"

"Not physically. His psychotherapist says—"

"His what?" Had she gone daft? Liam stared at the boy. "He's not even six months old. Why would he need one of those?"

She laid the child down on the bed, boxing him in with pillows and covering him with a fuzzy blue blanket embroidered with a train.

"I told you this was a matter of life or death. Kyle has serious emotional issues."

"Christ, what in-depth conversations could he possibly be having with a shrink?"

"Liam, these are his formative years." Her voice hitched. "Kyle is withdrawn and unhappy. According to his doctor, he isn't bonding properly. This kind of thing could ruin his life."

Liam inspected the now sleeping baby's demeanor. "He looks perfectly normal to me."

"What ails him isn't visible on the outside," she protested. "Spend time with Kyle, and you'll see that his emotional development is thwarted by the lack of an active male figure in his life. We cannot allow him to suffer, Liam."

"Are you serious?"

"Try to keep up." She placed a hand over her trembling lips. "He needs a family, a loving mother *and* father—together—to give him a sense of stability and security."

So that's what she wanted, to play happy family? Liam felt sick. "Let me be clear about one very important thing: If the paternity test bears out, we'll share custody, not a life. You and I will never be together again. Until we have the results, I've nothing more to say."

Turning for the door, Liam swallowed his shock. If he had to deal with Gwyneth for the whole of Kyle's childhood, *he* would need a bloody psychotherapist. He wished to hell he could wake up from this nightmare and find himself lying next to Raine.

Raine.

Just the thought of her caused something to shatter inside him. His plans, hopes, and dreams of a future with her and Hammer looked precarious. They'd worked so hard and come through so much together already. Now, it seemed as if he was losing them. No relationship—especially one less than a day old—could withstand such a test.

At that realization, a giant fist reached into Liam's chest and squeezed his heart.

Gwyneth grabbed at his sleeve. "You can't turn your back on our son, Liam."

He whirled on her. "How the hell do you expect me to react? You come here uninvited, tell me I've knocked you up, and that the boy you claim is mine suddenly needs a daddy. You honestly expect me to drop the life I've made since our divorce and play family man? With no proof?"

"I'd hoped you would be happy," she sniveled. "You're too noble to take your anger out on our innocent baby."

He refused to pack his bags for the guilt trip she kept trying to take him on. "As soon as the boy wakes, text me. I'll swab his cheek, then return you to your hotel. I'll call you once I have the results."

"I don't have a hotel," she confessed. "I'd hoped we'd be moving in with you."

He tried hard not to choke.

"I know now you've found someone else…" Gwyneth sniffled. "Is she very pretty?"

"You will *not* be living with me, and anyone in my life is none of your business." His voice was brittle as ice. "I'll arrange a hotel for you and the boy. Text me when he wakes."

"The boy?" she gasped. "Kyle is your son."

"That remains to be seen."

Before she could say another word, Liam left without a backward glance. As he strode down the corridor, he palmed his phone, quickly reading the messages Hammer had sent. *A pacifier?* Calculating bitch.

He fired a message back to Hammer.

Liam: Heads up. I haven't taken out the trash yet. Meet me in the bar as soon as you can. I'll fill you in.

Chapter Six

Hunched over a glass of scotch at the bar, Liam anxiously waited for Hammer. The burn of the single malt warmed his belly but didn't calm the turmoil or the ache behind his eyes. Despite their intention to come clean with Raine over dinner, Liam realized that extricating himself from Gwyneth might not be as simple as he'd hoped. He should have known. When had anything ever been easy with that woman?

He glanced at his phone. What the devil was keeping Hammer? No doubt he was still in the sack with Raine. Liam tensed, his anger building again. *Can't go there. Fuck.*

Picking up the tumbler, he rolled the amber liquid, watching it swirl within its glass prison. Liam felt just as trapped.

Lost in thought, he didn't realize Hammer had joined him until the man plopped down on the barstool beside him.

"Why is Gwyneth still in my club?" Hammer groused.

"The baby fell asleep. I told her to text me when he wakes. I'll get them out then."

Hammer sighed in resignation. "The sooner the better. Having Raine and Gwyneth under the same roof makes me nervous."

Liam nodded. "If Raine found my ex, I'm afraid she'd draw the worst conclusion."

"Gwyneth having a baby on her hip wouldn't help. And I don't want Raine talking to that manipulative viper. She'd eat our girl alive. Unless she's changed?" Hammer raised a brow in question.

"She's trying to convince me she has. But she's still a manipulative bitch, just more subtle."

"So your meeting with her was fun?"

"Shoving my dick in a blender would have been more enjoyable."

Hammer cringed, then gripped the open bottle of scotch and took a long pull. "That good, huh? Tell me what happened."

"Not shockingly, Gwyneth claims the baby is mine."

Hammer swore. "Is it? I mean…can you tell?"

"Not by looking at him. He's got brown eyes and brown hair, but it doesn't prove a thing."

"What does she want from you?"

"She's got it in her head that we're going to reunite and be a family." Liam shuddered. "Apparently, Kyle has emotional problems because he has no father. At least according to the boy's psychotherapist."

"Fucker, please." Hammer rolled his eyes. "A shrink for a baby? She thinks you're going to buy that shit? What else? Maybe you'd better start at the beginning."

Liam shared the details of his run-in with Gwyneth, but he was barely halfway through before he could feel Hammer's rage.

"I don't give a rat's ass how much proof she brought. Documents are forged every day," Hammer erupted. "You're not buying into her bullshit, are you?"

"Of course not. I told her I needed a paternity test."

"Damn straight."

Hammer seemed to calm slightly, so Liam told him the rest.

"The only thing that's keeping me from tossing her to the curb is that baby," Hammer grumbled. "Even I'm not that big of a prick."

"She's always called you the spawn of Satan, you know."

Hammer laughed. "I'm happy to oblige her and play the part."

"Speaking of obliging her, I need to find her a hotel."

"Let her find her own place to stay." Hammer scowled.

"She could have found one last night but didn't. That tells me the only way she's leaving Shadows is if I drag her, kicking and screaming."

"The good news is…we've got plenty of rope and ball gags." An evil smile tugged at Hammer's mouth. "Do me a favor. Find Gwyneth a hotel close to the airport so she can climb on her broomstick and fly back to London faster."

"I'll do everything I can."

Hammer chugged from the bottle again. "You know she wants more than a daddy for this kid. How much money?"

"She didn't ask for any, just me by her side, helping her to raise emotionally stunted Kyle. God, I'm going to puke. I have to talk about something else. Tell me, how's our girl?"

"Raine didn't eat much breakfast. I'm still worried about her, and that fucking pacifier didn't help." Hammer growled. "You have no idea how shocked I was when she slammed that damn thing on the table and asked me if you had an adult-baby fetish."

Liam choked. "I hope you told her no."

Hammer smirked. "Yeah. Don't worry, I did. It wasn't a lie, right?"

"Wanker," Liam replied with half a snort. "Look, about tonight… After dinner, I've been thinking… Let's show Raine the house. The fact that I bought her a home should make her feel more secure in our commitment. That also gives her a safe place to stay, one Gwyneth knows nothing about, in case my ex lingers nearby."

Hammer smiled. "Great idea. Is the remodeling done?"

"Not quite. But I'll give the foreman a call and tell him to clean up a bit when they're done for the day. We'll tell Raine we intend to move in by Christmas and to start thinking about what she wants in her new kitchen."

"Double ovens, for sure." Hammer nodded. "She's going to be thrilled."

"I think she will be, too. Where is she now?"

"Still sleeping in my room."

Snakes of jealousy slithered through him, hissing, just as they had in the car.

"I guess you finally got to finish what you started on our

way back, then?" The words spilled off Liam's tongue before he could stop them.

Hammer turned and stared. Liam didn't see anger or guilt in Macen's hazel eyes, just pity. That stung even worse. Liam wished he could take back the snide remark.

"Stop right there." Hammer held up a hand. "I took her to breakfast. When we returned, we both climbed into bed. I only held her and stroked her hair until she fell asleep. Even if I'd had sex with her, why would it matter? We *share* her. You know there will be times I'm not around and you'll want her. Vice versa." He shook his head. "I think Gwyneth being here has brought up bullshit you haven't dealt with."

Liam tossed back the last of his scotch. "Now who's psychoanalyzing whom?"

Deep down, he knew he hadn't resolved his bitterness for Gwyneth, but Liam didn't want to sit here and dissect his emotions. "How did your talk with Bill go?"

Hammer shrugged. "He threatened… I threatened. Bottom line: I told him if he showed his face at Shadows again, I'd put a bullet through his head."

"Sounds like a bloody good idea to me. I'll load the gun." Liam smirked.

"It's already loaded and waiting in the top left drawer of my desk." He took another swig of scotch.

Liam heard footsteps behind him. Had Raine awakened and overheard their conversation? Adrenaline slammed through his body. He and Hammer both whirled.

Beck walked toward them with a grin, clutching a white paper bag. "How are you holding up, Daddy?"

Taking the outstretched bag, Liam looked inside and spied the test kit. It brought relief…and dread. Whether he was ready to face fatherhood or not, he'd soon find out the truth. "I'm doing better now that you brought this. Thanks."

Pulling the kit from the bag, Beck arched a brow. "I can collect the sample now, if you'd like."

"The baby's sleeping at the moment," Liam replied. "Tell me what I need to do, and I'll take care of it after he wakes."

Beck nodded, then walked Liam through the necessary steps to gather the DNA. He also provided the name and phone number of a lab tech, Tom, who would run the sample and give Liam the results twenty-four hours later.

"By tomorrow, you'll know whether you're free and clear or writing child support checks for the next eighteen years." Beck shrugged.

"No shit," Liam grumbled.

"Where is your ex, by the way? I want to check her out." He winked. "See if she's really as psycho as you two say."

"We've got her stashed in one of the back rooms." Liam jerked his head in that direction. "But we still need to find a place to put her."

"Put her? You mean like…stash a body?" Beck blinked. "You already killed her?"

"No. We haven't fulfilled that fantasy yet," Hammer scoffed. "We need to find her a hotel room. She's convinced that she and the baby are moving in with Liam."

Beck turned livid. "Don't tell me you're fucking dumping Raine to placate your ex-wife."

"Bloody hell. No!" Liam barked.

"Good. Then I won't have to kill you." Beck shoved a hand into the pocket of his jeans and pulled out a ring of keys. After plucking one off, he handed it to Liam. "Here. This is a key to my condo. Your ex-wife and the kid can stay there for a few days since I'll probably be holed up at the hospital."

Liam blinked. He and Beck hadn't exactly hit it off, but he appreciated the gesture. "I'm… Wow. Thank you."

"No thanks necessary." Beck nodded at him. "You need all the help you can get."

"You're not wrong there," Liam grimly agreed.

"If you want to cause your ex some pain, I've got a nice big toy bag in the bedroom closet." He leered.

"I'll bet." He snorted at the sadist. "If I have to touch her to use those, then no thanks."

Beck chuckled. "I've got to run. Text me if you have any questions. Hell, text me and let me know how Raine's doing."

"Will do," Liam replied, surprised by the emotion thick in his throat. "I appreciate all you've done, Beck."

"You can thank me after we find out that kid's DNA doesn't match yours." He saluted, then turned and rushed out the door.

They sat quietly for several long minutes, Liam digesting the conversation. Then he turned to Hammer. "Is there something you're not telling me about Raine? About Bill?"

"Not at all," Hammer assured. "I'm just thinking… I know you said Gwyneth didn't ask for money, but she's got to have a price."

"She's got more money than god, Macen. She's here for *me*." Even Liam could hear the defeat in his own voice.

"Well, then, I guess for the first time in her pampered life, Gwyneth's not going to get what she wants."

"I could give a shit what she wants. I'm more worried about Raine."

"We're going to take care of her tonight," Hammer reassured.

"What if it turns out I do have a son? Will she still want me then?"

"Of course. Raine's heart is huge. There's room in it for me, you, and Kyle. If he's yours, she'll love him, too, because he's a part of you."

"Thanks. I needed to hear that." Liam sighed. "I want you to know that no matter how the test comes out, I am committed to you and Raine. I'll do whatever I have to, but I won't let Gwyneth come between us."

"Now you're talking." Hammer smiled and raised the bottle.

They drank a toast, and for the first time all day, Liam felt as if he had a bit of solid ground beneath his feet.

"Listen, why don't you go back to my room and slide in bed with Raine," Hammer suggested. "She's missing you. She could use the reassurance."

"I'd like that." Liam was damn grateful for the suggestion. He needed to feel her wrapped around him, breathe in her warmth. "I'm not very centered at the moment. I may sound like some damn Nancy, but just being near her calms me, Macen."

"It's the same for me." Hammer nodded, then grim determination lined his face. "I'll be in to join you two shortly. First, I want to talk to Gwyneth."

"I don't think that's a wise idea." It wasn't that Liam didn't appreciate his friend's help, but things were already fucked up enough without Hammer shoving his stick into the pot and giving it a big stir. "I'd rather you let her be."

"I know, and I understand why. But she's put on her best face for you. She might slip up with me, give some hint about why she's suddenly so eager to make you three a family."

"You're only going to piss her off. And if she comes screaming down the hall—"

"I'll cuff her to a cross and duct tape her mouth shut before I let that happen." Hammer's lips curled in a wicked smile.

"And you'd enjoy every fucking minute of it, too, no doubt." Liam stood. "I'll put this DNA kit in my car so I'm ready when the baby wakes and I've moved him far from Raine. If you can't possibly live without grilling Gwyneth, I won't stop you. But for Raine's sake, keep the fatalities in the war zone to a minimum, will you?"

"Boy Scout's honor." Hammer smirked.

Liam rolled his eyes and stood, tucking the sack under his arm. "We both know you were never a Boy Scout, mate. I'll be back."

* * *

As Liam left the bar, Hammer stood. Squaring his shoulders, he marched down the hall, jaw clenched. The day had been a fucking circus. He itched to keep all the animals in line with his whip, but circumstances prevented that. He didn't like things being out of his control.

The thought of waiting twenty-four hours before he knew whether Liam had gotten Gwyneth pregnant seemed as interminable as a life sentence in prison. Which was where Macen would find himself if Raine's father made good on his promise.

While Hammer had competent, cutthroat lawyers, he knew paying off Raine's father for so many years made him look guilty. Innocent men didn't resort to bribery. Even if Raine testified that Hammer never touched her sexually when she was a minor, the DA could claim Raine suffered from Stockholm syndrome or some other bullshit to convict him.

At least Liam would be here to care for Raine if the worst came to pass…unless Gwyneth sank her claws into him.

Pausing outside the newly renovated suite, Hammer dialed back his anger. He couldn't afford any chink in his armor. If Gwyneth sensed one, she'd go for blood. The bitch had come halfway around the world in hopes of ensnaring her ex-husband. She was in for a rude awakening.

He raised his hand to knock. *Fuck that.* Instead, he turned the knob and sauntered into the room.

With her blond tresses falling down her back, Gwyneth hummed a soft melody. Her relaxed posture looked smug. In fact, the succubus had a serene air, as if she believed her conquest was imminent. If Hammer let her anywhere near Liam, she'd suck the life out of him.

But she was on his turf, and Hammer intended to get the answers he sought and put her in her place.

He cleared his throat, and Gwyneth turned with a start. When her gaze fell on him, her warm greeting vanished. Ah, she'd been expecting Liam. He gave her a cold smile.

She snapped her polite mask in place over all her flawless ivory skin, big eyes, and plump pink lips. But he saw the calculating cunt lurking underneath.

"Macen, I wasn't expecting you. I'd ask you to come in, but since you already have…" She sent him a little shrug. "What a surprise."

Sauntering to the bed, Hammer studied the dark-haired boy. Cute kid, but he saw no particular resemblance to Liam. But then, he knew shit about babies.

"It's a surprise to see you, too." He raised a brow at her. "But since you've come all this way to *my* club to see Liam, didn't you think you'd have to deal with me?"

"I didn't anticipate you barging in. I see now that I should have." Gwyneth's tone, while passive, held censure.

Time to draw the battle lines.

"My place. My rules," he pointed out.

"Indeed." Her expression looked placid and matched her noncommittal tone.

Hammer bet she was biting back what she *really* longed to say. Once upon a time, she wouldn't have bothered, but Liam was right; this 2.0 version of Gwyneth seemed stealthier.

"If you've come to talk, I'm sorry. Now isn't a good time."

She swept a hand toward the sleeping baby. "Jet lag has taken its toll on Kyle. He's just like his father. You know how Liam needs his sleep. Another time." She glided forward as if to usher him out the door.

Hammer met her halfway and wrapped his fingers around her arm. "I prefer now." He hauled her into the small bathroom and closed the door behind him, leaning against the wooden surface to trap her in. "Here will do. So we don't wake the baby."

Gwyneth's eyes narrowed almost imperceptibly. "Kyle will be unsettled if he wakes alone in a strange place."

"We'll make this quick, then, sweetheart." Hammer slid a slow, appraising stare down her body, before settling on her breasts. "I see you spent Liam's alimony on a good cause."

The air around them shifted slightly, and he sensed her subtle rise of temper. He smiled again.

"I know that isn't what you came to discuss."

Macen licked his lips and stared as he captured a few strands of her blond hair, rubbing them between his thumb and finger. He dragged her closer. Heat rose from her body.

As much as he hated the whore, he'd play the seduction card if he needed.

When he glanced down at her breasts again, her nipples had peaked. A pink flush blossomed on Gwyneth's cheeks. He spied a barely perceptible tic of her arm, as if she fought the urge to cover herself.

Bingo.

"What exactly did you want?" She tried to jerk away.

Hammer didn't let go.

"Remember the night you tried to seduce me?" he murmured as he continued to fondle her hair. "Do you still think about it? Wonder what if—"

"I have no idea what you're talking about. I'm sorry if you misunderstood my attempt to make my husband's best friend feel welcome."

"You know, the year I came to visit Juliet's grave after you and Liam were married. Surely you haven't forgotten that night."

Gwyneth refused to meet his direct stare. The pulse point at the base of her neck accelerated. The blush in her cheeks darkened.

Hammer released her hair and brushed his knuckles across her jaw. He relished the opportunity to make her squirm.

She jerked from his touch. "I'm afraid I have."

"Liam and I were in the study, hitting the scotch hard. You joined us."

"You must be mistaken."

Funny how breathless she sounded.

"Oh, but you did, sweetheart. Liam went to bed not long after that. And you climbed in my lap. That ring a bell?"

Her face tightened for a moment, then smoothed again. "I do recall tripping on the leg of the coffee table and falling onto you. Is that what you mean?"

Hammer laughed—long and loud and totally at her expense. "So you just happened to straddle me? And rub your pussy all over my cock?"

She tossed her head primly. "I merely attempted to stand again and had difficulty finding my balance."

"For nearly seven minutes?" Hammer scoffed. "I've had shorter lap dances."

Another flush swept up her face, this one angry. "You think rather a lot of yourself. I never tried to seduce you."

Without warning, he gripped her shoulders and spun her against the door. Pressing his body against hers, she gasped. Nudging his knee between her thighs, he rubbed it against her pussy.

Gwyneth's breathing turned suddenly shallow, telling Hammer she was either pissed off…or aroused. He didn't care which. Either would make her reckless.

"Maybe you should have. You still look beautiful."

"You're standing too close." She braced her hands on his chest, as if she meant to push him away. But she didn't.

Hammer glanced down at where she touched him. "What are you doing with your hands there, sweetheart? You going to unbutton my shirt? Cop yourself a nice feel?"

She yanked her palms from his shirt as if he'd scalded her. "Don't be ridiculous."

"So you only wanted me when you were married to my best friend?" He sent her a mock look of pain. "I suppose it's not as much fun unless you're betraying someone you profess to love."

"You bastard." She gritted her teeth, then raised her hand to slap him.

Hammer snagged her wrist and shook his head. "Don't be a bad girl, Gwyneth, or I'll have to take you over my knee and spank you."

Her nostrils flared, along with her eyes. "I don't play your depraved games. Did you come simply to insult me? If you have no point, let me out of this room."

He'd definitely rattled her. Time to finish her off.

"You know I don't obey commands. I give them." He released her wrist, his stare drilling a hole into her. "How much?"

She understood exactly what he meant, and the little air of triumph he'd seen earlier returned. She batted her lashes. "How much what?"

"Stop playing innocent. You're not good at it," he bit out. "How much money will it cost for you to take the kid, leave the country, and get out of Liam's life for good?"

Somehow, she managed to look stunned. "You think this is about money?"

"You bet your ass I do."

Gwyneth frowned. "I'm disappointed you think I'd be satisfied by something so vulgar. I just want Liam. After all, Kyle needs his father."

"Then I suggest you approach whoever knocked you up and talk to him. Because that baby isn't any more Liam's than he is mine."

Gwyneth shook her head. "Kyle *is* his. I don't expect you to believe me, but I brought proof."

"You brought documents you doctored."

"The baby is Liam's," she reiterated between clenched teeth. "I've been chaste since the night we spent together after the benefit."

Hammer couldn't stop himself from throwing back his head and laughing. "Please. You'd fuck the stick shift in your Ferrari if you thought it would get you off."

She shot him an icy glare before lifting her chin indignantly. Then she pinned her mask back in place. "I've changed, Macen.

I'm not the same woman I used to be."

Hammer could test that claim in a matter of seconds. While being lied to by the pretentious whore pushed every one of his buttons, he wouldn't let his anger get the best of him.

He slid his thigh once more against her pussy, increasing the pressure. She tensed, then wriggled ever so slightly.

Hammer gripped her hips to help her along, grinding her onto his leg. "Tell me again how much you've changed."

She didn't quite manage to bite back her gasp as she stared at his mouth for a long moment. Animosity and anticipation hung in the air, sharp. Strained. He waited.

Finally, Gwyneth pushed at him and tried to close her legs. "Get off me this instant."

He didn't budge, just kept nudging her cunt against him. "I'm still waiting."

"For what?" Her breath hitched.

He took perverse pleasure in watching her struggle to control herself. Her pulse still pounded visibly in her neck. He felt her trying to pull herself together.

"For you to prove how you've changed." He stared her down, thumbing her collarbone and raked his gaze over her even harder nipples. "Because you look pretty aroused to me."

Her entire demeanor turned like a chameleon changing its color. Her perfectly waxed brows pinched together in a practiced look of anguish as she shoved at him. "Don't torment me. You can't fathom all I've been through. But I hope, for Liam's sake, you'll try."

Macen didn't buy it for a second. "All you've been through? You mean, all you've caused."

Gwyneth gave a delicate sigh, her slender shoulders sagging as if she needed to unburden herself. "I wasn't a good wife. I know. But my life has been hell since Liam and I separated. I've learned."

"Oh, really?" Hammer placated.

"I'd give anything if I could go back and undo the damage I've done. I've lived with the terrible guilt for destroying our marriage."

Hammer doubted she was capable of something as deep as guilt.

"I love our son…but every day I look at him, Kyle makes me realize how much I still love Liam as well." She paused for dramatic effect. "I always will. So I've come here hoping that we can be reunited and become a family with Kyle."

While it came as no surprise that Gwyneth meant to wheedle Liam into her life, watching the manipulative wheels spin in her head made Hammer's stomach roll.

"I'll do whatever I can to make it right," she confessed. "I'm simply not sure what that is."

"You want my advice?" Wow, did she have nerve.

Her chin quivered. "I'm determined to prove to Liam that I've changed."

Hammer doubted there was any hope of that.

"He's the sort of man who will be an active father to his son. And for Kyle's sake, it's imperative they foster a relationship now."

"You think the kid needs him, huh?"

"Maybe you think I'm foolish to believe that Kyle's emotional well-being is in jeopardy." She sniffled delicately. "But without his father, my little boy will suffer a lack of knowledge, understanding, bonding—love—that only Liam can give."

Hammer didn't doubt that Liam would fill those roles without exception…*if* he were Kyle's father.

"So will I." Gwyneth reached up and cupped his face, surprising Macen. "You and I… Well, there's always been a certain friction between us. I regret that. You're Liam's best friend. I'm his wife, so—"

"Ex," Hammer cut in.

She smiled tightly, as if dismissing that technicality. "You'd certainly like to continue to have him in your life, as would I. So let's put our hostility aside and bury the hatchet."

Was she fucking serious? Gwyneth certainly wanted him to think so, based on the pleading note in her voice. He tried not to snort in her face.

He'd let her assume she'd hooked him—for now.

"Actually, I'd like to bury the hatchet, too." *In your head.*

"Really? Oh, thank you, Macen." She stepped toward him and hugged him tight. "I'm so relieved. Maybe…you'll help me convince Liam that I love him so we can be a family?"

Hammer had to swallow the urge to puke, but he managed to keep his expression benign. "You'll have to do that on your own. I'll never lift a finger to help you hurt him again."

She drew back as if he'd slapped her. "You're still a bitter, selfish man, thinking of yourself rather than Liam. Pity."

"And you're a manipulative hag, so we understand one another."

Resignation crossed her face. "You know…early this morning, I was sleepwalking. I inadvertently stumbled into Liam's room."

Stumbled, my ass.

"When I woke, I was so excited to see traces of Liam. Then I discovered a woman is staying with him. I smell her perfume on you, too. I gather you're…sharing her?" She sent him a pitying expression. "Macen, what will you do when she becomes your next Juliet?"

At her low blow, a violent rush of fury surged up his body and slammed through his brain. Hammer tensed, curled his fingers into fists. If he didn't, he would wrap them around her neck and squeeze until every ounce of life left her body.

He stared her down, willing his expression blank. "You've got a good nose."

Gwyneth smiled, reminding him of a fucking politician—all flash, no substance. Total bullshit. "Well, I'm sure your little fling will pass before the poor girl does anything tragic. But Liam's heart is too big to be content with your leftovers forever simply to help you recover from your terrible mistake."

Hammer held in a snarl. "I thought we were ending our hostility, Gwyneth? Insulting me and my late wife doesn't seem very friendly at all."

"Oh, Macen." Somehow, she managed to look torn as she reached out to him and cupped his arm. "You're misunderstanding me again. Of course that's not what I meant. What I'm trying to say is that my heart will fulfill Liam in every way. And for his sake, I worry about you. I think it's time you found a woman who can love you for good. Or haven't you been able to find one?"

Hammer had never hit a woman in anger. *I might make an*

exception for you, you snatch-faced cunt.

Clinging to the last thread of his temper, he pasted on a smile. “Since we’re starting over, I presume we’re speaking honestly?”

“Of course,” she replied with a look of innocence.

“I told Liam not long after you two tied the knot that you were a scheming whore. I hated to be proven right, but I wasn’t surprised at all.”

Hammer watched Gwyneth waffle between a contrived shock and her usual haughty ice-queen demeanor. Her body tensed with an almost palpable hum. “I beg your pardon?”

“You’ve got two choices,” he drilled her in a calm, low voice. “One, you tell me exactly why you’re here. Once you do, I’ll write you a big fat check. Then you’ll haul your ass back to London so that neither Liam nor I will ever see, hear, or speak to you again.”

She peeled back her lips in a scathing, humorless smile. “You can’t afford me.”

“You sure you don’t want to try me? Give me a price and see if I’ll meet it.”

She scoffed. “No. I’m here for Liam.”

“Well, you’re going home empty handed, sweetheart. He stopped caring about you the minute he found you taking your personal trainer’s dick up the ass while you blew his boyfriend. Liam doesn’t love you. He will never love you. And he will never, ever consider being a part of your life again. I’ll make sure of it.”

Her little smile sent a warning prickle up his spine. “We’ll see.”

Chapter Seven

Behind Raine, the bed dipped. As she lay on her side, an arm slipped around her waist. Moist breath on her neck, stubble grazing her nape, and a familiar, woodsy scent drew her up through the layers of consciousness. She woke to the feel of a hard male body, warm and naked, spooning her against him.

Liam. Raine was intimately familiar with his touch. His musk—like the man himself—was a seduction. Alluring. Everything about him flirted with her senses, tempted and drew her in. Hammer felt completely different. Sharp, aggressive, darkly masculine. Unyielding.

Liam pressed his ready erection against her backside as he filled his hands with her breasts and groaned. "I didn't mean to wake you…"

"I'm glad you did." She lifted her heavy lids, expecting to see Hammer lying next to her, where he'd been before he'd stripped her down and tucked her in. Instead, she only saw the glowing numbers of the clock, noting that it wasn't even ten thirty. "I guess I drifted off. Where did Hammer go?"

"He's got a club to run, remember?" Liam pulled her to him, clutching her close. "I missed you."

She snuggled back against him. After his odd mood in the car this morning and his stinging refusal to touch her, having him here was an unexpected but reassuring surprise.

"I missed you, too."

"You feel good," he breathed in her ear.

As he spoke, the scent of Scotch hit her nose. He'd been drinking?

She turned in his arms. "Is everything all right?"

His grave expression took her aback. His dark eyes burned. "I need you to kiss me, Raine."

She met his stare, unblinking. Usually, he held her and pressed his lips to hers if the urge moved him. But now, the gravity in his voice said he needed her—and he didn't often admit that aloud. Was he feeling guilty about his rebuff this morning? Maybe, but this felt like more, like him reaching out for her love.

The woman in her responded. Maybe she should still be angry or hurt, but Liam had been her rock since their first day together. She sensed that now he needed her to be his. She ached to know why, but it wasn't the time to interrogate him.

Raine cupped his face. "Always."

She laid her lips over his in a soft caress, testing her welcome and his hunger. He tensed as she leaned in, then breathed through the initial brush of her mouth. He grabbed her hips, kissed her in return, but he didn't move or make a sound through the achingly gentle press of lips. His fingers tightened on her. Long and slow, he inhaled as if drinking her in. Raine wondered what troubled him.

She pulled back enough to search his face. "Liam?"

"My sweet love," he whispered against her lips, then rolled her to her back and covered her body with his own. He tasted of the tart, smoky Scotch he'd consumed—and of desperation.

Clutching her nape, he held her still for his pleasure and delved into her mouth as if he could fuse them together. He didn't test or apologize with this kiss. As he crushed her mouth beneath his, he claimed her, screaming "*mine*" without saying a word at all.

Raine jolted. From the moment Liam had taken her into his arms as a lost girl aching to feel like a woman, he'd cradled her in his sure hands, always steady and strong, beside her, supporting her, helping her grow, and never asking for anything in return—until now.

Carnal and thorough, he ate at her mouth. She felt his trembling, tasted his longing. He wasn't asking her for help. Obviously, he had no intention of telling her what upset him. But in that moment, it didn't matter.

Flowing around and under Liam, Raine opened and gave him everything. She had a million questions, but they didn't matter now, when everything about his demeanor told her that she'd become his life preserver in a raging sea. He entreated her by laving his tongue against hers again and again. He held her tight.

Time slid by, endless and meaningless, until he robbed her of breath and she turned restless in her own skin, until the ache to have him deep took over and she clung, spread her legs beneath him, and moaned for his next touch.

His swollen cock, hard and hot, slid against her sex. Raine basked in the intimacy as liquid heat rushed between her thighs.

"Liam…"

As if he realized he'd all but pounced on her, he pulled back and did his best to smile. "Did you rest well?"

The warmth of his body matched the concern in his voice.

"Yes," she assured. "Did you get some breakfast?"

"I'll eat a hearty lunch," he promised.

Raine hated the thought that he'd gone without food. "I can make you something."

When she moved to roll out of bed, he pinned her beneath him. "Stay with me."

It was a command, brooking no refusal. She didn't often see this side of her indulgent Liam. The only time she'd seen him uncompromising, he'd been very upset.

As if he realized how out of character he'd behaved, he tried to smile. "Tell me about your breakfast with Hammer."

It set off all her alarm bells. "It was fine. I'm sorry you weren't able to join us. Did you get everything taken care of?"

Liam tensed. She felt the spike of his anxiety all the way to her bones, especially when he nuzzled her neck again, as though needing the comfort of her skin. Raine wanted to give it to him, but she desperately needed answers.

"What's going on?" She struggled to put some space

between them so she could sit up.

He used his body to keep her down. "The business I need to attend to is more complicated than I thought. I don't like that it's made you doubt how I feel. I hate that I'll be busy—and probably preoccupied—for another day or two. Hopefully, no more than that."

Searching his dark eyes, she felt a flutter of fear low in her belly. "You'll still be with us at night, right?"

"I'm hoping so. I promise I'll do my best. I'm clearing my schedule tonight so that Hammer and I can take you out for a romantic dinner. Would you like that?"

Normally, she would, but the thick air of tension rolling off Liam made her insides knot. Something told her this invitation was more likely an apology or a precursor to bad news, rather than simply an amorous gesture. Raine didn't like the worry notching up inside her…but she couldn't seem to kill it.

She pressed her lips together. "Will you have to go back to New York?"

Liam cocked his head, then brushed his fingers down her cheek. "Don't be putting the cart before the horse, love. Relax, will you?"

Liam wanted her to believe everything was wonderful when it wasn't. Because he'd reached out to her, she was trying to give him the benefit of the doubt. She was certainly willing to hold and love him if he needed her. But she refused to be placated.

Raine pushed at his shoulders until she made enough space to roll away and sit up. "What's happening with you? With us? I'm scared."

He cupped her chin. "There's nothing to be scared about. The last thing in the world either Hammer or I want to do is leave you. I don't know of any reason I'll have to return to New York, so set that worry from your mind. Like I promised, I'll do my best to be with you as often as possible. Trust me, I don't feel whole when I'm away from you."

His words warmed her. She felt the same.

Raine bit her lip and nodded. She'd let her insecurities get the best of her again, even though they'd both tried to reassure her. Maybe she just had to stop waiting for the worst and believe that whatever was happening didn't mean the end of them.

Maybe they were trying to protect her from something. No idea what, but God knew they both had the instinct.

"Can I do anything to help? I feel useless."

"No. This situation will work itself out, but I'll have to be on hand to steer it in the right direction. Believe me, I'm not leaving you. I never want to."

The heartfelt vow made her sigh before he swallowed the sound with a searing kiss. He held her lips captive under his as if nothing in the world mattered more than making love to her mouth and cocooning her heart. Her uncertainty began to melt away.

Then he urged her to her back, covering her body with his own. He stroked her waist, easing down to the curve of her hip with his big hands before drifting up again to caress the plump weight of her breasts. Her breath stuttered. Her body caught fire again.

He loves me. They love me. It's going to be all right.

She repeated the litany in her head, wanting so desperately for it to be true.

Raine caught his face in her hands, stilling his invasion as she held his gaze and lost herself in his dark, compelling eyes.

Tension tightened his face. His expression turned somber. "Nothing matters more to me than you, Raine."

She tried to treasure the moment, but she still felt his disquiet churning the air between them.

God, why did he keep downplaying whatever was going on when she could plainly see how much it worried him? But questioning him again would get her nowhere.

"How long can you stay?" she asked instead.

"Never long enough to get my fill of you. Reach back and grab the headboard."

Yes. Please…

Raine needed him—his time, his affection, his passion—so she didn't hesitate.

Her breath caught when he pushed up and hovered, staring down at her. He pinned her hips, spread her wide with his big body, and slid his velvety-hard erection along her opening, back and forth, nudging her aching clit. Raine tried to wriggle under him. Needing more contact, more of him.

"Please, Liam. Please. Fill me. I want you inside me."

"Not yet. Patience."

"But—" Her cunt clenched hard as he ramped up the friction on her bundle of nerves, his unswerving stare drilling down into her. She trembled. Beyond being wet and ready, she needed to feel close to him. To bond with him completely.

"I said not yet. Hold on tight, Raine. Don't move and don't come until I tell you."

He looked every inch the Dominant he was. She realized he needed more than a sweet tumble from her. He craved control of this situation, likely because he couldn't control whatever troubled him. And because he needed to own her.

"Yes, Sir," she breathed, giving him what he sought and giving herself over.

He bent his head to her breast, drew her nipple between his lips, and held the erect tip between his teeth before sucking it into the heat of his mouth. The delicious pull reached down to her pussy, like an invisible cord.

Liam plucked at her precisely and perfectly, in exactly the way he knew would make her melt in need and want to beg him for more pleasure. Then he gave her other nipple the same treatment, not stopping until she whimpered for more.

God, she loved it when he did that. Raine grabbed at him, plunging desperate fingers into his hair and rolling her hips, silently pleading.

"I told you, don't move. Grab the headboard now."

As she complied, he gave a shove of his lean hips and spread her thighs farther. Then he sat up enough to push her legs back, exposing her completely. He stared at her slick opening, making her wait for him, as he fondled the bud of her clit.

He worked her patiently, his free hand sliding up her body to pluck at her nipples again as he circled her needy button with his fingers until her breath hitched, until she felt a flush suffuse her, until the electric thrum of her heartbeat roared in her ears.

"You're close." It wasn't a question; he knew.

"Yes." She writhed under him.

"Spread your legs wider. Plant your feet on the mattress."

Raine did it eagerly, ready to welcome him deep inside her. Less than eight hours ago, he'd made her scream out in pleasure.

The way she needed him now, it felt as if she'd been waiting a decade. His impatience to tear open the condom and roll the latex over the head and down the smooth, thick shaft said he felt the same.

"We're getting you on some damn birth control tomorrow," he grumbled.

She loved the idea of having Liam and Hammer spontaneously, of feeling them bare and intimate inside her. "I can't wait."

"You'll take all of me, love," he growled before guiding himself to her drenched pussy. Without pause, he thrust deep.

Raine gripped the rungs of the headboard with all her strength. Her back arched, and she tossed her head with a wail, feeling every delectable inch of him slide home.

Liam didn't give her a second to catch her breath as he withdrew, then slammed back inside her. Raine shrieked as rapture drizzled like warm syrup through her veins. He held her captive, so completely open to him all she could do was feel each stroke stripping her of composure bit by bit.

He braced himself over her body, staring down at her with those burning eyes again, his jaw tight, his breath sawing in and out of his chest. His hips pistoned as he slammed inside her with a dizzying rhythm. Every stroke drove her higher. She felt desperate for the end yet wished it would never come.

Liam clutched her, plowing hard, fast. Repeatedly. He gripped her hips, his lips crashing over hers as if he would starve without her. Every touch dripped with a desperation that swept Raine up and along with him, rushing toward the terrible beauty of a stunning demise. He'd told her she couldn't move, couldn't climax until he gave her permission, but she trembled with the urge to thrust against his onslaught and release headlong into the bright agony he gave her.

Just when she felt too close, he eased back, totally in control, and dangled her over a chasm of yearning so deep she couldn't stop herself from begging.

"Please, Sir. Liam…" she panted. "Oh…please? Please!"

"Hold fast. Not yet."

She mewled, clenching the slats harder, her body bucking, searching, needy. She loved this man—and everything he did to her. "I'm falling. Oh, god, Liam. I'm falling and I can't—"

"No," he barked. "You'll stay with me now. Wait for it."

Raine felt like a powder keg ready to explode. She could feel each ridge and every inch of him sliding against her flesh as he cleaved rhythmically inside her pussy. The friction burned her. She gasped. Every stroke sent his hard chest rasping over the tender flesh of her breasts.

She cried out once, then again, as he buried himself deeper still, gripping her hips and tilting her up for his pleasure. The powerful muscles of his shoulders, hips, and thighs bunched with effort. Pheromones surrounded them, and the animalistic hunger in his eyes consumed her. Everything about this moment—about this man—ignited her. Pleasure gripped her, squeezing out the need for everything but the agonizing release Liam held just out of her reach. When it came, she didn't know how she'd survive.

"Fuck, Raine. Come for me. Now!" he roared as he surged up again and thrust his hand into her hair, forcing her to stare into his eyes.

Lightning caught her blood on fire. The conflagration gathered, burned, centering right where they joined. Then he pushed her over the edge with his next stroke, and she shattered, flinging herself headlong into the abyss and screaming his name.

But she wasn't alone. Never again because Liam was right there with her as he emptied himself of seed, worry, anger, pain. In return, she wrapped her arms and legs around him, giving him all her love.

Their bodies pressed together beneath a sheen of sweat as the sounds of their ragged breathing hung in the room. Bliss filled Raine's every pore. The haze of rapture left her languid and limp.

"I needed that, love," he admitted between harsh sighs.

I know. "I did, too."

"Oh, Raine…" Liam leaned in to kiss her gently.

The muffled ring of his cell phone from his pants puddled on the floor sent him cursing and scrambling across the bed, shattering their enchantment.

As Liam silenced his phone and shoved it away again, Hammer surged into the bedroom. The fact that he'd burst into the room didn't startle her. His furious glare did. He darted a gaze between her naked body and Liam disposing of his condom and donning his pants. The rolling waves of tension pouring off Hammer as he sucked in a rough breath seized her with anxiety.

"Looks like you two had fun," he drawled.

She swallowed a lump in her throat. "We did."

It felt awkward admitting that to one lover when she'd just been busy with the other. Had she and Liam done something wrong? The three of them hadn't had any time to establish do's and don'ts. Hell, they'd only committed to trying to make this ménage work last night. Prior to that, they'd coupled off for sex—and jealousy had constantly brewed.

If she stopped to think about it, it made sense that each would demand some one-on-one time with her. Both men had sworn that if she shared her affection equally, nothing would ruin their relationship.

After this morning in the car, and now seeing Hammer's face, she had doubts.

She frowned, searching for the right words.

Hammer sat beside her on the bed, brow quirked. "Problem, precious?"

She swallowed her questions. No sense in borrowing more trouble. They had enough. "No."

Except… It dawned on Raine that Liam hadn't truly answered any of her questions before he'd taken her to the heavens.

Raine glanced between the two men. They shared some look, a silent communication she would probably never understand. After years with Hammer, she'd developed a sixth sense when it came to his moods. Something was wrong. He'd been upset since before they'd left the lodge. Now he was seething. And he didn't want her to know.

She'd had more than enough of their subterfuge. But Raine refused to sit on her hands and wait. She needed to figure out what they were hiding.

Liam eased onto the bed again and rolled beside her to cup her breast.

Raine watched Hammer as Liam thumbed her nipple. Macen didn't give any outward hint that Liam's touch bothered him. Instead, he threaded his fingers through her hair and kissed her.

"Is something wrong?" she asked as she stared into Hammer's stark face. "You're…tense."

A faint flash of surprise skittered through his eyes—or maybe it was guilt.

"Just dealing with crap around the club," he dismissed with a wave of his hand. "I didn't leave my frustrations at the door and should have. Did you get a little rest?"

"Something I need to help with?" Raine ignored his question.

"I asked if you got some rest," Hammer pressed her with a look of censure.

Now, they were both being evasive.

"I did. What is—"

"If Hammer needed your help, he'd be sending you out the door to tend to some task or another," Liam said in a soft, steely tone that warned her not to refute him.

"I would." Hammer nodded. "You deserve a day off. There's nothing so important that it can't wait until tomorrow."

If that's true for me, why isn't it true for you?

"Why don't you go start the shower for us, Raine?" Hammer suggested.

"I had one before breakfast."

"But not with me." Hammer dropped his gaze to her naked flesh. His nostrils flared, drawing in the scent of sex lingering in the air. Liam might be done with her for now, but Hammer hadn't even started.

She swallowed and darted a gaze to Liam. His unreadable face didn't tell her if Hammer's demand bothered him.

"All right."

Before she could climb out of bed, Liam skimmed a soft thumb over her cheek, then kissed her forehead, her nose, her lips. "Thank you, love. I enjoyed my time with you. I'll see you tonight."

"I can't wait." God, she hoped she got some answers then. They were driving her batty.

Hammer pulled her into his arms, onto his lap, and held her tight against his chest. His hold felt almost desperate, too.

Then he claimed her lips. As she surrendered to his potent kiss, Raine wished the three of them could have stayed at the lodge, far from the stress that now consumed the men she loved. Then she wouldn't have to deal with the fears and uncertainty eating her alive.

Bittersweet moments later, Hammer helped her up and gave her butt a playful swat. "I'll be in to join you in a minute."

Raine felt their eyes on her as she made her way toward the bathroom. A strange foreboding filled her. Intuition told her that life as she knew it was about to change.

* * *

As Raine walked away, Liam rolled out of bed and shrugged into his shirt. She'd shut the bathroom door, but he waited until he heard the stream of the shower pounding tile before he turned to Hammer.

"Raine is waiting on you, and the baby is awake, so we don't have much time. Tell me what happened with Gwyneth. You look like you're ready to stroke out, mate."

"Why the fuck did you say 'I do' to that vile whore?"

"I was listening to my cock then, not so much my head."

Hammer scrubbed a hand through his hair. "Based on what you told me, the woman I just saw wasn't the same teary, contrite one who begged you to parent with her. She tried to tell me she'd changed. When that didn't work, she pleaded with me to end the friction between us and start over so I'd help her get you back."

"Oh, for fuck's sake," Liam moaned. "She's a head case."

"And when *that* didn't work, she basically told me Raine would be my next Juliet, that you'd get tired of my sloppy seconds one day, and I'd never find a woman who loved me."

Liam clenched his jaw. "I'm ready to kill the bitch myself. She is still alive, isn't she?"

"Yes, which wasn't my first choice."

"Bollocks. So I need to watch my back?"

"And your front, too. I was her only potential ally, but by the end of our conversation, she'd burned every bridge with me. Now she has no other option but to bring her *A* game with you."

"She can try, but I won't be playing by her rules," Liam spat, but he still tasted her bitterness on his tongue. "I can't believe she had the nerve to toss Juliet in your face like that."

"Oh, I can," Hammer snarled. "Desperate times call for desperate measures, and for whatever reason—which I seriously doubt has a fucking thing to do with that baby—Gwyneth is beyond determined to get you back."

Liam clenched his jaw. "Don't worry. I'm right beside you with Raine, mate."

Hammer nodded, then darted a gaze toward the bathroom. Anger continued to roll off his frame, and Liam couldn't help but worry if Macen would sate some of his frustration with Raine.

"Pack up Gwyneth's shit and get her the fuck of out here." Hammer sounded viciously mad. "*Please*."

Liam had rarely heard such distress in Macen's voice. Clearly, the fear of losing the closeness they'd just begun developing with Raine was consuming Hammer, too.

"I will. Take care of Raine."

Christ, he wanted to tell Hammer to treat her gently, to be kind and loving, and to keep the beast inside him at bay.

"I'll occupy her in the bedroom until I get the all-clear from you." Hammer clapped him on the shoulder, then eased into the bathroom and quickly stripped off his clothes.

Liam had to dig deep and trust that the man would keep his emotions in check with their girl. He inched toward the open portal and watched the muted shadows of naked skin moving beyond the glass doors. He held his breath, expecting Hammer to shove Raine against the wall and claim her in a fierce rush. Instead, Macen simply wrapped his arms around the woman they loved and clutched her beneath the spray of water as if nothing else mattered.

With a sigh, Liam turned, stepped into his shoes, then left the room.

As he left Hammer's bedroom and passed through the man's office, he tried to savor the bliss he'd found while lost inside Raine. He'd sought solace for his worries and found it wrapped in her arms, along with a sense of balance, home…love.

As he exited into the hallway, he squared his shoulders and dragged in a deep breath, bolstering himself to do battle with Gwyneth. No doubt, she'd be more than stirred up when he dragged her out of Shadows, especially after her verbal spar with

Hammer.

Macen had been rattled, so their altercation must have been more vicious than even he'd let on. Juliet's suicide was still a gaping wound in Hammer's psyche. He hadn't let go of the guilt. And blast Gwyneth for knowing that fact and using it against him. It was why Hammer clung to Raine so tightly, why he sheltered her a bit too much. Someday, they'd have to deal with that.

Right now, enough was enough. Liam was ready to battle the dragon.

Gwyneth seemed willing to do or say anything to get him back. Why? She hadn't given a shit about him when they'd been married. And he wasn't buying that she simply wanted to atone. She might want a family for Kyle, but why the sudden urgency? Gwyneth had known she was pregnant over a year ago. Why wait until now to decide the time had come to be a family? Why arrive in the middle of the night and demand they start their domestic bliss that moment?

As far as he was concerned, once he dropped off this kid's DNA swab, he'd be counting every minute of the next twenty-four hours.

Suddenly, Gwyneth rounded the corner at the end of the hall. He cursed under his breath. She looked startled to see him, then pasted on a look of wilted relief.

Liam frowned. Where the hell was the child? Had she left him alone in the room?

"Oh, thank goodness it's you." She raised a palm to her heart, gliding toward him.

"Why are you roaming the halls? I told you to stay put." Liam ate up the remaining distance between them. No way would he have her near Hammer's office—and Raine.

"I had to find you." Gwyneth looked ready to burst into tears. "Hammer accosted me, and the things he said… I've never been so insulted or humiliated in all my life."

"I know all about your run-in." Liam gripped her elbow and tugged her toward the room she occupied.

"Only Hammer's side of it. I'm begging you to hear me out." She sucked in a deep breath, clearly preparing to launch into a tirade. Then her whole body stiffened. "Liam, I… How could you do this to me?" she gasped and covered her offended nose. "You reek of sex."

"Damn good sex, in fact," he quipped as he propelled her down the far hallway and pushed her into the bedroom, barely resisting the urge to slam the door.

Glancing toward the bed, he saw the baby playing safe and sound with his plush toys, still surrounded by pillows. For the love of god, if Kyle was Liam's flesh and blood, he'd have to do something to protect the lad from his inept mother.

"Pack your things," Liam ordered.

Gwyneth jerked from his grip and spun to face him, somehow managing to look both horrified and betrayed. "I came all the way from London to tell you about your son and confess that I still love you. And you…you just…" She reached out for him, curling her fingers around his shoulders, entreating him. "Liam, she's not for you. I'll take care of all your needs."

He shrugged her off. *I'd rather become a eunuch.*

"Anything you desire. Everything. I'm here for you. Don't do this to us!" she sobbed. "I know if you'll give us another chance that—"

"You had your chance. Stop your bleating and move," Liam growled.

"That tart you and Hammer are f…" She hesitated as if biting back the f-bomb. "Sharing. Perhaps she's fun to play with, but you need love. An immoral slut can't give you that."

With every fiber of his body, he wanted to defend his lass. But Liam knew Gwyneth too well. Doing that would only put a bigger target on Raine's back.

Liam didn't reply, just narrowed his eyes and jerked his chin. "Do as I say. And make sure you get everything because you're not coming back. Then gather up the baby. You've worn out your welcome here."

"Where are we going?" Gwyneth blinked, wiping at her tears.

"I've arranged a condo for you and the boy for a couple of days." He bent to fold up the playpen. "You even have a view of the ocean."

Gwyneth stared up at him with seeming devastation. "Don't stow us away like forgotten baggage. Stay with us."

"I have a life, Gwyneth."

"But…" she stammered and glanced over her shoulder toward the baby. "Don't you want to spend time with your son? Get to know him?"

"If he's actually my son, I will. Now start packing or I'll do it for you."

"At least let Kyle have some playtime—"

"Don't try me," Liam warned.

"This is Hammer's doing, isn't it?" She pursed her lips into a flat line. "He's angry that I rebuffed his advances."

"What?" Liam stared at her as if she must be crazy.

"Yes, your *best friend*—the man you share that woman with—he…touched me." She shuddered. "That's what I've been trying to tell you. He pushed me against a door and…" She dissolved into trembling tears. "I barely escaped."

If Hammer had touched her at all, it was to play games with her head. Obviously, it had worked. Liam wanted to tip his hat at his friend.

"Well, then, let's get you far from Hammer. He won't be able to bother you at the condo."

"I'm shaken. I-I can't seem to gather myself. I need you to hold me."

"You'll pack up and come with me now, or I'll forgo the condo altogether and take you and the boy straight to the airport. We'll let our lawyers sort out this mess."

"Liam, please. Listen to me." She shook her head imploringly. "I never once considered putting lawyers between us. I don't want money or documents about parental rights. I want a full life for Kyle. I want my son to have his father. I want my husband back."

Gwyneth might be singing a different verse, but it was the same song. He'd grown weary of these lyrics.

"I've told you more than once that until a paternity test tells me I fathered that boy, I don't believe you. And I don't care what you feel for me."

Tears spilled down her cheeks. "I brought *our* son here to show you that I love you and I've changed. W-when did you become so heartless?" She thrust her hands on her hips. "This is Hammer's influence. He's leading you down a terrible path of emptiness and depravity. My love can save you."

Her "love" had already fucked his life up once. The thought of giving her the chance to hoodwink him again…no. Even being near her now made him crave a shower.

"I'm giving you sixty seconds, Gwyneth. Get your shit together or I'll be dragging you out of the club empty handed."

She opened her mouth to argue. Something on his face must have convinced her that was unwise. She snapped it shut and began shoving her belongings into a designer suitcase. Kyle's things she tucked into the diaper bag. When she scooped up the baby, he started fussing.

Gwyneth shot Liam an icy glare. "If you're satisfied, I'm ready."

Repressing a smile, he snatched up her suitcase and the playpen, then led them down the hallway, toward the front door. As they passed the bar, Seth turned, coming face-to-face with Gwyneth. Sauntering into her path, he flashed her a cynical smile.

She didn't return it. "I might have known you'd be here, too." Turning to face Liam, she flashed him a look of pity. "Obviously, you've been lonely since our separation. I can't think of any other reason you'd surround yourself with your most debauched friends. My poor Liam…"

He rolled his eyes.

Seth just laughed. "I'm doing well. Thanks for asking, Gwyneth. I wish I could say that it's good to see you, but I could go another hundred years without the privilege." He turned to Liam. "You finally getting her the fuck out of here?"

"I am."

"Hot damn. We'll throw a party. After the exorcism, of course." With a smirk, Seth sidestepped Gwyneth and continued down the hallway, whistling as he left.

She stared after him for a moment, then turned back to Liam and shook her head mournfully. "Oh, Liam. I should never have left you."

"I'm so glad you did."

He all but pushed Gwyneth out the front door. Having her in a common area worried Liam. Hammer should be occupying Raine now, which distressed him for other reasons. But even if

Macen couldn't control his beast, she'd be safer with him than with Gwyneth.

Once outside, he raised his key fob to unlock the doors of his Escalade. After tossing her suitcase and the playpen into the back, Liam closed the hatch, then turned to find Gwyneth staring at him with a wounded expression.

"Well, looky here." That familiar voice turned him to stone. "It's the slick Mick who's fucking my daughter."

Liam whirled to see Bill strolling toward them across the car park.

"Get in the car, Gwyneth," he demanded.

His ex-wife froze and stared at Bill. Why didn't she ever bloody listen?

Liam didn't have any more time to insist again before he stepped in front of Gwyneth and Kyle to glare at Bill. "What the hell are you doing here?"

"Just paying you and Master Pervert a friendly visit." Bill leaned and settled his stare on Gwyneth, undressing her with his eyes. "Is this another kinky whore you tie up and beat? She sure is pretty."

Gwyneth gaped indignantly. "How dare—"

"Shut up," Liam snapped, wanting to slam Bill's teeth down his throat. No woman should have to endure Bill's vile nature. And his protective instinct now extended to Kyle. "Get in the bloody car."

"Did you knock this one up?" Bill winked. "Good job. Maybe you'll plant a seed in Raine's belly soon, too. I've always wanted to be a grandpa. I think I'd make a good one, don't you?"

"So you could try to rape that child, too?"

Bill waved him away. "Don't make me out to be some villain. Master Pervert popped Raine's cherry when she was underage."

Liam surged forward and lunged in Bill's face. "Hammer never touched—" No, he didn't owe Raine's father any explanation. Nor would Bill believe the truth. Blood boiling, he shoved a finger in the old man's face. "Turn around and leave while you still can, Kendall."

"Does my daughter know you're fucking this blonde, too? 'Cuz I'll bet Raine will get pissy if she finds out you're shoving your deviant dick into this beauty's juicy cunt," Bill taunted gleefully, then turned to Gwyneth. "It is juicy, isn't it, honey?"

She clutched Kyle tighter to her chest and glanced nervously at Liam.

"Get in the bloody car, Gwyneth," he growled. "Now!"

Finally, she scurried into the backseat with the baby, then quickly shut and locked the door.

Liam narrowed his gaze on Kendall. For the hundredth time, he wondered how the sorry sack of shit had had any part of making their beautiful Raine.

The violence Liam wanted to unleash on the man scared him. He'd seen the photographs of the abuse this animal had heaped on her. It made him crazy that Bill continued to breathe. Liam had to beat back the urge to fix that.

"Did you think Hammer was kidding when he said he'd put a bullet in your head? I'd be happy to do it in his stead. Turn the fuck around and leave. You won't get another warning."

Bill plucked a toothpick from behind his ear, seemingly unconcerned, and picked at his tobacco-stained teeth. "I ain't going anywhere without my money."

Cold fury poured through Liam. "Your money tree has dried up, old man. Fuck off."

"I don't think so. You two don't get to plow my daughter every which way for free. If you freaks want to keep boning Raine… Well, Hammer has been paying for the pleasure since she was seventeen. You two will have to keep paying."

With a roar, Liam snapped and grabbed Bill by the scruff of his grimy shirt. As he slammed the devil against the SUV, the car rocked. Gwyneth shrieked. Kendall's mouth fell open in shock, the toothpick tumbling from between his lips. His face turned red, making the scar Raine had slashed across his cheek look even whiter.

"She's not a whore," Liam spat. "And the thought of you trying to be her pimp is revolting. If you talk about the woman I love like that again, I will kill you myself." Liam dropped Kendall to his feet.

The man scowled at him furiously. "Pay me. Or you'll all be sorry."

Finally, the shitbag skulked across the parking lot, heaved

into his truck, and pulled away.

The wind ruffled Liam's hair, holding a bit of a nip. He dragged in the air, hoping it would cool him down. No such luck. He prided himself on being a man in control. Bill Kendall made him want to strip away his civility and murder the miscreant with his bare hands.

As he rolled out of sight, Liam scrubbed a hand down his face, then yanked his phone from his pocket. He fired off a text to Hammer about Bill's visit, as well as his threats. He also advised Macen that Gwyneth was clear of the club before tucking his mobile away.

Liam closed his eyes. *When is this bloody day going to end?*

Forcing himself to carry on, he climbed into the driver's seat. At least delivering his ex-wife to Beck's would mean one fewer problem.

He glanced in the rearview and spied Gwyneth's pale face. He suspected she'd heard every word of his exchange with Kendall, especially since the window beside her was open an inch or two. Hammer must have left it cracked. Liam muttered an inward curse.

Swiveling in his seat, he turned to see his ex buckled up with Kyle still clutched in her arms. She looked honestly shaken.

"Are you both all right?"

Gwyneth remained silent for once.

Liam frowned. He didn't know much about babies, but he'd watched the telly. "Do you have a car seat for the boy?"

She froze. "No. I… The airlines lost it. They promised to call me when they found it."

Liam gritted his teeth. "We'll stop and get one, then. He isn't safe otherwise."

With a curse, he started the engine and pulled away from Shadows.

Two blocks later, Gwyneth cleared her throat. "Is that horrid man actually the father of the woman you and Hammer share? Is Raine her name?"

"I won't discuss her with you—ever. She's none of your business."

"I'm on your side, Liam. I found that man positively frightening."

"Drop it," he warned.

She ignored him. "I hope that man's psychotic tendencies didn't pass to his daughter."

Liam gripped the steering wheel so tightly his fingers turned white. He bit back a vicious roar.

Gwyneth cupped his shoulder. "We've both made mistakes, haven't we? I'm more than willing to forgive yours, darling."

He shrugged off her touch. "Don't bother. And I told you, I'm not your darling."

She sent him a pouty expression. "I don't understand. You were so distraught by my unfortunate lapse of judgment, yet you seem perfectly content to let Hammer defile Raine, whom I gather you care for. Why is that? Is she with him now?"

He tensed. Jealousy rolled through his belly in a horrifying wave. Liam knew he had to control his irrational urge to hoard Raine for himself or he'd lose her.

"I finally see what's going on." Gwyneth seemed to measure her words. "You're looking for some solace or belonging in this wanton relationship. But you can't possibly love a slut you *share* with Hammer. Thankfully, Kyle and I are here to rescue you. We'll give you the true happiness you're searching for."

Liam tried hard not to let his anger override his sense. But if she called Raine a slut one more time… Only a few more miles, and he'd be rid of her.

"Are you listening to me?"

"I am." Liam glared at her in the rearview mirror. "Trouble is, you're not listening to me."

"Of course I hear you. But I'm confident you'll make the right choice." She smiled back at him, her face glowing with conviction. "After you've spent time with your son—with me—and see how much I've grown as a wife and a mother, you'll understand. I'm never giving up on you, darling. Never."

Chapter Eight

Raine tiptoed down the hall. She wasn't exactly sure where Liam or Hammer had gone. Neither had told her. Neither behaved like himself. Liam had been preoccupied and distressed all day. Hammer had been covering for him earlier. Then, something had happened to send his temper flaring, too. He hadn't wanted her to know it, but please…

She really wished she could ask them straight questions and get straight answers. She'd been trying that all day. No luck. Evasions, sidestepping, maybe even outright lies—anything but the truth. Ironic after the way they'd stressed honesty in particular with her at the lodge. She'd be incredibly furious and hurt…except they'd continued giving her their love and affection. First, Liam had made love to her as if she were his only lifeline. Afterward, in the shower, Hammer had gripped her with the same desperation.

Something had definitely gone wrong between their last incredible joining at the cabin and the time they'd awakened her. It had only been going more wrong all day. Raine was convinced now more than ever that they meant to protect her.

And if she wasn't going to get answers from them, the time had come to find someone who might talk. Beck was probably prepping for surgery now, but Seth was just down the hall. Of course, given his allegiance to Liam, her little game of twenty questions might not be well received. But any information he gave her was more than she had now.

Breath held, she crept to Seth's door and knocked, hearing him engaged in low conversation behind the portal.

"Come in," he shouted.

Biting her lip, Raine turned the knob and pushed the door open. She spied him sitting behind a little makeshift desk in the corner of his room that seemed overly small for his tall frame. He swiveled around in his chair with the phone pressed to his ear and waved her in.

"I'll have to call you back," he told whomever he talked to. "Yeah. That would be great. Thanks." He hung up.

"Have I come at a bad time? I can come back."

Now that she saw his tawny brow raised and his knowing stare, he clearly wasn't under any illusions about why she'd come.

He gestured to the edge of the bed—the only other soft surface in the room. "Sit down."

Raine couldn't fail to hear the command in his voice. She cut to the chase. "You know why I'm here."

"I've got a pretty good idea, yeah." He crossed his arms over his chest and hooked one ankle over the other. "But shoot."

She settled herself on the corner of his rumpled bed and folded her hands nervously in her lap. Most of the time, his face was so friendly. Golden hair in a banker's cut, laughing green eyes, Seth was always ready to lend gentle support or tell a good joke. He seemed like everyone's friend…until he slipped into Dom mode.

He'd done that so easily with her, and it had taken him little more than a heartbeat. He wasn't in Dom stance or wearing leathers or even telling her to kneel. Yet she felt that commanding part of his nature surround her. He'd make some woman a wonderful, if exacting, Dom someday.

"They're hiding something from me," she murmured.

"And?" He neither confirmed nor denied.

"It's killing me. It's affecting us."

He paused, measuring his words. "You're worried."

She nodded. "I'm working on believing they love me and

telling myself they don't intend to leave me."

"We've covered this. They do and they're not."

Even if she'd heard it before, his words eased her fears a bit. Seth didn't know all the nuances of their relationship or Hammer's and Liam's feelings, but he knew the important things. He'd know if they'd gotten over her or intended to find the door.

"Look..." He held up a finger. "I know what makes Hammer and Liam tick. It wasn't easy for the two of them to swallow their pride and hash out a peace, but they did it for you. Then a breath after their truce, they began working together to break through your walls. Why would they do that?"

"Because they love me," she murmured.

He nodded. "Hopelessly in love, yes."

"Then why aren't they talking to me? I've tried to ask questions. I'm not getting answers."

"So you're going to stomp your foot and make demands?"

"No," she defended herself, then sighed. "Okay, I got mad at the gas station, but once we got home, I really thought about it. I told Liam I was scared."

Seth stood. "You made yourself vulnerable. So you actually did learn *something* over the past couple of days?"

Raine shrugged. "I tried."

He slanted her a dry expression. "Yeah, after making demands didn't work. But it's progress, little one. Go on."

"I don't know what else to do or say. Liam seems to be...shutting down one minute and clinging to me in desperation the next. Hammer spent half the car ride trying to distract me, but then he disappeared for a bit and came back incredibly pissed off. They're not usually moody like this. Everything feels wrong."

He shrugged. "And you think you deserve an answer right now?"

When he put it that way, she sounded bitchy. "It would be nice if they at least said something to put me out of my misery."

"It's human nature to want what you want when you want it. But is that giving them the best of your submission?"

He had that Dom talent to ask questions designed to take the starch right out of her spine. "Damn it."

"Liam would give you a red ass for that." Seth grinned.

"I know. He likes ladies." She managed not to sigh dejectedly.

"He does. But you knew it, just like you knew that if you asked what was bothering them and they didn't answer right away, they must be protecting you from something."

"But I don't need to be protected. I'm a grown woman. I can handle it."

"They might *need* to protect you. Did you think of that? Can you let them?"

"Yeah, but—"

"No. Either you trust that they have your best interests at heart or you don't. And if you don't, why are you with them?"

When he gave her that logic, it sounded so obvious and straightforward.

"I do. I love them both." She gnawed on her lip for a moment and tried to put her thoughts into words. "I feel safe with them. I can't breathe without them."

His gaze softened as he approached, dropping a hand to her shoulder and crouching until they were eye to eye. "Raine, they won't cater to your every want. There's a reason for everything they do, but accepting that is part of being submissive."

She sighed, her gaze hitting the concrete floor. He was right. "Okay, I may not always behave like the submissive I should, but they're not letting me fulfill my role—to comfort and help them. I feel useless."

"You can't give them your love and support unless you know the situation? Think about that."

Hell, Seth was right again. If she were truly giving herself to them, she would trust that they'd tell her everything when the time was right. She'd be giving them her heart and soul through it all.

Her independent nature didn't make that easy.

"You're right." She sighed, feeling somewhere between lost and stupid.

"Follow where they lead you. Let go of your control. They won't let you fall. They've worked too hard for your progress."

"Why is it so hard to do that?"

He chuckled. "If it were easy, submission wouldn't be a

journey. You're still learning. It's not easy being a Dom, either. You have to let them do what they've been wired to do all their lives—protect you, communicate when you need it, honor and love you. They'd walk a hundred miles over broken glass to keep you safe. But you have to remember, it will be in their time frame, not yours."

His answer made Raine nod miserably. "You're right. I can't stand to see them so upset, to watch them struggle against whatever's happening and do nothing. I just… My head keeps going back to places that scare me." She closed her eyes, remembering the terrible rejection in Liam's stare as he'd watched Hammer fondle her in the car. "Liam was so jealous earlier today."

"Yes, he was, and that's an issue he has to work through." Seth stood, paced. "I've known Liam a long time. After Hammer moved out here, I spent a lot of my weekends with Liam. He doesn't give his heart away freely. Hell, hardly at all. He can be a very private, closed man. But the fact that he fell for you so quickly and completely told me even before I met you that you must be a special woman."

Raine didn't think there was anything particularly special about her. She was simply a woman in love with two men and lucky enough that they loved her and one another enough to accept that.

"But given Liam's past, trust isn't easy. Jealousy is," Seth pointed out.

His past? "Oh, his ex-wife."

The one who'd cheated on him so horribly. Sometimes, Liam seemed so sure of himself that she forgot he was a man with his own insecurities.

Seth nodded. "Gwyneth is a part of his problem. The bigger part is you. Did you ever think it's been daunting for Liam to know you've been in love with Hammer for close to an eternity?"

It hadn't really occurred to her. She'd fallen for Liam so quickly. It had been as easy as taking her next breath. One minute they'd been talking in her kitchen about the cuts on her fingers from broken china. The next she'd been pouring out her heart to him and hoping he didn't feed her any more pickles.

Then suddenly, she'd been wearing his collar and…

How could she not love Liam? He'd listened to her, sheltered her, treated her like a desirable woman, and done his best to help heal her. Knowing she'd failed to see how she could comfort and love him more made her feel ashamed. In fact, she'd approached this whole day more like a woman lost in her own insecurities than a sub who wanted to surrender herself to her two loving Doms.

"It's got to make him wonder, Raine, where he stacks up in your heart. Will you ever love him as much as you do Hammer?"

"Of course! If he has to wonder that, then… Oh, I've fucked up."

"Language, little one." He shot her a warning stare.

"I know but it's true. Every time I think I've learned something, I turn around and screw it up again." She beat her forehead with the heel of her palm. "I haven't been the submissive they need today."

He laughed. "The day isn't over. You still can be. Consider what I've said. Follow your heart. Be open and loving and—this will be tough for you—patient."

Raine wanted to be annoyed with Seth, but he already knew her too well. She speared him with a glare, but a smile lurked under it all. "Ugh."

He pulled her to her feet and gave her a brotherly hug.

She embraced him in return. "Thank you, Seth. I know you didn't have to do this."

"I did. You might have kicked me in the balls if I refused to help you."

She giggled and rolled her eyes. "I'm so scary."

"Let's just say I wouldn't want to cross you, little one. Now go. I need to make some phone calls. And you have some Doms to suck up to."

Raine sent him a soft smile of thanks. "Yes, Sir."

* * *

With his handgun tucked beneath his suit coat, Hammer hovered over a bank of monitors in the security room, watching live images from the parking lot, as well as the external doors.

Liam's text about Bill stalking the parking lot enraged him. Hammer didn't see any signs of the wretched asshole, but he couldn't shake an ominous feeling.

Leaning back in his chair, he closed his eyes and pinched the bridge of his nose. Stress and lack of sleep were taking their toll. He'd resisted napping for fear another crisis might arise, as if there hadn't been enough already.

Thankfully, Liam had removed Gwyneth from the club, but that nightmare was far from over. And with Bill's reappearance, Macen felt a choking need to protect Raine that wouldn't subside.

Rising, he strode down the hall, back to his office. He grimaced at the stack of mail awaiting his attention. The phone calls he had to return didn't hold much appeal, either.

He'd barely settled into his chair when he heard a knock on his door. Hammer raised his chin as Raine peeked her head into the room.

"Do you have a minute?" She wore a solemn expression that told him she had something heavy on her mind.

Fuck, what does she know?

Clearing his throat, he nodded. "I've got all the time in the world for you."

As she stepped into the room, she quickly glanced around. "Where's Liam? I was hoping to talk to him, too."

"He's not here, but come in. Shut the door and tell me what's wrong."

Hammer stood and rounded his desk, unable to fight the urge to wrap Raine in his arms and promise her everything would be all right.

She closed the door behind her, looking oddly nervous as she glided toward him, dressed again in the jeans and T-shirt she'd worn to breakfast. He tried really damn hard not to notice how the word *RECKLESS* on the tight red cotton stretched across her breasts.

Taking a few steps forward, Raine suddenly stopped, then sank to her knees before him and cast her gaze to the floor, legs spread, palms atop her thighs.

Hammer stood mesmerized. The breath caught in his lungs. A lump of pride lodged in the back of his throat. His rigid cock jerked demandingly beneath his zipper.

She didn't say anything, simply waited for his acknowledgement. He gaped for words, then opted for a moment of silence to savor the incredible sight. Yes, she had knelt to him before, but always when he'd instructed her to. She'd never simply offered her submission to him like a gift.

Finally, he stepped between her knees and smoothed his hand over the top of her head, petting her dark, glossy hair. A shiver rippled through her at his touch.

"You look breathtaking, precious. To what do I owe this honor?"

Slowly, Raine raised her head to meet his stare. "I'd like to talk to you and Liam, Sir."

Christ, her soft voice even sounded submissive. Her open expression seemed to welcome him inside her soul. He wanted to wrap her in his arms, spread her legs, shove his cock inside her, and fuck her to a gasping climax. Then he'd take her to his bed and start all over.

Hammer clenched his jaw and untangled his fingers from her inky hair. He needed to break physical contact with her until he could tamp down the fantasies searing his brain. Raine had come to him with something on her mind. He had to listen to her before anything else. Then maybe he'd strip her down and ravage her.

Part of him hated that plan. Somehow, Hammer had managed to suppress his inner beast when he'd showered with Raine earlier. He'd had her naked and to himself exactly once before. The primal male animal inside him remembered every bit of that night he'd fucked her bareback and raw. Today, as he'd slid his soap-slick hands over her supple flesh, those memories hadn't been good for his restraint because that hadn't been the time to plunder her. Now wasn't, either. The snarling, clawing demand to make her his slave still thundered through him. Without Liam here to balance him, how long would he be able to keep this need at bay?

"I'm sure Liam will be sorry he missed whatever you intend to say. If you'd like to talk to me, I'll gladly listen."

She seemed to weigh her options at length. "I can talk to him about it later, I suppose."

"Or I can," Hammer offered. "Whichever you prefer."

"Thank you."

She dipped her head again, and he couldn't stop staring. Or wanting.

"Look at me, precious."

Raine complied easily and naturally. A million times, in his dreams, he'd imagined her like this, surrendering her power to him. The reality was so fucking heady he nearly staggered. She just glowed with an undeniable purity that radiated from her heart.

"You have no idea how stunning you are right now, do you?" As a slight pink hue rose in her fair cheeks, he grazed her with his knuckles.

Raine tried to look away and smile past his compliment, but Hammer settled a finger beneath her chin, forcing her to focus on him. To his relief, she didn't fight him or turn away.

"You make me feel that way," she murmured.

Hammer sent her an encouraging smile. "What do you want to talk about?"

Crossing his arms over his chest, he waited. No doubt, she'd come to ask more questions about Liam's recent troubles. Raine had likely been eating herself alive with worry all day. A rush of guilt slammed Hammer. He was far more to blame than Liam for putting her through this turmoil. Tonight couldn't come soon enough.

She hesitated slightly, as if unsure of her words. She licked her lips. At the sight, the beast inside him jerked against his mental chains again, growling to sink his teeth into the arch of that soft pink bow of a mouth and devour her whole. He certainly didn't relish dodging questions he couldn't answer.

"I know there's something more going on than a problem involving Liam's work. I suspect you're keeping whatever's happening to yourselves because you're trying to protect me."

He'd known she was too clever to keep in the dark for long. Hammer arched a brow at her. "Protecting you is our job as Dominants."

"I know," Raine quickly affirmed. "As much as I don't like how it feels to be left out, I also have to trust that you and Liam will tell me what I need to know when the time is right."

She struggled between stubborn old habits and the unchartered submission she now gave. Though turning over her control surely chafed her independent side, Macen knew she wouldn't give up simply because of the discomfort. Not his Raine. He smiled.

"We've already decided." He trailed his fingertips down the hollow of one cheek. "We'll explain everything at dinner tonight. We just need you to be patient a bit longer, while we get some facts straight and tie up some loose ends. Will you do that for us, Raine?"

Some of the weight left her shoulders. "I'll do my best. You know I'm struggling."

"I would have never guessed," he drawled fondly.

She sent him a smile. "You and Liam taught me at the lodge that I had to be honest."

They had, and now he felt like a grade-A asshole for convincing Liam to withhold the truth from Raine until they'd dealt with Gwyneth.

"So…" she went on. "After a pep talk from Seth, I came to tell you how I'm feeling."

Damn it, Liam had been right all along. Macen bit back a curse. He hadn't given her enough credit. Instead, he'd assumed she hadn't had time to embrace the lessons they'd taught her over the last few days. Staring at her now, with her heart in her eyes as she confessed her worries, Hammer wanted to kick his own ass. His decision to shield her from the ugly truth stemmed from his own inability to trust in their new commitment, not hers.

Hammer knelt and cupped her chin, drilling his gaze down into hers. "I'm sorry the time hasn't been right to tell you yet. We never intended to hurt or worry you."

"I know that logically. But I feel confused and anxious. You're making me crazy."

The drastic change in Raine's demeanor floored him. She spilled her emotions without anger or confrontation. Neither throwing dildos nor—thank goodness—running away.

Hammer felt something shift inside him. For years, he'd been her protector, caring and providing for her. Then he'd claimed her as a lover, taking her body and giving her pleasure.

Now, he finally felt like her Dominant.

"I know it's been a difficult day. Balancing our protective instinct with your independent streak is…an interesting endeavor."

"You mean, I'm a pain in your ass." She grinned before she turned serious again. "I'll admit I want answers. I accept that you're not ready to tell me and trust that you will when it's time, but it's so hard for me not to go down the path of insecurity and fear." Tears welled in her eyes, and she tried to blink them away.

God, she'd made herself so vulnerable and she was fucking beautiful.

"Shh," Macen murmured as he gathered her in his arms and helped her to the sleek leather couch. Easing down, he settled her on his lap and sifted his fingers through her hair. "You've come so far, precious. I'm truly proud."

She stared up at him with a shy smile, as if he were her world. His chest buckled with the weight of emotion.

"I know coming to me today with your feelings took tremendous courage, but you're doing well," he went on. "Always remember, we'll do everything in our power to keep you safe, Raine. You're the most important thing in our whole world. I love you." Hammer paused and swallowed tightly. "I always have."

"I love you, too," she murmured softly, staring up at him, her big blue eyes brimming with faith and tears.

When a single tear slid down her cheek, Hammer bent and kissed the drop away.

Liam had told him just a few days ago at the lodge that the early days of his relationship with her had been a battle of wills. It had taken a lot of effort for Liam to break through her walls. Hammer wasn't surprised that Raine had confessed she didn't know how to cry and bleed in front of anyone.

You do now, and it's a glorious sight. Hammer kissed the top of her head.

More tears spilled from her eyes as she lifted her head to him. He couldn't resist brushing them away and taking her lips with his own. The primal need within prowled restlessly but let him have this moment. And as Hammer feasted on her tears, he mourned all the years he'd refused to give her the love she needed. He thanked God every day that Liam and circumstance had conspired to make her stay.

Wrapping her arms around his neck, Raine pressed against his chest. Hammer breathed in the scent of her sweet citrus shampoo and basked in the reverent silence they shared.

As he skimmed his fingertips down her back, Hammer held her. Liam deserved more than half the credit for Raine reaching this moment, and Macen wished his friend could be here now to witness their girl's progress.

Raine sniffed, then shifted to stare into his eyes. Hammer pressed his lips to hers once more.

"Feeling better now?" he asked.

"I think so. It's still strange, being so open and all."

Hammer nodded in understanding. "It will be, at least for a little while. Anything worthwhile requires practice."

"Well, that sounds nifty," Raine groaned.

He laughed. "You'll grow accustomed to freeing your emotions. One day, keeping them to yourself will feel as awkward as revealing them seems now. Whether you'll have half as much success curbing your sarcasm remains to be seen."

She chuckled. "Don't hold your breath."

"I know better," he assured her. "You've grown so much—and so quickly. Don't minimize your achievements; celebrate them."

A tiny smile curled her lips. She almost looked proud of herself. "I'm working on it."

Raine was, and he was thrilled for her. But that subversive part of him just wanted to lay claim to her again.

Hammer drew in a steadying breath and set her on her feet. He couldn't let her confuse progress with sex. And he didn't need to derail her thoughts now with pleasure. Hopefully, there would be time for that tonight.

She stood as if she'd unloaded the weight of the world off her shoulders. "Thanks, Macen."

"You're welcome. We've got all afternoon before dinner. What are you going to do?"

Heaven help him if she said she wanted to spend the time between the sheets with him. He didn't think he'd be able to stave off his primal side.

"Actually, I need to run a ton of errands. I've neglected getting groceries. I've got a package to drop at the post office. Then the drugstore…that kind of stuff."

Unease skittered through Hammer's veins. Bill was out there, somewhere.

Macen glanced at the pile of paperwork on his desk. He felt the weight of his silent phone tucked in his pocket. Stay and wait for Liam's return or go with Raine and make sure she stayed safe?

"I'll come with you," he offered.

She frowned. "Why? You hate errands. I think the last time you picked up your own dry cleaning was before I got a driver's license."

That was probably true. "I'd like to spend time with you."

"And I'd like to stop somewhere and get some sexy lingerie for tonight so it will be a surprise." She batted her lashes.

Damn, he hated to argue with that. Besides, Bill had been spotted twice at Shadows. The sick fuck was mad at him. He wanted money, not Raine. She'd probably be safer elsewhere, in broad daylight, in public.

"Keep your phone with you," he advised. "We're going to leave about five thirty, so you'll need to be back and ready before then."

"Can't wait." She pressed another kiss to his lips.

Macen looked forward to the chance to come clean with her about Gwyneth, the baby, Bill—everything. "Me, too."

With her hand in his, he walked Raine to her car, scanning the parking lot and the surrounding buildings. No sign of Bill or trouble. He kissed her lips softly and watched as she pulled onto the street. God, he hoped that asshole showed up now that Raine had left. Hammer withdrew the gun from his back and pocketed it. He was ready.

Chapter Nine

The minute Liam pulled into the car park at Beck's condo complex, he turned to Gwyneth. Finally, he could take control of the situation. She was no longer blindsiding him or tearing into his best friend. He didn't have to shield Raine from his ex-wife here. No more reacting or putting out fires. She'd be on his turf, following his agenda, playing by his rules.

Let's see what you're all about, shall we?

The doorman beeped them up, and as they entered the condo, sunlight streamed through the wall of windows lining the entire back of the place with incredible views of blue ocean as far as the eye could see.

"Liam, this is lovely. A bit cozy…" She glanced around the small space as she wheeled her suitcase in, gliding her fingertips across the back of the leather sofa. She rounded the bar toward the kitchen, fingering the door to the balcony and looked out with delight. "But Kyle and I will be happy here temporarily until the three of us find something together."

Carting in bags of groceries, he turned to glare at her. He was tired and bloody hungry and he didn't have much patience for the manipulative wench being deliberately thick. But he intended to set her straight—once and for all.

Liam set the necessities on the kitchen counter, along with

Kyle in his new carrier. He put away the food and staples, watching Gwyneth sigh like the cat that ate the canary. No doubt, she had something planned.

Finally, she rolled her suitcase with the playpen folded on top into the only bedroom. Grabbing an apple and a few crackers, Liam snacked, happy to not be in the same room with his ex-wife, even if it was only for two minutes.

He'd barely finished the last bite when she called for him. "Oh, Liam…"

"What?" he bit out.

"Can you set up Kyle's playpen in the bedroom with us?"

The apple that had tasted so good on the way down suddenly turned sour. "I'll set it up, Gwyneth. But I've told you I'm not staying here."

She just sent him a smile that said she found his delusion adorable. "Thank you."

As he bent to set up Kyle's temporary bed, the babe began to fuss. A whimper at first, then a loud little pant or two. A sniffle, a huff, then the boy began to wail.

Liam sent Gwyneth an expectant expression. She sidled closer to him, ignoring the baby's cries and drawing a fingernail down his shoulder. "I appreciate it."

"I'd appreciate it if you'd see to Kyle. My head is hurting."

"I'll rub your neck the way I used to," she offered, brushing her body against him.

He tried not to shudder. "No. Find out what ails the boy." When she still hesitated, he rose and pinned her with a glower. "Now, Gwyneth."

She didn't look at all contrite or compliant, reminding him that his ex-wife didn't have a submissive bone in her body. Instead, she huffed out a breath as she exited the bedroom and called over her shoulder, "We must talk about us soon, darling."

He'd told her repeatedly that he wasn't her darling or remotely interested, but playing blonde was all part of her game, no doubt.

As Kyle continued to fuss, Liam glanced around the corner of the bedroom, into the kitchen. Gwyneth had taken to rocking the boy in his car seat and trying to shush him. Besides lacking submissive bones, she also seemed to lack maternal ones.

"Is the boy hungry?" he asked.

"I don't know."

"Aren't you his mother?"

She sent him an annoyed sigh. "Are you finished with the playpen yet? Perhaps he wants to nap again. Or maybe it's all this drooling. So messy."

"Is he teething?"

"It seems so."

But you don't know? Liam scowled. Definitely time to dig deeper and find out what game Gwyneth played.

With the playpen complete, Liam lined the bottom with a blanket from the bed, then left to find Gwyneth on the couch. Kyle still sat fretting in his car seat at her feet while she filed a fingernail. The tyke gnawed on his fingers, slurping and grunting, seemingly starved. Gwyneth seemed more concerned by her cuticles.

"I've set Kyle's playpen up in the bedroom."

"Good." Gwyneth glanced up, a little smile curling her lips. "Come, sit next to me. We have our whole future to discuss."

When she patted the couch beside her, he scowled. "As soon as I take Kyle's DNA sample, we'll talk."

"Now?" Gwyneth blanched. "Surely we need a doctor for that."

"No." Liam patted his pocket. "I've got the test kit right here."

She opened her mouth to argue again, but Kyle interrupted with a lusty howl that demanded their attention.

"I think the lad is hungry," Liam pointed out.

With a perturbed sigh, Gwyneth rose. "He always is."

She walked right past the boy and into the kitchen. Sifting through the cupboards, she found what she sought and pulled out a new baby bottle and a can of formula. Kyle's protests went up another decibel.

She turned to Liam with a beseeching expression. "Can you rock him or something while I make his bottle? I'm beginning to wonder if he's coming down with a fever. He's so fussy. This absurd test can wait a few days until our child recovers."

Liam wanted to ask why she kept objecting to the test, but he had a suspicion. He refused to be played again. Time to turn the table.

"A fever?" Liam frowned. "Why didn't you say so? We can wait a day or two. Finish fixing the lad his bottle. I'll change his nappy on the sofa."

Surprise, then relief, darted across her face before one corner of her lip curled up. She couldn't quite repress her triumph. "Perfect, darling."

Gwyneth turned back to the stove, heating the bottle. Liam freed Kyle from the car seat and laid him across the couch. As he changed the baby, one little chubby fist snagged his finger, gripping with surprising strength. Liam smiled. *Are you mine, little man? No time like the present to find out...*

Glancing up to make sure Gwyneth was out of sight, Liam withdrew the kit from the pocket of his jacket. Tearing open the cellophane wrap, he withdrew the swab stick and slid his little finger across Kyle's face. As the boy opened his mouth, Liam ran the cotton tip gently against the inside of the baby's cheek. He only whined a bit.

Popping the sample into a slender plastic receptacle, Liam shoved the test kit back in his pocket. Mission accomplished in less than sixty seconds—with Gwyneth none the wiser.

Satisfied, Liam carried Kyle with him to the window, patting his back and murmuring softly to the cranky boy to calm him.

Gwyneth returned with the bottle. The second Kyle spied it, he began kicking and wailing impatiently.

"There." She handed Liam the bottle. "Would you mind feeding him? I need to take care of a few things."

He took the warm bottle and tilted Kyle back in his arm. "Fine."

She brushed her fingers through Liam's hair. "You're such a love, darling. Kyle didn't get much rest, so if you wouldn't mind putting him down in his playpen after—"

"Go on." The sooner she left the room, the better. "We'll manage."

She disappeared through the kitchen and into the hall as Liam paced back to the couch and sat with Kyle. He watched, fascinated, as the babe grabbed at his bottle, searching for the teat, and put it in his mouth himself.

"Whoa, tiger." He laughed. "Give me a second and I'll

help."

Kyle had other ideas as he latched on and greedily suckled, staring up at Liam with big, dark eyes as he concentrated on each pull. The tyke was cute. He'd give the boy that.

As Kyle slurped, Liam heard the clink of the shower pipes. The woman was grooming again? Liam rolled his eyes. He wouldn't mind a shower and some hot food, considering he'd been up since four a.m. and hadn't managed either one.

He relaxed into the buttery leather cushion as Kyle's eyes drooped heavily and his pulls slowed. Shortly, the lad sucked nothing but air from the empty bottle, so Liam gently eased it from his little mouth. Kyle's face scrunched up, as if he meant to start wailing again. As he parted his lips, it wasn't a cry that emerged but a sturdy burp. Kyle blinked, looking surprised. Liam chuckled and stood, carrying the boy to the playpen and tucking the fuzzy blue blanket around him. Kyle dropped off in seconds.

Liam wasn't sure how long the boy would nap, but he hoped to have a good hour to get to the bottom of Gwyneth's scheme. As soon as he found some more fucking food. God, he was starving.

Grabbing a cup of yogurt and a spoon from the kitchen, Liam ate and glanced around the condo. He spied Gwyneth's open purse lying on the counter and began to prowl through the black Versace hobo bag. He wasn't exactly sure what he sought, but he hoped to find a clue about her intentions—notes, correspondence, documents—anything. Other than cosmetics and some breath mints, he found it nearly empty…and surprisingly void of baby things.

Gwyneth had tucked her cell in one of the pockets. Picking it up, he scrolled through the device. No apps that charted child development or programs designed to entertain the wee one.

He launched her Facebook and scrolled down her timeline. Nothing about work, family, or even Kyle. Instead, he saw lots of shopping and trips to the spa. Of course, some people never posted about their personal lives or children for security reasons. Understandable, he supposed. She had a friend request from some young chap in London eager to show off his chest.

Liam frowned, then flipped to her text messages. James,

Colin, Andrew, Ryan. The list went on… At the bottom, a message from her sister. Gwyneth had wished her older sibling a nice holiday. He flipped open the message from the bloke at the top of the list to find some sexts and a close-up of him wanking himself. Liam quickly shut the window with a grimace.

After that, he could only imagine how dreadful the pictures on her phone's camera would be. He hoped to hell she hadn't taken pictures of herself masturbating and sent them back to the man.

The shower shut off, and he knew he didn't have much time to spare. But he couldn't be squeamish now if he wanted any clue about what his ex-wife intended.

Liam quickly scrolled until he found her camera roll. The images were chronological, listed by month and year. The more recent ones even listed days.

He chose the photo she'd last taken—a pair of Prada shoes—and began scrolling back. Food, spas, girlfriends, bars, and men. Lots and lots of bars. Even more men. Selfies of her partying at various London nightclubs, each with a different glass and a different fellow. Last week, the week before, the month before… He frowned. She'd been drinking it up three days after Kyle's birth? And somewhere called Paramount Bar two days before she'd delivered the child, when she was supposedly very pregnant?

Cursing under his breath, Liam shoved the phone away. So Gwyneth hadn't been the chaste flower she claimed since he'd seen her last at that bloody benefit. What he hadn't noticed was a single picture of Kyle—not sleeping or playing or looking cute. What mother didn't have a picture of her infant? Of course, Gwyneth hadn't seemed like a model for motherhood. Still, the fact that she lacked even one snapshot of the boy she'd nurtured inside her body and given birth to made Liam's suspicions whirl.

She'd tracked him down to introduce him to his supposed son and plead with him to become a family. In the absence of any other motive, Liam had believed her…somewhat. He'd been disturbed that she seemed to view the child as a nuisance more than a blessing. Of course, she'd once seen her husband in that same light. Still, he might have been persuaded to believe she'd changed a bit, maybe shifted her priorities since becoming a mother—until now. Everything on her phone just reinforced that she was the same good-time girl he'd divorced.

Not only did he wonder if Kyle was his son, Liam now wondered if the lad was even Gwyneth's. He had his doubts, which was a huge fucking relief. But if the kid wasn't hers, who did he belong to? And why had she tried to pass Kyle off as theirs?

The way Liam saw it, Gwyneth seemed almost desperate to have him in her life again, perhaps even recklessly inventing a son. What the devil was she really after?

Liam had no bloody idea. Time to turn up the heat.

He had no more than tucked her phone away when his own began vibrating in his pocket. He slid it free and checked the screen as he moved to the window.

"Seth, talk to me."

"Well, hello to you, too, asshole." His friend laughed.

"Sorry. I don't have a lot of time. Gwyneth is getting out of the shower."

"Did you get her dirty?"

"No. Fuck no. Would *you* touch her?"

Seth made a gagging noise. "The thought made me throw up in my mouth a little."

Liam rubbed at the back of his neck. "Me, too."

"Turns out her father actually is terminal," Seth confirmed. "Cancer. He's not expected to live much longer. Maybe a month at most."

"No shit, huh?" *So his ex-wife occasionally did tell the truth.*

Liam wondered if she'd been honest about anything else. Had he misjudged Kyle's parentage? Was it possible he'd fathered the boy after all? His gut said no, but…

"Lots of speculation in the business section of the paper about what will happen to his empire," Seth continued.

"Gwyneth and her sister have never been interested in actually working, so I'm not surprised. Anything more about Kyle's birth?"

"That's where things take a weird turn. I'm coming up empty handed. There are no recent births recorded under the name Kyle O'Neill, which is already odd. I also looked up Kyle Sinclair, just to be thorough. Nothing within the last six months.

Then I tried to cross-reference Gwyneth's name as the birth mother. No record of that, either."

Which meant the birth certificate she'd shown him earlier today had likely been forged.

"If Gwyneth had given birth, she should be listed as a mother on that baby's birth certificate," Seth explained. "Can you think of another name she'd be using?"

"No. She's always used Sinclair." Even when they'd been married.

"Liam…I've got to tell you, I'm not even sure this is her kid."

"I'm thinking that myself." In fact, Liam was almost convinced.

"That's all I've got so far. I'll keep looking and let you know if I find anything else, but I'm not expecting much more today. The UK is eight hours ahead of us, so all official government offices are closed for the night."

"I appreciate all you've found." Liam hung up and sighed. He needed a game plan to make Gwyneth talk—and fast.

The snick of the bathroom door opening and a soft rustling sound made him turn. And stare.

Gwyneth stood before him in almost nothing. What little scraps she wore were siren red. The bra, if he could call it that, sloped over her shoulders with delicate scalloped straps. The quarter cups cradled the underside of her enhanced breasts, exposing her tight pink nipples. Below the long, lean line of her abdomen that didn't bear a single stretch mark, a tiny scrap of peekaboo mesh cupped her hips—and completely exposed her waxed mons.

If that body has ever been through pregnancy and childbirth, then I'm the bloody Pope. You've yanked my chain long enough, woman.

She struck what she thought was a seductive pose, sliding a hand into her fluffed hair now spilling in wide curls around her shoulders, batting her false lashes and pursing her red-painted lips in a pout. Liam felt his stomach buckle.

Gwyneth flashed him a come-hither smile and turned slowly to reveal her wiggling ass, adorned with a red, silky bow just above the pert cheeks, bisected by her lacy thong. The ensemble looked like something out of a Frederick's of Hollywood catalog, but Gwyneth couldn't get even the slightest rise out of him.

Swaying, she faced him once more, curling her lips coyly. "Liam..."

She approached on red patent stilettoes, tiptoeing in six-inch heels secured by cuffs around the ankles, drawn together with a black silken tie like a corset. Everything about her looked overblown and ridiculous. She was trying far too hard to seduce him.

When they'd been together, she'd often tried to control him with sex. She hadn't seemed terribly interested in the sex itself. Liam didn't imagine for a second that he alone flipped her switch in some way she couldn't live without. So what the bloody hell did the woman want? Him, he supposed. Or more likely something *from* him.

Either way, her desperation would make it easier to manipulate her until he got the answers he sought.

Then his nightmare grew more real as she settled awkwardly onto her knees before him, her back stiff, her thighs spread as if she tried to emulate a submissive pose she'd seen on the Internet. Unfortunately, in those knickers, he could see the bare lips of her sex. He grimaced.

Liam had no doubt Gwyneth had never attempted such a position in her life.

What. The. Fuck?

"What do you think, darling?" Gwyneth purred as she caressed her way up her thighs, as if wanting to display all her treasures there just for his taking.

Somehow, he managed to paste on a smile. "Well, this is unexpected."

"I've missed you. I wanted to show you *all* the ways I've changed and prove that I've learned to embrace your needs."

Liam stared down at her, trying not to snort. She didn't know the first thing about his needs. But if she wanted to hand over her control, he'd use it to get some answers and give her an experience she'd never forget.

Standing above her, as immovable as a mountain, legs parted, shoulders squared, Liam folded his arms across his chest. "My needs?"

She bowed her head in a parody of surrender before she peeked up at him from under her fake lashes. “I understand now. I’ve read all about them and I want to give you my submission.” She licked her lips. “Make this the best you’ve ever had…Master.”

Gwyneth had no idea what she was talking about. He stared at her throat and fought the urge to shake the silly bitch until her teeth rattled. “You want my Dominance, do you?”

“Mmm. I like the sound of that,” she moaned.

“Are you sure? I’ve changed, too. My tastes run dark now.”

She paused, then flashed him a mega-watt smile. “Yes. Yes! Dark sounds lovely.”

You think that now. Just wait…

“Please give me a chance… Since we have Kyle now, you and I should begin a new life together. I’ll surrender everything so you know I’m serious. Let’s try, darling. Do it for me. For Kyle…”

He should scene with her for the baby’s sake? Twisted logic. Liam shook his head. He couldn’t look too eager, but he intended to have fun with this. “I suppose.”

“Wonderful.” She cupped her breasts in her hands for him and moaned. “I’ll satisfy you so completely you won’t ever want anyone else.”

Liam tried not to sneer. “You’ll need a safe word, Gwyneth.”

“I know what that is.” She nodded, as if excited by her own ability to read a website. “It’s a word I say if things get too intense. Then we’ll stop and we discuss.”

“Usually, but not in my case. If you say your safe word, I’ll know that my needs are too much for you and we’d be better off apart. If you say it, everything stops…forever.”

“I won’t need it. I’ve been looking forward to this since the moment I saw you again.”

“Your safe word is…” *Infidelity.* “Abstinence.”

“Why that?” She reared back.

“Because you would never say it while you’re having sex, now, would you?”

“No,” she breathed. “I wouldn’t. You are clever. Liam, this is an exciting game.”

"Game, yes." He managed not to roll his eyes as he gestured her across the room. "Come to the living room."

She sauntered across the kitchen, swinging her hips in an exaggerated sway, making the floppy bow at the small of her back bob. With a kittenish smile, she tossed him a saucy glance over her shoulder. When she reached the sofa, she turned and leaned back, unhooking her nearly nonexistent bra. Her breasts didn't move as she flung the garment away.

Pinching her own nipples, she sent him a teasing stare. "Do you like what you see?"

"I'm in charge, girl. You don't talk unless I give you permission. I didn't tell you to strip."

"But don't you want me naked?" She shoved her knickers off, then slid them back and forth over her pussy with a groan.

Liam tried not to wince. "Stop. You're not allowed to touch yourself without my permission."

"I'm not, at least not with my hands. You can do that for me."

Not in a million years. "Drop the knickers. Put your hands behind your head, girl." He twisted his face into his most serious Dom expression and waited until she complied. "Good. Now stay right here. I need some special toys for our…game."

"Toys?" She sounded as excited as a child at Christmas.

"I told you not to talk. Are you ill-equipped to handle me? Do we need to stop here and now?"

She shook her head frantically and pressed her lips together. Thankfully, she didn't say another word.

Spinning on his heel, Liam whirled back through the condo and into the bedroom. Sure enough, in the back of the closet, he found a big, dark duffel bag. He hoisted it onto his shoulder. Heavier than fuck. Liam smiled for the first time since arriving here. Now he could have some fun. He'd bet the good doctor kept an arsenal of interesting shit.

Shutting the bedroom door behind him, he returned to the little living room. Gwyneth had splayed herself out on the back of the sofa, long legs spread wide. "I know I'm not supposed to talk, but I wanted to show you that I waxed just for you."

He couldn't look. "Quiet! I've told you to hold your tongue. We were going to start with pleasure, but now…" He shook his head in mock regret. "Well, it's punishment for you."

She gasped. "Will it hurt?"

"It will now."

Liam was almost thankful for the months he'd spent as a sadist after his divorce. At the time, he'd thought that inflicting pain on subs who craved the hurt might release the resentment he felt toward Gwyneth for her betrayal. But it hadn't, and he realized he wasn't the kind of man who simply enjoyed doling out torture. For his ex-wife, he'd make an exception. Not that he'd hurt her physically in any lasting way. But fuck with her mind? He couldn't wait.

"Turn around. Bend over the sofa." When she hesitated, he sent her a warning glare. "You're trying my patience."

Finally, she turned, still looking at him over her shoulder, as if she didn't quite trust his mood…or him.

"Head down." Once she'd complied, he sidled closer and growled in her ear. "Hands at the small of your back."

She shivered and arched, pointing her ass in the air. "As soon as I show you this."

Gwyneth grabbed her cheeks and eased them apart. Idly, he realized she'd even waxed and bleached there. He leaned over her back so he didn't have to see that again.

"I didn't ask you to show me anything." When she didn't respond, he curled his fingers into her hair and tugged, knowing it stung her scalp just a bit. "Did I?"

"Oh, Liam… You have changed. Y-you're so thrilling."

"Excellent. Just think, Gwyneth. Every day will be like this for us if I come back to you. Would you like that?"

She nodded, her skin flushing.

"I'm sure you would. You'll surrender your will to me and beg me to use you like the dirty slut you are."

Gwyneth froze. She'd never heard him talk like this. Probably never even imagined he could.

Liam sent her a cold smile. "Won't you?"

She peeked back at him. "I…um, yes."

"Head down," he warned again. Reluctantly, she turned away and focused on the couch cushions again. "Say it. Beg me to make you a dirty slut."

She struggled for breath now. "Liam… Why are you using

that terrible slur?"

Because that's what you called Raine. "It's a term of endearment to a Dom. Say it or give me your safe word."

He heard her swallow. Her entire body tensed. She fought herself. Balk and risk losing him or say something that went absolutely against her grain? On the one hand, if she bailed now, he could end this farce, have a hot meal and a shower, then hold Raine in his arms. On the other hand…jerking Gwyneth around was more than a wee bit of fun.

"Make me your dirty slut, Liam," she breathed out, sounding as excited as someone holding toxic waste.

"Who am I?" He tugged a bit harder on her hair.

"Master."

Liam grimaced, then reached into Beck's bag of tricks and rummaged around. Not surprisingly, he found exactly what he needed.

"Yes. I'm the Master. You're the slut. See?" He shoved the impression paddle he clutched in Gwyneth's face. "What will your skin say when I smack your ass with this?"

She stared at the leather implement, then blinked, looking horrified. "S-slut."

"Isn't that perfect?" He hissed in her ear. "While I punish you, I'll mark you. Everyone who sees this ass for the next few days will know who and what you are."

Bracing himself on the small of her back, he raised his arm and waited. Her body tensed. She squeezed her cheeks together. Gwyneth wasn't submissive. Surely, she would safeword now so he could walk away from her "romantic" overtures. In twenty-four hours, when the swab in his pocket proved Kyle wasn't his son, he'd never have to see her again.

Nearly ten seconds passed. She said nothing. He stared at her taut back as she held her breath. Did she really not intend to balk?

So be it…

He flung his arm down, snapping his wrist. The paddle met her flesh with a resounding smack. Gwyneth screamed and buried her face in the sofa cushion, muffling the god-awful sound. The word slut blossomed in a red welt across her stark white flesh. Liam smiled in satisfaction.

"Do you want another?"

"No!"

"Then stand up."

Stiffly, she rose to her full height. She turned to him with an accusing glare, moisture welling in her eyes. Liam wondered if those were the first genuine tears she'd ever cried for him.

"You did well," he praised softly. "Your ass will be a lovely shade of red for days." He wended around the sofa and eased down, setting the paddle on his right and pointing to a spot on his left. "Sit here."

Gwyneth frowned and followed with slow footsteps. Apparently, she'd already realized that sitting on leather was going to be bitterly cold and hurt even more.

Beside him now, she sank gingerly toward the sofa. The instant her ass made contact, she stood again. "I don't think I can."

"Breathe through the pain. It's much easier than childbirth, and you survived that so well."

She shot another glare in his direction.

"Or do you need to say that safe word? Like I said, I know that what I want now may be too much for you."

Her face bunched up with determination, and she eased back down to the couch with a hiss. She wriggled, seeking a comfortable position, leaning on the unoffended cheek.

He slung an arm around her shoulder to set her flat again and nestled his lips against her ear. "Struggle for me. I like to watch you endure."

Finally, she stilled, her whole body tense, eyes closed, shoulders halfway up her neck. "You do?"

When she squeaked the question, Liam bit the inside of his cheek. "Hmm. I'd like to see a bit more." He reached around the side of the sofa and dragged the duffel to his feet. After a quick search inside, he found something else she was guaranteed to hate.

He unwrapped the little metal implements from their plastic packaging and handed them to her. "Put them on, slut."

She tensed, her eyes narrowing. No doubt, she hated that word. Finally, she dragged her gaze back to the object in her palm. "What are they?"

"I thought you'd researched for me." He sent her a disappointed scowl.

"I-I did. I just…" She shook her head. "I can't recall. Jet lag's got me a bit."

"They're Japanese clover clamps." He sent her a raised brow. "For your nipples."

Shock crossed Gwyneth's face as she looked down at the molded metal. She studied the shiny pair of clamps, then turned them over in her hand with a frown.

He grabbed them and squeezed the sides. "Open them like so. Set your nipple between these rubber pads, then let go. They'll pinch a wee bit."

"Oh." Her face tightened. "All right, then."

When she took them from his hand, she looked less hesitant. *That won't last long...*

He sent her a benign smile. "You're doing fine, slut."

She bristled again for a moment before she smoothed her expression and squeezed the sides of the clamps, trying to line them up with the hard tips of her breasts. Then she drew in a steadying breath and slowly let go.

Her eyes flew open. Her breath hitched. She looked at him as if he'd gone mad. Her high-pitched keening followed. She sounded a bit like a braying donkey.

"Help me. I can't…" She gasped again and yanked the metal contraptions off. "Please!"

"You're not ready for this?" He took the clamp away with a scowl, then tossed both on the coffee table. "Gwyneth, I've got to tell you… I don't know if we'll work out. I like a sub's struggle through the pain. So far, you've done little but complain."

"I'll get better," she vowed. "I need practice. Maybe…if we share a little pleasure first, then I'll be able to do anything." She reached for his zipper.

Before she could touch him, he snatched her wrist in his tight grip and scowled at her with a thunderous expression. "You don't have permission to touch me."

"Permission? I can't be with you if I don't touch you," she wheedled. "This game is confusing, Liam."

"Try to open your mind. Maybe we can work up to these

tasks soon. For now, let's try something that doesn't involve pain."

"Yes." She latched on to his offer immediately. "I'd like that."

He sent her an indulgent smile, knowing she'd hate what he planned next even more. "Wait right here."

Liam rose and went into the kitchen. It took him a moment to search for a bowl, but he found one that would work well enough, then filled it with water and set it on the floor in front of the sink.

Repressing his smile of evil glee, he sauntered around the corner and hovered just inside the kitchen. "Come to me."

With a wince, she did her best to rise from the leather sofa. But her raw backside stuck to the surface. She whimpered as she peeled herself free and rounded the arm of the couch.

"Stop," he commanded. "You misunderstand me."

She sent him a quizzical stare. "I'm coming to the kitchen, like you asked."

He shook his head. "On your hands and knees."

Gwyneth blanched. "You mean…crawl?"

"Precisely, slut. And wiggle your ass for me like you did when you were wearing your little bow."

Her eyes bulged out. She gaped at him. "That arouses you?"

"As long as you're the one crawling to me."

She mulled his words for a long moment, clearly trying to decide if he meant them.

"I've given you an order," he told her. "You know your choices. Don't keep me waiting or I'll get the paddle and I'll be forced to smack your other cheek."

Immediately, she fell to her hands and knees. Her head dropped. Her shoulders sagged. He almost had her right where he wanted her.

She winced and hissed with each little movement over the hardwood. It seemed to take forever, but she finally reached his feet.

"Now follow me into the kitchen. I've got a treat for you."

Gwyneth didn't look like she quite believed him. Liam ignored her skeptical stare and walked her to the bowl, holding her by the hair at her nape as if it were her scruff. She gave the bowl a bewildered stare.

"Drink," he commanded. "Show me what a sweet little bitch you are. Lap up your water, then give me a happy bark."

"A bark? Like a dog?" She launched to her feet. "Are you mad? This is ridiculous!"

He shot her a narrow-eyed glare, chest out, fists on his hips. "That's not your safe word."

"I can't… I'm not a dog." She shuddered. "It's too vulgar."

"You're not one for puppy play?" He mocked a disappointed frown. "I suppose it's important I know your limits now. I'll grant this has been a tough day for you. But I hope you'll be in a better frame of mind for this tomorrow."

She sent him a stilted smile that told him hell would freeze over first, but she didn't say a word.

"Why don't we try some pleasure for now?" he suggested. "You haven't earned it precisely, but I see some effort. I'll reward that."

She sent him a relieved smile. "Yes, please. Kyle is in the bedroom, so I suppose we can't go there, but we have the sofa or the table or—"

"Show me how ready you are first." He pulled out a chair. To his delight, the seat was made of a hard, solid wood—no cushion.

Gwyneth looked at it fretfully. "Can I have a towel or a pillow?"

He shook his head sternly. "If you sit, there might be an orgasm in your future."

At that, she perked up and eased slowly into the seat. Immediately, she regretted her decision and cringed. Liam pressed his lips together to hold in a laugh.

"Wait here." He meandered back to the bag of tricks and took his time searching through all the goodies inside. He wasn't exactly sure what he was looking for but then…yes. He found the perfect toys.

Withdrawing the items he needed, Liam headed back into the kitchen, setting one on its side on the kitchen counter. *This ought to finish her off…*

"Spread your legs and brace your feet on either side of the chair's legs," he told her as he sauntered closer once more. "Nice and wide. Just like that."

She did so quickly, as if she couldn't wait to show him what lay between her legs. In fact, she looked proud of herself.

Yes, you were born with a vagina. Congratulations... Now you'll find out it doesn't always get you what you want.

Liam knelt at her feet, carefully positioning himself outside her spread thighs, then wrapped one cuff around the leg of the chair and her ankle, strapping them together and securing the Velcro. Crouching on the other side of her body, he repeated the process.

With her restrained to the chair, he rose to his full height and grabbed the other item, unwrapping it with a grin. Then he turned to her, holding it in his outstretched hand. "Suck this, slut. Get it wet. Then I want you to shove it in your cunt, nice and deep for me."

Hesitantly, she took the dildo in her hand. Neon orange and the size of a freakishly large porn star, she stared down at the silicone, frozen. "It's so large."

"Indeed. Does it make you hot? I can't wait to see you take it all."

"It won't fit," she argued.

He scowled at her. "Of course it will. You've had a baby. This is much smaller than Kyle's head, so you should have no trouble. Now stop being a mouthy slut and do as I say."

Her mouth gaped open, then closed, only to open again. She sighed, then lifted the big tool to her lips. She looked more like she braced herself to suck a lemon than a phallus.

No matter how wide she parted her lips, she couldn't wrap them completely around the dildo. She licked her lips, sighed in frustration, then tried to tongue the silicone. Grimacing at its taste, she finally resorted to drawing it close to her mouth and spitting on it gently.

Liam had to bite back a laugh. She'd probably never spit in her life, likely even refused to do it for the dentist. Well, she did spit after a blow job.

He smirked. "You're doing fine. Yes... Now put it in your cunt."

Gwyneth looked even more hesitant. "Really, I don't think—"

"I didn't ask you to think. I asked you to fuck that. To please me. All you're doing is flapping your gums. How is that submission?"

She swallowed hard as she lowered the dildo to her opening. She wasn't nearly wet enough to even try. Of course Gwyneth wasn't aroused. What got her hot was being adored. She enjoyed that far more than actual sex.

As the silicone phallus touched her folds, the tip of it seemed to eclipse most of her pussy. A glance told him that she'd have to defy the laws of physics to make this fit.

Wearing a look of concentration, she pushed a little. Then a bit harder, shifting in her seat and wriggling, before wincing.

"Keep going. Shove that in your wee hole. Stretch it. Make it burn for me," he encouraged.

She dropped the dildo to her side with a frustrated sigh. "Liam, shut up. You must know it won't fit."

"Shut up, is it? That doesn't sound submissive at all," he scolded.

She glowered at him, then tried to fix her expression. "What's so wrong with normal sex? Let's reconnect before we try dirty and deviant. I want to touch your skin, hold you close, feel you inside me. Maybe we can make another baby."

Liam cringed, then tried to recover. "Are you safewording out, then?"

Gwyneth huffed. "Stop with these silly games. Honestly, bark like a dog? Do you really find that arousing?"

"No." He grinned. "I've never engaged in that particular kink in my life. But watching you try amused the hell out of me. How does your ass feel, by the way?"

"This was all a…game to you?" She gaped.

He just smiled. "You kept calling it one, so…"

Her face flashed red as she ground her teeth together and screeched. "You bastard! You heartless, cruel—"

"You've yanked my chain all day. Consider this quid pro quo."

"I didn't humiliate you!"

"Two years ago you did. Today, you've disrupted my whole life. I'm on to you." He leaned over her chair and wrapped his hands around the back, mostly to prevent himself from strangling her, and hovered right above her face. "I don't think Kyle is my son. I'm not even convinced he's *your* son. You don't care for him properly, and you don't give a shit about his welfare. The DNA swab in my pocket will prove that by tomorrow."

"You took the sample without my permission?" Her face distorted in horror.

"I had your permission. You also gave me several excuses why I should wait. I simply chose not to."

She closed her eyes and clenched her jaw, then seemed to swallow down her anger. "Never mind. Darling, you and I share a more sophisticated love than these foolish games imply. Let's rekindle it. Carry me to the sofa, and we'll make love like we used to. I miss—"

"Shut up and listen." He gritted his teeth. "We don't share a 'sophisticated love.' We don't share anything at all. I don't care what you do, where you go, who you fuck, or how you choose to live. There is no you and I, Gwyneth, and there never will be again." He tugged on her hair and glared into her face. "And for the record, even if I'd been without sex for a century and you were the last woman on earth, I wouldn't touch you again. Ever."

She paled for a moment before her eyes blazed with indignation and a terrible fury. "How dare you! You can't treat me like I'm less important than your gutter-fed whore. I am an aristocrat, damn it! Fourteen generations of Sinclairs have reigned with kings and married royalty."

"Why did you come, Gwyneth? Why did you go to the trouble of borrowing a baby and flying halfway around the world? Why do you want me back? It must be pretty damn important."

Her face closed up. "I've told you. You've chosen not to believe me."

Liam would have liked a real answer to his question, but it wasn't worth spending more time in her company to find out. "I never will."

Then he left, not looking back.

* * *

Raine parked in a visitor's spot in the parking lot at Beck's condo complex and cut off her little sedan's engine. She glanced at her phone and grimaced. The line at the post office had been stupidly long and slow. The dry cleaners had taken twenty minutes just finding Liam's and Hammer's things. And she'd dithered too long over lingerie for tonight.

She'd been texting Hammer off and on all afternoon. He'd grumbled that they didn't have his favorite sandwich fixings for lunch, so she'd also grabbed fresh subs for the men. He and Liam, who had missed breakfast, must both be hungry. She'd have to scratch groceries off her list for today or she'd be late for dinner. Just this last stop and then she'd be with them for a hopefully peaceful evening.

Raine unbuckled the big fruit bouquet from the front seat, then darted out of the car and around to the other side. As she lifted it from the passenger's side, she balanced the basket, her phone, and her car keys, then headed into the lobby of Beck's building. She hoped he enjoyed the goodies, but what else did a sub get another Dom as a thank-you-for-helping-me-with-my-submission gift?

The doorman greeted her warmly, obviously remembering her from her stay here last week, when she'd been hiding out after running away from Hammer and Liam.

Shoving the ugly memories aside, she smiled back. "Would it be possible to leave this in Dr. Beckman's refrigerator?"

The uniformed man flipped through the papers on his clipboard and nodded. "Sure. He added you to his list so you can come by anytime."

"I don't have a key."

"I'll get you in. Or his current houseguest can help you out, too."

Houseguest? Raine shrugged. Maybe he'd had someone visit him unexpectedly or was letting another doctor crash at his place. If that was the case, she'd have to be quiet.

"Thank you."

"This way." He led her through the secure double doors, across the lobby, to a bank of elevators and pressed the button. "You getting ready for the holidays, Miss?"

She smiled, optimistic that Christmas would be much better than her disastrous Thanksgiving, which had started with her migraine and ended with Hammer and Liam at one another's throats. "I'll be starting my preparations tomorrow."

They exchanged small talk until the door to the elevator on her right opened. As she entered and watched the doorman press the button for the penthouse, Raine inspected the fruit bouquet to make certain it was no worse for the wear after the car ride.

She almost missed the ding of the other elevator and the blur of the familiar man in the gray suit storming by. He shoved out the lobby's secure double door, and it closed behind him before she realized she'd just seen Liam, looking somewhere between determined and smug. A prickle of alarm skittered down her spine.

Raine frowned. What the heck was he doing at Beck's? Why would he visit when the doctor was in the middle of surgery? And had a houseguest?

The elevator door in front of her began to close. Raine stuck her leg out to stop it.

Hopping to keep her balance, she thrust the fruit basket in the doorman's hand. "Can you hold this? That was my boyfriend. Something is clearly wrong. One minute…"

She didn't give the doorman an opportunity to object, just darted out of the lift and ran down the hall. "Liam!"

He didn't hear her. He'd already pushed his way out the second set of doors into the parking lot and now pressed the phone to his ear. He paused, a deeply satisfied smile adding dimension to his sharp profile. What the hell was going on with him?

"Miss?"

Raine turned. The elevator began to beep. The doorman, wearing a slightly impatient glower, held the fruit bouquet.

When she looked back at the parking lot, Liam sauntered toward his car, still chatting on his cell. She frowned at his retreating back. The elevator's beep became an insistent buzz. With a little curse, Raine turned away. She'd see Liam in less than an hour. She'd ask him for an explanation then.

"Sorry." She turned back to the elevator and took the silent ride up twenty-something floors, ignoring the doorman's questioning gaze.

Once the doors parted, she made her way to the corner unit.

The guard pulled out a set of keys.

"Go ahead and knock. If the houseguest doesn't answer, I'll let you in."

Tapping on Beck's door and hoping a stranger answered was awkward, but she supposed he couldn't just barge in on someone staying with the doctor.

Raine lightly rapped her knuckles on the solid wood and took the fruit basket back in hand. "Thank you."

Suddenly, the door flung open. "So you're back, Liam? What is the—" The blonde standing there fixed her scowl on Raine. "Who are you?"

Raine couldn't breathe. Statuesque, sexy, and lean, the British bombshell looked as if she'd stepped off the pages of a lingerie catalog, especially wearing daring red peekaboo lace undergarments. Despite the woman's mussed hair, crimson lips, and gentle flush, the most terrifying thing of all was her familiarity.

Weeks ago, she'd Googled Liam's ex-wife. Now she wished she hadn't. She looked even more gorgeous in person.

The woman shifted her attention to the doorman, who gaped beside Raine, and gave him a haughty glare. "You may leave."

The doorman blushed profusely, then backed away, disappearing into the elevator.

"Gwyneth." The shell-shocked whisper fell from Raine's lips. She almost couldn't keep the heavy basket from slipping through her numb fingers.

"Who the devil are you? Oh, you must be the maid. You're impertinent. Call me Ms. Sinclair. Come back in twenty minutes. I'll need clean sheets and towels, and you'll—"

The sound of a baby wailing from inside the condo stunned Raine. Why would Liam's ex-wife be in Beck's condo with a baby?

"Oh, for heaven's sake." The woman rolled her eyes. "Never mind. Might as well come in now and get started."

She flung the door open wide and whirled around toward the bedroom. Her pert backside looked red and freshly branded. The word slut had been imprinted temporarily onto her cheek with some sort of impression paddle.

As if suddenly self-conscious, Gwyneth grabbed a blanket

from the back of the couch and began picking up all the implements of BDSM play scattered around the room. A dildo. Restraints with Velcro cuffs.

Stunned mute, Raine blinked and shuffled in. The sight only grew more disturbing. Clover clamps lay on the coffee table. The slut paddle sat on the nearby sofa. Gwyneth scooped those up, too, as the baby howled in the background.

Beck was a sadist, and this was his place. Gwyneth was his houseguest…except he was in surgery. The woman looked freshly flushed, and Liam had just exited the building, looking quite satisfied. Beck hadn't known the woman long enough to have fathered a baby with her. But Liam had.

Oh, god. She was going to be sick.

Gwyneth disappeared into the bedroom. Raine barely managed to unload the fruit bouquet on the countertop dividing the living room and kitchen. The other woman had since belted a robe around her scantily clad figure and picked up the baby. Dark curls and dark eyes. Raine could so easily see them as having come from Liam.

Had he decided to return to his ex-wife, the mother of his child? Had his lovemaking earlier today been a bittersweet good-bye? Did he and Hammer intend to sit her down tonight over dinner and tell her that Liam had a son and intended to take up with this bitch again?

"Why are you just standing there?" Gwyneth huffed. "You can start in the bedroom."

No way could Raine go back there. She desperately wanted to know if she'd find any more evidence of her passion with Liam. On the other hand, hadn't she gotten enough of an eyeful already? Seeing firsthand that he'd scened with her was bad enough, but to find out he'd taken the woman to bed and thrust inside her—

Raine swallowed the thought—and the resulting bile—as the day's events rushed back at her. Liam had been eager to leave the lodge this morning. To rush back to Gwyneth? Well, of course. Why wouldn't he want a woman who'd given birth to his child and still looked like a supermodel? He'd refused to touch her in the car. Maybe she'd mistaken his anger for indifference. Liam hadn't explained his mood. Obviously, Hammer had lied that the issue revolved around his business because he'd been temporarily covering for his old friend. Liam had fucked her as a kiss-off, and Hammer had been pissed about that. They'd spoken afterward, once Macen had told her to start the shower. Raine hadn't heard more than a hum of their conversation, but they'd exchanged fast, furious dialogue. Then Liam had disappeared.

Apparently to spend some "quality" time with his ex-wife.

The hurt cleaved Raine's chest, devastating her. Pain overwhelmed her until she couldn't breathe. Every second seemed to last a thousand years as she watched Gwyneth pat the baby and stare at her impatiently.

It wasn't this woman's fault that Liam wanted her more. But after Gwyneth had cheated on him, Raine would have thought Liam would steer clear.

Looking at the stunning vixen, Raine knew why he hadn't.

"Get moving," Gwyneth demanded.

"I'm not the maid," she muttered finally.

"Who the devil are you, then?" Gwyneth cocked her head to the side and sidled closer, seeming to examine her with sharp green eyes. "Raine?"

She lifted her head and glared back. So Liam had mentioned her. Raine didn't know if she was happy that she'd been worth his acknowledgment or pissed off that the man she thought she loved had spoken about his last lover to his once-ex-and-again-current squeeze.

"I don't have anything to say to you," Raine breathed.

"You must. You came to see me." The woman narrowed her eyes, shooting her another scrutinizing stare. "Did you see Liam as you arrived? What did he tell you about us?"

Us? Raine's stomach rolled again.

"Nothing." He hadn't even stopped to look at her. Raine had imagined that he simply hadn't heard her…but maybe he just hadn't wanted to bother.

Finally, a smile curled Gwyneth's lips. "He must have been in a hurry. He's so excited to begin our lives together again, this time with his son. This is Kyle."

Gwyneth grasped the baby's wrist and moved it to simulate the baby waving.

Hearing the woman confirm all her worst fears had Raine

backing up a step.

Pity crossed the other woman's face. "Really, Raine. What did you think was going to happen? You're cute, and I'm sure you have a great personality, but Liam needs more than you can give him. Did you imagine that he preferred you over me, especially when that meant taking Hammer's sloppy seconds?"

"He loves me." She tried to convince herself as much as Gwyneth.

The pity deepened. "Did he tell you that? Oh, poor girl. He is a silver-tongued devil. Of course he'd tell you what you want to hear so he could get you into bed, but now he and I are quite reconciled and—"

"You cheated on him." Raine frowned. The kind but firm man who'd told her about the painful dissolution of his marriage couldn't be this heartbreaking barracuda Gwyneth described.

"To get his attention." She waved Raine's concern away. "I thought he had a plaything on the side and… Well, the misunderstanding is all quite resolved now. And so happily."

Acute pain slashed through Raine. She staggered back another step. This couldn't be happening. It couldn't. Liam had never seemed like a liar, cheat, or player.

But how else could she possibly interpret Gwyneth's attire, all the implements of pain and impact play she'd seen…and, of course, the baby?

"Poor thing. You're crushed." Gwyneth managed to look contrite. "In your shoes, I'd be utterly humiliated. I'm not sure I'd speak to the bastard again. Liam is a man with dark tastes. He enjoys the hunt, the game. I'm afraid you haven't been much sport. From woman to woman, let me give you some advice: Wash your hands of him this minute, and he'll never have the power to hurt you again. I'll make certain he doesn't bother you anymore."

Gwyneth gave Raine what she supposed passed as a kind smile. It looked more like a shark flashing its teeth. Or maybe she just felt that way because this gorgeous woman trumped her every day and twice on Sunday. Raine knew she was never getting Liam back.

Did she really want to be his pity fuck or "pet" project anyway?

Betrayal washed a chill through her. Raine didn't want to believe Gwyneth, but with so much proof, how could she think otherwise?

A sob rose from the depths of her chest. Her whole body jerked. Her face crumbled. No way would she let this beautiful bitch see her cry.

Raine turned and ran from the condo and the building, tears blurring her vision as she climbed into her car. The old her would have run far and fast and never looked back. She wasn't even sure what this Raine would do as she drove away.

Chapter Ten

Hammer stood at the front door of Shadows, waiting for Liam to return. He hoped his pal made it back before Raine, so they'd have some time to talk—not only about Gwyneth but to discuss the best way to break the news about the woman's return to Raine at dinner.

When the familiar black SUV pulled into the lot, Hammer watched Liam bound out of the vehicle and hurry toward the entrance. As he approached, Hammer opened the door wide and shot the man an expectant stare. "Well?"

"Raine's still not back from her errands yet?" Liam sounded concerned.

"No, but probably soon. She's buying something sexy to wear for us tonight." He grinned, then sobered as they walked past the bar. "So, what's this story you have to tell me? Quickly, before she gets back."

"Oh, it's hysterical," Liam assured. "But first, I need to eat something before I pass out."

He turned to the kitchen, grabbed a bottle of water, and made a quick sandwich. As the two men headed toward Hammer's office, Liam began relaying all the gory details in between bites, savoring every word.

Hammer listened in shock and horror. "You found a picture

of a guy jacking off in her texts?"

"It gets better." As Liam took the last bite of food, he headed toward the bathroom. "I'm going to use your shower, mate, so I can keep talking. Wait until you hear what Gwyneth did after I talked to Seth."

"I'm not sure I want to." He winced. "Do I?"

Liam laughed. "I almost had the bitch barking for me."

Hammer blinked, then let out a deep belly laugh. "I've got to hear this."

Following Liam into the bathroom, Macen leaned on the edge of the vanity, keeping an eye out the window for Raine as his friend showered and described Gwyneth's "submission."

Hammer made Liam back up several times and repeat the humiliation he'd unleashed on the pretentious whore, laughing until his stomach hurt.

Liam stepped out and grabbed a towel as Hammer shook his head. "I would have paid money—good money—to have seen that. You didn't happen to record it on your phone, did you?"

"Damn, I should have, right?" Liam laughed.

"Hell, yeah. That thing would have gone viral in a matter of minutes." Hammer snorted. "So you got Kyle's sample dropped off and your cheek swabbed, too. Now we wait."

"Tom at the lab was expecting me and promised to rush it through as quickly as he could," Liam explained. "Thank god for Beck's contacts. I might have the results back early in the morning."

"Great. But after all the shit you found on Gwyneth's phone, do you think there's still any chance that baby is yours?"

"I can't say positively until we get the results, but I have serious doubts that he's even *her* kid."

"And even after all the humiliation you put her through, she still didn't tell you what the fuck she's up to, huh?"

"Nope." Liam shook his head. "Gwyneth stopped talking, so I left."

"Well, hopefully by this time tomorrow, all we'll have to worry about is getting her out of Beck's condo."

"I've got rope." Liam smirked. "When we find out the baby's not mine, I'll thank Beck for use of his place and toy bag, then tie Gwyneth up and haul her to the airport. Then we can get on with our lives…with Raine."

"Speaking of…"

"When did she say she'd be back?" Liam shot Hammer a worried glance.

"She didn't, exactly." It was after five o'clock, and she knew they planned to leave for dinner at five thirty. Hammer frowned. "Let me see where she's at. Maybe she got hung up in rush hour."

With furrowed brows, he pulled out his cell phone and launched an app. Liam stepped up next to Macen, looking at the screen. They watched a blinking green dot inch along a map of streets, coming from an all-too-familiar part of town. In tandem, both men raised their heads, sharing a look of abject dread before Macen swallowed tightly.

"Bloody hell," Liam groaned. "Why is Raine near Beck's condo? None of her favorite stores are near his place."

Hammer felt his blood run cold. There was no logical reason for Raine to be in that neighborhood, unless…

"Son of a bitch. I wonder if she stopped by Beck's."

"I hope not. After the mood I left Gwyneth in, she'd eat Raine alive." Liam scrubbed a nervous hand through his wet hair.

Hammer tried hard to connect the dots, dreading the implications. "It doesn't make sense. She knew Beck was in surgery. Unless she'd decided to ask him why we left the lodge so suddenly."

"Do you think she actually went to check out our story?"

"I wouldn't put it past her. Shit. Hang on a sec." Hammer punched another button on his phone. A snaking green line appeared showing the route Raine had taken since leaving the club. She'd stopped at the condo, all right. Hammer closed his eyes. His bowels turned to liquid.

"Oh, fuck no," Liam moaned.

"We'd better get ready."

"For Hurricane Raine," Liam replied before he flattened his lips into a tight line. "This is going to get ugly."

"Ugly isn't the half of it," Hammer agreed. "Looks like we're at DEFCON one, brother."

* * *

Liam hoped Raine would merely be pissed off. He could deal with anger, but if Gwyneth had crushed her tender feelings, that heinous witch would rue the day she'd ever met him.

Together, they watched as the green dot on Hammer's phone moved steadily closer to Shadows and decided to intercept her at the entrance. No one needed to overhear what she was likely to shout.

Liam had no illusions. He'd seen Raine rail at Hammer when she'd sneaked into his room a month ago and he'd rebuffed her for trying to seduce him. Today, he and Hammer would be lucky if all they had to do was dodge dildos.

At least the truth was finally out, the deception and misdirection over. Now he had to deal with the nagging stress wrought by Gwyneth, his not-quite-son, and Bill Kendall. But the bright spot? When Raine had discovered their cover-up, she hadn't simply run away, as she would've in the past. Even if she only came to Shadows to confront them, at least she was returning. They'd have the chance to persuade her they'd never meant to deceive or hurt her. If he and Hammer managed to end this evening with her heart still in their hands, he'd be eternally grateful.

But he worried that was too much to hope for.

Finally, Raine whipped her car into the lot and came to a screeching halt, straddling two parking spaces. Liam cocked a brow at Hammer. *That's our girl.* As his friend nodded grimly, Raine tore out of the car and slammed the door, storming toward the entrance of the club. Even in her fury, she looked breathtaking…but she might not take the compliment well just now.

She shoved the door open, her cheeks red but stained with silvery paths. A knife stabbed into Liam's heart and twisted.

From day one, she'd slipped under his defenses and into his very soul. Never had a woman created such chaos in his life. Or made him feel so much joy, immeasurable passion, and love—more than he'd realized he was capable of feeling.

What would his life be like if Raine were no longer in it?

When she caught sight of them, her bow mouth pursed. Fire

shot out of her eyes, and she looked ready to erupt like a volcano. "How fucking dare you—"

Hammer clapped a hand over her mouth. "Not one more word."

She screeched, struggling against his firm hold, tearing at his wrist to tug it away. She screamed behind his palm, still making enough noise to alert the whole club.

"We know where you've been. We know who you saw. We're going someplace private to talk about it," Hammer growled. "Settle down unless you want everyone to know our business."

If anything, her eyes flashed with more fury. She bit at him and glared, looking as if she'd like to boil the flesh off his scrotum.

Liam resisted the urge to cover his own balls and leaned into Raine's face. "Give us a chance to explain, love. Thirty seconds, and we'll be in Hammer's office. Then you can vent all you want."

Raine zipped that lethal glare at him, then tried to stomp on his toes. He managed to dodge her at the last second. *Bloody hell...* His wee lass had turned violent.

Damn it, he should have followed his instincts and told her about Gwyneth's phone call from the start. Hindsight was a bitch. If he could somehow make her listen, maybe he could reach her. At present, she was disinclined to do anything but tear his head off.

"You have a choice," Hammer snarled in her face with low, controlled tones. "Come with us quietly or…" He pulled a ball gag from his pocket and dangled it in front of her. "I know how much you love these."

Instantly, her eyes widened, all shock and blue lightning. Then they narrowed again. Behind his palm, she panted hard, her breath hot. At barely five feet tall, she didn't pose them any threat, but her temper was fearsome.

"What's it going to be, Raine?" Liam asked quietly. "You can walk with us…"

"Or we'll hog-tie you," Hammer finished.

"Either way, you're coming along. There'll be no more biting, stomping, or screaming. And no more swearing. Do you understand?" Liam asked.

Her little hands balled into fists, and she shot them both death glares. No doubt, if she'd been a man, she would have thrown a punch or two.

"You locked the gun away, didn't you, mate?" he asked Hammer.

"Yeah. She'll have to rely on verbal combat. Raine?" Tentatively, Hammer withdrew his hand, keeping it right above her mouth.

She stewed. And fumed. As she glanced at the ball gag again, she somehow managed to turn even redder. "Fine."

Liam felt as if they'd defused a bomb—at least temporarily. She was still liable to go off, but at least it would be in private. He was grateful that he and Hammer had talked this out a bit, and turned to his friend with a questioning stare.

Macen pocketed the ball gag and answered with a nod. Together, they each grabbed one of her arms and lifted her, carting her away from the common area and down the hall.

"Don't touch me," she hissed.

Liam's inner Dominant roared to life. *Like hell.*

They both secured their grip.

"I can walk," she insisted.

"We're going to help you," Liam crooned.

"You can shove your help—"

"Do we need that ball gag after all?" Hammer sent her a silky warning as they hit the hall, wending past the door of Seth's room, steps away from their destination.

"No," she spat.

Liam gripped Raine's arm tighter as they crossed the threshold of Hammer's office, Macen sliding in first and all but dragging her inside. Gripping the knob, Liam shut it, knowing her explosion was imminent in three, two, one…

As soon as the latch clicked shut, she yanked her arms from their holds and balled her fists again. "You both fucking lied to me. And I don't give a fuck about my language. You can both go fuck yourselves. But oh, that's right. Liam has already fucked me—and his perfect Barbie doll ex-wife. Were you taking notes? Making comparisons? I can't believe you didn't say a fucking word about that fucking bitch."

"That wasn't what happened at all," Hammer insisted. "Calm down and we'll explain."

She whirled on him. "Don't fucking talk to me like I'm a child. Though I guess you two have decided I'm as naïve as one. How long did you think you were going to keep me in the fucking dark? And that lie about Liam's business problems?" She rolled her eyes. "Lame!"

"So you don't want to hear the truth?" Hammer raised a brow at her.

"You can take your fucking truth and shove it up your fucking—"

"Love, listen to us. We—"

Raine spun around to Liam again. "Not only did you *not* tell me about your fucking ex-wife—nice lingerie, by the way; I'm sure you enjoyed that—but you have a son you never fucking bothered to tell me about. So are you packing your bags and leaving with them to live happily ever after? She's only going to screw you again, but maybe you enjoy that."

Betrayal fueled her angry speech. But their disillusioned girl believed the damning situation after a mere glance—without asking him a single question. In some ways, that cut Liam to the quick…but he reminded himself that only a week ago, his relationship with Raine had seemed hopeless and he'd ended things with her abruptly. Of course she would worry he meant to do the same now. She was giving up on him before he could hurt her again.

"I divorced Gwyneth with good reason. I would never want her back, and I certainly wouldn't leave you for the likes of her. That's the sincere truth."

"Oh, so *now* you're telling me the truth? But not earlier today in the car?" She wagged a finger in his face. "You two spent the last few days lecturing me until you were blue in the faces about honesty and communication and how great our relationship would be if we could all just trust one another. Blah, blah, fucking blah."

"Raine," Liam reassured softly because telling her to calm down would not go well. "Love, I don't want Gwyneth. I didn't touch her."

"Bullshit! I saw the nipple clamps, an imprint paddle, and

the fresh welt that said slut on her ass—not that I doubt *that* for a minute. Oh, I forgot the restraints and the elephant dildo. So if you weren't playing with her, you were…what? Recreating your good times and reminding her of all she'd been missing?"

Liam didn't falter. "No. If you'll stop losing the bloody plot, I'll explain."

"Explain what? She told me the two of you have worked out her 'lapse of judgment' that ended your marriage. Wow. So I guess paddling her was better than couple's therapy, and now all is forgiven. How long before you leave me to join her and be a family?" Raine challenged, as if waiting for the other shoe to drop. Of course she zoomed right to the worst-case scenario. In her case, it had happened every damn time.

"Oh, that calculating cunt," Hammer muttered.

Indeed. Gwyneth had played Raine perfectly. Like dominoes in a row, each felled the next in an inevitable chain reaction. But Liam had handed his ex-wife the means. His maneuvers—however well intended—had backfired.

"Why would you think she told you anything resembling the truth?" Liam asked.

"Because I already know you two lied to me."

"To protect you, yes. We're sorry if that upset you. But her lies were meant to confuse you and cause you pain," Hammer spat. "Don't let the doubt she planted in your head grow, precious. And don't give her *any* of your power. That belongs to us."

"Nothing she said is true." Liam sighed. "All she wants to do is separate me from you. You can't let her."

"Give me one reason I should believe you," she challenged.

"Do you think we would have planned to take you to dinner tonight to explain everything if we weren't going to tell you the truth?" Macen asked.

She shot him a skeptical glare. "Maybe it was taking you two that long to get your stories straight."

Liam leaned into her face, fusing their gazes together. "Because I love you, Raine. That's why you should believe me."

Liam had this one chance to convince her that he loved her with every cell in his body. If not, she'd let doubt overtake her and leave. But as long as he was breathing, he'd keep fighting for them.

Unfortunately, he couldn't read Raine now. Since she'd always worn her emotions on her face, that was dangerous. She hadn't dropped the f-bomb for several minutes, so he took that as a good sign. But he still sensed a palpable storm raging beneath Raine's surface.

She teared up. "You didn't even tell me about your son."

"I don't think he's mine," Liam countered. "Tell me what else Gwyneth said to you so I can explain everything."

"She pitied me. No, first she thought I was the maid. Then she said I was cute, but I couldn't keep you amused for long because you like the hunt, and I'd never provide you enough sport." She covered her face, and her body shook. Pain drenched every sob as she swiped at her cheeks and backed away. "I'm sorry I wasn't entertaining enough for you."

His worst fears had come to pass; Gwyneth had cut her to the bone. The knife in Liam's chest twisted harder as he watched Raine cry, longing to enfold her in his arms and kiss away every tear. Fierce and proud, she looked hauntingly lovely, even as she stood wronged and breaking before them.

He bit back a curse. If he had a do-over on this afternoon, he wouldn't have simply humiliated Gwyneth; he would have throttled her.

Liam darted a glance at Hammer, who looked as if he wanted to unleash his own form of justice on Gwyneth. But now, they needed to deplete Raine's anger and heal the devastation the bitch had inflicted—fast.

Hammer met his stare and nodded.

Without a word, Liam wrapped Raine in his arms.

She flinched and bucked against him. "Don't you touch me!"

He ignored her because she obviously needed the reassurance of his embrace badly. Instead, he nudged her against the wall as Hammer gathered her flailing arms and pinned them above Raine's head.

Liam cupped her cheeks in his palms and forced her to look at him. "Listen to me, Raine, and listen well. You've let Gwyneth crawl inside your head and dredge up your insecurities. Hear my side of things before you decide to do anything rash, like throw us away."

Liam explained everything, beginning with that bloody benefit. Raine took that in stride, sending him a shake of her head. Clearly, she thought he'd been an idiot. *Take a number and get in line...*

Explaining today's events, starting with Gwyneth's four a.m. phone call, proved much trickier.

"I didn't want to leave the lodge," he swore. "I never would have just for Gwyneth's sake. I don't give a shit about her. But I had a responsibility to find out if Kyle was mine."

"But you don't think he is?" Raine asked.

"I'm about ninety-nine percent sure, but I'll have proof of that by tomorrow."

"How?" She cut him a skeptical glare. "Something other than ESP or simply deciding that your ex-wife is a loon, I hope."

That segued into the stickiest explanation—him taking Kyle's DNA, fucking with Gwyneth's head, then walking out on her screaming and restrained to Beck's kitchen chair.

She rolled her eyes. "Please… Looking at her in that killer lingerie wasn't any sort of hardship. No living heterosexual man would turn her down. I can hear you still breathing. I know you're heterosexual, so—"

"I rebuffed her," Hammer cut in. "More than once. I refused her four years ago, and I did it again this afternoon."

Raine's blue eyes widened. "She hit on you?"

"More or less. I shut that down."

"I did, too," Liam added. "She took me by surprise when she popped out of the loo in that getup. I certainly didn't ask her to put it on."

"But hey, since she's wearing butt floss and you just happened to have full use of Beck's toys, why not relive the best parts of your marriage?"

Liam choked back a laugh. Even mad, his saucy wench had a quick wit.

"No. Gwyneth and I never engaged in anything remotely close to BDSM play when we were married. Today was the first time. And what you saw—the toys, the restraints, and the welt on her ass—that wasn't for any sexual pleasure or because I wanted her submission."

"He had to mindfuck her to get some answers because we owe them to you, precious," Hammer insisted.

"Exactly. I used her desperation and my Domination to manipulate her. I owed her humiliation, and trust me when I say she didn't enjoy it."

"She looked pretty damn satisfied when I saw her." Raine struggled against their hold again. "Let go."

He and Hammer held firm, knowing they couldn't give her any slack now.

"No." Macen gripped her wrists tighter.

Liam brushed the hair from her face. "Never."

"Seriously, Liam…" Raine gritted her teeth. "I don't believe for one minute that you shoved your Dominant side away when you married her. That would be totally out of character."

But he had. "After Juliet took her life, I did my best to deny myself the lifestyle that made her want to end everything. I buried my needs and swore I'd fly right. I knew abstaining wouldn't bring Juliet back, but I felt compelled to give her some penitence. It wasn't until after my divorce that I did some soul searching and realized I couldn't deny my nature forever. I need to be who I am."

"So you came here," Raine stated flatly.

"Eventually, yes. Then I met you, love. But that's why Gwyneth and I were purely vanilla. I didn't believe I should live a D/s life with my wife."

Raine didn't say anything for a long moment, but her lips began to quiver. "But D/s is okay for your whore? Got it." She struggled for freedom again. "I know my place. You can let go now."

Liam almost did. Damn it. No matter what he said, she only heard the worst. He understood that she was hurt and angry…but she made him feel as if she would never trust his love.

"When have I ever treated you like a whore, Raine?" Liam wanted to say more but wasn't sure what would convince her. He looked at Hammer, wordlessly asking for help.

"Never," the man growled. "And she knows that. She's thinking with emotion, not logic." Macen turned on her. "Listen to him. You know damn well where Liam's heart lies. Mine, too. We're both in love with you or we wouldn't be here fighting.

And don't you *ever* call yourself a whore again."

Looking slightly chagrined, she stopped trying to pull from their grasps. Liam wasn't sure they were reassuring her. Suddenly, he knew what would.

Liam sent a resolute glance at Macen. "I think we need to show her. Right now."

Hammer looked blank for a moment, then he caught on. A slow smile spread over his face. "Oh, yeah."

"Show me what?" she asked suspiciously. "Your penises? I've already seen those. If you two think you're going redirect *me* with sex and cool my anger with orgasms, think again."

Liam shook his head. "I'd like to, but no. We have something else in mind."

Hammer issued an evil chuckle. "And if we take you someplace, you can't act like a brat. Can you stop clawing, biting, and screaming for fifteen minutes?"

She leveled Hammer with a dry, derisive stare. "I don't know. Can you stop being an ass that long? You're on my shit list, too. You lied straight to my face."

Remorse settled over Hammer's features. "Yes, I did. And I'm sorry. Without consulting Liam, I decided the gas station on the side of the highway wasn't the time or the place to tell you about Gwyneth suddenly appearing with a baby. I wanted to wait until the three of us could sit down so we could tell you privately."

She sighed. At least she appeared to be mulling his words. "Don't ever lie to me again, Macen."

"I won't," he vowed softly.

She softened slightly, then raised her chin to scowl at Liam. "That goes for you, too."

"Lying to you was never an option for me," Liam assured as he leaned closer and brushed his lips over hers.

Thankfully, she didn't object.

"So…will you come with us and not raise a fuss?" Hammer settled his lips against the pulse point of her neck.

Raine gave a shuddering little exhalation, part resignation…and just the smallest part excitement. "All right."

"Wait here. I'll be right back," Liam instructed, then rushed down the hall to his room.

Yanking his suitcase from the back of the closet, he unzipped a side compartment and plucked the blue velvet box from inside. He flipped it open. Yep, the little gem still lay inside.

Though it had barely been two weeks since Liam had intended to surprise her, it seemed like a lifetime ago. Of course, chaos had ensued—a shit storm coming from every direction—and he'd never found the right moment to give her this gift. Maybe that had been for the best. The three of them had been through so much together. Liam felt a unity and rightness in surprising her with Hammer at his side. The time was now.

Liam hoped this would be the key to solidifying their future.

When he returned, Raine had sidestepped to put a bit of distance between her and Hammer. She wore a pensive expression.

He crossed the room and wrapped an arm around her waist. Hammer joined him and did the same. Together, they filed out the door.

Her posture was stiff as they led her down the hall, through the dungeon, past the bar, and finally outside. She didn't utter a word as they made their way to the Escalade. Discreetly, he scanned the car park for any sign of Bill. He noticed Hammer did the same. With Kendall popping up to extort more money and making veiled threats, they couldn't afford not to tell Raine for much longer. And Liam also suspected his old pal hadn't come clean about bribing dear old Dad. Christ, they'd have to cross that bridge soon, too…

One catastrophe at a time.

* * *

As Liam slid behind the wheel of his SUV, Hammer settled Raine in the front passenger seat, ensuring she was buckled in. Then he folded all six foot three of him in the backseat.

"Ready?" Liam asked.

How was she supposed to answer that? "Where exactly are you taking me?"

Liam sent her a secretive smile and pulled out of the lot. "You'll see."

She tried not to feel hurt that they intentionally kept her in the dark. After all, they behaved as if whatever they meant to show her would make her happy. She couldn't imagine what that would be. Sending Gwyneth off at the airport with a one-fingered sayonara, maybe. Of course, Raine could think of a hundred reasons Liam and Hammer would lie to her about what had really happened with the woman earlier today, but only one reason they would tell the truth.

Because they loved her.

After the strife they'd been through, Raine's head told her they did. Her heart *really* wanted to believe it. Was she so broken that she simply didn't know how?

The possibility filled her with wretched desolation.

She'd been so sure of their feelings for her at the lodge. If anyone had asked her last night, she would have insisted nothing could come between the three of them. How terrifying that at the first sign of trouble, she was questioning everything. Raine wished like hell she knew how to make it stop.

As Liam turned off Wilshire heading south on Crenshaw, he reached over and wrapped his hand around hers. Hammer caressed her shoulder. Raine didn't pull away, but inside she felt frozen.

She hated being this scared girl who didn't trust anyone. Other than her mother and grandparents—all of whom were gone—no one had shown her much kindness, at least until Hammer had taken her in. And then, he'd cared for her like a protective parent…while rejecting her as a lover. Liam was the first man to try filling both roles at once. In the last few days, Hammer had broken through the defenses he'd erected after Juliet's suicide and, like Liam, become her Dom in every sense of the word. She wanted to trust them both so badly now, ached to be cocooned in their love and reassurance.

But she just kept seeing Gwyneth's smug face, half-exposed breasts, and freshly paddled ass.

Had they really turned the woman down?

Lost in a chasm between painful hope and white-hot fear, she didn't know how much time had passed. Suddenly, Liam turned up to the gate of a posh residential district.

When she'd been a girl, she'd sometimes sneaked away

from her father and ridden her bike here, imagining herself in one of these big, character-filled houses. In her imagination, each one had been filled by a happy couple who looked on fondly while their children played on the manicured lawn, then enjoyed a hot meal every night before Mommy and Daddy tucked them into bed with kisses. Life was perfect here.

To Raine's shock, the gate opened immediately for Liam.

"We'll be there in two minutes," he said suddenly.

Her heart stuttered. "Where?"

Raine already knew there wasn't any thru traffic on this street, only more houses. Were they taking her to a private play party with the rich and famous? To meet some celebrity? Or…

She'd heard about houses that took in subs for training. Surely Hammer and Liam wouldn't drop her off like dirty laundry and leave her to be tutored by strangers…would they? No. They were too damn controlling. If they'd wanted to do that, they wouldn't have bothered taking her to the lodge.

"It's a surprise," he replied in a low, beguiling voice.

"A good one," Hammer added softly. "Relax."

She wasn't very good at that. They might be with her now, but the part of Raine that knew she'd never been half as pretty as Macen's usual conquests was petrified that Liam's nasty slut of an ex-wife would steal him from her.

Follow where they lead you. Let go of your control. They're not going to let you fall. Seth's words earlier rolled through her head. Instead of believing that, Raine had stomped her way back to Shadows, looking for a fight because that was easy. In fact, she could fight all day long. She'd spent most of her life fighting—her abusive father, her feelings for Hammer, and now these stupid insecurities about Gwyneth. She even wanted to fight against the bleeding wound inside her after Liam's remark that he wouldn't sully his wife with BDSM.

But Raine couldn't be mad at him because his commitment to her wasn't strong enough for marriage. She'd just been dumb enough to think they'd have a storybook ending. Yeah, because the princess in the tower always got it on with two guys.

Liam and Hammer cared, absolutely. They would appreciate the woman with whom they shared good times, a few laughs, and lots of mind-blowing sex. It was her fault for wishing that meant forever.

Raine withdrew her hand from Liam's and stared out the window, blinking away her tears while trying to hold herself together. Just a little while longer. She'd look at their surprise, then beg a headache when they returned to the club, lock the bathroom door, and cry this maudlin shit out of her system.

Then she'd just enjoy one day at a time with them, all the way to the inevitable end.

Liam made another left, and the houses just got bigger and bigger…until they passed one with a tennis court in the backyard. There, they made another left, onto a cul-de-sac. Toward the end of the street, Liam pulled into a U-shaped driveway lined by lovely manicured hedges with an interior filled by a patch of lush grass. A brick walkway, guarded by two marble statues of lions, bisected the foliage and led to the front door, illuminated by warmly glowing lights.

The house was huge but somehow still oozed charm. Big, beautiful windows dotted the front of the pale gray stucco façade. The French doors in the middle opened to a white Juliet balcony, which, along with a pair of traditional fluted columns, formed the portico over the massive front door with glass insets, which gave the house grandeur. Wrought iron planters spilling out with a profusion of colorful flowers framed all the other windows along the front.

Liam killed the engine. Hammer all but jumped out of the car to open her door. As he helped her out and Liam came around to take her other arm, Raine stared.

"Why are we here?" she asked them. "Do you know who lives in this place?"

"I do. Isn't it lovely?"

"Incredible." God, she'd give anything to stay here for even a night, just so she could pretend the house was hers.

Liam's smile turned brighter. "Then come with us."

Raine grew more confused with each step they took up the brick entrance, toward the front door. Had they rented it for the night since the lodge was so far away?

When the three of them reached the portal, Liam reached into his pocket. "Hold out your hand, love."

With a puzzled frown, she did. He set a small blue velvet

box in her palm, cupping the top of the soft case with his fingers and curling them around her own. "Raine, whatever you think, you mean everything to Hammer and me. We're not planning to be with you for a day or a month or even a year. We're committed to staying by your side, through thick and thin, day in and day out, sharing our lives with you. We love you, now and forever."

As his words melted her, Raine looked at their joined hands, then glanced into Liam's solemn face. "I don't understand."

Hammer wore a matching expression, cradling her hand from beneath so they completely surrounded her. "Liam is much better with words than I am, but everything he said is true. Open the box, precious."

Why would they bring her to a stranger's doorstep to give her a gift? Her heart started to race. A dangerous fantasy crossed her mind… But no. They couldn't possibly give her a gift like this.

"What is this place?"

"Go on," Hammer whispered as both men lifted their hands away.

Carefully, Raine gripped the sides of the box and tugged gently. It opened without a sound. Inside lay a key.

Raine stopped breathing as she looked first at Liam, then Hammer. More of that insidious hope filled her. She blinked away rapidly welling tears. "Y-you…" She shook her head. It wasn't possible. "It can't be."

Liam stroked his finger down her cheek and nodded. "I never seemed to find the right time to give this to you, but I understand why now. It's meant for all three of us. Put the key in the lock, love, and open the door to our new home."

Her heart skipped a beat, and the buzzing in her ears felt as if a swarm of bees had taken over her head. "You're serious? This is… It's…"

Raine couldn't finish her sentence through her onslaught of tears. She covered her mouth with her hands to hold in a shocked sob.

"Yes," Liam confirmed softly. "I know how long you've wanted a home to call your own, something that no one can take away. So I bought this for you. Regardless of what happens between us, this is your house. You'll always have these four walls and sturdy roof to shelter you, Raine."

"I-I can't accept this. It's too much. It's—"

"Too late," Liam cut in. "It's already done. The title and deed are in your name."

His words shocked her system again. She tried to comprehend, but her brain whirled. Time seemed mired in a slow, thick honey. Nothing made sense except the key in her hand and Liam's words echoing in her brain.

Hers. The house was hers. And Liam had done this for her.

"Oh, my god." Sobs wracked her body.

Had anyone ever done anything half as wonderful for her? Why would they?

Suddenly, Hammer nestled her from behind, wrapping his arm around her waist and holding her close against his chest. His warm breath brushed her ear as Liam stood frozen, studying her expression intently.

"Are you happy?" Macen asked.

She nodded. "I'm speechless. It's...amazing."

Liam looked relieved. Had he actually imagined she wouldn't be thrilled?

"You haven't seen the inside," he reminded her.

"It doesn't matter." She shook her head. "Whatever is inside is the most beautiful thing in the world to me. Why would you do this?"

Raine wasn't under any illusions. This wasn't some little one-bedroom cottage in the sticks. He'd bought her a palatial home. It must have cost a whole pile of pretty pennies.

"Because I wanted to give you everything," Liam murmured. "Especially the security you should have had as a child."

He was destroying her one word at a time in the best way possible. Had she really been wondering minutes ago if they could possibly love her?

"I always wanted to give you that, too, precious." Macen's voice cracked, thick with emotion. "It's why I took you in...and why I couldn't let you go. I should have bought you a place of your own years ago but couldn't stand the thought of not having you near me every day. I was afraid I'd lose you."

A cry filled with a confusing mix of shock, sorrow, regret, and delight tore from her throat. She launched herself into Liam's arms, pulling Hammer with her. From behind her, he held tight.

Tears slid down her cheeks as she trembled, the reality finally registering. "You really bought me a house?"

"I did." Liam pulled away and cupped her face, staring into her eyes with a fierceness she'd never seen before.

"When?"

He hesitated. "Before Thanksgiving."

Guilt tore through her. He'd never given it to her because she'd run away, been a defiant, difficult handful.

"I see the self-reproach on your face. Don't," Liam insisted. "It's worked out for the best. We're all meant to live here together."

Her tears started in earnest again. "That would be a dream come true."

"For me, too." Hammer leaned around to press a kiss to her cheek.

"Understand us, Raine," Liam went on. "You're not a whim. You're not a sport or a conquest for either of us. You're the center of our lives."

Before she could say another word, Liam claimed her lips in a kiss somehow tender and primal at once, teeming with painfully pure love. She wrapped one hand around his neck and opened to him completely. He felt so solid pressed to her chest. Raine couldn't imagine loving this man more.

When he broke away from her, the passion and fire still blazed in his eyes. "Forever, love. Don't ever question that again."

How could she? "Thank you, Liam," she whispered, her voice quivering as more tears spilled down her face. "Not just for a gift that's beyond amazing. Thank you for understanding me and what I need."

"You ready to have a look inside?" Liam grinned.

"Yeah." A big smile broke out across her face. "Beyond ready."

"One more thing…" Hammer turned Raine to face him. "The previous owners lived here for about thirty years. It might not be decorated to your taste. But you can make it whatever you want. It's empty, so I know we'll need to buy furniture, but if you want to redecorate the kitchen or bathrooms or whatever…then do it. That's my gift to you, precious."

Her heart split wide open for the second time tonight. "Macen, you don't have to do that. I'm sure it's beautiful the way it is. I don't need—"

"Let me. Liam has given us an amazing house to live in. Let me make the inside as beautiful as you."

That might be one of the nicest things he'd ever said to her. She started to cry again and pressed her lips to his for a slow, reverent kiss before her face got too sloppy again.

"I'm overwhelmed. You two are the most wonderful men who ever happened to me. I love you both."

"And we love you," Macen murmured. "Now open the door."

Chapter Eleven

Her fingers shook as she tried to align the key into the lock. After the third try, she finally managed and turned the handle. The impatient part of her wanted to shove the door open and run through the house. Another part wanted to savor every moment of this amazing dream.

Raine gave the door a tiny nudge, and it swung open, revealing one tantalizing inch at a time.

"I know we're not married, but…" Liam swooped her up in his arms, then carried her across the threshold.

She giggled as he set her down. Hammer stepped in and palmed the light switch by the door, flooding the expansive foyer with light. Raine could only think of one word to describe the place.

Wow.

The hardwood floors gleamed a pale cherry and spread down the long corridor and up the wide staircase to the second floor. A crystal chandelier hung above her head, minimal and elegant—perfect for the space.

An opening to her right revealed a family room with walls painted in a tranquil pale sage and built-in bookshelves a lovely dove gray around the white marble fireplace surround. Liam turned on the lights in the room, and she saw a traditional gleaming white mantel with intricate columns and moldings, making her *ooh* and *ahh*. On an adjacent wall sat the brace for a giant flat-screen. Raine could imagine comfy couches in here, reading by the fire, snuggled with Liam doing a Sunday crossword or watching football with Hammer.

Three French doors lined the back of the room, leading out to a cozy little sunroom that flanked the backyard and would let in a ton of natural light.

Drawn as if it were a beacon, Raine wandered toward the space with her mouth hanging open. She couldn't have imagined a more beautiful house if she'd tried.

"Look to your right," Liam murmured.

Raine whirled. And gasped. "Oh, my god…"

The family room extended a good twenty-five feet. Moldings at the ceilings and baseboards were pristine and substantial but somehow just right for the space. Three cottage windows, topped with leaded-glass eyebrows, would let in more sunlight on the far side of the room. Two built-in shelving units, arched and obviously original to the house, had been restored lovingly.

"Everything is…perfect. When was the house built?"

"Nineteen fourteen." Liam smiled as he guided her around the room with a hand at the small of her back. "Since I bought it, I've had the plumbing and electrical brought up to code. The house was in good shape, but I've had the necessary minor repairs completed. Most recently, the contractors have been painting."

The faint smell of it lingered in the air, and Raine nodded in amazement at all his choices. "It's as if you read my mind, Liam."

Hammer watched her intently, seemingly pleased by her response. He sauntered closer and dropped a kiss on her mouth. "We want you happy."

"How could I be anything else?" She feathered her lips across his, then turned to Liam and sank into his kiss for a sweet moment.

They continued the tour by peeking into a powder bath at the end of the foyer with floor-to-ceiling polished travertine and a large oval mirror. Funny that a bathroom should look regal, but this one managed.

Across from the family room sat a formal living room, complete with a black baby grand. It opened to an expansive dining room with more French doors leading to more gardens. Silk drapes, pale gray walls, and classic moldings all framed a beautiful eight-armed fixture made of a fascinating blend of a white rustic wood and glittering crystal.

Toward the back of the dining room, a leaded-glass door drew Raine's attention. She tiptoed toward it. Her head told her this was now her house. Her shock told her not to touch or break something that belonged to someone else. Carefully, she pushed at the door.

Hammer grabbed her arm. "Brace yourself."

A little warning gong resounded through her. She could easily dial back her expectations since the house had already far surpassed anything she'd imagined.

She smiled his way, then Liam's. "Whatever is behind this door will be great. I can make anything work."

Nodding, Hammer cupped the curve of her waist before his palm took a slow slide down her ass. "Good girl. Go on."

Tummy tightening, Raine poked at the swinging door. As it opened, Liam flipped on the light. She filed into the space, seeing a sizeable butler's pantry immediately to her left. Then the portal swung wide, and she spotted the kitchen.

Her jaw dropped. She couldn't speak.

Gleaming marble floors, medium-toned walnut cabinets, every appliance known to man. She wandered around the room, checking out the Sub-Zero refrigerator built in behind faux panels to match the rest of the room, the convection and conventional ovens, the six-burner gas cooktop… *Amazing.* This was a cook's paradise, complete with two sinks, one in the huge island that seated three on wide, black leather barstools. A wine fridge, a storage rack for stems, and a lovely door that led to the backyard. This kitchen just kept on giving.

"Anything you want to change?"

She wasn't terribly fond of the black granite counters, mostly because she suspected they would be a bitch to keep clean. But spending time here would be a treat. "No."

Hammer faced her and leaned down until they stood eye to eye. "You forget how well I can read you. Let's try again.

Anything you want to change?"

Raine didn't want to seem ungrateful, but Hammer was insistent. "The countertops."

A wide smile spread across his face as he sauntered over to Liam, who looked about ready to burst with his grin. They high-fived one another.

"What's that about?" she asked.

"We both guessed you'd feel that way, love," Liam supplied. "I had a feeling when I bought this house that the kitchen would be your favorite room, but I saw you wanting something brighter that matched your personality."

The fact that he'd thought of the interior design in such detail touched her. In fact, they looked very pleased with themselves. She was pretty happy, too.

At the far end of the kitchen, a long, narrow room housed a full-sized washer and dryer, a long countertop for folding, and a stainless-steel sink for industrial cleaning. A kitschy ironing board pulled out from the wall. Whoever had built the house really had thought of everything.

The kitchen led to a pale yellow breakfast nook surrounded by three walls of windows that overlooked the backyard. When Liam flipped a switch, light flooded the back patio. A pool glimmered just outside. Raine couldn't wait to walk out and see it.

Through a back door, the three of them pushed their way into the moonlight. Raine blinked and stared at their own personal Shangri-La. *Unreal...*

The pool lay like a blue oasis across the yard, long, curved, and serene, surrounded by a spa, fountains, and classical urns filled with ferns and flowers. Giant palms swayed in the slight breeze all around the pool like solid sentries, ensuring privacy.

"You know what I was thinking when I first saw this yard?" Liam asked with a grin.

Raine scanned the space. Surrounded by the house on one side, the towering plants and full shrubs on two more, and another two-storied structure she couldn't identify, the pool and patio were completely private. Even the gazes of nosy neighbors in their big houses on either side couldn't penetrate the wall of greenery. Only someone in a helicopter could see them. Maybe.

She shook her head at Liam. "That I won't need a bathing suit."

His smile widened and turned devilish as he cupped her breast. "Exactly. I mean to fuck you out here. A great deal."

Hammer ambled up behind her and wrapped an arm around her waist. Then his hand drifted down to cup her pussy. "Hmm. I see more than one surface I can bend you over and fill you with my cock."

Raine gasped. Her head rolled back on Hammer's shoulder. Liam moved in and trailed kisses down her neck, then reached into her shirt and pulled one breast from her bra and over the V-neck. The wind barely caressed her nipple before he engulfed it in his mouth. As she gasped, Hammer lifted her swishy skirt, tucked his fingers under the elastic of her panties, and began rubbing her clit.

"God, that's so fucking sexy," Hammer groaned as he watched Liam suck on her nipple. "You're so wet."

Her body felt wide open to them. The pleasure they never failed to bestow sent her head reeling, her body aching…her soul pleading for more.

"Spread your legs." Macen nudged at her thighs with his fingers. "And no more panties."

"This bra is in my fucking way," Liam snarled. "Damn it to hell, I can smell her."

They were driving her mad, dousing her body with ecstasy, flooding her veins with heady desire. She wriggled against Hammer's fingers for more friction.

"Why don't we help each other?" Hammer suggested.

Liam didn't hesitate. "Deal."

Before Raine could question what they meant, Hammer unhooked her bra at the back and pulled it away from her breasts, leaving them to dangle, while Liam reached under her skirt and pulled her panties down to her ankles.

"Step out," Hammer commanded.

Raine did so automatically. Did they really mean to fuck her right here? Right now?

"Shirt off," Liam insisted.

She took that to mean yes.

Swallowing hard, heart racing, she followed orders, tugging

at her shirt to yank it free. The minute it cleared her head, Liam tugged her bra off and tossed it onto the patio, beside her shirt and panties.

Taking a step back, Liam looked on as Hammer fingered her pussy under her brief skirt as the moonlight gleamed down on her bare breasts.

"So fucking lovely. I think it would be a prettier picture without the skirt, mate."

With a growl, Hammer popped the button at the small of her back and tried to tug the zipper down. It wasn't easy one-handed, and he gave a frustrated grunt.

"A little help here, please."

Liam sauntered close again. "My pleasure."

Raine's heart pounded furiously as he wrapped his arms around her waist, finding the zipper as his lips locked over hers. He took the kiss deep and sweeping. She had trouble breathing as the sensations and their scents overwhelmed her.

After a brush of cotton down her thighs, she stood completely bare between them. Liam cupped her breasts and thumbed her peaked nipples, approval gleaming in his dark eyes as Hammer continued to work her clit dangerously close to orgasm. A flush rose up her body. She whimpered in a little plea and felt herself utterly melting.

"Jesus…" Hammer sounded impatient. "I'm dying to be inside her hot little cunt."

"As much as I love her lush breasts…" Liam drawled, then curled his hand around her waist and caressed down to her bare backside. "I find myself desperate to bury my cock in her ass."

Hammer nipped at her neck, the bite filled with a reckless impatience that only jacked her desire up more. "I don't think I have a damn condom with me."

"I only have one," Liam murmured as he inflicted love bites all around her aching nipples. "And I don't have any lube."

That was bad news. Terrible. The worst.

With a groan, Hammer stiffened. Raine felt his displeasure—largely in the cessation of the rhythm of his fingers.

She keened, long and loud. "Please…"

"Precious." He dusted the sensitive spot just under her ear with apologetic kisses. "We'll have to go back to the club. The one and only fucking time I'm not prepared…"

"Wait! I just remembered I am." Liam nipped at her hard peaks. "Let's tour the bedroom."

"Fuck yeah," Hammer breathed.

The guys gathered up her clothes—none of that silly donning-garments for her. Raine's pussy ached, but she prayed they'd give her relief soon. And in her new house… What could be sweeter?

They couldn't run upstairs fast enough. At the top, she had a sense of an elegant landing, gorgeous built-ins, three open doors leading to what she was sure were perfectly wonderful bedrooms, a big roomy bathroom between, then a step up to the biggest bedroom.

The master.

As they turned the corner, Liam turned on some lighting, which glowed above the crown molding, providing soft ambiance to the whole enormous room. The size shocked her almost as much as a plush bed smack-dab in the middle, complete with pristine white sheets. A massive nightstand sat nearby in the otherwise empty room.

Liam nudged her toward the mattress. "Get on the bed, love."

"And spread your legs," Hammer added.

Raine didn't dare disobey—and she didn't want to. But as she moved toward the bed, she had too many questions to stay mute. "When did you…?"

"Prepare the room? Weeks ago, not long after I bought it." He shrugged. "I planned to bring you here as soon as the time was right and spend the night enjoying you in every way possible. But I think this will be even better." With a little smirk, he opened the top drawer and reached inside. "Catch." He tossed a condom Hammer's way.

Macen caught it one-handed, then sent her a feral smile. "You're dawdling, girl."

Liam pulled another condom and a tube of lube from the drawer and set them both on the gleaming surface. "A bit faster, if you please."

It wasn't exactly a request. Her stomach knotted with excitement.

Raine eased onto the bed, the cool sheets at her back. Propping herself on her elbows, she parted her thighs just enough to tease them and watched as they came toward her in tandem.

Yes. God yes. This was what she needed… The two halves of her heart working together to make her whole. And they needed her to be open to them. After having so many events out of their control today, they'd want to exercise their power. They would require it.

The men sent one another a stare she couldn't quite read, but Raine had little doubt they plotted something that would eventually bring her pleasure. She couldn't wait.

At the edge of the bed, Liam tsked and shook his head. "That will never do."

"Not at all," Hammer concurred as he wrapped one hand around her thigh.

On the right, Liam did the same. Then together, they spread her wide, exposing her pussy to their hungry stares. Their savage smiles made her blush.

"Love me," she breathed.

Liam caressed her hip. "We do."

"But we'll tell you again if you need to hear it." Hammer lifted her leg. Gravity bent her knee, and he set her limb down again, foot planted on the mattress, then stared at her pussy. "Pretty."

"I like that." Liam arranged her other foot down on the plush surface, somehow spreading her even wider.

"You're intentionally misunderstanding me. I mean, make love to me," Raine entreated. "Take me. I felt as if I belonged to you both last night." Before Beck's emergency surgery, Gwyneth's intrusion, and the secret-baby scare. "I want that again."

"You don't give orders and ultimatums." Hammer's smile disappeared, replaced by a commanding passion she was beginning to learn well. He skated his fingertips up her thigh, trailing lip-bitingly close to where she needed their touch. A shiver zipped down her spine. "Now, it's our way."

"It is." Liam's voice sounded rough. "You'll drown in the pleasure we give you. In return, you'll give us every one of your whimpers, moans, and screams. We will hear exactly what our lovemaking does to you, Raine. Do you understand?"

"Yes…" Their words and demeanors were unraveling her. "Yes, Sirs."

A corner of Hammer's lips kicked up in a grin. "You haven't behaved very submissively since you stormed back into Shadows, full of accusations. That changes now."

Right now. Raine heard him loud and clear.

"Yes, Sir."

"Better." He grazed his knuckles over the bare pad of her pussy.

She raised her hips to him, shuddering as she remembered the way they'd shaved her yesterday. Again today in the shower earlier, Hammer had seen to the task himself with a pride in ownership that probably should have pushed every feminist button inside her. Instead, it just turned her on.

Raine whimpered. He gave her an evil chuckle and pulled his hand away. She bit her tongue. Neither demanding nor whining would get her anywhere. As much as she hated it, he would force her to be patient and wait.

The thought had barely crossed her mind when she felt Liam slide his shoulders between her thighs and work his way up to her needy sex.

She tensed, held her breath—and spread even wider for him.

"That's a girl…" Liam breathed against her wet flesh.

His first lazy swipe through her drenched folds had her groaning and blindly reaching for him. She couldn't repress the urge to drive her clit against his tongue to feed the impossible ache as she bucked against his mouth. Hammer had other plans.

He rounded the bed and caught her wrists in one of his big hands, pinning them to the mattress as he stood behind her. He bent and captured her lips with his own as his free hand wrapped around a sensitive breast.

She was burning, every nerve ending aflame and crying out in agonized bliss. Another whimper tore from her lips, only to be swallowed by Hammer's lips as Liam continued tormenting her cunt.

He added fingers, one at a time, slotting between her swollen folds as he suckled and teased her pouting clit with his relentless tongue.

As if eager to add to her suffering, Hammer tore his mouth from hers to nip at her taut nipples, a scrape of teeth followed by a hard, sucking pull. On fire now, Raine arched her back and wailed for them, an incoherent plea.

"That's it. That's what we want to hear," Hammer murmured, his mouth still pressed to her breast. "Give us your cries."

Raine mewled out again when Hammer sank his teeth into her tender nipple, just enough to send a tingle of pleasurable pain radiating through her. At the same time, Liam wrapped his lips around her clit, sucking with a beautifully brutal draw and proving that he and Hammer maneuvered together like a perfect team.

They were both completely dressed—feasting on her naked body with their mouths, teeth, fingers, and tongues, pushing her to the edge. Every nibble, touch, suck, and probe confirmed the fact that they were determined to command not only her mind and body—but every last shred of her control.

Liam drove his fingers deeper still, twisting until he settled over the hidden knot of nerves inside her before strumming the sensitive spot with an exacting pressure. The roar of pending release began to throb in her ears.

"Please," she gasped, arching her hips from the mattress again, longing to rush over the edge of release.

"Are you ready to come for us?" Hammer taunted.

"Yes. Oh, god, yes."

Liam's mouth never left her clit as he raised his gaze and drilled her with a dark stare, his hooded lids heavy with lust. Virile and seductive, he worked to bring her pleasure. The sight unraveled her self-control.

Then Hammer plucked at her nipple, gently twisting as he settled his mouth close to her ear. "When you returned to Shadows and threw your little fit, did you ever think there might be another side of the story? Or did you simply believe everything Gwyneth told you?"

Raine moaned, her pending orgasm simmering just below a boil. Hammer wanted to talk about this *now*?

"I'm sorry," she blurted.

"I didn't ask if you were sorry; I asked if you believed her."

"Kind of…" Raine squeaked as Liam continued that unrelenting quest with his tongue. "The horrible things she said made sense at the time."

Liam lifted his mouth from her, giving his lips a slow lick that made her belly tighten and dip. "So, love…"

No! Don't stop. Can't we talk later? She sent him a pleading stare, which he ignored.

"You just assumed I'd fucked Gwyneth?" he asked. "I'm curious… Am I the only one you don't trust or does that extend to Hammer as well? Maybe you lack faith in love altogether?"

That wasn't true…not really. Well, maybe a little. She sighed. She'd never been good with trust, not when almost everyone had let her down.

"What else was I supposed to think? The evidence that you'd scened with her was all over the condo. And Gwyneth's red fuck-me ensemble didn't exactly make me feel better. Coupled with the fact that you walked right past me in Beck's lobby after I called your name… I didn't know what else to think."

"I didn't hear or see you." Liam frowned. "When have I ever ignored you, Raine?"

In the car earlier today. But pointing that out wouldn't be wise. Or kind. He'd had extenuating circumstances. And normally, he made her feel like the center of his world.

Now, Raine regretted accusing him of screwing the shrew before she'd asked a single question. Knowing Liam had bought her this amazing house in the hopes she'd share it with them, she felt even more contrite.

"Almost never." Guilt further cooled her desire. "I'm working on learning to trust both of you. But I have to fight myself everyday to believe I'm worthy and that love won't hurt. I've never experienced the kind that wasn't painful."

"I see." Liam resumed strumming her clit with his fingers as he pinned her with a hard stare. Raine worried they had more questions poised on the tips of their tongues.

"Let me guess." Hammer leaned in close, his lips drawn in a tight line. "It was easier and more comfortable to fall back into old behavior than to implement anything we taught you at the lodge."

She bit back a little huff. "I wasn't rational. I didn't exactly make a conscious effort to lose my temper."

"You didn't think at all. You closed yourself off to us," Hammer chided.

"And you won't be doing that again," Liam warned. "You're not allowed to hide yourself or your feelings. Hammer and I will always strip your walls down and lay you open, raw and naked, like you are now. Do you understand?"

Raine knew they meant every word.

"Yes, Sirs," she murmured, feeling duly scolded.

Bending back to her pussy, he swiped his tongue over her flesh. Raine jolted with renewed sensation and moaned. In an instant, he ramped her back up until she needed so badly for them to cover, devour, and fill her.

Instead, Liam paused again. "By the way, if you want this climax, you'll have to swear you'll never shut us out again."

What? They commanded her, ruled her desires, and controlled her body. Now they wanted her to make a promise she likely couldn't keep? Didn't they know she'd say or do almost anything right now for the shimmering orgasm just out of reach?

Raine didn't believe that if she uttered a few easy words, they'd shower her with bliss. No way. They'd want more. Way more. And when Liam's fingers got busy again, she *really* couldn't find the patience to figure out what. Instead, she gave them a keening little cry.

"Is that a yes or a no?" Liam asked with a quick slap to her cunt.

A deep burn seared her folds. Raine hissed as the fire spread outward in a slow, stinging slide.

"Convince us you intend to communicate honestly." Hammer arched a dark brow.

Liam swooped in low, giving her a long, torturous lick before backing away again. "Or will Hammer and I take turns edging you for the next month?"

God, that sounded awful. She groaned in desperation. "Yes. I'll communicate."

"Rationally and calmly," Hammer insisted.

Liam nipped at her inner thigh, his fingers plying her clit with maddening circles. "Without yelling or sounding as if you're from the gutter. You know I don't like that language from you, lass."

She did. She knew. "It slipped out. I'm sorry. It won't happen again."

"It best not." Liam laved her clit slowly.

The friction kept her achy and needy. Raine had no idea if she could keep her promise, but she'd have to try damn hard because she couldn't possibly make it another thirty seconds without this orgasm.

"No." She shook her head frantically. "Communication. Honesty. Trust. Got it."

Hammer leaned into her face, his expression sharp, exacting. "Tell me why we should believe you."

"I want you," she gasped out.

He tweaked her nipple again. "That's a given. I can see the flush turning your skin rosy and smell your sweet pussy."

That wasn't helping her train of thought. Panting, Raine closed her eyes and tried to gather her wits. "No, I mean I want to make you both happy, please you, make you proud. I know I lose my temper, but deep down, that's all I want. Please…"

"Hmm. Your words make me even harder, precious." He caressed her cheek, and she opened her eyes, her lashes fluttering.

"That's true for me as well," Liam agreed, then settled his mouth over her pussy again, the torture-by-tongue igniting a fever of hitched breaths and ecstasy poised right on the precipice… Abruptly, he pulled away once more, his lazy fingers replacing his tongue.

She writhed, her legs twisting as she moaned long and low. "Please…"

"Not yet," Hammer murmured as he toyed with her nipple, then shot Liam a knowing smirk.

What now? She dug her nails into Hammer's hands, arching, trying to cling to sanity.

"Why don't you think you're worthy of us, Raine?" Hammer demanded.

"What?" How the hell was she supposed to answer that?

Liam pinched her clit. "You heard us. We're waiting."

Raine's hips shot off the bed. She knew their game, and it

sucked. They wouldn't relent until she talked, so she squeezed her eyes shut and dragged in deep breaths that did absolutely nothing to calm the raging fire inside her.

"I'm not the type either of you are attracted to."

"Type? What do you think we like?" Hammer demanded.

Plastic Barbies whose IQs are smaller than their ring size. "Come on. Marlie was beautiful, but Gwyneth leaves her in the dust. They're both gorgeous, blonde, and—"

"Void of a heart or soul," Liam interrupted.

Hammer crossed his arms over his chest. "So you measure your self-worth by comparing your physical appearance to women who mean absolutely nothing to us?"

Apparently, this answer interested Liam since he paused his torture again.

Frustration set in. "They were clearly easy to ogle and fu… Um, screw."

That made Hammer scowl. "And even easier to forget. Damn it, Raine. I've been in love with you for six fucking years."

It would have been nice if you'd told me, instead of turning me away and making me feel ugly.

"And I fell hard and fast for you in a way I never had. But …" Liam shrugged, then quirked a brow toward Hammer. "That complicated everything."

Macen sent him an ironic smile. "Complicated or not, I'm still glad."

"I'm glad, too." She bit her lip and turned to Hammer. "How I've felt about you is no secret. But you surrounded yourself with Marlies for years. I wasn't ever going to be tall or blonde or look like I'd spent hours at the salon. My mom left when I was young, so what I knew about makeup could fit in a thimble. I couldn't compete. I didn't know how to try."

She closed her eyes. God, she hated dredging up this icky shit. It made her sound weak and feel wretchedly inferior.

"Your honesty was very nice, precious," Hammer praised, letting go of her wrists.

No, it was embarrassing and sucked big monkey balls.

"Open your eyes," Hammer insisted. "No hiding."

Raine weighed the pros and cons of complying. But she

couldn't not face them forever. And if she wanted that orgasm Liam dangled like a sweet carrot, she would have to fall in line.

She opened her eyes and stared at the crown moldings. They really were lovely and… Why was Hammer removing his belt? She'd barely wondered before Liam's warm breath wafted over her aching pussy. Then it almost didn't matter.

"We're proud of you, love." Liam sent her a satisfied smile, then lowered his lips to her clit again and sucked gently.

Raine melted against his mouth. *Finally…* Had she told them what they wanted to hear? It seemed so, and she thanked her lucky stars they intended to put her out of her misery.

She stretched, luxuriating in the rise of bliss again, needing and squirming and trying to catch her breath.

When she grabbed for Liam's hair, Hammer gripped her hands and pulled them above her head again. Her eyes flew open wide as she craned her neck in time to see him wrap the belt around her wrists like makeshift cuffs.

"If you need rope, mate, it's in the nightstand," Liam murmured against her weeping folds.

"Good man." Then Hammer drilled her with a command. "Don't move."

Raine held her breath, not even daring to shake her head. Oh, she loved bondage, and they both knew it. That persistent ache behind her clit ramped up again, and she shot him an imploring stare, even as Liam opened his mouth against her and ate at her hungrily once more.

Macen returned in moments with a length of silky white rope. He tied it to the end of his belt, then secured the length to the bedframe and stepped back to admire his handiwork with a self-satisfied smile.

As if she wasn't in total sensual distress, Hammer settled onto the bed next to her and smoothed his fingers through her hair. She raised her head, silently asking for a kiss.

He skimmed a slow gaze over her face and shook his head. "What else led you to think you weren't as attractive as Marlie or Gwyneth?"

"Macen…" she whimpered. *Stop talking. Let me come.*

At her whine, Liam released her clit and pinned her with a warning glare. "Answer him."

She gave them both a long-suffering sigh. They weren't going to budge until she talked. "It's probably stupid…but none of the Doms at Shadows ever seemed interested in me. I know their opinions shouldn't matter. It's just…I always figured I must be unattractive since no one even wanted to play with me."

Hammer's expression clouded with guilt. "I'm to blame for that. When you first arrived, I declared myself your protector. Everyone respected the fact that an underage girl was off limits. When you turned eighteen…" He grimaced. "I got hit up three times during your party alone. I'm still approached regularly. I refuse everyone. It's not you."

His words hit like a slugger's bat to her psyche. Her jaw dropped. "I had no idea."

"I concealed the information for a couple of reasons. You needed someone to watch over you, and I didn't want you mixed up with some player who might screw with your head or bruise your tender heart."

Like Zac, who'd taken her virginity.

Macen could be an ass, but he was a natural-born defender. In a way, his protectiveness was touching.

He looked uncomfortable. "And…I didn't think I could stand to watch anyone else touch you. I was selfish, and I'm sorry if hoarding you made you question your worth."

Liam grinned, rubbing his fingers around her clit again in aimless circles. "Raine, I took you under my wing because you needed it. And because I couldn't resist you. You're lovely."

Their attention now made her *feel* lovely. She smiled—and maybe even glowed a little.

"Thank you for being honest," she murmured to Hammer, then turned to Liam. "And for being so kind."

"Let us show you how beautiful we think you are," Liam murmured before laying siege to her pussy once more—sucking and licking while penetrating her empty sex with nimble fingers.

Raine cried out in delight and curled her hands around the taut leather belt, holding tight as she endured his stunning assault.

Then Hammer added to her torment, bending to her and laving her nipple. She let out a long moan as he sucked deep and feasted on her heavy breast.

The teasing game they'd played—taking her to the brink of release only to deny her—had stripped her of restraint. Pleasure pelted her from every direction at once. She couldn't contain or control it. Raine simply hung on for the shuddering breakneck ride.

Liam scraped his teeth over her throbbing clit. With an agonized groan, she fought the rising desire because they hadn't given her permission to come. Hammer continued the double assault, devouring her lips, her neck, her breasts like a hungry wolf. Together, they forced her headlong toward oblivion. Thrashing between them, Raine moaned and pleaded as they ripped every ounce of pleasure from her.

Aware of Hammer leaning over her, she whispered in hoarse desperation, "Please…Sirs. Please."

He paused, and she glimpsed pride in his smile—along with a bit of sadistic joy. "You've earned this one. Come hard. Give Liam your pleasure."

Before he'd even finished speaking, the rush of blood and desire burst into a writhing euphoria that sent her soaring. As her sex clenched, a guttural scream tore from her throat. Liam suckled her clit and rubbed at her most sensitive spots with his clever fingers. He drew her pleasure out with precision. It was nothing less than exquisite torture. Cries of rapture tore from her throat as she called their names.

"Fuck," Hammer cursed as he cupped her face. "You make me want you so damn bad. I'm going to pack your pussy full, precious."

Even as Liam stroked his tongue gently over her throbbing bud, drawing a lingering sweetness from the climax and easing her down, Hammer's vow ratcheted her back up again. Shock waves pinged through her body.

Liam eased back from her cunt and rose. "I'm going to do the same to your ass, love. We're going to fill you so completely, you won't know where you end and we begin."

Oh, pretty please with sugar on top…

"You better be ready to dig your nails into my shoulders and scream. And we'll do everything we promised…" Hammer smiled. "As soon as you show us that you won't hide behind the defenses in your psyche anymore."

Show them how? "I'm working on my trust issues."

"And the best way to do that is to submit." Liam climbed onto the bed beside her.

"Isn't that what I've been doing?"

"When you're in the mood," Hammer poked. "We all know that when Liam had you collared, you only gave him pieces of yourself and only on your terms."

It was true. She hadn't given Liam all of her soul. He may have forgiven her, but she still struggled to forgive herself.

Hammer skimmed a knuckle across her cheek.

Liam stroked her abdomen, her thigh. "If your focus is on submitting to us, you won't be so quick to scurry behind your walls again because it will hurt to shut us out. You'll have a void only we can fill."

"You know I want to please you." Raine licked her lips nervously. She didn't know exactly where he meant to take the conversation, but she had some worrisome ideas.

Liam gave her a devilish grin. "How soon we fill those your aching voids is up to you."

Hammer leaned onto his side to check her hands. Once he'd massaged her fingers and wrists, he settled beside her again with a satisfied nod. "All you have to do is tell us five things you love about yourself."

"Five things that…" Was he serious? "Right now? I'm naked and bound to the bed and you want to play armchair—"

"Hit a nerve, did we, love?" Liam arched his brows before his expression turned downright insistent. "Name them. Now."

She'd rather be waterboarded. "My self-opinion doesn't have anything to do with us."

"Wrong." Hammer shook his head. "The way you perceive yourself affects you so it affects our relationship."

"You're filtering again, Raine," Liam pointed out. "You're deciding that your self-image isn't important. That's not your choice to make. You're not allowed to close off parts of yourself and only give us what's comfortable."

"Step outside your comfort zone," Hammer instructed. "For the last time, Raine. Tell us five things you love about yourself."

"I love working in the dungeon and cook—"

"Stop." Hammer narrowed his eyes in warning. "Not the

things you enjoy. You seem fixated by what Marlie and Gwyneth look like. Tell me five of your own physical attributes you appreciate."

Couldn't they pour hot oil over her? It would burn just the same. Dreaming up a handful of characteristics she liked about herself could take all night. But she was naked, cuffed, and at their mercy. She had nowhere to hide.

She sucked in a deep breath. "I like my boobs."

"Like or love?" Liam asked.

For herself, she didn't care much, but… "I love them."

"Why?" Liam quizzed.

"Because they bring you and Hammer pleasure."

"That they do." Liam chuckled. "Same goes for the rest of you."

"This isn't about *us*," Hammer pointed out "We want to know what *you* love about yourself."

Um… "The color of my eyes."

"So do we. Keep going," Liam encouraged.

"My legs."

"Tell us why," Hammer urged.

"I like their shape, though I've always wished they were longer."

"You're perfect just the way you are," Hammer assured. "You always have been."

Raine paused, running through a litany of additional possibilities. She didn't like her hair much. It was so dark brown, almost black. And it wasn't as thick as she'd like. Her smile? A million other women had one similar. She could grow nice fingernails, but men didn't care much about stuff like that. Her skin had always been so fair, and she wished she could carry at least a little tan, but she just burned. Her nose and her cheeks had always seemed simply average. Her chin was a bit too square, her mouth a hint too wide. Apparently, she'd pretty much exhausted the list at three.

She darted a nervous glance between Hammer and Liam, then shrugged. "That's all I can think of."

Without a word, Hammer untied the rope and released his belt, freeing her wrists. He rubbed her hands, working the blood back into her fingertips.

"Kneel on the floor," Hammer ordered.

She wanted to ask why but bit her tongue. Neither of them looked thrilled that she'd come up short. Did they mean to punish her?

After scooting off the bed, she sank to her knees and spread her thighs, resting her hands atop them. *Let's get this over with.*

"Since you're having trouble thinking of more than three aspects of your appearance you love, let's try another angle. Hammer and I gave you some affirmations at the lodge, Raine," Liam reminded. "Recite them to us now."

She blanched and issued an inward scream. "I'd rather list more things I love about myself. I'm reasonably smart. I can be funny—"

"You had your chance. The affirmations, if you please," Liam insisted.

Ugh. Raine had memorized every damn word but loathed having to spit them out again. "They make me feel awkward and uncomfortable."

Actually, they made her itch. Liam and Hammer knew that.

"Because you don't believe them yet. Say them enough, and you will." Hammer shot her an expectant smile.

Might as well get this over with... Raine resisted the urge to roll her eyes. "I will open myself up and share not only my needs but my emotions."

"*Every* need—from tampons to kisses," Hammer reiterated.

"Especially your fears, joys, accomplishments, and worries," Liam added.

I know. I know. I'm trying to figure out how...

"I will be totally honest at all times without fear of embarrassment or reprisal. Nor will I hold back for fear of hurting someone's feelings."

"You know we expect total honesty. Without fail," Liam emphasized.

"Is that clear?" Hammer asked in that damn hard-assed Dom voice that turned her on.

"Yes, Sirs." Raine swallowed tightly. They'd already dealt with that mantra a bunch at the lodge.

"Next one," Liam prodded, gesticulating with his finger.

She sighed. "No one has control over any aspect of my life

unless I choose to give them my gift."

Hammer nodded. "Just remember, you can take back your control any time you want, Raine. But don't decide to toss in the towel just because things get uncomfortable."

Been there. Done that. She'd hated the T-shirt. "I understand, Sirs."

Liam frowned. "Today, you handed your control over to Gwyneth. You gave her the power to hurt you, didn't you?"

"Yeah." She hadn't meant to, but Raine now realized that she'd let Liam's bitch-faced ex climb inside her head.

"Last one," Hammer murmured. "You're doing really well, precious."

Raine nodded and tried not to wince. On the surface, this declaration seemed like it should be the easiest. Somehow, it hurt the most. "I deserve happiness and love."

Without a word, they knelt beside her, surrounded her.

"You do." Liam brushed her hair back over her shoulder and cupped her chin before he pressed his lips to the pulse point on her neck. "We hope you'll let us fill you with our love and happiness, Raine."

"Every day," Macen echoed.

A single tear slipped down her cheek as she raised her hands and cupped each of their cheeks. "I'll always try to share my emotions and fears with you two—without yelling or cursing. I can't promise I'll never hide behind my walls, but if I'm not aware I'm doing it, tell me. I'll work hard to come out…or let you in."

The broad smiles that lit up their faces were almost blinding. They hugged her, and Raine felt something shift deep inside. It wasn't this house's beauty that made it a home because her home would always be in their arms.

"I think you're catching on," Hammer teased.

"Yeah, yeah." She flashed him a playful pout.

"We're proud of you, love. Keep your faith in us. We won't let you down." Liam kissed her so gently she almost melted.

Hammer stood and extended his hand. "I think it's time to christen this house properly. What do you say?"

"I agree." Liam got to his feet, too, and reached out for her.

She took their hands. "I'd love that. But there's a problem."

Chapter Twelve

"Besides my blue balls?" Hammer quipped.

"That's a problem we can fix." She flirted with a little grin. "But you're overdressed for the occasion. Here I am, all naked, and no one is joining me."

They both rushed to tear off their clothes, and Raine had to repress another smile. Today's conversation had been difficult. She'd made a huge mistake earlier, but Liam and Hammer had calmed her, talked to her, explained. The resulting dialogue hadn't been easy, but it had been fruitful. Now she felt like the three of them stood on more solid footing. And they had an absolutely beautiful house in which to start their forever.

Then the sights around her completely derailed her thoughts. Hammer yanked off his shirt, exposing a pair of broad shoulders and a wide, muscled chest that never failed to make her hot. Beside him, under him, she felt so small and feminine and protected. Then Liam shucked his pants, and her breath caught. Under his lean shoulders and the muscles bunching all the way down his back, his body tapered to the most sigh-worthy ass she'd ever seen on a man. Taut, lightly dusted with hair, and just round enough for her to want to bite.

She gave a happy little shudder of a sigh.

Suddenly, Liam turned to Macen. "Look at her, gawking at

us like we're a couple of slabs of beef."

Raine felt a flush rise on her cheeks. "You can't blame me. You're both incredible. And not just to look at."

"As much as I've enjoyed fucking you when you're mad, pliant, or solemn, I think I'm going to enjoy it a lot more when you're happy." Hammer wrapped an arm around her and guided her toward the bed, then glanced at Liam. "Hurry up, man. I don't know how long I can wait before I start without you."

Liam laughed, then kicked free of his underwear before lunging at her and grabbing her face. He crushed her mouth under his.

Macen's lips feathered up her neck before he breathed against her skin. "You're going to be so well fucked, precious."

Raine's breath caught. "Promise?"

They merely smiled, and Liam nodded. "If you're not able to walk out of here, oh…what a pity that would be. But we'll carry you."

She never wanted to leave this golden house that represented all their tomorrows, but she knew they had to return to duty and Shadows—at least until they could furnish this place and move in.

"I like the idea of being carried." She strolled closer, wrapping her hands around their cocks at once and giving them both a long stroke. "Let's see if we can make that happen."

Hammer hissed out a curse. Liam groaned, his face contorting with pleasure.

"I think my balls are turning blue, too, mate." His voice already sounded gruff.

"That's it." Macen stared at the little foil packet in his hand and tore open the condom. "Why the hell haven't we managed to get you on birth control yet?"

"I wondered the same thing earlier today," Liam said as he slowly rolled the thin latex over his ready erection.

"I have an appointment next week." She'd hoped to surprise them at Christmas, but it seemed like the perfect time to tell them. And she couldn't wait to feel them bare and deep, raw, without barriers, spilling inside her. Someday, maybe they'd tell her to stop taking birth control and…

One step at a time.

For now. Raine drank in the sight of their strong, masculine bodies. Already, their faces were sharp and flushed with desire. The mere sight of them made her heart race and her sex weep with need. Liam watched her with a lusty stare as he slathered lube over his proud cock with long strokes. She shivered in anticipation.

"Bend over the bed," Hammer demanded. "Let Liam prepare you so he can fill that sweet ass of yours."

Raine didn't hesitate. She bent, legs slightly spread, and rested her head on the thick mattress. She didn't have to wait long before she felt him—smelled him—just behind her. Her body turned tense and needy.

"Liam…"

In answer, he palmed the small of her back, then traced his finger down the line of her spine, that velvet touch skimming close to her rosette. She arched with the movement, then stilled. God, she was beyond eager to feel him taking her in the most dominant way possible. She craved his possession, that tender way he somehow managed to use her thoroughly.

He touched his lubed fingers to her tightly drawn tissue, rimming it, coaxing her open. Raine tossed her head back, grabbing the sheet as his fingers probed insistently, silently urging her to cede to him. To submit.

Raine groaned with a shaky exhalation. Closing her eyes, she focused on relaxing every muscle in her body. She started with the frown creasing her forehead, then moved down to her shoulders, her back…little by little until she unclenched and arched even more, offering herself up.

Liam clutched her hips. "So beautiful. I love having you open to me."

Hammer leaned in and tucked her hair behind her ear. "I can see you trying to please us. It's stunning…"

Their touches and praise nearly made her purr from the back of her throat as she turned her head and managed to capture his thumb with her teeth and suck it inside her mouth.

Hammer growled. "That tongue…"

She circled his digit with the tip and sent him an inviting stare—until Liam slipped in another finger and made her gasp.

"Please hurry." She wriggled her ass at him.

"Greedy minx," Liam chided.

Hammer leaned back and watched with fire blazing in his eyes. "That's it. Let him ready your velvet walls so he can slide balls deep inside you."

"I'm bursting to do just that." Liam breathed harshly. "How does that feel, Raine?"

"So good…" She groaned. "I'm ready. I need you. Please."

"Good. I can't wait," Liam growled as he helped her upright. "Every time with you is…" He shook his head on a rough sigh as he met her stare. "Only enough to make me want you more."

Raine's heart skipped as he eased behind her to sit on the edge of the mattress. He drew her between his masculine, slightly spread thighs. His cock stood straight up, as if reaching for her.

She wrapped her arms around him and filtered her fingers through his hair. "It's the same for me, Liam."

He didn't speak again, simply pinched her nipples, then laved his handiwork before drawing them into his hot mouth. Raine held tight as he alternated between one breast and the other, a frantic, thorough tease.

Hammer sidled up behind her, his body heat seeping into her skin. He palmed her ass and nipped at her lobe. As she turned her face to meet his kiss, Liam dragged his lips across her stomach, soft, stinging little nips with a flare of tingles that awakened her skin. Hammer possessed her mouth, stroking deep inside as Liam flicked the tip of his tongue over each of her erect nubs. She was happily drowning in them and the desire swirling inside her.

Liam ripped himself away. "Now, Macen."

Before she could process what he meant, Hammer pulled back and bit at her lower lip. The sting excited her even more as he gripped her hips and turned her to face him—only to find him stroking his hard cock. Her body trembled in anticipation.

Liam grabbed her around the waist and lowered her to his lap. The tip of his hard cock pressed against her sensitive rosette. Raine's whimper only seemed to urge him on, and he pushed against her fragile rim. She arched and opened. The smoldering pressure built. Pleasure flashed inside her as he breached past her barrier. As he slowly eased inside, stretching and filling her with thrill and pain, Raine keened to the rafters.

* * *

As Liam worked Raine onto his cock, Hammer's balls tightened. A vivid memory of squeezing through her tight little ring and thrusting into nirvana filled his head. His blood thundered.

Ecstasy skittered across her face. Her eyes fluttered closed. Her head fell back, exposing the graceful arch of her neck as Liam thrust deep. Her soft, needful moan made Macen's cock jerk.

Damn, he'd caged his desire this morning when he'd told her to strip and climb into bed for a nap after breakfast. The shower they'd shared when Raine had come to him smelling of sex had rattled his restraint, especially when he'd put his hands all over her wet skin. Mere minutes ago, he'd sweated, watching her shatter under Liam's insistent mouth. Though he'd ached for a taste himself, Hammer had held back.

Now, his self-control was shot to hell.

Hammer cupped her pussy, dragging his fingers over her hard little clit. She gasped.

"Oh, shit. She just clamped down on me." Liam dug his fingers into her slender hips as he yanked her up his shaft, then shoved deep inside her. "So fucking hot and tight."

Hammer gritted his teeth, wanting to feel her close around him, too. *Claim. Now. Fuck yeah.*

Liam glanced at him, then paused his voracious thrusts to recline on the bed. Hammer supposed his urgency—or insanity—must have shown, and thanked fuck Liam could read him.

"Lie back against his chest," Macen demanded, guiding Raine down.

She did, blinking at him with big eyes that didn't just turn him on but also inside out. He gripped her pale thighs, spreading them wide and draping them outside Liam's. Her musk pervaded his senses as her hips tilted up. He stared at her bare cunt, pink, glistening, swollen, and pouting—just waiting for him to slam deep. Macen knew how fucking perfect she'd feel.

"There." He stepped between her thighs and traced a

fingertip from her navel down, down…all the way to her eager clit. He toyed with her. "Now you're splayed out the way I want you, precious. I'm going to drive inside you and feel your cunt ripple around me as you melt between us."

He parted her shimmering flesh with his thumbs, spreading her open even farther, and fastened his mouth over her drenched folds, eating at her clit, drinking her in.

After years of coveting Raine, he'd barely had her a handful of times—certainly not enough to cool his fever. In fact, every time, she'd heated him up hotter. Right now, it raged inside him.

"Please, Macen," she whimpered, threading her hands in his hair. "Oh… God, I can't—"

"You can't what?" Hammer snarled, furious at having to pull his tongue from her.

"I-I can't wait."

The supplication in her tone burned him. "To feel us plow into your soft, slick body together?"

"Yes," she cried.

"You want us to fuck you?" He bit into the tender flesh of her inner thigh, then laved the imprints of his teeth and watched the welts rise.

Raine keened out a high-pitched screech. "Macen…"

"Is that a yes?"

Before she could answer, Liam pinched her nipples. As she gasped, he planted his feet on the mattress, spreading her legs wider. He thrust long and slow into her ass with a groan. "Beg Hammer to fuck your pretty, tight cunt. And hurry it up."

"Please. Macen." Her high-pitched plea sounded beautifully desperate. "Please… I need you, too."

Something inside him snapped.

Gripping his cock, Hammer nudged his blunt head against her sweltering pussy. He didn't wait another second before he gripped her hips, then shoved up and inside her—balls deep in the first tight thrust.

Jesus… Like heaven.

"About damn time…" Liam moaned. "Fuck her. Hard."

With pleasure.

He surged into her again. Her fragile body yielded, taking every inch he slammed deep. She wrapped her legs around him with a cry. Her pussy contracted. Her blue eyes glazed in ecstasy as her fingers bit into his shoulders. He growled.

Below them, Liam drove into Raine's ass. The friction of them both buried deep burned. Her back arched. Macen thumbed her clit. Raine shuddered and cried frantically, bucking, clamping down, so close to coming undone.

Hammer slapped her pussy. "No. Don't. You do *not* have permission."

Raine mewled as she rippled around his cock, then dragged in a breath. *Too close…* With a curse, Hammer pulled back.

She shrieked, writhing and trying to force him deeper. "For the love of… I can't take this. Fuck me!"

"When we're ready," Liam insisted in her ear.

Hammer withdrew completely and glowered at her. "You don't make the demands. I told you to hold back."

Raine scowled at him. Before he could reprimand her, her expression dissolved. She whimpered and stabbed her nails into Liam's thighs.

The other man hissed, grabbed her wrists, and crossed them over her body and under her breasts. "Stop that, hellcat."

Hammer bent and bit down on the fleshy mound above her clit.

Raine's scream filled the room. He watched, seeing the moment her pain turned to bone-melting bliss, witnessing the little red marks on her vulnerable, bare pussy. He caressed the pretty brand.

She trembled, breathing hard, fast. Her feverish blue eyes begged, telling Hammer that he'd become the devil and her savior all at once. He sent her a sinful smile.

"Please…" Her voice sounded hoarse, raw.

His inner beast loved stripping her down to a pale, pleading mass.

Take her. Now.

"Damn it, Macen," Liam cursed impatiently.

Hammer clenched his fist. No fucking way he could wait now. He needed to finish this, annihilate her defenses, remind her who she belonged to.

Cock in hand, Macen impaled her again in one long stroke. She thrashed between them, pinned, immobile, helpless. He fucking loved it.

"Help." Tears welled in her eyes. "I'm on fire. The burn is…too much."

"That's exactly how we want you." Hammer reared back and plunged deep again, sending her grinding up and down on Liam's cock. "Burn hot and high for us."

"I am," she gasped. "Oh, god, I am."

With a grunt, Hammer unleashed the last of his restraint, plowing into her at a blistering pace. Their skin slapped. Sweat broke out at his temples, between his shoulders. His whole body coursed with need. Raine closed her eyes with an animal cry, working between them. Liam's length rubbed his own through the thin barrier of her skin, back and forth.

Hammer grabbed her hips, snarled, bent his knees to work deeper. A low, guttural cry tore from her chest, and he relished the sound.

Now. Hammer didn't refuse his inner beast's demand.

As he drove fast and hard into Raine, she yelped and she tossed her head from side to side. Hammer hovered over her, bracing his palms flat on the mattress. With every plunge inside her, her breasts bounced in his face. He bit and sucked at her.

Beneath them both, Liam shuttled Raine up and down his cock, a frown creasing his face. Raine's eyes were closed, but her mouth split wide open in a silent scream. Grinding into her, Macen tried to work deeper than his last stroke, deeper than ever, plant himself inside her forever.

Own.

Claim.

"Who do you belong to?" Hammer seethed out the words between clenched teeth as he fucked into her tight walls again.

"You and Liam, Sir," Raine panted, grinding her hips against them.

"Yes." His fingers tightened on her thighs, and Macen knew they'd leave bruises on her fair skin. He loved the idea. His next hard thrust felt impossibly deeper. "Ride your Masters' cocks. Feel our power and strength surging into you."

"I feel it. I feel everything!"

"We own you, precious. All of you."

Hammer bit her breasts again. Her screams filled the air. He snarled in satisfaction.

"Macen," Liam snapped.

Hammer blinked and found his friend glaring in a furious scowl. His eyes narrowed. Liam better not be killing his buzz.

"A bit easier, mate," Liam insisted. "Let's make sure our girl knows she's *loved*."

Darting a glance over Raine's smooth, writhing flesh as Liam rocked inside her, Macen caught sight of the red imprints of his teeth stamping her. He spied even more at the arch of her mound and inside her thigh. The Dom inside filled with pride, but the man winced. Fuck, they were christening the house, cementing their bond, not using her to the fullest. Tender Raine was new to being shared. And as a fresh submissive, she wasn't ready to be anything near a slave he could brand at will. She might never be.

Hammer looped the chain around his inner beast's neck and yanked hard. He withdrew, leaving only his crest throbbing inside her as he tried to catch his breath, slow his thoughts.

What was it about Raine that drove him to the brink of insanity? He'd marked Juliet before, numerous times, but never compulsively. Not with the intensity Raine conjured inside him. What the hell did that mean?

"No!" Raine struggled, screamed. "Don't you dare stop. I need more. I need you both now."

Macen wanted to give Raine what she begged for, felt need breathing down his neck. But he'd also asked Liam to keep him in line and not let him break her.

Sweat ran in rivulets down his chest. He eased inside her gently, panting, undecided. He flicked a questioning stare Liam's way.

"It's all right, brother," Liam reassured with a nod. "Let's let our girl fly. What do you say?"

"Yes!" Raine broke free of Liam's hold and pressed his palms over her breasts. "I need you both. I'm dying without you..."

Liam pinched her nipples. Raine's soft kitten moan brought Hammer back to the present. Yes. They needed to set her free, then follow her into ecstasy.

Focused on Raine's pleasure, Hammer rocked into her,

finding a steady rhythm that alternated with Liam's. When he glided his thumb over her clit once more, Raine sighed blissfully.

With every stroke, he picked up the pace. The sounds of their flesh slapping accompanied by Liam's grunts and Raine's whimpers echoed in the cavernous room. The musky scent of sex surrounded them.

As she clutched and released his driving shaft in impending climax, tingles shot up his spine. He tossed his head back, jaw tight, and roared at the searing ecstasy burning through his bloodstream.

He might not be marking her at the moment, but the memory of those he'd left now and the first time he'd taken her to bed rolled through his mind. Nothing like knowing Raine looked as if she belonged with him… Even the thought was decimating his self-control.

"Say the word, man," Hammer rumbled. "I'm on the edge."

"Right there with you," Liam assured, his voice low and torn, as he squeezed Raine's breasts and thrust up beneath them. "Oh, love… You feel so perfect. I don't want this to end. But you've brought us to our limits. Are you ready?"

Raine clawed at Liam's arms. "More than ready."

"You want it?" Hammer knew she did, but he craved hearing it again.

"Yes!" she croaked.

Macen gritted his teeth and staved off his need to come for just a moment more. "Tell us how much."

Her eyes flew open. Her pools of blue had darkened. Her expression speared him with fire that shot straight to his balls. "I fucking need this. Let me come for you. God, let me…"

"Do it," Liam barked. "Come. We want to feel you. I've got to have it."

As soon as Raine climaxed, she would drag him over the edge with her.

Beyond eager to feel the painful, exquisite death of this sweltering demand, he bellowed as he drove inside her again.

"Now!" Hammer commanded her.

Her body seized on their cocks, strangling so tight he couldn't move or breathe. *Fuck yeah.* Blackness swam in his vision as he tried to delve deeper into the molasses grip of her cunt. Rapture gripped him by the balls, squeezed his heart, and flattened him with a steamroller of pleasure even as he soared into a blinding, piercing euphoria he'd never experienced.

Oh, he'd never get enough of this.

Liam let out a ferocious roar as he pumped into Raine from behind while she spasmed around them, her velvet walls fluttering and clutching, and howled out her release in an endless hoarse cry that echoed even after she fell silent.

As the three of them lay, panting and sweating, in a tangled heap, Hammer floated back to earth one boneless limb at a time. He loved the feel of her body, steaming and lush, pressed against him. He felt dead and yet more alive than he'd ever felt in his life.

"Holy crap," Raine gasped, sounding dazed.

Liam fought to catch his breath. "What the hell just happened? I only thought I'd had my mind blown before."

"No idea what that was," Macen added, skimming a palm down Raine's thigh. "But I can't wait to do it again."

"Amen." Liam laughed.

Raine giggled. "I'm going to love playing house with you boys."

Telling himself he'd remind her soon that he wasn't a boy at all, Hammer wrapped his arms around her waist and pulled her with him, slumping to the bed on his side. Liam turned in tandem as Raine slowly opened her eyes. Love, pure and unfiltered, reflected there. Hammer felt Liam's hot breath spilling over her shoulder as he cupped her breast.

"We love you, Raine," Liam whispered in her ear.

"Forever," Hammer added solemnly.

A soft, contented sigh slipped from her lips as she closed her eyes. "I love you both, too."

One at a time, they eased from inside her. Liam rolled out of bed first, returning with a warm washcloth. Hammer stood and watched for a moment as his pal cleaned her off with such gentle reverence. Drugged by contentment, Hammer sauntered to the bathroom, trashed the condom, and returned to join them in bed.

As their bodies pressed together, Liam skimmed his hands over her soft flesh. Raine smiled softly. Hammer tugged a strand of her hair and watched as she forced her heavy lids open, peeking up at him beneath her dark lashes. Christ, she was beautiful.

"Yes?" she croaked.

"We haven't forgotten your earlier rant…" he began, biting back a smirk. "Fourteen fucks, one damn it, one bullshit, one regular shit, and you called me an ass."

"Tsk, tsk, Raine," Liam added.

Raine blinked. "But I was—"

"A very bad girl," Liam scolded in her ear. "We'll have to broaden your vocabulary and work harder on your communication skills."

She arched a brow as she peered over her shoulder.

Hammer expected her to toss out some smartassed comeback, but he tugged on her hair, cutting her off. "Don't go there."

She barely managed not to roll her eyes. Life with her would never be easy, but then…anyone could do easy. Hammer lived for a challenge. Raine would give him one every day.

"There will be repercussions, lass," Liam warned.

"Yes." He yawned, suddenly feeling twice his age. "But not right now. This feels too good. But soon. Very soon."

Raine let out a low moan just as a cell phone began to ring. Hammer felt Liam tense.

What the fuck now?

If Gwyneth was calling to cause more shit, Hammer would drive to Beck's place and set the bitch straight for good.

Raine rose up on one elbow as Liam rolled out of bed. Macen could see the anxiety crawl across her face.

He pulled her to his chest and placed a kiss on her cheek. "Don't worry, precious. If that's Gwyneth, she won't get the chance to hurt you again."

She tensed as Liam pulled out his phone.

Confusion wrinkled the man's forehead as he pressed it to his ear. "Beck?"

* * *

Liam pressed the phone to his ear and closed his eyes, rubbing at them with his thumb and forefinger. Every time the damn phone rang, something else fucked up was about to happen. "What's going on? I thought you'd be in surgery."

"Me, too. The hospital in Cleveland took the donor off life support, but apparently the patient is hanging on. They're anticipating another eight hours or so. Looks like the surgery might not happen until tomorrow. So I went back to my condo."

That rattled Liam. "My ex-wife is there."

"Right. I was focused on getting some decent sleep, and I'd forgotten." Beck hesitated. "What a hellacious, stick-up-her-ass—"

"I know." Liam sighed. "Neither Seth nor Hammer can stand her. Raine had the misfortune of running into Gwyneth earlier. It didn't go well. We've been…talking about it since."

Beck chuckled. "With your pants off, I'll bet."

In fact, Liam wasn't wearing a stitch now, but he didn't admit that. "The baby is swabbed. I doubt he's mine, but when I prove that tomorrow, I'll move my ex-wife out of your place and put her on a plane back to London. I know it's an inconvenience, but I'll gladly put you up in a hotel room tonight."

"No worries. I've got a house to crash in, man. The condo is just for convenience. But that's not why I'm calling. When I met Gwyneth, she was rocking Kyle and crying. And behaving like a shrew, but she was worried, and I digress… Anyway, once I proved my medical credentials, she let me examine the kid. I'm no pediatrician, but something is definitely wrong. He's running a fever and throwing up green. We're at the emergency room now. I hate to ask this of you, especially since you don't think this is your kid, but I have to get some shut-eye before this surgery, and she's falling apart."

"And you want me to come there?" Liam challenged, then rolled his eyes.

"I think it's a good idea."

Liam was so bloody exhausted. A decent meal and a night in bed with Raine and Hammer were all he wanted. But Gwyneth was in an unfamiliar hospital, surrounded by strangers in a city she'd never visited. Even if Kyle wasn't her son and she lacked mothering instinct, she still seemed to care for him on a basic human level…maybe more. Would he want to be stuck alone in a waiting room, pacing the floor, anticipating news that might come in five minutes or five hours?

That sounded like the worst torture.

Yes, he'd wanted to humiliate Gwyneth, but that didn't mean he wanted anything to happen to the boy. And maybe, if she was truly shaken, her defenses would be down and he'd finally get some answers.

"I'll be there in less than thirty."

"Thanks," Beck said.

"Thank you for taking care of Kyle and letting me know."

When they hung up, Hammer glowered, appearing as if he'd like to grind his teeth into dust. Raine had gone quiet.

"You have to go," she murmured, clearly wanting an explanation and not asking.

Was she so disappointed that she wouldn't ask? Or was she trying to show him her trust? Liam wished he had time to puzzle through it now. Nothing was more important to him than Raine, but damn it if life hadn't prevented him from having the time to make certain she felt emotionally secure.

"I do and I'm sorry about dinner," he said with regret, dressing as he explained the situation.

She opened her mouth, then closed it. He thought for sure she'd clam up and force him to drag an answer out of her, but she surprised him.

"Kyle is a baby. Whether you're his father or not, he needs someone to champion him."

"I'm not going because I want to," Liam swore.

"I know." She nodded solemnly, and he believed she did.

He pressed a soft kiss to her lips. "I don't know how long I'll be. The emergency room is never quick."

Hammer wrapped an arm around Raine's shoulder. "I'll take care of her. Don't worry."

That set his mind at ease…mostly. He worried about Raine crawling down another mental black hole. Thankfully, she wouldn't be alone, but then he worried about Hammer's tendencies as well. "I'll do my best to be back shortly."

"But…" She bit her lip. "You haven't slept or eaten enough. I'm worried about you."

Liam's heart softened at her words. Raine's submission showed so well here. She wanted to take care of the people she loved—feed and nurture and ensure their wellbeing. She'd make an amazing mother someday, and he couldn't fail to notice the contrast to Gwyneth. He'd been praying Kyle wasn't his son mostly so that he didn't have to parent with his ex-wife. But taking in Raine's soft concern while standing in the house they'd soon share, he hoped someday that he and Hammer would fill her belly and these bedrooms with their children.

He wondered how Macen would feel about that after losing a pregnant Juliet…

"They have a cafeteria, love." When she would have objected, Liam laid a finger over her lips. "Granted, it's not your cooking, but I'll be all right for a night. I can doze in a chair if I need. Don't worry about me. Just keep working on all the things we've discussed here. Will you do that for me?"

She sent him a slow nod. "Or I could come with you, help out—"

"No," he and Hammer both answered at once.

Raine reared back, looking a bit hurt. Liam took her hands. "There's nothing you can do there but worry, and I'd rather do that for all of us."

"Besides…" Hammer cut in. "You met Gwyneth. She's a vicious, scheming cunt. I don't want to give her the chance to hurt you again."

"Precisely." Liam nodded.

"She took me by surprise. That's all. I can handle—"

"But you shouldn't have to," Liam shot back.

"Precious." Hammer turned her to face him and stroked her cheek. "That woman is probably already thinking of other ways to run you off. Don't make it easier for her. It's tempting to say that you simply wouldn't believe her, but she's a master of manipulation."

"And your heart is far too delicate to have to deal with the likes of her." Liam handed Raine her clothes. "Let me drop you and Hammer off back at the club. Cook him some dinner. He's looking a little peaked," he tried to tease. "I'll be back in two shakes."

She clearly didn't like it but nodded and pulled on her clothes. Hammer followed suit. Within a few minutes, they were all walking out the door and locking it behind them.

Hammer buckled her into the front seat again, and this time Raine reached out for Liam's hand—a far cry from their drive over. He and Hammer *were* opening her soul. Maybe not as quickly as they'd like, but he had to believe that someday she'd feel deep in her heart what he knew: the three of them belonged together.

"I'll make you a hot meal when you get home," she promised. "And I'll miss you."

"I'll miss you, too, love."

Hammer clapped a hand on his shoulder. "Don't worry about a thing here. Just make sure Kyle is all right and deal with the bitch."

* * *

Down the hall, Evanescence pounded as Raine glanced at the clock in the kitchen. Though working the dungeon, she'd escaped for a few calming moments in the kitchen. She stirred the batter for Hammer's favorite apple spice muffins. Just after midnight. She pressed the phone lying beside her on the counter to make sure she hadn't somehow missed hearing from Liam. Nothing. She'd left two voice mails and half a dozen texts. She'd received no reply.

Her stomach tightened. It wasn't like him not to respond at all.

As she prepared the muffin tin and dished the batter inside, Raine wondered what could be taking him so long. Yes, the emergency room could be slow and crowded, but he'd been gone over three hours. Did that mean the little boy was seriously ill? Or… Frowning, she slid the pan into the oven, then tapped her palm nervously against her thigh. What if Gwyneth had somehow manipulated or lied her way back into Liam's good graces? Raine couldn't imagine him falling for that. But she was clever.

What if the woman had done something more sinister than merely deceive Liam? Gwyneth seemed awfully determined to have her ex-husband back, and Raine had no idea why. How far would she be willing to go?

Setting the timer on the muffins, Raine turned and took her

sugar cookies off the cooling rack, then headed to the pantry and the refrigerator to see what other ingredients she had. And honestly, she'd really like to know if she only had enough time before Liam returned to make brownies…or whether she should start something more involved like a lemon meringue pie.

She wrinkled her nose, wishing he'd just walk through the door and put her out of her misery.

"Raine?" Hammer walked into the kitchen and shut the door behind him, taking in all her cooking with a scowl. "You're baking in fet wear?"

Her heart skipped, and she ignored his question. "Did you hear from him?"

"Not yet."

"So he didn't call or text you? I've been trying for the past few hours, but I'm not reaching him at all. It's beginning to freak me out."

Hammer relaxed a bit and pulled his phone from his pocket. "Neither of us has had a spare second to charge our phones for over twenty-four hours. Mine is just about dead. I'll bet his is, too."

That made sense but somehow didn't comfort her at all. "True."

"So…you're baking?"

Raine understood his question and hated to worry Macen, but if she lied about this, especially after their time together earlier today, he'd be beyond disappointed and have every right to punish her but good. Besides, they'd all had enough drama for one day. "Just a little."

He sniffed. "Apple spice?"

At his almost hopeful question, she managed a smile. "For you."

"Hmm…" He sidled closer and dropped a kiss on top of her head. "I knew there was a reason I loved you."

She gave him a little elbow. "It better be for more than my kitchen skills."

"You have other stellar qualities." He slid a hand under her skirt and cupped her pussy. "Are you sore?"

Discerning the point of his question wasn't hard. She flushed. "Nothing I don't like and didn't enjoy."

Lust lit his eyes, and he looked ready to pursue something more appropriate to the bedroom than the kitchen. "Well, precious…"

But Raine just couldn't focus when she was this worried. "Macen." She pulled away and began to pace. "What's taking him so long?"

He shook his head. "We don't know yet. He'll tell us when he comes back."

"What if he doesn't?"

Hammer frowned. "He bought you a house for the three of us to live in. What part of that says he's bailing on you? We really have to work on your trust and confidence—"

"That's not what I meant." She huffed, then crossed the kitchen again. "I believe he wants to be here with me, with us. It's her I don't trust."

Understanding lit his eyes. "You shouldn't. But Gwyneth can't do anything to Liam. He's in public and he's far bigger than her. They have armed security there. He's fine."

"I'm having a hard time believing that she would somehow acquire a baby who looks enough like Liam and is the right age, fly halfway around the world to rekindle whatever she thought they had, only to give up the second he said no."

"You understand he completely humiliated her, right? I doubt she'll keep pursuing him after what happened this afternoon."

"I don't think she'll just shrug it off and go home. She's after something."

Hammer sighed. "Well, it's not money. I offered her a chunk to go away. She refused."

Raine shook her head. "I don't think it's about money, either. If Gwyneth never loved Liam in the first place, why go to so much trouble to trap him into a relationship? What is she up to? Revenge?" She paced again. "I don't like any of this. It gives me a bad feeling."

"Raine…" He cupped her shoulders and tried to give her a soothing caress down her arms.

She refused to be placated and shrugged him away. "It's all I can think about. I'm worried. If she's half as terrible as you say, then she's got some trick up her sleeve. I just know it."

Before he could waste his breath trying to calm her with another platitude, Raine crossed to the pantry and grabbed the ingredients to start a piecrust. She suspected it was going to be a long night.

Hammer grabbed her arm, exerting just enough pressure to make her pause. She glanced at him over her shoulder.

“Don’t.” She bristled.

“Put the flour down. Now.”

That low and commanding tone grabbed her belly and squeezed. He’d given her an unequivocal order. Raine really wanted to argue that she needed the distraction baking provided, but that voice wouldn’t let her.

With a little sigh, she set the flour back on the shelf and turned to face him, head bowed. “Yes, Sir.”

He crooked a finger under her chin. “Let me take your worries away. Come with me.”

Chapter Thirteen

After seeing the state of the kitchen and the anxiety humming off Raine, Hammer knew his assurances were falling on deaf ears. She'd convinced herself that Gwyneth posed Liam some imminent danger and nothing would keep her from worrying.

Raine needed a break from her disquiet, a way to get out of her head. Hammer had the will and the means to provide that.

Holding her hand, he led her down the hall.

She resisted. "Where are we going?"

"To the dungeon. I intend to give you what you need."

A little frown wrinkled her forehead. "What I need is for Liam to come back."

"Until he returns, I'll take your mind off your worries…and everything else."

Raine took a moment to sort through his words, then gave him a breathless nod.

As they entered the dungeon, members glanced their way. Hammer ushered her past most of the equipment inside, then pulled her to a stop at the same spanking bench on which Liam had claimed her virgin ass a few short weeks ago. Then, he'd seen his friend take what Hammer had always hoped would be his, and caustic anger had rolled in his veins. Feeling cheated, he'd watched, barely blinking, until the deed was done.

Now, Hammer gripped the sturdy frame of the spanking bench and began dragging it to the center of the dungeon, beyond eager. Around him, the club members did a double take. Their stares skidded off him, then came to a screeching halt on Raine, waiting self-consciously beside him. As he came through with the bench, patrons parted like the Red Sea, acting as if they were about to witness a miracle. Hammer felt the *OMG* hanging in the air.

In six years, he'd never once scened with Raine. No one had since he'd declared her under his protection…except Liam after the disastrous public punishment Hammer had assigned last month when she'd tried to seduce him. Beck had botched that, of course, giving his Irish pal the chance to step in and claim the girl. As far as the members knew, she belonged to Liam—and him alone.

Hammer intended to set the record straight and nurture the bond of love the three of them finally shared. Besides, publicly staking his claim on Raine using the same piece of equipment Liam had held a certain poetic symmetry.

The sound of paddles and whips from surrounding scenes faded. Doms paused, moving closer to caress their subs and stare. Some long-term members simply smirked as if they'd been waiting for Hammer to pull his head out of his ass and acknowledge his feelings for Raine.

He clenched his jaw. He'd fucking give them something to see.

"Everyone is looking at us," she murmured.

Hammer turned and quirked a brow at her. "Because you're stunning, precious."

"I'm sure it's because you rarely play in public anymore. And to them, you've never touched me."

"It doesn't matter why they're staring. Let them," he whispered, noting the flicker of nervous excitement on her face. "You'd like that, wouldn't you?"

Raine scanned the crowd. "Maybe. I don't know. The time Liam took me in front of the others, he had me so focused on him the crowd faded away. I hardly remember anyone there. Just him. And you."

Hammer already knew she was going to love it. He bent close to her ear. "Come on, my little exhibitionist. Let's get you splayed out and cuffed up so we can fuel more speculation."

Raine set tentative fingers on his chest. The way her gaze clung to him, uncertain yet seeking reassurance, stirred his Dominance.

"I'm not here to please anyone but you and Liam. I don't give a dam…um, darn what anyone else thinks as long as they know I belong to you two."

"By the time we're done, I won't leave a single doubt in anyone's mind."

She blinked, and he caught the heartbeat accelerating at her neck. "What exactly do you—"

"Plan to do to you?" Hammer interrupted with a wolfish grin.

"Yes. I'm excited, but I don't think I can… No whip for me, please." She shuddered. "That scares me."

Because it made noises that convinced her he'd inflict tremendous pain and leave gashes in her flesh. He could—but not with her. Never. Naturally, he'd respect her limit…for now. It was a Dom's nature to push, but he'd do that later.

"I know pain isn't going to enhance your submission."

Raine nibbled her bottom lip. Worry and nerves ate at her composure, but she nodded.

Hammer palmed her face and snared her gaze. "Talk to me. What's going on inside your head?"

"I'm still worried about Liam," she answered in the same hushed tones. "Why hasn't he called?"

"If something were wrong, he would find a way to reach us."

"But… shouldn't we wait until he can join us?"

"Liam is with you, precious. Right here." Hammer patted her heart. "I want you to feel him through me. Do you understand?"

More tears formed in her eyes. "I'll try, Sir."

"You'll succeed. Now make us proud." Macen brushed away a tear that had spilled over her thick lashes.

She sniffled, surprisingly tense. "What if I can't do this, Macen? I mean, the right way." She struggled with her quiet words. "I want this. God, I've wanted it since I first started fantasizing about you."

A rosy blush stained her cheeks.

"And when exactly did you start doing that?" Hammer drew the pad of his thumb over her bottom lip, desperate to know.

Raine darted a shy glance away. "Since I understood what this place was and why I was so drawn to you. Probably about two weeks after you found me in the alley."

She'd begun to star in Hammer's fantasies even before then. Once the bruises and cuts from her father's abuse had healed and Raine had stopped looking at Macen as if he were another monster with a cock intent on hurting her, he'd started dreaming about the beautiful girl handing herself over to him. Two thousand three hundred and some odd days—and the same number of long, empty nights—he'd burned to bring her to his dungeon and stake his claim.

"You weren't the only one," he confessed, then scowled. "But lusting after a girl who hadn't yet reached the age of consent made me feel like a sick fuck."

His desires had only increased as he'd watched the girl finish growing into a woman. For years, every day had been an exercise in restraint and creativity, conjuring new ways to deny himself the pleasure of Raine.

"That didn't make you a pedophile, Macen. I was seventeen, not five," she reminded pointedly. "I still ache for you, you know."

"I hope you always do, precious. My feelings will never change."

"Then help me, please." Raising those big, trusting blue eyes to him, she curled her fingers around his lapel. "My head is whirling with what-ifs. What if I fail you because I can't turn off my brain?"

"Let me worry about that." The weight of him taking her to subspace for the first time rocked Hammer deep. No way would he fuck this up.

"I want to, but you've scened with so many subs over the years, most of them far more experienced. I don't know exactly what to expect," she whispered.

Conscious of all the eyes still on him, Hammer pulled her

into his arms and pressed a kiss to her forehead, longing to push the chaos and apprehension from her mind and replace them with reassurance and love.

"The only way you'll fail me is to not try," Hammer assured. "Do you trust me with your body, your safety?"

"Completely."

Her answer filled him with masculine pride. "Then let me guide you. I won't fail you."

"Yes, Sir." She sighed, closed her eyes—already trying to give herself over.

Pressing his lips to her neck, he slowly loosened her corset. When it slipped from her breasts, he eased back, watching the material fall loosely around her body. The sight of the wicked red bite he'd left on her flawless flesh a few short hours ago burned desire through his veins, seizing him with the urge to mark every inch of her and show the world she belonged to him. Tracing his finger over the welt, Hammer bent and laved his tongue over the swollen impression.

"I'm going to mark you again, precious," Hammer murmured against her breast.

He felt her shiver before she reached up to slide her fingers through his hair. "I want that."

Lolling her head to one side, Raine exposed her slender neck to him in invitation. Macen didn't refuse. He nipped a trail of tiny red blotches as he worked his way toward her mouth. Stopping, he hovered over her lips, tasting her warm breath as he deftly tugged her corset free, letting it drop to the floor.

"What do you call me?" he prompted against her lips.

"Sir. I want that, Sir."

"Very good." He cupped her nape and drew her in, holding her captive to his stare. Then he melded their lips together, sweeping deep inside, drinking in her heady power, her luscious control.

A collective gasp echoed through the dungeon, followed by a buzz of hushed whispers. Hammer had no doubt his heated possession of Raine's mouth, along with his choice of a partner, would keep tongues wagging for days.

Once upon a time, no one had batted an eye when he'd entered the dungeon with a sub. Hell, he'd had a different one damn near every night. But this past spring, Hammer had finished a session with a crop, then reached for his zipper and a condom, only to see tears of agony swimming in Raine's eyes. The sight had been a jagged stake through his heart.

He didn't even remember the other woman's name, but he'd never forgotten the debilitating hurt on Raine's face. After that moment, he'd more or less stopped sceneing in the dungeon.

And he'd never—ever—kissed any sub with such passion.

Now, he ignored the whispers of the others and took Raine's mouth again. He'd spent too many years burning for the chance to publicly declare her his. To hell with the rest of the world.

Hammer deepened the kiss and felt his everyday persona begin to slip away…and his natural Dominance take over. His shoulders squared. His chest expanded. Then he fisted Raine's inky mane as he growled out his possession, took her tongue, and dragged her small body flush against him.

As he claimed her mouth harder still, his lips stung. Raine's fingers dug into his scalp. Her nipples tightened, and Macen longed to tear off his shirt to feel them against his bare chest.

He dragged his palms down her back, around her waist, as he ate at her mouth. Twisting the small button of her skirt free, Hammer slowly eased the zipper down and pushed at the garment. It fell down her legs.

As he released her mouth, he fused his gaze all over her. He exposed the lovely red ridges—signs of his possession—he'd left earlier on the inside of her snowy thigh and the pad of her smooth pussy. Those brands called to him, tempting him. He couldn't resist that lure.

Around him, the crowd murmured louder, clearly noting the imprints, too. No doubt they were speculating even now that he'd left those bites on her tender flesh. Hammer's nostrils flared. Satisfaction filled him.

He inched in close to Raine's ear. "Step out of your skirt."

"Yes," Raine replied. "Sir."

She'd finally called him Sir in a voice loud enough for everyone to hear. Pride wasn't the only thing of Hammer's that swelled as she affirmed to all around her that she belonged to him. And amid the escalating murmurs, he couldn't help the gratified smile that pulled at his lips.

With a graceful elegance, Raine stepped from the puddle of clothes at her feet, then cast her gaze toward the floor. God, she'd become the epitome of submission, clearly striving to represent him, as well as herself, in a light so positive it was all but blinding.

Hammer's world narrowed to only her. He'd always suspected she'd be utterly amazing, but watching her now stirred his Dominance all the way to its depths.

"Climb on the bench."

She raised her eyes first, reflecting the total trust and faith she had in him. When she extended her hand, Macen helped her kneel on the leather, moving in close behind her as she bent and settled her body over the extended padded surface. He dragged his fingertips down the line of her spine in a whisper-soft touch. Goose bumps peppered her flesh. Turning her head toward him, she focused on his face as he traced indiscriminate patterns over her skin, then issued a soft sigh and closed her eyes.

"You're like velvet," he murmured, feeling her tension begin to bleed away beneath his fingers. "Supple. Silky. Warm. Are you ready to take my pleasure and my pain?"

"Yes, Sir."

Raine's reply was so soft Hammer almost missed it. But he caught the note of anxiety in her tone. A tiny ripple of tension made her flesh quiver as she waited. Hammer studied her, considering the girl with a frown. She'd come out of the gate so brave. He refused to let her worry or cower now and cling to her power.

Flinging his hand in the air, Macen sent it crashing down and landed a brittle slap across her ass. His palm caught fire as a thin wail tore from her throat. His cock, strangling within the confines of his trousers, twitched as he drank in her cries.

"I can't hear you," Hammer barked.

Raine's head snapped up. She sucked in a shuddering breath. "Yes, Sir."

Skimming his palm over the imprint blossoming all angry and red, Hammer bent to whisper in her ear.

"Let my burn sink into your bones," he commanded. "Take my pain. Let it wash over you and carry you away."

Leaning out to watch Raine's face, Macen continued to

caress the sting away as she lowered her head once more and worked to calm her breathing. Dialed in on her every nuance, he noted that the little line between her eyes he'd spied at breakfast had grown sharper and deeper.

"I'm trying, Sir."

"You're doing well, precious. I couldn't be prouder of you."

Hammer moved to the side of the bench and caressed his way up her torso before wedging his hand beneath her breast. He teased her nipple between his finger and thumb. Raine's breath caught on a moan. The line between her brows began to smooth. Hammer smiled.

She'd done a hell of a lot more than try. Raine had processed that slap as if she'd been a well-trained sub. Sometimes, like now, she utterly amazed him.

"Thank you, Sir." Her voice quivered. A new frown tugged at the corners of her lips.

One well-placed spank wasn't going to erase her concern for Liam. Hammer knew he needed to help Raine empty her mind by overloading her with sensation.

Feathering kisses down her shoulders, back, and ass, he punctuated each with a fiery scrape of his teeth. He bit into her hip and sucked for a long, satisfying second, then pulled at her flesh as he eased away.

Raine squealed and jolted, her legs flailing involuntarily and almost clipping Hammer in the jaw. He grabbed her ankles and pressed her feet back on the padded surface, then laved his tongue over the soft flesh of her ass.

"Sorry, Sir."

"I know it wasn't on purpose. Are you still with me?"

"Yes, Sir."

"That's my girl."

Because he intended to get a lot more physical with her, Hammer fastened the cuffs attached to the embedded eyebolts on the frame around her ankles one at a time. As he did, he caressed her skin, keeping a constant physical connection of reassurance.

He was her lifeline, and in more ways than Hammer could really admit, she was his.

"Such a lovely sight," he murmured. "Spread your legs wider for me."

Raine readjusted her knees, opening herself up for him—and the watchful eyes of every club member around her.

"Yes, that's it. So pretty and pink. So wet and inviting," Hammer praised before bending in close to her ear. "You're on display, Raine. Everyone is admiring you. Can you feel their hot stares? Feel the heat of arousal from the men you thought never saw you? They see you now…all helpless and bound for me."

Raine mewled as she slowly opened her eyes, glassy and not quite focused. Hammer smiled. She'd begun to fall away under his hand so easily and trustingly. It wouldn't take much more for her to sail off into subspace—where he intended to send her.

"Close your eyes," he demanded softly.

Her lids fluttered shut, and Hammer pressed a tender kiss to each, then moved behind her once again.

The sight of her bound, spread, and wet for him staggered Macen. He fought the urge to unzip his pants and drive his cock into her soft cunt. Instead, he traced the lips of her labia with his thumb and forefinger. Raine's body rippled. She whimpered. Her pussy clenched at the empty air.

He drew his sodden fingers to his lips and licked them clean, savoring her tart spice.

Hammer smiled as he rounded the frame again, never taking his eyes off her. The delicate lines and feminine angles of her body as she waited for his command made his cock ache and his blood surge.

Bending near her head, he cuffed each of her wrists in the same leisurely, reassuring fashion. Once she was firmly secured to the bench, Hammer twisted his fingers into Raine's hair and tugged, urging her to lift her head off the leather padding. Staring into her smoky blue eyes, he settled his gaze on her lips, slightly parted and ready to be kissed.

The further Raine drifted into her submissive place and ceded to him, the more power Macen absorbed. As he descended into his Dominance, time slowed. The club and the patrons receded, blurring into the background. But every detail about Raine grew sharper, more defined. He heard her every breath, catalogued the heaviness of her lids, dissected her hint of a smile, absorbed the submissive plea in her eyes as she silently begged for more.

"Your safe word is Paris. Take a deep breath and clear your mind, precious. Focus on my words and all the sensations I'm about to bestow on you."

She issued a soft sigh and nodded.

"Good girl," he whispered and kissed the bow of her pink lips.

Stripping off his shirt, Hammer studied the assortment of impact toys lining the table next to him. He chose a thick, heavy flogger. Testing its weight in his hands, he rubbed the wide leather falls between his finger and thumb. Buttery. Supple. Exactly what he needed to free her mind.

Hammer sensed the crowd around him flowing back to give him space to move. The chants of monks mingling with a techno beat faded away. Otherwise, the dungeon sounded eerily quiet, serving to heighten his focus on Raine.

Gripping the cool metal handle in his fist, Hammer raised the flogger before settling the tip of the falls over Raine's shoulder blades.

She started with a little gasp and tensed.

"I've got you. There'll be no pain. Your body is safe in my care. Let your mind follow."

Her soft, consenting moan resonated in his head as he slowly dragged the long leather ribbons down her back, letting her grow accustomed to their feel. As he ate her up with his gaze, she shuddered, gave a longing sigh, then arched in supplication. But the heavy rise and fall of her chest told him she was still alert and mentally processing far too much.

"Unwind for me, precious," Hammer murmured as he skimmed his broad hand over her back. "Focus on my voice, my hand, the pleasure I give you—and nothing more. *Nothing.* Do you understand?"

"Yes, Sir," she replied with a breathy whisper.

Though Hammer knew her very well as a woman, he was still learning her as a submissive. But he had every reason to believe that giving her permission to let go of her worries would help her find that lovely place in her head where her troubles floated away.

"Let go for me, Raine. Let me take you where you need to be."

Hammer dipped his hand between her legs and circled her clit with his thumb. Her whole body twitched. As he swept his fingers through her hot nectar, her hips rolled in time with each drag of his digits. She was doing exactly as he'd asked and surrendering beautifully.

"You're wet and aching for me, aren't you?" When she moaned, Hammer smiled. *Such a satisfying sound...* "You'd like me to drive my cock into your tight little cunt and make you come, wouldn't you?"

"Yes..." Raine strained against the cuffs and ground into his nimble fingers.

"In time, I will. You belong to Liam and me—now and forever. We own every inch of you, and that includes your screams of ecstasy. No one hears them except us."

Hammer's proclamation caused a flurry of loud whispers to fly through the dungeon. He ignored them and directed all his attention and energy to the rhythmic sway of Raine's slender hips. He reveled in guiding her pleasure.

As Macen drove two fingers deep inside her sweltering core, she gave a high-pitched cry that gripped his cock and pulsed in his brain. The rest of the world dissolved.

"That's it, Raine. Hand your control over to me. It doesn't belong to you."

With every moment that passed, her pink folds shimmered more. Her essence flowed. The spicy scent of her cunt nearly made Hammer groan.

He withdrew his fingers from her clutching walls, then dropped to one knee behind her. Dipping in low, he swiped his tongue over her glistening folds, striking her clit with the tip. Her intoxicating flavor exploded on his taste buds.

Raine mewled long and loud. Her nub of nerves hardened beneath his lips. Christ, he wanted to stay here for hours and lap her up while her cries resonated through his brain. But this scene wasn't about what he wanted, but what she needed.

After one more deliciously long stroke, he savored her, then slowly stood, smoothing his palm down her ass in a long caress. Raine gave him a pleading groan. The depth of her frustration seared him.

"Yes, precious. That's exactly what I want... You suffering

under my hand," Macen cajoled. "Because you're mine to tease, please, torture, and enjoy."

At his words, her spine dipped. She lifted the firm curve of her ass in the air, ready for whatever sensations he heaped on her next, and melted against the leather-topped frame. *So fucking perfect…*

Hammer raised the flogger and gripped the handle firmly, feeling his biceps bunch from the weight of the bulky falls. Swinging his arm out to the side, he landed the thick bands over Raine's ivory ass with a heavy thud.

Raine *aah*ed, flinched. Branding every detail of her response into his brain, Hammer brought the leather down again as he memorized each flex of her thighs, gasp of breath, clench of her ass. She turned rosy. Her breathing accelerated. Macen smiled. She didn't like outright pain, but when he peeked around to her face, the subtle pinch and smoothing of her brow told him she loved the fuck out of this little sting.

Flicking his wrist every so often, forcing the leather to land with an extra bite, he watched as Raine processed the added sensation with an occasional frown. But it wasn't long before she strained against her cuffs, arching her ass higher into the air in a silent petition for more.

Hammer heard a familiar, soft chuckle and glanced to his left to find Seth had stopped sceneing, too, and now gazed on with interest. He gave Macen a nod, then resumed his study of Raine's face once more.

The lull between whacks clearly frustrated her as she cried out and tugged at the cuffs around her wrists.

"Ask for what you want," Hammer instructed.

Her arms and legs quivered. As he peeked between her thighs, he noted her slickness now coated her entire pussy. She'd swollen with need, gone from pink to a flushed rose pouting for attention. Macen's mouth watered.

"Yes, Sir," she mewled. "Please. More."

Crouching behind her, Hammer leaned in and captured more of her tart, tangy taste. Then he flattened his tongue and swiped over her lush folds and all the way up to the small of her back.

Raine squealed and bucked, panted and gasped. He pinned her in place with a wide palm splayed across the top of her ass to still the writhing roll of her hips.

He rounded the spanking bench and bent until they were face to face. "More what?"

"Everything."

"I can do that, sweet sub," Hammer assured before he gripped her hair and took her lips in another savage kiss. He drank down every ounce of her surrender, letting it fill all the empty places inside him he'd never allowed another sub to touch.

Tapering away, he released her hair and stood. She relaxed on the bench now. His chest expanded, and a potent rush of power blasted through him. Fuck, he wanted his whip—his go-to toy. He knew he could kiss her with it so sweetly and send her flying. But she'd asked him not to use it, and he wouldn't betray her trust.

Clenching his jaw, he strode to the back of the bench again. The scent of her feminine musk filled his senses and lingered on his tongue like a drug. Lovingly, he brushed his fingers over the imprint of his slap. The mark still stood visible but blended beautifully with the warm, reddened flesh of her backside.

Dominance. Control. Peace.

Drawing the flogger back, Hammer landed the heavy falls across her pale flesh in a steady, throbbing rhythm again. And again. And again. Time lost all meaning, measured only by each deliberate stroke and the subtle jerk of her body.

Her soft moans echoed around him, coalesced in his brain, and pulsed through his body. Each second sharpened with crystal clarity, magnifying the rising energy inside him. Nothing else mattered. No one else existed. Time stood still for this one moment.

"Tell me where you're at?" Hammer asked, his voice rough and husky.

"In the clouds," Raine sighed, her tone laced with serenity.

"Go farther, precious. Sail past the stars," Hammer demanded softly. "I'll bring you back when it's time."

As he continued to strike her ass with the wide falls, he looked for any signs of distress and found none. Her ass was a pretty red. Neither her hands nor feet looked purple. All good.

Her dreamlike moans amplified his senses. Hammer

reviewed the scene—what he'd done, how she'd responded mentally, emotionally, physically. Though he still focused on her with a keen hyperawareness, Raine no longer reacted to the flogger landing on her flesh.

He'd never taken her to subspace before, and the power she'd willingly ceded ignited every cell in Hammer's body. He held tight to the priceless trust she'd placed in his hands and fought the urge to slide out of his own head, into Dom space. Once he'd learned the submissive in her well enough, after he knew her every reaction… Yes, then he'd slide into his own delicious place and fully consume her power as he sent her even beyond the stars.

That day would come. Soon.

"Are you still with me, precious?" he murmured, watching her eyes gently flutter.

"Yes," she whispered breathlessly.

"That's my beautiful girl," he praised.

Sending the flogger over her already fiery red flesh, he could feel her slip away almost as tangibly as if she slowly released his clutching hand.

"She's gone," Seth finally murmured softly.

"Excellent." Hammer smiled but didn't stop.

Mesmerized by the give of her flesh beneath the falls and the deepening red of her backside, he felt a weight lift from his shoulders. He'd given her what she needed, had crafted a quiet place inside her mind where she could escape the chaos.

Keeping her suspended in that peaceful euphoria as long as he dared, Macen finally laid the flogger aside.

Staring at her welted flesh, he fixated on the slick cream coating her pussy. Raine called to every primal cell in his body. She had surrendered herself mind, body, soul—and it still wasn't enough. He needed more.

Own.

Take.

Claim.

Bending, he kissed the hot flesh of her ass, felt the throb of it beneath his lips. The need to feel her soft pussy surrounding his cock had him gritting his teeth. Not here. Not yet. He'd enjoy the razor's edge of need just a bit longer. When she was ready… Oh, he'd gorge on her.

Tormenting himself further, he uncuffed her ankles, then laved the rippling welts across her skin. He tasted her heat, gently bit into it, before begrudgingly lifting his lips from her blistering flesh.

Hammer stood and moved to the front of the bench and quickly freed her wrists. Raine still didn't move—didn't flinch—even when he brushed his fingers over her cheek and through her hair.

Placid and free, she floated in the safe haven of subspace, somewhere far away from everyone, especially Gwyneth and the problems the bitch had wrought.

Like a slow-rising wave, pride rolled over Hammer. He'd taken her there, dissolved her worries and fears, and given her the sweet gift of peace.

His chest expanded. He couldn't suck in air fast enough as he breathed through his urge to let loose a primal roar. Instead, he clenched his jaw and gently lifted his limp beauty from the bench.

As he turned, he was almost startled to see the crowd still gathered, still staring, approval all over their faces.

Cradling Raine close to his chest, he held her for a long moment, simply gazing at the peace on her face. Then Hammer turned and walked out of the dungeon, intending to bring her back gently and sate a few cravings of his own.

* * *

Beck met Liam in the car park and ushered him through a doctors' entrance that led to the emergency room. As they walked the maze of corridors, he updated Liam on Kyle's progress.

"I don't really know more than what I said on the phone," Beck offered. "But like I said earlier, we give priority to babies, especially when they projectile vomit green and we can't find any obvious cause."

Liam didn't like the sound of that. "So it's serious?"

"Could be a sign of a liver problem or a twisted stomach," Beck replied. "Both can be deadly in infants if they aren't caught early enough. Those are worst-case scenarios, of course. Hopefully, it'll turn out to be something more benign, but we won't know without further testing."

Deadly? Liam staggered at that news. "Where are Gwyneth and the baby now?"

"Kyle is with a nurse having blood drawn. Mom was agitated and disrupting treatment, so security escorted her to the waiting room."

"Why doesn't that surprise me?" Liam shook his head.

Beck rubbed at his chin. "Just for the record, I haven't decided yet if your ex is merely a drama queen or just fucking crazy."

"As a loon, mate. I'm all but convinced I never really knew her."

"Well, she's a looker. I'll give her that much, but I wouldn't fuck her—and that's saying something." Beck grinned.

It was. "Do you think Kyle will be all right?"

"Honestly?" He shrugged. "I don't know."

"Poor little guy. And I thought I was having a rough time of it." He raked a hand through his hair, feeling as if he'd repeated the motion all day.

"And it will probably get rougher. His doctors will likely insist that Kyle get a barium bottle to test his upper gastrointestinal tract. It won't be pleasant, but the test is vital if there's a blockage."

"So we could be here for a bit, then?"

"I'm thinking so. I've pulled strings where I can, but it's a busy time, and the labs are backed up. The tests simply take a while. And this is where I leave you. Just carry on to the end and turn right. You'll see the waiting room. Gwyneth's in there. I need to get out of here and sleep, at least for a few hours." The doctor clapped him on the shoulder. "Later, man."

"Thanks, Beck. I'm in your debt."

As the other man waved him off and disappeared into an elevator, Liam found the waiting room. He pushed the door open and spotted Gwyneth pacing by the window and wringing her hands, obviously distraught.

When she turned again and caught sight of him, she rushed over in a soiled T-shirt and jeans, then threw herself in his arms.

She smelled terrible.

"Oh, Liam. Thank god you're here. I'm so worried and fatigued. I've had no idea what to do, the name of a doctor to call. I would have rung you, but after this afternoon, I didn't think… Then that surly man came…" She looked close to dissolving into tears.

"Steady, Gwyneth. Take a seat and tell me about it," he soothed as he took her elbow and led her to one of the chairs in a corner.

There was only one other person in the room, but zero privacy.

Liam waited until she finally settled herself into a chair before dragging another to face her. He dropped into it. "I'm glad that Beck stopped by his condo and could help."

"Yes, I am, too. I didn't mean to sound ungrateful." Gwyneth started wringing her hands again. "I'm just so worried."

He laid his palm over her fingers and squeezed. "Tell me what's happened with the lad."

Gwyneth sniffled. "After you left, Kyle developed a fever. He'd been listless and fussy most of the afternoon. But when he woke from his sleep, his nappy was dry. He felt hot. Next thing I knew, he started vomiting green everywhere. I-I didn't expect it. He doesn't eat much more than formula, so I didn't know…" The tears started up again. "I tried everything I could think of. I rocked him. I sang to him. I wrapped him in cool cloths. I even tried to smash up crackers and feed him some. I'd just decided to call an ambulance when Dr. Beckman walked in. You know the rest."

"Crackers?" Liam looked at his ex-wife as if she finally had lost her mind. "That's what you thought to give a vomiting baby?"

"I thought it would soothe his stomach. It works for me. I didn't know what else to try. What do I know about babies?"

Maybe the truth would finally come out… "You *are* his mother, aren't you?"

She avoided his probing stare, reaching for a box of tissues on the table beside her, and blew her nose daintily. Back ramrod straight, she flew out of the chair to the rubbish bin. Rather than return to her seat, she resumed pacing.

"Gwyneth?" Liam refused to let her ignore the question.

"I-I…" She turned back to look at him, a flush staining her cheeks. She gave an exhausted sigh. "Liam…"

With just one word, Gwyneth asked him for mercy he didn't feel.

He cocked a brow at her. "Tell me."

With slow, reluctant steps, she crossed the room to him again. "Oh, bugger it all."

He remembered hearing exactly this tone of voice after he'd caught her cheating. His hackles rose. "Sit. Explain. Now."

She took her seat again, squirming gingerly to avoid sitting on the cheek where he'd paddled her, and reached out to pat his knee. Their gazes tangled, and she must have seen that he'd reached the end of his patience.

Gwyneth drew her hand back. "I'd like to start by saying I never meant this situation to get quite so out of hand. But…Kyle isn't your son."

Liam fought back a smile of triumph. "We didn't actually have sex after the damn benefit that night in New York, did we?"

"When I suggested you come to my hotel room, you didn't say no. But you passed out just after you took off your trousers." And she looked put out about that.

Relief hit him square in the chest. Good to know he didn't have to disinfect his dick again. "Kyle isn't your son, either. Is he?"

"No." She took up her hand wringing again. "He's Kitty and George's."

"Your sister?" She'd just married as he and Gwyneth had divorced.

The puzzle pieces of her deception began to slot into place. She'd developed this elaborate ruse and manipulated him. And she'd destroyed Raine's piece of mind. For what? Liam couldn't yet comprehend her purpose.

How could he have ever believed he had feelings for this selfish, miserable bitch?

The anger he'd tamped down earlier heated from a slow simmer up to a roiling boil.

"You're so void of a conscience that you'd deceive me

about fathering a child? You've got some fucking nerve. After the way I found you cheating, I guess I shouldn't be surprised that you lack a basic understanding of what's right and wrong." He stood abruptly, shoving his balled-up fists into his pants pockets.

In another corner, the other person in the waiting room cleared his throat and hurriedly left.

"Oh, Liam…" She sniffled. "Don't be angry. Give me a chance to explain. Then you'll understand."

Liam swung back to face her and fought for control. "No, I won't. What the bloody hell is wrong with you, Gwyneth?"

"With me?" Nose red, eyes swollen, she stabbed her finger at him. "What about you? You've let Hammer corrupt you and become a vile pervert."

Coming from her, that was almost a compliment.

"I don't give a flying fuck what you think of me. But you destroyed every shred of feeling I ever had for you by treating the woman I love with such contempt."

"That ill-kept guttersnipe? You've come down in the world. She's a—"

"Be very careful about the words you choose." His voice went frosty with warning. "Another insult and I won't be responsible for what happens."

Liam strode away from her to calm his thoughts and pulled out his phone to give Raine and Hammer the good news. Naturally, his battery was dead. *Fuck.*

She approached him from behind. "I'm sorry. I'm distraught, not thinking clearly. You have no idea what I've been through."

"It's of your own doing," he reminded in a rough tone.

He wanted to say more, but the man who'd left the waiting room returned, wiping water from his lips and sending them a sideways glance.

"I didn't mean any harm," she insisted. "I just needed you to marry me again for a few weeks."

Liam barely managed not to choke. "Marry *you*? Again? You've gone fucking mental. I bloody well learned my lesson the first time." He grabbed Gwyneth by the wrist and hauled her back to her chair. "Why would you think I'd agree?"

"Well, I didn't mean forever." She gave him a petulant frown. "I thought if I dropped my knickers and enticed you again, you'd enjoy it. And I'd inherit a company worth a billion pounds."

His jaw gaped open. Now he knew she *was* mental. "What are you yapping about?"

"My father is dying. He's been trying to decide whether to leave his company to Kitty or me. Of course, we'd both inherit money, but he said he's still choosing which one of us to leave his business."

Liam still couldn't discern where he fit into this scenario, but one question smacked him in the face. "What do you know about running a company, especially one that size?"

"Nothing." She bit her lip and paused, as if just realizing that practicality. "But I've already lined up a cash-rich buyer. Kitty foolishly thinks she should run it herself. If she's going to be that ridiculous, she doesn't deserve anything."

Liam perched on the edge of his chair. "And what does all this have to do with me?"

"Well…Daddy thought you kept a firm hand on me and was more than a teensy bit upset by our divorce. To inherit the company, I have to prove I'm 'responsible and less impulsive.'" She dropped her voice, mocking the elderly man. "Because apparently droning out her vows to an insipid idiot and spitting out a kid makes Kitty dependable. Anyway, my father said that he'd leave control of the business to me if you and I remarried. Other than sex, I had no idea how I was going to convince you to take me back…"

That was Gwyneth logic. Nothing she did should shock him anymore, but this blew his mind. "So you decided to kidnap your own nephew and use him to coerce me?"

"It actually started when I agreed to do my sister a favor. We'd planned one last trip to New York for my father. He so enjoys the city. But at the last moment, his doctors said he wasn't well enough to travel. I convinced Kitty and George to press ahead with the trip. When we arrived, Kitty spent the first two days crying. She's been having some postpartum thing." Gwyneth waved her hand in a dismissive gesture. "Anyway, George decided a romantic cruise might cheer her up. He asked me to watch Kyle."

Liam frowned. He'd thought her critique of George had been rather harsh—until now. What sort of daft prick would leave his child with Gwyneth? "And? You thought—just in case seducing me didn't work—that while they were vacationing, you'd use their own son to try to screw them out of a billion pounds?"

"Really, Liam…that's unfair."

He growled a curse. "Sounds pretty accurate to me."

"Being responsible for Kyle every day and night has been so difficult. Do you know how impossible it is to get any sleep with a baby? And now that he's so terribly ill…" She started sobbing again. "Oh, it's awful. I look a fright. I can't remember the last shower I had in peace. My nerves are shattered. I don't know why anyone would want to breed." She shuddered.

Liam had never been more ecstatic that he hadn't gotten Gwyneth pregnant.

"What should I do? He's seriously ill. What if the worst happens?" she sobbed.

"You'll have to live with the consequences of your actions." Something she'd had almost no experience with. "Why are you confessing all this to me now?"

"I've been out of my mind with worry. I can't deal with the stress. You can usually fix any situation, so I hoped if I told you everything, you'd help me. I don't know where else to turn…" She dissolved into tears once more.

Liam shook his head. "The doctors will give Kyle all the help he needs. But you're beyond help. I can't believe what you've done."

"It started out innocently," she protested. "Once Kitty and George set sail, I found myself in New York. I just wanted to see you again. I tried the apartment. When I couldn't reach you there, I lowered myself to visit that terrible club Seth belongs to. Of course, you weren't there, either."

"And someone there told you where to find me?" So much for member confidentiality. A head needed to roll for that.

"It wasn't her fault. When I appeared with Kyle at that…place, everyone assumed Kyle was yours." She winced, staring at him with green eyes, begging for forgiveness. "I just carried the assumption along. Then everything snowballed, and I found myself having to come up with even bigger explanations—"

"Lies." He corrected.

She frowned. "Not…completely factual statements, I'll admit."

"Fucked-up fabrications meant to disrupt my life."

She sighed. "Don't be a martyr…"

He glowered at her furiously, not trusting himself to speak—or not to throttle her. "Anything else, Gwyneth?"

"That's it." She dabbed at the tears rolling prettily down her cheeks. "Can't you see how I'm suffering? Help me."

Gwyneth never had been good at focusing on anyone but herself.

"What about your sister? Does Kitty even know her son is sick?"

She stood and resumed pacing, wringing her hands again. "I rang Kitty before you arrived. Their ship docks in Galveston early in the morning. They've already scheduled a flight from nearby Houston that lands at LAX shortly after noon. Thank God. I'm too exhausted to keep up this pretense. And you've become so surly."

Liam felt a ridiculous amount of relief at her statement. But one thing still bothered him. "Why the hell didn't you just ask me for help? That's what a normal person would have done."

She gaped at him. "You were so angry about my little fling with the trainer. He was pretty, and he didn't mean anything to me. But for some reason, you were quite put out. Why would I believe you'd help me, especially since I needed you to marry me again?"

At least Gwyneth had figured out that he wanted nothing more to do with her. Since she usually couldn't fathom a man not being madly in love with her, that was progress for his ex-wife.

"We'll never know now, will we?"

Chapter Fourteen

Silence filled her head. Raine felt the press of lips to her forehead, a caress of her shoulder. She drifted on a cloud of warmth, surrounded by an odd peace. Nothing cluttered her mind. It was a nice change. She breathed, feeling too lethargic to do more.

"Are you with me, precious?"

Hammer. She recognized his voice, his term of endearment. He trailed kisses down her neck. Raine was aware of him, but sensation didn't quite penetrate her haze. She should probably answer him, but when she tried, she only managed the softest moan.

"Come back to me now," he coaxed. "Open your eyes. Look at me."

Raine didn't want to. She enjoyed the peaceful void. Almost nothing penetrated her quiet except his affection. But under that cajoling note, insistence laced his voice. Something inside Raine didn't want to disappoint him.

Slowly, she became more aware of her surroundings: soft sheets on her tender backside, a warm quilt tucked all around her, Hammer's bare torso pressed against hers as he leaned over her.

"Raine… You looked beautiful submitting to me. Everyone

in the club now knows you belong to Liam and me, and you did us so proud. Let me know you can hear me."

It took a lot of effort, but she managed to nod.

"Good girl. Open your mouth." Hammer brushed her lower lip with his thumb, and she slowly complied.

Gently, he pushed something thin past her lips and placed it on her tongue. Instinctively, Raine closed her mouth around the little square. She smelled the chocolate mint candy before she tasted it. Rich, sweet, with a hint of bite… She moaned.

"You were amazing. Everyone saw you in a beautifully submissive light, especially me. I couldn't have asked you to surrender more perfectly. I'm humbled by your trust."

You made me feel like I was flying. I loved giving you my control. Let's do that again. "Macen…" was all she managed.

The chocolate melted and the flavor coated her tongue. Her head began to rise to the surface after what felt like a long submersion under her blanket of peace. The heater blew warm air over her face. The whiskers on Hammer's cheeks abraded her jawline as he nipped gently at her neck, her lobe. His hot breath feathered across her skin.

"I've imagined you giving yourself so openly to me a million times. You were better than all my fantasies," he praised, leaving little love bites on her neck.

"So good for me, too," she whispered.

By will alone, she lifted her heavy lids to see Hammer hovering above her, his hazel eyes looking so green, the beginnings of a dark beard fanning over his face.

A knock sounded at the door. Raine frowned.

"Come in," Hammer called as if he knew exactly who was intruding.

Seth opened the door and hustled in, holding a cold can of soda and their scattered clothes from the dungeon. He set the garments on the nightstand and handed the can to Hammer.

"Thanks, man."

Seth nodded. "You're welcome. Have fun."

With a wink, Seth was gone. She liked the guy. He seemed kind, straightforward, easygoing. Liam had good friends.

"Drink some of this." Hammer helped her sit up and popped the top of the can.

Raine's head was still swimming a bit as she braced herself upright and surveyed her surroundings. Hammer's room. Before today, the only other time she'd been in this bed, he'd been fucking her into oblivion, like a primal animal in heat over and over… She'd spent most of her time lately in Liam's room. In Liam's bed. In Liam's arms.

Now everything had changed.

Hammer helped her sip the drink. The bite of the cold and the effervescence hit her tongue, tickled her nose. Caffeine jolted her within moments. Or was that just her brain kicking in again?

She stared at the can. Seth had brought it, not Liam, who hadn't been there for the scene because he'd gone to the hospital with Gwyneth and the sick baby. So Hammer had done his best to shut off her head and tune out her worry.

"Has he called you?" Raine blurted.

Regret tightened his face. "No. But Liam is fine. He's coming back. Don't worry."

She really wanted to believe him. Their relationship was worth nothing if she didn't have faith. Hammer had never been one to mince words or pull punches. If he thought Liam could be lured away, he wouldn't say otherwise. And her gorgeous Irishman would have never bought them a house in which to build their future if he planned to leave.

"I know you're right. I just don't like it," she murmured.

"Liam would be touched by your concern, but he wouldn't want you to worry."

Raine pondered that. "I know that, too."

Hammer brushed the hair from her cheek. "How do you feel?"

"Relaxed. Good." *In heaven.*

He cupped her nape, and his lips climbed up her neck. "Not too tender anywhere?"

Experimentally, she flexed and wriggled. Heat flared over her ass, upper thighs, and the small of her back. But a comforting warmth spread all through her body.

She snuggled down in the bed a bit more, barely resisting the urge to close her eyes again and find that alluring peace. "Sensitive. But it's…" She sighed, sent him a little smile. "Nice."

A wicked grin curved his lips before he dragged the blankets down, baring her to the waist. He cupped her breast and latched on to her nipple, giving it a deep, hard suckle. An unexpected electricity zinged through her body, zipping through her veins, zapping her clit. Her eyes flew open wide. She sucked in a breath. Hammer's touch always felt insanely good, but Raine had never experienced this hypersensitivity. Ten seconds ago, she hadn't been thinking of sex at all. Now?

As he pulled his lips away, she arched up and wrapped her arms around his neck with an imploring groan. "Macen…"

"How about now?" he taunted, pinching her nipple and filling her with another burst of sensation. "I can make you feel a whole lot better than nice, precious."

* * *

"Please…"

Raine's whispered plea went straight to his cock.

Oh, hell… Hammer hadn't expected to give her anything except aftercare, but the instant she'd melted into him and he'd tasted her skin, he had fixated on one thing—and one thing only. In fact, he'd make it far more than nice. He'd fuck her until she clawed his back, screamed her throat raw, and fell to the mattress in exhaustion.

He kicked the covers aside altogether and tore into his zipper, shoving it down with a hiss of breath. "You enjoying that endorphin high?"

She blinked, wide-eyed as she watched him undress with a lick of her lips. "Is that what I'm feeling?"

So fucking innocent in some ways, and he shouldn't enjoy corrupting her this much. "You bet it is. I'm going to do everything in my power to make sure you don't come down anytime soon."

Hammer rolled out of bed long enough to shove his pants to the floor. The sight of Raine in his bed, on his sheets, wearing the marks of his teeth on her breast, her thigh, her pussy… Fuck if that didn't drive him out of his mind. He craved putting more of his brands on her pretty skin.

"Is that what you want, too? Yes or no?" he asked.

Every cell in his body wanted to merge with her, make it clear in no uncertain terms that he owned her.

She blinked up at him, blue eyes clinging, berry nipples hard, breathing shallow.

"You know what I'm asking, Raine. How much I'm asking. Yes or no?" He enunciated each word clearly.

Because he didn't know how much longer he could hold back. If she was too tired, sore, or scared, he'd have to take himself in hand and hope like hell that would sate him enough to leave her alone. But no way could he unchain this side of him without her consent.

Somewhere in the back of his head, reason screamed at him. This wasn't a fabulous idea. Liam wasn't here to pull him back if he got out of hand, and he'd sworn to keep himself in check. Hammer cursed, raking a hand through his hair.

He was strong, damn it. In control. He didn't need a fucking babysitter. Raine was precious to him, and he'd never break her. He could enjoy himself a little, then pull back. No harm, no foul. No problem. Right?

Raine bit her lower lip, watching him shyly, almost the way she had before he'd ever touched her…just like she had when she'd harbored a mad case of hero worship that had driven him to the brink of sanity because he'd been unable to sate his desire for her.

He could sure as fuck do something about it now.

"Raine? Answer me."

A coy little smile creased her face as she lifted her hands from the bed. They fluttered around her, brushing aside her hair, spreading the dark mass over his white pillow, before she set her palms on the upper swells of her breasts.

And began to feel her way down.

Hammer nearly grabbed her wrists to stop her. No one was going to put out the fire he'd kindled except him. But Raine merely cupped her breasts, barely thumbed her nipples before gliding her hands down her stomach. Goose bumps broke out all over her skin. Her nipples drew up tighter and harder. She gave a little gasp and looked at him helplessly. Then she bent her legs and grazed her fingertips inside her thighs until she cupped her knees. Slowly, she nudged her thighs apart, easing them wide just for him.

Once her pussy lay totally open and wet, she dropped her hands to her sides. Hammer stared at her plump mound and swallowed a growing knot of lust.

"Always," she whispered, soft and inviting.

A wave of primal possession swept up his body, a tsunami of thick, visceral demand. It sizzled across his skin, seared his veins, shook his heart, and slammed down his cock.

Before sanity vanished, Hammer managed to grab a condom from the nightstand and rip it open with shaking hands. As he rolled it down his aching length, he wondered why the hell he couldn't harness this fucking urge to conquer her in every possible way. The force wasn't totally new—he'd felt stirrings of it with Juliet—but the need had never been as overpowering and instinctive as it was with Raine.

"Oh, precious." Hunger roughened his voice. "You have no idea what I'm going to do to you."

Raine's eyes widened. "I can take everything you want to give me, Sir."

Hammer prowled onto the bed, homing in on her splayed thighs. "We'll see."

He didn't give her time to respond before he dipped his head low and bit into the supple flesh of her thigh, leaving his mark opposite the one he'd welted at the house.

She tensed beneath his lips, her body rippling with a gasp—a breathy sigh of passion and pain. Raine arched off the sheets.

If she meant to entice him, she fucking succeeded.

The musky scent wafting from her cunt made his mouth water, but the urge to press her flesh between his teeth drove a need even more potent than his desire to taste her. Hammer wanted to consume her, lick her welts, and listen to her unbridled cries.

Dragging his tongue over the swell of her hips, he circled her hipbone like a shark. Then with a carnal growl, he gnashed her tender skin between his teeth. Raine jolted, shrieked, then held her breath for a long moment before releasing a throaty wail.

"Yes, precious. Let my burn sink deep," Hammer lauded as he dragged his tongue over the marred flesh in soothing swipes.

Power, sizzling and savage, flared through him, tearing at his self-imposed restraint. As he gripped Raine in a brutal grasp, white halos appeared around each of his fingers. She'd have five bruises on each hip tomorrow. Hammer made a mental note to strip her down then and inspect them, kiss them…add more.

Narrowing his eyes, he inched his way up her body with a predatory stare. As he settled his hips between her thighs, a flicker of a smile curled at the corners of her mouth. Raine froze, watching, waiting, breathless.

With a thunderous roar, Hammer drove past her wet folds and deep inside her, all the way to the hilt, in one rough stroke.

He pumped into her, once, twice, again and again as the angry red welt he'd left on Raine's breast earlier snared his gaze. She needed a matched set. In fact, she should always wear his symbols on her pale skin. Even the thought charged his veins with white-hot lust.

His need to mark her warred with his need to fuck her. He shoved into her again, gnashing his teeth, then pulled out of Raine's soft pussy with a roar. She whimpered at his loss, moaning in protest when he released her hips as well.

"I'm not done with you yet," Hammer taunted as he stretched his body over hers. "Fuck, I haven't even begun."

Slanting his mouth over her lush breast, he kissed her unmarred skin, then sank his teeth into her flesh just above her nipple with a low groan of bliss.

"Macen…" Raine panted. "Yes. Oh, god. Yes."

Lifting his head slightly, Hammer watched the ruddy mark darken on her snow-white skin. Strumming his thumb over the impression, he inched higher, then claimed her soft, parted lips in a harsh kiss.

Raine opened farther for him. Hammer nipped her bottom lip, giving a sharp tug, before releasing her mouth. He settled his lips against her slender neck and fastened his teeth over her skin inch by inch, leaving behind a trail of crimson brands. She whimpered, moaned. The sounds only fed his boiling demand.

He eased down, looking for smooth flesh that needed his possession. Her collarbones. Sweet. Delicate. His…

As he bit down against the thin bone, Raine's screams echoed off the walls, reverberating in his ears. The faint taste of copper slithered over Hammer's tongue. He pulled away, studying his handiwork. A droplet or two of crimson dotted against her milky flesh.

Her breathing came faster. Her nipples turned harder. She looked at him like he was a fucking god who could give her the world.

Oh, yeah. Fuck yeah. She'd look at that wound for days and remember it. He would, too.

"Tell me what you want, Raine," Hammer demanded before sucking at the tiny puncture.

"You, Macen. All of you," Raine groaned as she writhed, rolling her hips under him, taunting him. "Fuck me. Hard. Please."

Rocking back on his knees, he settled his cock against her rosy pussy, nestling the crest right against her glistening folds. And he waited. She thrashed, but he stilled her with an unyielding grip on her thighs. He watched her opening flutter around him as if she tried to suck him in and pull him deep.

Hammer smiled as he drove inside her in a single, merciless thrust.

Raine gasped and groaned. "Harder, Macen. Deeper… Yes!"

As he slammed into her again, Raine sank her teeth into her bottom lip. Christ, she was amazing, his fucking dream come true.

The first time he'd ravaged her now seemed like a distant memory. Of course, the amount of alcohol he'd consumed at the time had numbed most of the brilliance stunning him now. Just as he had in the dungeon, Hammer focused on every movement of Raine's body: the wrinkle of her brow, the gasps that expanded her lungs and raised her breasts toward the heavens before they shook and bounced as he slammed into her small, soft body.

The blood on her collarbone beaded again. As he slid on top of her once more, Hammer shoved his arms under her and curled his hands back toward him, over her shoulders. He pounded her pussy and fixated on her unblemished clavicle. He leaned in, opened his mouth, hungry for another taste.

Something in the back of Hammer's brain kicked him. He

wasn't a goddamn vampire. He'd never gotten off on blood. Why was he so obsessed now? It didn't matter. He had to pull back, cage this vicious need riding him so hard.

Stilling inside her, Hammer sucked in a deep breath. Shame. Remorse. Guilt. They all flattened him like a freight train. "Christ. I'm sorry, Raine. I didn't mean to—"

"No," she gasped as she gripped his arms and dug her nails into his flesh. "Don't stop. Please. *Please.* I need this…need you to do this to me."

He more than liked the idea of her craving the hard edge of his touch. But he couldn't use her this roughly—not given how small she was, not with the day she'd had.

"No, precious. What you need is to be pampered and loved."

"If you do that right now, I'll kill you," Raine cried. "When you let yourself go, I feel needed. You and Liam give me purpose, make me feel adored. Something in me would die if I couldn't give you what you craved. Give me all of you. Let me serve your needs, Macen."

Submissive to the core. Raine had shown the vulnerable side she desperately hid from everyone…except him and Liam.

"Use me," she urged. "Do whatever you need. I'm yours."

Her beseeching tone clawed at his precarious restraint. She needed him to fill all the dark recesses inside her, just as much as he needed her to fill his.

"You want it all?" He surged deep into her again.

"Yes." She rolled her hips up to him.

"Every last bit?"

"I do. Please…I'm begging."

Yes, she was, and it sounded so sweet.

"Fuck!" He roared as he jerked from inside her, then grabbed her waist and flipped her to her stomach. "Get on your hands and knees. Now."

Raine rose on all fours, presenting her narrow back and fiery red ass to him. She looked so defenseless, pale and small, head bowed and wordless. Hammer felt the snap of all rationale.

Smoothing his palms over her warm backside, he landed a feral slap across her ass and watched the rosy flesh turn flaming red instantly. Raine howled out. Her screams burrowed into his soul, pouring life into the jaded, dormant crevices inside him.

Still not satisfied, Hammer bent to lick the handprint. As his tongue abraded her skin, Raine writhed and moaned, riding the high of the burn he'd inflicted.

Clutching at her hips and stilling her sway, he bent and sank his teeth into the heated flesh of her ass. And again he felt their shared perfection descend deep inside him.

Hammer slapped at her thighs. "Open. Wide. Take me, Raine. Take all of me."

She spread for him immediately as Hammer ruthlessly dug his fingers deeper into her sides. He plunged into her cunt and drew her burning cheeks flush against him for a long heartbeat. She clutched at his cock with her aching softness and a sensual cry. His eyes rolled back in his head.

Pure, intoxicating heaven.

"Head down, my sweet sub," Hammer ordered, his tone unbending. "Keep that beautiful ass poised high in the air."

As Raine obeyed, Hammer's chest expanded. He slid his hands up her back and wrapped his fingers around her shoulders, digging them into the wells of her collarbones. Raine's heartbeat pulsed beneath his fingertips.

Everything about the siren had haunted his fantasies for what seemed a lifetime. And now he knew exactly why.

She was built to take him. He'd convinced himself the first time he'd fucked her that she couldn't handle him. Now…Raine was fucking all he'd ever sought.

With her head down, she pressed her cheek against the mattress. Her ebony hair fanned out in silken skeins over his sheets. The long line of her rippling spine covered in pale, soft skin shredded the last of his control.

"Scream for me, precious. Fill me with your submission. Your love."

As Hammer slammed into her like a man possessed, he bit at her back, sucked at her flesh. Raine's cries of rapture echoed through his head, urging him faster, harder, higher.

God, he fucked her in one of the most submissive positions he could think of…and it still wasn't enough. More. He needed it. Now.

Macen pulled her arms behind her back, capturing her wrists in one hand at the small of her back before gripping her hair in his fist. An arc of pure power sizzled through him.

With each new thrust, Hammer ground his hips upward, trying to fight his way deeper.

"Macen!" Raine cried. "Please. I need—"

"I know exactly what you need," he said between heavy breaths as sweat poured down his face. "And I can't wait to feel you shatter around me. Clutch my cock tight and suck me in more."

"Yes," she screamed. "I can't…hold—"

"No!" he thundered. "Not yet."

Releasing her hair, he leaned back and slapped her ass. The sound of the crisp crack resonated through his head, made his balls draw up.

Everything about her set him on fire. The flames licked down his spine, racing through him in a sizzling rush. Reaching around the swell of her hips, Hammer wedged two fingers around her clit. As he rubbed the hard nub, she bucked against the friction and slammed back against him with an incoherent moan. Her cunt rippled and quivered around him.

The rush of release tore through him.

"Now," he commanded. "Come for me now, Raine. Hard! I want it all."

Hammer held her wrists in a vise-like grip as he circled the sensitive nub with his thumb again and again.

Raine sucked in a powerful gulp. Her entire body tensed. Then she bowed, lifting her head off the bed, arching and keening and swelling around him.

The muscles of her fiery pussy contracted in hard spasms. Raine screamed his name. Hammer slammed into her shuddering body and released a savage roar, coming into the latex barrier with a spine-bending force that blew him away.

Though he was her Dominant, she stripped him raw. Never had he imagined a woman could utterly decimate him the way Raine did because she was the missing half of his heart. She completed his soul.

As she rippled and clenched around him with aftershocks, his cock jerked. Panting, sweating, Hammer wrapped his arm around her waist and tumbled to his side, toppling her over with him, onto the bed.

Still coupled together, he held her as their breathing slowly evened out. Brushing the hair back from her nape, he pressed his lips against her sweat-soaked skin. Sliding his tongue over her flesh, he tasted salt and breathed in Raine's musky-lily scent.

"I love you, precious, with every cell in my body."

"Mmm," she moaned, then turned her head to kiss him.

He leaned into her soft, warm body, sliding his tongue into her mouth. As he swept deep inside her, she utterly surrounded him, and he groaned.

"I love you, too," she murmured, her stare tangled up in his.

Replete and totally satisfied, he pulled her in and held her tight. Peace settled over him. With a sigh, he closed his eyes.

* * *

One a.m. had come and gone by the time Kyle had consumed the barium bottle Beck had warned him about. Then the little guy had X-rays taken and more tests administered. Liam had been at the hospital for nearly five hours when the pediatrician on duty finally declared that Kyle wasn't suffering from a life-threatening illness but merely a virus. *Thank God.*

Liam exchanged few words with Gwyneth when he finally dropped her and Kyle off at Beck's condo. After escorting her up and helping her settle Kyle, he ignored the fact that his ex-wife looked as if she had something to say and all but ran out the door.

Despite his weariness, Liam found the energy to smile. Gwyneth's schemes were behind him. Kyle would be reunited with his parents in a few hours, and Liam hoped the boy wouldn't actually require a real shrink because of his aunt's scheme.

Best of all, he would never have to see his she-devil of an ex-wife again.

On the drive back to Shadows, exhaustion slammed him as if he'd run face first into a brick wall. He kept himself awake by blasting the air conditioning in the car, despite the December chill, and counting the moments until he could return to Raine and Hammer. Then he'd strip, shower, crawl into bed, and sleep for a week.

As soon as he shared the happy truth about Kyle.

Until then, Liam mulled over the past twenty-two hours. What was it about money that drove people to senseless acts of mayhem and maliciousness? Try as he might to understand, Gwyneth's intrigues still boggled him. What had she imagined she'd do with him if she'd persuaded him to marry her again? Divorce him after he'd outlived his usefulness, Liam supposed. After she'd utterly ruined his life, of course.

Deciding he'd never understand the woman, Liam let go of the thought and concentrated on better things, like Raine and Hammer.

How lucky was he to have both his best friend and the woman he loved in his life? Their joining at the lodge had been incredible, but the pleasure they'd exchanged at the new house earlier had transcended any bodily experience and cemented the promise of their future. Of course, what they shared was far more than sex. Their ménage fed his mind, spirit, heart, and Dominant soul. They still had problems to face; Liam had no illusions. But the three of them were a team. They balanced one another. If they all remembered that, somehow they would always find their way together.

The house would be a foundation for their new life. Raine's stunned reaction had both warmed and convinced Liam that he'd done right in buying the place. And nothing could have surprised—or thrilled—him more than when Hammer had offered to furnish and take care of any other renovations Raine wanted. Now it would be not simply the roof Liam had put over her head to help her feel secure but the home in which they'd all stake their futures.

Relief filled Liam when he pulled into the lot and saw Shadows' ornate red door. Even in the wee hours, the place was still half full with members' vehicles. He grabbed a spot and hurried inside.

Hammer and Raine didn't appear to be working in the dungeon, but the thumping rhythmic beat of the music filled his ears. The primal screams and moans of both pleasure and pain surged a renewed vigor through his veins. The thick scent of heated bodies and sexual arousal swarmed his senses, so heady he could almost taste it.

Seth sat curled up on one of the oversized couches, giving aftercare to a pretty redheaded sub whom he'd wrapped in a blanket within the circle of his arms. The second he caught sight of Liam, he kissed the sub's forehead and sent her on her way.

As Liam crossed the floor, he heard some of the chatter around the cavernous room. Only a few words filtered through. Members talked excitedly about how intense the scene earlier had been. But as he passed, those conversations ceased abruptly. Some Doms simply stared. Jesus, had the rumor mill found out about Gwyneth and his "son"?

When Liam reached Seth, he nodded to his buddy from New York. "I see you're adapting to Los Angeles well."

"I won't lie. The girls are pretty, and the weather is damn nice."

Liam half expected Seth to rib him about his entertaining, soap-opera life again, but the man didn't. "Glad to hear it. You seen Raine and Hammer?"

Seth paused, and all of Liam's instincts flared. "They scened earlier in the dungeon."

Just the two of them. Liam heard Seth's unspoken message. Something between anxiety and annoyance prickled at him. But Hammer was Raine's Dom, too. He'd sometimes need or want her. At least that's what his reasonable side told him.

The other side flamed hot with a blinding streak of jealousy.

"And?" he managed to ask.

Another pause, this one longer. "It was…intense."

Liam didn't particularly like the sound of that. "Meaning?"

"Raine flew hard and fast. I think she must have needed it."

After the day she'd endured, likely so. The evasions and the lies, his ex-wife and the baby, their row… All of that would combine to set her off-balance. She would have wanted someone to take that away from her, even if only temporarily, and to center her.

But damn it, his day had been far fucking worse. Every bloody event had blindsided him. He'd managed to brace himself through one train wreck after another—none of them of his creation. Had either Hammer or Raine thought for a moment that he might need the opportunity to control *something* today?

"You look pissed off," Seth observed. "But you've always

agreed that Raine's needs come first. I'm sure she can't wait to be with you again. Don't be jealous."

That felt like telling him not to breathe, and he battled with himself. If Hammer had been gone and Raine had needed Liam's support, Dominance, or affection, Hammer would absolutely have insisted Liam give her whatever she required—no questions asked.

Why, then, Liam wondered, was he feeling betrayed? He turned to his friend. "I didn't ask your opinion about what I should think."

Seth held up his hands to ward off any argument. "Just telling you how I see it."

He didn't care. Instead, he fought for calm. "When did Hammer and Raine finish?"

"A little over an hour ago, I think."

So plenty of time for Hammer to have taken complete advantage of Raine. No, given her aftercare. She'd probably needed that, too. "Where did they go?"

"To his room." Seth looked reluctant to make that admission. He scooted to the edge of the sofa and looked Liam in the face. "I know you didn't ask me, but seriously, you've got to deal with this. You're trying to play cool, but I can see it's eating you up. You two *share* her. Equal time, equal surrender."

True, and if Liam felt as if he'd received the same affection and devotion from Raine that Hammer did, maybe he'd be all right with the fact that his best mate had done god knew what to his girl when his back had been turned.

Liam nodded, not trusting himself to say much more. "I'll talk to you later."

Seth grabbed his arm. "Don't go in there half-cocked. You're exhausted, and you've had a lot on your mind. Take a drink. Unwind. Remember what's important."

The man wasn't wrong about his exhaustion, Liam mused. Maybe he needed to take a step back and clear his head. The last thing he wanted now was another drama, especially one he created.

With a hesitant nod, Liam allowed Seth to nudge him toward the bar.

"What'll it be, mate? Single malt, right?" Nick, the

bartender, stood before him with a cheery fucking smile Liam just couldn't bring himself to match.

"Aye, straight up."

"I'll take a water," Seth added.

The minute Nick placed the tumbler in front of him, Liam lifted it. His hands shook as he tossed the liquor back. The burn seared its way down his throat yet did nothing to thaw the ice freezing his chest.

"Another?" the bartender asked.

"Nah." The booze would only make him wearier, and he still had to find Hammer and Raine, explain his night at the hospital with Gwyneth. But he had to tuck away this irrational anger first, remember that Raine was not his exclusively.

"You missed Raine and Hammer center stage earlier," Nick said. "They scened for a good, long while. One of the most amazing connections between a Dom and a sub I've ever seen."

A shockwave of anger jolted Liam where he stood as he tried to process Nick's words. Liam resisted the urge to smack his pretty-boy Australian teeth down his throat.

Instead, he tapped the counter. "I've changed my mind. Another."

"Sure thing." The bartender poured again and frowned. "Hey, are you okay?"

He ignored Nick and tossed back the drink, then turned away.

"Did you see Hammer take Raine in the middle of the dungeon earlier?" he overheard one Dom ask another.

"No, but I heard about it the second I walked in the door," the other answered. "About fucking time, if you ask me. They've been hot for each other for years."

"Yeah, and it showed. That scene was an act of pure Dominance. She subbed out for him just like that." The stranger snapped. "Like she'd been falling over for him for years."

"In a way, she has. I wonder where Hammer's Irish friend fits into all this."

No shit. Liam wondered that himself. Or if he even did.

"Hammer declared that he and Liam own her," the first Dom said. "But who knows?"

Who indeed?

Liam slammed his empty glass on the bar with a scowl. One of the Doms looked up and noticed him, then elbowed his peer. Both men quickly melted into the crowd.

Heart thudding in his chest, Liam couldn't breathe. His jealousy returned in spades to bury him where he stood, somehow stunned—though he probably shouldn't be.

"Don't jump to conclusions," Seth warned. "Those two are talking out of their asses."

"Actually, I think they're spot on, Seth. Now if you don't mind, fuck off." Liam pushed away from the bar and left the dungeon. It was high time he found the pair of them and confronted whatever was going on.

Chapter Fifteen

The little bit of Liam still capable of rational thought understood that he'd lost the plot. But Hammer sceneing with Raine—without him—felt like a boulder breaking his back. Suddenly, logic had left the building. And he didn't give a shit.

Would their relationship always be like this, him feeling like a third wheel in their twosome? Yes, Raine claimed to love him, too. Why didn't he quite believe it? Probably because he couldn't figure out what the hell he gave Raine that Hammer didn't. Liam couldn't think of a single thing. Now it seemed as if they'd just been waiting for him to piss off somewhere so they could fuck without him.

They'd done more than fuck, though. Hammer had claimed her with the members of his club as witness, and Raine had probably been all too eager to kneel for Hammer in front of everyone they knew.

Liam cursed. He sounded like a maudlin pansy. Time to shove down his heartache and man up.

As he stomped down the hall, he tried to clear his head, but all he imagined were the sounds of Raine's moans and pleas for Hammer to take her in every way. Jealousy flared hotter than a furnace. Were Hammer and Raine laughing at him? Rolling their eyes at how fucking predictable and gullible he was? He must be, after all. How else could Gwyneth have succeeded in duping him for nearly two years?

Raine didn't need him. She had her house now—and the one man she'd always wanted.

But she needs you, too.

And his best fucking mate?

Hammer loves you. He's still your friend.

Who happens to want your girl.

But all to himself? Hours ago, Hammer had insisted that Liam spend some much-needed time with Raine. Had Macen thrown a hissy when he'd realized that Liam had made love to her? Not at all.

Liam didn't know what to think anymore as he made his way toward Hammer's private rooms.

When he reached the door to the office, he opened it and crept inside. The soft glow of a muted desk lamp lit the place. He stood frozen as he strained to hear the sounds of sex from the adjoining bedroom. When only the tick of a clock intruded, he crossed the room and carefully opened the door to Hammer's quarters.

The heavy aroma of sex filled his nostrils and slammed into his brain. When he'd last touched Raine, he'd found that scent erotic as hell. Now, it choked him, cloying and thick.

As he forced himself into the room, he saw that half of Hammer's bed lay empty. Light seeped under the bathroom door as he stepped closer to where Raine sprawled out in sleep.

She'd kicked off the covers and lay naked on her stomach. The pale light of a bedside lamp illuminated her body. At first, Liam couldn't wrap his mind around the numerous mottled bruises in the shape of fingertips and palms, the myriad bites impressed into her skin everywhere, and her bright red ass.

Raine looked a lot like she had the first time Hammer had taken her to bed and used her so brutally, just before Liam had swept her away from Shadows to protect her at the lodge. This time, Macen had welted and marked her even more.

Son of a bitch...

A red haze spilled through his head. His fists curled in rage, nails biting his palms. The bathroom door opened, and Hammer came toward him. Liam didn't pay him any attention until the man stood almost in front of him and braced a hand on his shoulder.

Liam jerked away. "Don't fucking touch me, you bastard."

"I—" Hammer scowled and sighed. "Oh, hell. Not here. Let Raine sleep. Let's—"

"I'm not ducking into the damn bathroom again," he interrupted, struggling to keep his voice low. "I'll need room to knock your fucking block off."

"Fine. Let me get my pants. I'll meet you in my office."

Even now, Hammer thought to dictate to him. *I don't bloody think so.*

Instead, Liam stared at Raine, completely covered in Hammer's marks of possession—the impressions of his teeth, the imprint of his fingers, the welts from his flogger, the chafing at her wrists and ankles from his cuffs. She looked like she'd been mauled by a beast.

Liam shook his head. All those marks, and none of them his. Just like she would never be…

That reality smacked him in the face with the force of a two-by-four.

He staggered out of the bedroom, through Hammer's office, and into the corridor outside. Liam slammed the door and braced himself against the wall, struggling against the urge to plow his fist through the drywall.

Hammer hadn't been satisfied by merely claiming Raine in front of everyone when Liam hadn't been around to show her—or anyone else—his Dominance, too. Of course not. The wanker had dragged her back to his room and fucked her like an animal, savagely marking her all over.

The door beside him opened, and Hammer stuck his head out.

"What are you doing out there? Come in here where we'll have some privacy."

"I'm done listening to you, you rotten bastard," Liam cursed. "How could you?"

"Calm down," Hammer urged. "We'll talk about this."

"Save your breath. I already know about your public claiming of Raine. The whole damn dungeon is talking about how incredible it was. You couldn't fucking wait for me to leave, could you?"

Hammer snorted. "What? I started the scene in the dungeon because *she* needed it."

"Raine did? Ha! More likely, *you* needed it. I know you, Macen. You couldn't wait to unleash your inner beast on her." He gave in and punched the wall in a satisfying crack. Agony exploded across his knuckles—and he didn't care. "I'm thinking you didn't quite finish, mate. You missed branding a few spots. Shall I leave you to it?"

A tic in Hammer's jaw was Liam's only indication that his mate felt anything. "Oh, goddamn it. You had your chance to mark her this morning, but you—"

"Didn't attack her like a fucking animal."

"What's going on?" Raine poked her head out the door, belting a robe around her small waist. "Liam! Oh, thank god you're back." She sighed in relief and stepped toward him, arms outstretched.

Liam pinned her with an angry stare that warned her not to touch him.

She stopped in her tracks and glanced between him and Hammer. "What's going on?"

"Why do you care? I can plainly see who you'd rather be with," Liam accused. "Don't mind me. I'll go on being invisible."

"Don't you *dare* make her feel guilty because you can't get over your shit," Hammer roared.

Liam snapped his gaze back to Macen. "My shit? And have you gotten over yours? You're pulling all the same tripe you did with Juliet, but now you've gone off the fucking deep end." He grabbed Raine and ripped the robe open, flicking his gaze over her marked skin. The imprint of Hammer's teeth on the soft pad of her pussy made him want to hit again—and not just the wall. "Look at her. Bloody hell…"

Raine grabbed the sides of the robe and belted it again, hiding herself from him. She looked chastened and guilty and furious all at once.

Fine time to care that you stabbed me in the heart.

Hammer stepped in front of her protectively. "You don't get to make her feel small or regret what she needs."

Gaping, Liam stared at the two, then stepped back. He'd been pointing out how wretchedly Hammer had treated Raine, yet the man acted as if she needed protecting from him. Liam would never raise a hand to her, never hurt her. But Macen already had.

Raine peeked around Hammer's shoulder. The look in her eyes said he'd wounded her tender heart. How the hell had he become the bad guy?

"Liam," she began. "We never intended to upset you."

They hadn't, he realized. He ducked his head and shook it as cold reality slipped over him. "Because you never thought of me at all. I've been a fool, actually believing I was an important part of our threesome. I see now that you're a couple, and I'm just in your way." He looked at his bleeding hand, a symbol of his bleeding heart. "I can't be second choice for you, Raine. Or just your third, Hammer. You have what you both want: each other. I'm done."

He turned his back on them and walked down the dark hall. He wanted nothing more than to shut out the rest of the world. If this wretched torment was love, they could have it.

"Liam, wait! Please listen…" Raine. He heard her footsteps scampering after him.

He just kept walking.

"For fuck's sake," Hammer bellowed. "Pull your head out of your ass. We need to talk this out."

Liam didn't answer, simply shut the door between them.

Once alone, he flipped the lock and sank onto the bed. He couldn't breathe. He felt like he'd run into a solid wall of pain. His chest felt constricted. Panicked, Liam tore open his shirt, convinced he was having a heart attack.

Bracing his elbows on his knees, he bent his head and pulled in a rough breath. Maybe he was overreacting to Raine and Hammer. But no matter whose collar she'd worn or who had taken her to bed first, she would always be Macen's girl. That knowledge imploded his chest. But hadn't she told him that from the start?

He trembled. A sweat broke out across his brow. What the fuck would he do next?

Hammer began banging on the door. "Don't pout like a

bitch. Get out here and talk to our woman like a man."

She's your woman. "Go fuck yourself."

"Jesus, you called me a fuckwit last week. If the shoe fits, buddy…"

So now Hammer wanted to insult him on top of it all? *What a pal.*

"You're going to wake up tomorrow and feel like an asshole," Macen continued into his silence.

You'd know all about that…

Hammer sighed impatiently. "You need time? Fine. You know where to find us. I'll be taking care of Raine's crushed heart, fucker. Thanks for that."

Heavy footsteps receded down the hall. A door slammed. Of course his best mate was leaving him and taking the girl. He'd expected that all along.

Silence closed in on Liam. Now what the fuck did he do with himself? He supposed he could go take that shower he'd wanted on his drive home. Alone. He'd climb into bed alone, too. And wake up alone. Maybe it was better that way.

But it felt fucking terrible.

Liam stared at the blank wall in the dark room. Nothing here was his. The mattress and the bedding? Hammer's. The furniture? Hammer's, too. Even the four walls belonged to the man. Suddenly, Liam felt as if he didn't belong here at all. He'd drive to the house he'd bought…but that wasn't his, either. He'd given Raine the keys. He felt too bloody tired to drive back to the lodge. Besides, her ghost would be in every room. The lodge would be temporary, anyway. Where would he live? He'd closed the apartment in New York.

No idea how long he'd sat there, staring into oblivion. Next thing he knew, Raine eased into the room and sat beside him. Fucking Hammer. The bastard must have given her his key.

He couldn't deal with her right now, couldn't bear for her to see him so raw. "Raine, just go back to Hammer. He'll take care of you. He always has."

Liam wanted to do right by her. Even now, when his heart was breaking, he tried to find the courage to let her go so she could be happy. After all, it wasn't her fault she was in love with someone else. She'd told him that before he'd ever once kissed her. He'd been stupid to hope he could snare her heart, too. He had no one to blame but himself.

"I need you every moment of every day, Liam. I've been going crazy with worry for you. Please, listen. I'm sorry. This is all my fault—"

"Every time my back is turned you're fucking him, giving to him in a way you've never surrendered yourself to me." The accusation slipped out, fueled by a mix of fury, ugly jealousy, and fatigue.

"That's not true," she protested.

"We both know it is. Whatever you feel, you'll never love me even half as much as you love Hammer."

Raine sent him a horrified stare, then threw her arms around him. "If I've done anything to make you think that, I'm so sorry. It's not true. Will you just listen?"

Liam didn't answer. Maybe she'd feel better saying whatever she needed to. Or maybe she'd finally realize he was right. He'd rather gouge his eyes out than hear this, but he shrugged.

"I was worried sick about you with Gwyneth. I didn't know what she could do to hurt you more, but I'm sure she could think of something. I couldn't be with you and I couldn't do anything for you. I hate feeling helpless. So I began baking and…Hammer found me. He realized I'd worked myself up. He helped me get out of my head and—"

"What did you bake?" Liam wasn't even sure why he asked.

"Sugar cookies. And muffins."

"What kind?"

She hesitated. "Apple spice."

Hammer's favorite. Of course. That just pissed him off more. "Did you ever once ask what I like? No. Date scones, Raine. Not that it matters."

"You always ate whatever I put out and I thought…" She closed her mouth and drew in a breath. "You're right. I didn't ask. I'm sorry, Liam. I'll make date scones for you."

"Don't bother." *Would she?* He hated feeling this vulnerable. And angry. Christ, he was snapping at her for acting on her feelings. Liam closed his mouth. Better to stop now.

"It's not a bother. I bake Hammer's favorites because I want to please him. I would gladly do the same for you because I love you."

Now she was just feeling sorry for him.

He stood. "It doesn't matter. Just go. I need a shower and—"

"Something to eat, someone to take care of you." She rose beside him and put her arms around him. "That's why I'm here. I'll give you whatever you need."

Liam couldn't miss the soft persuasion in her voice.

He broke from her hold and swiped at his face. "It's Hammer you want. Look at yourself, Raine. Christ, you're so bloody in heat for him. Do you even care what he does to you?"

"I'm fine," she assured. "He didn't hurt—"

"You all but accused me of treating you like a whore earlier. Hammer's the one who treats you that way. There's barely an inch of you he hasn't branded. Next you'll be telling me you liked it."

"I did."

Those two words went off like a bomb inside him. She loved Hammer so much that she'd gladly wear the symbols of his touch. Liam shook his head. He'd treated Raine so gently—like a fucking princess—and he'd held back for so long because she looked delicate. Her feelings were even more fragile. He'd been afraid to hurt her.

What an idiot he'd been.

"I won't lie." She'd dropped her chin and said it so quietly he almost didn't hear it. "I needed it."

From Hammer. Just not from him. "And you got it."

"I needed what he gave me, Liam. And he needed to give it to me." She raised her head to meet his stare. "I'll take him in any way he chooses—soft, sweet, hard, passionate, rough, dirty—because he touches my soul."

"Well, then you should go." He gestured her out the door. "Hammer is more than capable of seeing to your every craving and desire."

"You do the same for me. I'd be proud to wear your marks, too, Liam."

He couldn't bear her mollifying words as he looked at her sadly. "I've already given you my whole heart, Raine. It's obviously not enough."

"Not enough?" she asked in teary incredulity. "Liam, you're everything to me. I love you with every beat of my heart. I need you more than my next breath."

The impact of each word reverberated like a blast through him. God, he needed her, too.

"And you know how hard that is for me to say," she sobbed.

Liam did. He held back his own tears.

Even when he felt abandoned and betrayed, he feared crushing her heart. He loved her more than he'd ever loved Gwyneth or anyone else. Raine might be the submissive in their relationship, but she wielded so much power. She could annihilate him.

Instead, she smiled tremulously at him. "I love Hammer. I admit it. But I love you, too, Liam—every bit as much."

He wanted to believe that and didn't know if he could. And he was too fucking overwrought to deal with it now. "It doesn't feel that way, Raine."

"Then let me prove it," she insisted. "Don't tell me no because I'll fight for you, the way you fought for me."

"Christ… Stop."

"Punish me if you want to. I'll take whatever you mete out. But I need you to understand one thing." She took his face in her hands and melded their gazes. "Any time either you or Hammer wants me, together or alone, I'll submit to my Masters because I belong to you both. You're the two halves of my heart."

He struggled to put distance between them, get away from that insistent stare delving into him, seeing all his bleeding insecurities. Even as he stumbled toward the shower, Liam felt the gut-deep need for Raine to wrap her arms around him and love him the way she did Hammer.

Raine followed him. "Tell me what you need, Liam."

"I'm fine." Would she ever give him the same open body, heart, and soul she gave his friend? If he let her in again, could she?

"You're not, and I won't leave you when you're half starved, exhausted, and hurting. You never left me to drown in my own worries, even when you felt as if I'd betrayed you, even when I wasn't giving my submission to you. Even when you uncollared me, you tried your damnedest to stay by my side. I won't do less for you. You want to know what you give me? Why I love you? Because you listened, you understood, and you loved me no matter what. I've never had that once in my life. No one has ever just held me and accepted me as I am. I've learned about love from you. I may not have been good at showing you, but you've taught me more about the kind of person I want to be. I'm not leaving. And I'm not letting you go."

Her words touched him in places he didn't want her to reach right now. His first instinct was to grab her and clutch her like a lifeline, take comfort in her nearness. But she stood before him bruised and tear-stained and defiant. He didn't bloody know what to do. He didn't even know what to think. A few weeks ago, at the first sign of his rejection, the girl would have run away. Now, she was a woman, standing her ground, refusing to give up on him. That had to mean she felt *something*.

"Raine…"

"Do you want to keep arguing or let me help you undress and get showered? I'll do whatever pleases you, Sir."

Against his will, her concern for him burrowed under his skin. There was the lass he'd first fallen head over heels in love with.

"I've been taking care of myself for years, Raine. I can still manage."

"Of course you can. But you don't have to," she replied softly. "I'm not here merely to see to Hammer's needs. You have them, too. Do you have any other objections before I take care of you?"

He didn't have the energy to keep arguing. And in truth, he didn't want to. "Fine. Run me a bath, sub. While I'm soaking, I'd like a grilled cheese sandwich and a glass of cold stout."

She gave him a radiant smile. "I'll be happy to do that, Sir. While I'm gone, think about what else you need and how else I can serve you."

Her words bowled him over. Never had he expected the spitfire to give him this sort of total submissive devotion, especially after all he'd blurted in a fit of furious jealousy. Now, Liam couldn't find a word. He might have given her a house, but Raine had just handed him her soul. And he knew damn well she didn't give an iota of herself easily. Nothing could have told him more eloquently that she understood him, trusted him…loved him.

Remorse burned through his veins. Still, she stood before him, radiating her willingness to give him anything, everything. His Dominant side thrilled with a million possibilities. If he weren't so tired, he'd savor every damn one. Right now, he simply wanted to touch her.

"Raine…" He cupped her face, his thumb caressing across her cheek. "Love."

She closed her eyes and nuzzled into his palm. The visible relief on her face amazed and humbled him.

What the hell had he done to deserve her?

When he dropped his hand, Raine sent him a shaky smile, then stepped to the soaking tub and started the taps. As she waited for the water to turn warm, she approached him on soft footfalls. Her silky pink robe caressed her unbound breasts, belted at her tiny waist, brushed her thighs. Lace framed her lapels and wide cuffs. Soft, feminine…so like the woman herself. Despite being wrung out in every way, he ached to sink deep inside her again.

Never taking her stare from his, Raine stopped before him and fingered the top button of his shirt. "Can I undress you, Sir?"

Liam swallowed. "You may."

She smoothed her palms across his chest, all the way to his shoulders, before working his buttons. One by one, she freed them from their moorings, not so slowly that he'd call her actions seductive…but not so clinically that he'd call them sterile, either.

The gravity in her stare pulled him in deeper to her as she released the second button, the third… Then he lost count, reveling in Raine's attention.

As she pulled the last one free, she fanned her palms up his bare chest, pushing the shirt off his shoulders. He shrugged out of it, letting it fall to the floor. Liam felt his breathing accelerate, his heart start to thump.

Raine turned away long enough to check the temperature of the water and set the stopper down in the tub. She rummaged around in the cabinet and found some vanilla bath beads and some sort of oil. After pouring both into the filling water, she stashed them away again and turned her entire focus on him once more.

Liam felt it in her stare as she approached him again, then dropped to her knees. The thump of his heart became a drumbeat of a thud—hard, fast, insistent. She bowed her head, and he couldn't resist running his fingers through the silky hair at her crown as she worked at his laces and pulled his shoes free. His socks followed.

Then she reached for his zipper.

Fifteen minutes ago, he would have thought he'd be too exhausted for this. But she'd barely touched him, and he was hard as a post. *Bloody hell.*

Raine dragged the little tab down. Liam held his breath as the teeth hissed in the silence, looking at her as she stared up at him, her eyes big blue pools of surrender.

His chest expanded as he dragged in a rough breath and curled his hands into fists as she eased his pants down his legs, past his feet, leaving him bare. Neatly, she folded every garment and set them on the counter behind her, then rocked back on her heels to give him another submissive glance.

"Let me double-check your bath water so I can see if it needs adjusting," she murmured.

He didn't really want her to leave his side. In fact, he was ready to ditch the bloody bath and give her all his attention. But her expression told him that she not only wanted to give to him now, she needed it. God knew he wanted to be on the receiving end.

He dropped his palm to her crown again and caressed her. "Go ahead."

Raine gave him a little smile before she rose to stick her hand in the bath. After taking more than a few showers together, she knew what temperature he preferred. The fact that she cared for his pleasure, down to this level of detail, warmed him.

She fussed with the taps, increasing the heat from the faucet. Liam watched her bent and diligent in assuring his comfort. Why did that turn him on so damn much? He'd never noticed whether Juliet had cooked or bustled after him. Gwyneth hadn't possessed a caretaking bone in her body, and he'd never missed it a whit. But for as long as he'd known Raine, the sight of her doing anything domestic for him had lit some flame inside him.

Maybe because she'd always shown her feelings for Hammer by taking care of him and he wanted the same for himself. Maybe because, despite what he'd told himself in the beginning, he'd always wanted Raine forever.

That realization set Liam back on his heels.

She turned to him. "I think it's ready. I'll make your sandwich."

As Raine walked past him to swish out of the room, he grabbed her by the wrist and pulled her against him. His hard cock bobbed between them, brushing against her silken robe as he took her by the waist and thrust another hand in her hair, then captured her lips with his own.

She yielded to him instantly, bracing herself by clinging to his shoulders and tilting her head to accommodate his stroke inside her mouth. He tugged on the robe and pulled at her hair as he ate at her, starving for her taste. He bit at her lower lip, then seized her, gorging on the sweet, giving flavor of her kiss again.

Raine moaned, trembled in his arms, and opened herself to him. He could almost feel her working to keep her walls down. Liam couldn't remember a time she'd ever put so much effort or heart into her submission.

Panting, he broke away and stared down into her face, her flushed cheeks and swollen lips. Besides being so beautiful she blinded him, she lay so open to him in every way. It stilled his heart. With every move and touch, she stoked the Dominant need inside him.

The past twenty-four hours had been one blindsiding shock after another. This had to be the most amazing of all.

She didn't move or say a word, just blinked up at him as if awaiting his every command.

Damn near moved to silence, he cleared his throat. "I'd like that beer now. And the sandwich."

Raine nodded. "I'll be right back. If you'd like to start soaking, I'll be in to help you soon."

Help him? Liam wasn't sure what that entailed, but it sounded bloody nice. He could think of a thing or two he needed help with… As he glanced down at his engorged cock, he thought it might be a great idea to start there.

Shaking his head, he stepped into the deep tub with a sigh.

Perfect. Raine knew him well, and he took comfort in that.

He sank back, eyes closed, and let his spine melt against the back of the tub. He wasn't sure whether he'd had his eyes closed for two minutes or ten when he heard the water cut off.

Raine bustled over to him with a steaming sandwich oozing cheese and well toasted, just the way he liked it. In the other hand, she carried a frosty mug of black beer.

With a smile, she set both on the wide ledge of the tub. "Anything else?"

"Stay with me."

Maybe it wasn't a fair request at nearly three in the morning, but Liam didn't want her to leave, couldn't fathom spending the rest of the night without her.

"Of course." She didn't hesitate. "Can I wash your hair?"

He all but sighed with bliss. "I'd like that."

"Then I'd like to do it for you."

As he took a bite of the gooey sandwich with a hint of crusty sourdough and chased it with a gulp of the stout, he watched her flit to the cabinet to find his favorite shampoo, then disappear. He'd scarfed most of the sandwich and downed the beer by the time she returned with a big plastic cup and knelt by him at the side of the tub again.

Without a word, she turned on the tap once more and filled the cup with water. Liam watched her as she rose and protected his eyes with her hand, tilted his head back, and sluiced warm water through his hair. He groaned at the slice of heaven.

Raine lathered his hair, massaging his scalp, lingering at his temples, easing the knots at the base of his neck. Everything she did somehow soothed and invigorated him at once. He'd been wiped out when he'd arrived at Shadows, but the longer she touched him, the less he had any interest in sleep.

After long minutes of her luxurious care, she rinsed the suds from his hair, then swept the empty plate and glass onto the counter. She stood on her tiptoes, reaching into the cupboard above the toilet for a fresh towel. He smiled. Such a wee thing, and so willing to please.

When Raine turned back to him, she held the towel open, inviting him to walk inside. "If you're ready…"

Beyond ready. Liam jumped to his feet, displacing the water in the tub with a mighty *whoosh*. He stepped out and into her open arms, every part of him softening to her touch except one. She patted the water off his shoulders, chest, and back before he ducked to let her soak up the excess moisture from his hair. Circling around him, she dried off his back, his buttocks, his legs, even dabbing at his feet before she crawled around to the front and dragged the towel down his abdomen, up his calves and thighs, circling his impatient cock.

The moment she dragged the terrycloth over his raging staff, he moaned. Jesus, the woman pushed every one of his buttons. He wanted the chance to push hers.

Raine set the towel aside, then prowled in the cabinet again. Her little robe whispered up the back of her thighs, barely covering that lush ass.

"Almond or honeysuckle lotion?" she asked over her shoulder.

"Fuck the lotion, lass. I want you in my bed."

She flushed a sweet, rosy pink. "Any way you want me."

Liam grabbed her by the hand. He couldn't lead her out of the bathroom fast enough. Even that seemed too slow, so he turned and lifted her against his chest, fusing their lips together. Automatically, her legs wrapped around his waist as she opened to his hungry onslaught. God, she was such a tiny thing against him but so full of passion.

He begrudged the dozen steps it took to reach the bed before he set her on her feet and sprawled across the mattress. He propped his head up on one hand and stroked his cock with the other.

He heard her breath hitch and smiled. "Raine?"

At the side of the bed, she sank to her knees and bowed her head. "Yes, Sir."

There she went, pushing his buttons again. She'd never bowed for him voluntarily, and here she was, offering him all of her so beautifully. He watched her, roughing his hand up his cock a bit faster, trying to assimilate all his thoughts and yearnings into a coherent sentence. *Bloody hell…*

"You say you love me?"

She lifted her head long enough to meet his stare…and sneak a glance at him palming his cock. Then she jerked her head down again. "I do."

His breathing picked up, and his heart beat so fast already Liam wondered if it would rattle out of his chest. "Show me. Make love to me. Tell me how you feel with your body."

Chapter Sixteen

Light spilled from the bathroom, illuminating Raine as she rose. She trembled and bit her lip, looking vulnerable as she stared at him stretched out before her. The little furrow appeared between her brows. He'd given her a command that wasn't easy, and anticipation tightened Liam's chest as he waited to see what she would do.

She slipped onto the bed next to him, and he released his cock. He couldn't do anything to it that she couldn't—and make him feel much better. But Raine didn't start there; she merely braced herself on his chest and gazed into his eyes.

"I'll do my best," she murmured. "Because I love you."

Liam absorbed her vow as she dropped a kiss to his chest, his jaw, one cheek, then the other. A fleeting press of her lips in each spot had him closing his eyes… He barely had time to process how moving he found every touch before she gave him another brush of a kiss elsewhere.

Raine climbed farther up his body until her face hovered over his. Dark obscured her expression. Liam hated that he couldn't see what lay in her eyes.

"Turn on the lamp," he insisted.

She didn't hesitate before she did as he bid. Soft light poured from the fixture on the nightstand, spilling over the bed.

"Better?" she asked.

He nodded. "Come back where you were."

When he held out his arm to her, she settled into the crook instantly. Now he could see all the curves and delicate lines of her face. Her expression held nothing back. Raine wasn't sure how to give him what he'd asked for, but that stubborn chin and her determined mien told him that she'd give her all trying.

That effort alone warmed him. She wanted to please him. Hell, she already was. But he let her continue because he needed to feel her love in the most tangible, visceral way.

Raine eased closer, her warm breath spilling onto his lips. "Because I love you."

He'd barely comprehended her whisper before she layered her mouth over his. Liam tasted her solemn vow as he parted her lips and climbed in deeper. Yes, he'd asked her to give to him, but he found himself impatient for more—for all of her. Thankfully, she didn't seem to mind, just complied with his wordless demand, stroking his tongue with her own and cradling his face in her small palm.

Liam couldn't keep his hands to himself. His fingers found their way into her hair, tugging slightly to change the angle of their kiss. The other curled between them to yank at the belt of her robe until it slithered apart.

As he reached under the silky garment and skated a palm down her hip, she pulled back with a little grin. "Because I love you."

Then Raine eased down his body, lying half atop him, and bent her head to take one of his nipples in her mouth, flicking it with her tongue and teasing him. A jolt of desire buckled him. He'd never thought of the nubs as particularly sensitive, but he'd been damn wrong. The minx had proven him wrong.

She eased one thigh between his, and he felt her knee barely graze his balls. The heat of her naked pussy blasted his hip. She pressed her soft breasts to his side and wriggled her damp folds against him with a little moan. A blaze of need flared inside him, and Liam grabbed handfuls of her silk robe, trying not to tear it off her body and mount her. Letting her love him in her way was sorely testing his control.

With a hiss, he cupped her nape and pressed her head into his chest. She took him deeper, laving his sensitive flesh. Liam groaned hoarsely. He'd already been hard. Now, Raine made him ache for her touch and the sharp, divine release only she could give him.

In his arms, she squirmed until he eased up on his hold and kissed her way to his other distended nipple. As she worked it into her mouth, another jolt of sensation zapped him. Desire pooled low in his belly, revved his blood. God, the woman drove him mad.

With another lap of her tongue, she pulled away. He wanted to protest. The Dom inside him ached to take over and command all her satin flesh for his pleasure. But he needed to know how else she intended to make love to him.

Raine gave him a shy smile, then dropped her gaze to his chest and started feathering her lips down his sternum, down his abdomen, down even lower…

She nipped and licked at the skin around his navel, avoiding his cock throbbing for her attention. Every muscle in his body went taut as she teased the skin of his stomach, dipped her tongue into his belly button, then breathed over the sensitive head.

Dear fucking hell, how long did she expect him to lie back and do nothing? Was she proving her love or simply tormenting him? It felt like a fine line. He began to sweat.

Propping herself up on her hands and knees, Raine shimmied down his body. He caught a mere glimpse of the bite marks on her breasts, saw a few on her neck. They'd infuriated Liam when he'd been convinced she'd never love him the way she loved Hammer. But now that she'd invited him to leave his own, Liam found himself staking out her skin, seeing where he could brand her as his, too.

Then she chased all thought from his head as she caressed one of his thighs and dipped her head to drag her teeth over the other. She sucked at him, giving him a little love mark. Then another farther up. Another inward. And another just under his balls.

Unable to stop himself, Liam tangled his fingers in her hair.

"The amount of teasing I'll take has its limits, love. Remember the expression about paybacks."

She tipped her chin up, resting it on his belly. If she turned her mouth, it would be right on his cock. *Damn it, woman...*

Instead, she simply grinned. "I'll keep that in mind, Sir."

Suddenly, the door opened. A shadow darkened the portal. Liam would have recognized the shape anywhere.

Hammer dragged a chair into the room, at the side of the bed, and stared at Raine on top of him, putting her little mouth all over him. "Work your magic, precious. Bring him back to us."

Liam couldn't miss the approval on Hammer's face. His acceptance and Raine's openness touched him. After the meltdown earlier, instead of rubbing his nose in his mistake, they'd simply cared enough to understand, forgive him, and love him back.

Emotion lumped in his throat, clogging him. He loved them both. The two most important people in his world.

Liam sent Hammer a grateful nod, then the man plopped into his chair with a wink.

"I asked Hammer to join us because you're a part of us," Raine murmured. "There's nothing of mine that belongs exclusively to him, especially my heart."

"I can feel that in your touch," he managed to choke out.

"Good. Take whatever you need from me, Liam." She wore every emotion in her big, blue eyes. "Because I love you."

A few days ago, she hadn't yet told him what was in her heart. Now she couldn't seem to say it enough, and that moved him more than he had words to express.

And then he didn't think anything because she took his cock in hand. Her eyes fluttered shut as she closed her lips around him with a moan. Her tongue swirled. Liam felt her devotion as she worshipped him with her mouth.

All the blood left his head, rushing south, right to the center of the pleasure she heaped on him. Her head bobbed as she laved him up and down, sucking him deeper with every pull, then stroking his crest with the flat of her tongue, only to ease back and work the little spot just beneath before starting the cycle all over again. Liam gritted his teeth and shoved his hands into her hair once more, so fucking ready to throw her onto her back.

"Raine…" he growled out, desperate to urge her faster.

She answered him by scraping his sensitive head with her teeth ever so gently, cupping his balls…and pulling away.

"Am I proving my love to you?" she asked in a husky voice.

He fisted her hair and dragged in deep breaths. "You're proving how well you can test my restraint."

"I might be. But it's only because I love you. I don't want you to ever doubt it again."

It was all he could do to hold in a groan. "Our wee lass has turned into a tease, Hammer."

His best mate laughed. "She's teasing the fuck out of me. I can only imagine how you're feeling. Good luck with that, man."

"I'd have better luck if she lost the robe."

"I'd be more than happy to." Raine pulled it off her shoulders in a slow caress, then tossed it to the floor.

Liam groaned. Hammer did the same. Then Liam heard the hiss of a zipper and saw Hammer freeing his own cock to stroke its length. Then Raine eased one of her thighs over his body, straddling him, and leaned forward until the tip of his cock nudged her opening. He stopped thinking. God, he'd give anything to take her bareback.

But she leaned forward and braced her hands on his shoulders, bending until her plump breasts swayed in his face. Liam's mouth watered. He loved her nipples something fierce—big and hard and sweet.

He captured one between his lips and gave it a mighty suck. Raine gasped and threw her head back. Liam watched her arousal climb, transfixed. Her lips and cheeks turned rosy. She softened everywhere. He couldn't wait to be inside her.

But Hammer's telltale bite mark taunted him, a red beacon mere inches from his mouth. He found himself nipping at the flesh just beside it.

"Yes," she panted. "Yes. Please let me feel your teeth, Sir."

Everything inside him jerked to plant his mark on her. He gripped her arms as his mouth hovered just over the pristine spot he wanted to call his own, the territory he wanted to look at tomorrow and know with pride that she wore a part of him.

"Aren't you sore, love? I don't want to hurt you."

"You'll hurt me far more if you don't. *Please…*"

Fuck, how was he to say no to that? And why would he bother?

Liam sank his teeth into the firm flesh of her breast, right beside Hammer's brand. He sucked hard, bit deep—and felt need grip him mercilessly by the balls. Raine whimpered and dug her fingernails into his scalp. Her whole chest moved as she breathed with him, his teeth still steeped into her skin.

He fucking didn't want to let her go, but he pulled back to ensure that he wasn't hurting her. The rapture on her face made his restraint vanish.

Raine *did* want his marks, didn't only want Hammer's. Liam couldn't wait to give her more.

"Scoot forward and lean closer," he demanded.

She did it without question. Liam gripped her hips and bit at the underside of her breast, nipped at her ribs, dragged his tongue up her belly. Then he caught sight of the impression of Hammer's teeth on her pussy. Instead of feeling jealous that another man had left his brand on their girl, Liam imagined how erotic it must have been the moment Hammer felt her most tender flesh giving way to his unyielding need.

Liam wanted that for himself and almost thanked Hammer for the excellent notion.

"Closer," he barked at Raine. "Give me your pussy."

She rushed to comply. "Thank you, Sir."

Her heartfelt reply and total appreciation for even the idea of his teeth on her tender pussy ratcheted up his ache even more. He couldn't get his mouth on her fast enough.

Stroking her clit with his tongue for a long moment and hearing Raine catch her breath sent a heady rush through Liam's bloodstream. She was a goddamn drug, and he'd become a fucking addict. He didn't care. The moment her flavor hit his tongue, something in him snapped. The most primal part of his nature roared.

Easing back, he let his bottom teeth barely graze her clit. He kept her hanging there, balancing on a knife's edge. Her thighs tensed. Wetness gushed. Her pleading moans rang in his ears.

"I need this," she whimpered. "I need you. Liam…"

He planted his teeth in the fleshy pad above her clit and bit down ruthlessly. She screamed. Her body jerked as if he'd hooked her up to a live wire. For a moment, he worried that he'd hurt her. Then she reached for her nipples and pinched them hard, tugging, twisting, squeezing.

The sight had him sucking at her mound, then testing the fleshy pad with his bite once more.

"Yes. Yes!" she cried. "I want to see you there tomorrow. Because I love you."

"I love you, too, Raine. I need to be inside you." He sounded gruff, impatient.

She didn't care at all. She slid down his torso. Liam caught sight of the fresh marks in an angry red directly above the most vulnerable place on her body.

That damn near made him berserk.

He clutched her hips, anticipating that moment he could thrust deep and lose himself inside her. All he needed was a bloody condom and…

But Raine kept inching down, then arched back, unerringly setting her swollen cunt against his naked cock. He dug his fingers in deeper, resisting the urge to sink in and damn the consequences.

In the back of his head, Liam knew that was the most animal part of him wanting to mark her in the most human way by filling her belly with his seed. She'd let Hammer do it once, but this wasn't a pissing match. Raine hadn't given him free reign over her body like that. Frankly, he'd expect Hammer would have something to say about it, as well.

Last month when she'd worried Hammer had gotten her pregnant, Liam had been willing to raise that child as his own. But the notion of swelling her belly with *his* baby… He gritted his teeth, wanting nothing more. It surprised him that so soon after Gwyneth had scared the hell out of him with a "son," he'd be so eager to truly conceive a child. Not just any child—one with Raine. That made everything different.

Someday…

"Let me get a condom, love." He reached for the drawer of the nightstand.

"I don't need one. I'm willing to give everything to you. Because I love you."

Then Raine pushed her hips back, and his cock sank past her wet opening, deep into her core without any protection at all. The friction blazed through him, almost as hot as the reality of the trust she was giving him and the depths of her love.

"Jesus, Raine!"

As she took him to the hilt, she mewled. "If you don't want this, tell me now."

Her voice quivered. Her pussy rippled. She was already close. Damn it to hell, so was he.

"I want you this way," he confessed. "More than anything. I love you so much. Aren't you in the middle of your cycle, love?"

"Pretty much," she whispered.

And she still wanted to be with him this way.

Hell, Liam wasn't going to last, not feeling heaven all around him, not seeing his marks on her, too. Not knowing that with this climax, they could cement their futures together in more ways than one.

But he had one problem…

"Hammer." He tried to catch his breath. "Mate, I won't take her bare if you're not ready for this."

"Oh, don't let me fucking stop you from the best sensation ever." Macen's voice had become a rough growl. No doubt, he was close, too.

That was all Liam needed.

"Give me your body and your love," he demanded of Raine. "Ride me hard."

She keened out her answer, then dipped her hips and thrust him deeper, taking him from hilt to head and back again with every sway of her hips. Liam clenched his jaw and dug deep for restraint.

A half dozen strokes in, her cunt all but strangled him. She dug her nails deep into his shoulders. "Sir, may I come?"

"No," he snarled. "You wait for me, love. We're going to feel this together."

Her aching cry filled his ears. Hammer's rough breathing followed. Liam heard his own low growl.

He slid his thumb over Raine's clit. Hard, poised, ready. Damn it, he wanted this to last, but every drag of her walls over his bare cock drove him dangerously close to the brink.

From beneath, he tried to thrust up as he yanked her hips down onto him. In the back of his head, Liam realized he was fucking her without finesse. She'd be even more bruised tomorrow. He'd see those discolorations, be reminded of this heady, life-changing pleasure and…

What had infuriated him an hour ago now set off his desire as if someone had lit the fuse on the bomb inside him.

Liam flipped Raine to her back and shoved his way back inside her in one unrelenting thrust. She looked up at him as if she was lost and only he could save her. Orgasm was seconds away. He felt his spine tingling, his balls drawing up, his breathing change, the ache sharpening.

"Last chance," he managed to say. "I can pull out."

Raine shook her head. "Because I love you."

Those words flipped the switch on Liam's self-control.

"Come!" he shouted, driving into her ferociously, shuttling in and out of her body at a dizzying pace.

Almost instantly, Raine seized up and wailed, her entire body clenching down to suck him in deeper.

"Fuck…" Hammer groaned harsh and low.

Liam felt everything inside him give way as his cock jerked, ecstasy shot through his system, and he spilled every bit of himself inside her. Spasm after spasm of pleasure rocketed through his body, giving him the fuel to pump her until he felt spent and dry—and so desperately fucking in love, he knew it would never end.

* * *

After a luxurious bath, Raine lay flat on her back, happily cuddled between Liam and Hammer. Both had rolled to their sides and propped their heads on their palms. She resisted the urge to pinch herself. With everything terrible that had happened today, it spoke volumes about their commitment to one another that they'd all ended up in the same bed, sharing a soft conversation, wearing matching looks of contentment.

Liam added an extra dose to her happiness when he related everything that had happened with his ex-wife at the hospital while they'd waited to learn about Kyle's illness.

"You mean, after all Gwyneth's bullshit about that kid being your 'love child,' he's not only *not* yours but he's not even hers?" Hammer looked ready to throttle the woman.

Liam gave his friend a tired smile. "Exactly. I guess she thought I'd marry her just because she wanted me to or out of the goodness of my heart. Who knows? She wanted something so she expected the universe to fall in line. I'm glad it's all behind me. Now that the truth is out in the open, she'll return Kyle to her sister, take herself back to London, and…I don't expect to hear from her again."

While Raine couldn't be happier that Gwyneth had come clean, one thing bothered her. "And what made her decide to suddenly tell the truth?"

Liam paused. Exhaustion lidded his dark eyes and pulled at his firm mouth. "She was rattled enough by Kyle's illness that she couldn't be bothered to keep up the façade any longer." He leaned in and brushed his lips over hers. "You don't look convinced, my suspicious wench."

Raine didn't want to be suspicious, but something sounded off. "So she was just going to give up? She hijacked a baby, falsified birth records, came up with a whopper of a lie, and…" She shook her head. "I don't see her quitting. It's a huge fortune."

"Well, the DNA test is due back in a few hours, anyway, and the jig would be up. She knew that."

Granted, Raine had only met Gwyneth once, but that didn't sound like her at all.

Hammer palmed her abdomen with a frown. "I hear what you're saying, but what else could she do to Liam?"

"I don't know, but some people would do a lot more crap for a lot less money."

"True," Hammer agreed. "But in this case, I think Gwyneth is played out. She doesn't have any other moves."

Maybe not obvious ones, no. But the woman's whole plan had been pretty unexpected and unbalanced. Raine wouldn't be surprised if Liam's ex had something else up her sleeve. Then again, childhood with Bill Kendall had made Raine naturally wary.

"I don't think I can stay awake anymore, love." Liam lay

back and closed his eyes.

Most of this day had been truly awful for him. Like, the worst day ever. She understood why he'd reached the end of his energy and wanted it over.

She leaned in and brushed a kiss on his lips. "I love you. I can't wait to move into our new house together. Thank you."

"Love you…" he muttered.

In the next breath, he began to snore.

She smiled fondly, then turned to glance Hammer's way. "He's wiped out."

Macen frowned and rubbed at his eyes with his thumb and forefinger. "I'm afraid I'm not far behind him. Hell of a day."

"Yeah," she sighed. "Let's not wake up later and have this much drama."

"You got it, precious." He curled an arm around her. Then from one breath to the next, he dropped into a deep slumber, too.

And despite the fact that the December temperatures had dropped tonight, sandwiched between Liam and Hammer, she might as well have been curled up in a furnace. And the three of them definitely needed something bigger than a queen bed.

It was her last thought before she succumbed to fatigue, as well.

She woke with a start to some god-awful chainsaw-like noise. Heart racing, she sat up in the dark room, wondering what that sound was. Then she realized it wasn't a power tool at all but Liam and Hammer grinding out dueling soundtracks of some of the loudest snoring she'd ever heard. A glance at the bedside clock told her she'd barely been asleep for an hour.

Sighing, she tried to lie back and catch more shut-eye. Liam rolled to his side and tried to take his third of the bed out of the middle. With his mouth near her ear, it only increased the decibel level of his snoring. Hammer decided to fight someone in his sleep, and Raine ended up with knees and elbows in her back. As they closed in on her, her body temperature went from toasty to roasting.

There'd be no peace in this bed tonight—or what was left of it.

Shaking her head, she crawled out from between them and pulled on the robe she'd discarded while making love to Liam earlier. He was naked next to Hammer, who wore only his boxer briefs. They looked cute in bed together. What a shame she didn't have her phone to snap a picture. If she did, though, they'd paddle her ass silly.

Raine pulled the sheet over the two of them. She could find her own bed, she supposed, but she found herself incredibly exhilarated by the promise of their future. The house, the love, the way they'd worked through more of their issues… She didn't want to sleep now; she wanted to live.

They wouldn't be up for hours yet, but she could make their coming morning much better than the one they'd just had. Hammer had his apple spice muffins, but she intended to make date scones for Liam.

Grabbing her laptop, she rushed to the kitchen while searching for a recipe. Orange and date scones, no. Maple and date, no. Bacon and date scones? Oh, just hell no. Finally, she found a recipe that sounded edible. If he didn't like this version, she'd try another next time until she got the pastry right.

She bustled around the kitchen and grabbed her ingredients. Self-rising flour, baking powder, salt, sugar, butter, eggs, milk—check. Dates…no. She glanced at the time on her computer and debated. Go to the store now or wait until sunrise? Raine sighed. She was awake and wanted to get these baked, try one herself before she unleashed them on Liam, just in case they sucked and she had to start over.

With a little curse, she tiptoed back to Liam's room, tossed on some yoga pants, a T-shirt, and some flip-flops. She searched the club until she found her purse, phone, and car keys. It had become an old habit of hers to inform Hammer before she left, but he looked so peaceful sleeping. She'd run out to the twenty-four-hour market just around the corner and be back in less than half an hour. They'd never miss her.

Pushing her way out the club door, she heard it click shut behind her. The parking lot was fairly well lit and mostly empty. Of course, her little compact sat there, along with Liam's Escalade. Hammer kept his Audi in the garage out back. Some of the other cars she didn't recognize, except Beck's Mercedes. When had he arrived?

With a shrug, she glanced past what looked like Seth's rental and a van she'd never seen, then strode to her four-door. She'd just pressed the button on the fob to unlock it and opened the door when someone behind her growled, put a brutal hand over her mouth, then shoved something hard against her ribs.

Chapter Seventeen

Hammer rolled over in bed, not fully awake, but floating in and out of sleep. As he breathed in, the scents of Raine, sex, and something unfamiliar filled his senses. Slitting open one eye, he saw that he wasn't in his own room but Liam's.

Hammer remembered exactly why. Raine had climbed on top of his friend and ridden Liam like a goddess until it seemed Liam's hurt and insecurity had melted away. Watching and listening to their erotic melding, Hammer had stroked his own cock and joined their shared orgasm by coming all over his stomach in a hot, spine-tingling rush.

Rolling to his side now, he slung his arm around Raine and snuggled close. But when he tried to palm her breast, he caressed an expanse of flat, hairy chest instead. Jolting awake, Hammer jerked up. Christ, he'd been snuggling Liam.

His cock instantly deflated. Good thing he hadn't tried to tap that.

He shook his head. What a wake-up that would have been.

Glancing around the shadowy room, Hammer searched for Raine but didn't see her. He peered toward the bathroom. The light was off. The door stood wide open. Where the hell had she gone at just after five a.m.?

Grumbling, Hammer inched off the bed and grabbed his

pants. As he meandered out of the room, he zipped up and left Liam stretched out on the bed, snoring like a lumberjack.

As Hammer made his way down the hall, light spilled from the kitchen. He frowned. Raine never ate this early. Hell, she was rarely even awake. Was she baking because something had upset her? He couldn't imagine what. A few hours ago, she'd showered Liam with love and exorcised the jealous demon inside him. Raine should be basking in her achievement, not burying her sorrows in dough. Things were good between the three of them now. At least Hammer thought so.

Yeah, and you thought Juliet was on the same page as you for years. You learned the hard way never to assume anything.

If something was bothering Raine, Macen swore he'd press her until he got to the bottom of her distress and fix it.

Rounding the doorway, he found the kitchen empty, other than counters cluttered with bowls, measuring cups, and various baking ingredients all surrounding her laptop. Hammer fingered the track pad until her screen illuminated. A recipe for date scones?

He scrubbed a hand through his hair. Had she ever made anything with dates? Not that Hammer could remember, and especially not at the ass crack of dawn. Darting a gaze over the ingredients on the counter, he scowled. It looked as if everything lay out, waiting for Raine's baking magic…but she'd simply walked away.

Hammer felt the hairs on the back of his neck prickle. Surely she wouldn't have run away again. Would she?

With a sick feeling in the pit of his stomach, Hammer turned and sprinted down the hall. As he burst into Raine's room, he flipped on the light and flung open her closet door. Her clothes hung in a row, just as she'd left them. He knew she hadn't taken any of her things from Liam's closet; he would have heard that. A wave of blessed relief washed through him.

But as Hammer turned off the light, he couldn't shake the uneasy feeling seeping through his bones.

"Damn it, where are you, Raine?" he whispered.

The state of the kitchen stuck in his head. She never left it cluttered or untidy, much less abandoned a recipe like that. He strode back to the mess, then compared the recipe to the items on the counter.

“She didn’t have any dates.” He scowled and stormed toward the back door, his keys jingling in his pocket with every step. If Raine had gone to the grocery store in the damn dark without telling him or Liam… Hammer shook his head. He’d redden her ass another shade darker.

Shoving the heavy metal door open, he stepped out into the cool night air. Raine’s car sat beneath a floodlight. But the driver’s side door stood wide open. Her purse littering the ground blasted Hammer with ice-cold fear.

Sprinting to her car, he found her personal items spilled haphazardly across the pavement. Her keys gleamed in the driver’s seat, and her cell phone lay upside down on the floorboard. His heart thundered in his chest.

Raine would never leave her things here voluntarily. Hammer looked around for anything that might tell him what had happened. What could have transpired in Shadows’ small parking lot? A mugger? A rapist?

Bill?

Son of a bitch.

“Raine!” Hammer screamed, hoping she might be nearby and hear him, scream in return.

Nothing but silence.

Panic bled through his veins. “Oh, god. Raine! No, baby. No.”

Racing toward the club, Hammer yanked his keys from his pocket. At the door, he trembled as he tried to open the lock. Dread crawled up his spine and wrapped around his throat, choking the air in his lungs.

“If you have her, you cocksucking motherfucker, I’m going to kill you,” Hammer vowed as he yanked the door open. “Liam!” he bellowed, tearing down the hall. “Liam!”

The doors to Beck’s and Seth’s rooms banged opened simultaneously as both men stood blinking at Hammer. Roused from sleep, they looked startled and confused.

“What the hell are you yelling about?” Seth asked with a scowl.

“For fuck’s sake. Are you two idiots arguing again?” Beck shook his head in disgust. “Keep it down before Raine has both sets of your balls hanging from the kitchen window like wind chimes."

Hammer ignored their comments. "Liam!"

As he thundered down the hall, his friend emerged with his pants half zipped and looking disoriented. "What the bloody… What's wrong, Macen?"

"She's gone," Hammer choked out, trying to swallow the fear and anger lodged in his throat. "I'm worried Bill has her. Her car's in the lot. The driver's door is open, and her stuff spilled everywhere. She wouldn't have walked away and left her wallet, her phone, her…"

Macen's whole body trembled as he gripped Liam's shoulders, needing to ground himself with something solid.

"No. That can't be." The same horror Hammer felt filled Liam's voice and stare.

"I don't know how long she's been gone," Hammer barked, trying to contain his panic. "I woke up maybe five or ten minutes ago and found her missing."

"Oh, fuck. If it's Bill…" Beck growled, pinning Hammer with a knowing stare.

The doctor knew exactly what Bill Kendall was capable of since Hammer had called him the night Macen had discovered Raine in the alley. The two had slipped a sedative in her soda so Beck could examine her. Hammer had taken photos to document the horrific abuse she'd endured at the hands of her *loving* father. Liam had seen the pictures just last week. He'd also had the displeasure of meeting Bill, so he understood well the urgency to find Raine.

Swallowing tightly, Liam gripped Macen's arm. "The security room, mate. The cameras will tell us if that piece of shit has our girl."

As all four men raced down the hall, an ominous déjà vu crested through Hammer. He swallowed back the urge to vomit.

"What was Raine doing in the car park alone during the wee hours?" Liam asked.

"I think she intended to bake something." Hammer unlocked the door, flipped on the lights, and hurried inside the private room. "There's flour, sugar, and other shit all over the counters, but I think she needed an ingredient she didn't have." He scrubbed a hand over his face as he sat in front of a bank of wide monitors. "I can't believe she didn't wake one of us up to go with her."

Liam paled. "What was she baking?"

"Something she's never made. Date scones, I think," Hammer growled.

Why did Liam care? Bill could well have taken the woman they loved. Macen didn't want to focus too keenly on the brutalities she could be suffering at this very moment. He just wanted her back.

"God, no." Liam's voice cracked. "Oh, love… Not the scones."

"Why not?" Seth asked. His brows slashed as he stared at Liam, who looked more shaken than ever.

"She wanted to make them for me." Guilt and remorse roughened Liam's voice.

Struggling to keep his own emotions in check, Hammer rewound the security feed from the parking lot. "We never had the chance to tell her that Bill had been sniffing around. She went out to that lot, never imagining…"

God, now he wished he'd made the time.

Liam curled his hands into fists. "I thought we could protect her."

Hammer had, too. They'd been wrong.

When he found the right file and hit play, no one in the room said a word, just stared at the monitor. As Raine hurried from the back door, the time stamp showed four forty-six a.m. Hammer glanced at his watch. Quarter past five now. His gut clenched at the thought of all the terrible things that could befall her in nearly thirty tormenting minutes.

On the monitor, she made her way toward her car. A tall figure dressed in black and wearing a baseball cap stepped into view, sneaking up behind her. Hammer's stomach pitched as he watched the man grab her. Raine fought, throwing an elbow, stamping on his foot, struggling like a mad thing, using every trick she'd learned in the self-defense classes in which he'd enrolled her. When she turned on the man, still fighting, she tried to knee him in the groin, but he held her down. Raine attempted to shove the heel of her palm into his nose but only succeeded in flipping the hat off his head. Startled recognition had her jaw dropping, her eyes widening.

The face and glowing blue eyes Hammer had hoped never to see again filled the screen.

"I knew it," he roared, turning toward Liam. "That motherfucker has her."

Liam nodded grimly. "Wind it back."

Hammer jerked his attention to the screen once more. Without the hat to conceal Bill's expression, an evil sneer consumed his face. Chills froze Macen's every muscle, rolling through him in a debilitating wave.

Liam pressed the rewind button and homed in on Raine. She snapped her hand toward Bill's cap, knocking it to the ground. Hammer could clearly see the bastard's bulbous nose and the long white scar bisecting his cheek—a result of a wound Raine had given the son of a bitch over six years ago, when she'd last fought not to let her father take her innocence and her life.

The image played on, and Raine shot a frightened glance at the security camera mounted to the nearby lamppost.

"She knew we'd come here. Our brave little…" Liam's voice cracked.

Cold fury filled Hammer with an even colder purpose. He and Liam knew the enemy and had no doubt what Bill was capable of. He'd do whatever it took to rescue Raine. And if her father's head start was too big to overcome… Macen ground his jaw tight. He'd kill the fucker so slowly and painfully Bill would grovel for death.

"Your brave little sub clearly wanted the cameras to catch her assailant," Seth concluded as they watched Bill jam something that looked like a cell phone against Raine's ribs.

Hammer leaned forward, trying to decipher the mysterious object in Bill's fist. The man suddenly slapped his hand around Raine's arm, twisting it behind her back. Her mouth opened as if gasping in pain.

Rage thundered through Hammer as Bill yanked her tight against his round belly, drawing the hand with the black square up a few inches under Raine's ear. A stun gun. He could kill her with that. *Oh, dear god.*

Unable to look away, even knowing what would happen

next, Hammer gnashed his teeth as Bill pressed the probes against Raine's neck. Her body spasmed, then she fell limp into her father's arms. He carted her toward a dark van, jumped in, and rolled out of the lot.

"*No!*" Liam shouted, his face distorting in agony. "Oh, Raine."

Hammer lost it. Bolting out of the chair, a feral roar ripped from his throat before he slammed his fist on the metal desktop. Every cell inside him seemed to detonate like an atomic bomb. His body shook with uncontrollable rage.

"How do we find her?" Beck asked.

"We?" Hammer arched a brow.

"Yes," Beck insisted. "If she needs a doctor…"

"Bill Kendall is a dead man," Liam vowed.

"Fuck yes. He is. We end this now," Hammer agreed.

"Guys, we need to call the police," Seth interjected. "You've got video proof that Bill kidnapped her. If we zero in, we might even be able to get a plate number off that van."

Macen didn't want to involve the authorities yet. When the police found Bill, they'd merely arrest the prick and let him live through a trial, during which Raine would have to recount everything her father had ever done to her, as well as the violence he heaped on her now.

Liam had it right; Bill Kendall needed to die. Hammer wanted to end his miserable existence. The end more than justified the means if it meant they could bring Raine back home. But no way would he sit at the club with his thumb up his ass, answering a shitload of questions while the wheels of the justice system creaked along at a snail's pace.

"No," Hammer barked. "I know exactly where Bill is. He's sitting at home, waiting for me because he wants his paycheck and he's using Raine as bait. We're going to pay him a visit. You stay here on standby. We'll call you if we need to show the police the footage."

Understanding curled Seth's lips into an icy smile. "Got it. Get out of here. Just make sure you all wear gloves. Fighting fingerprint evidence in court isn't easy."

"I've got gloves in my medical bag," Beck assured. "I'll get it and be right back."

"I'm throwing on the rest of my clothes and grabbing my gun," Hammer announced as the three men darted out of the room, leaving Seth to wait for their call.

He dressed frantically. Liam and Beck must have done the same as they all met up within two minutes. Finally, with his pistol tucked into the small holster at his side, he raced with the other two for Hammer's car. Piling in, Macen turned to them. "We get Raine out. Whatever happens after that is self-defense. Got it?"

"Bloody fucking right, it is," Liam growled.

Beck nodded grimly. "Bill charged you when you attempted to call the police, Hammer. We both saw it."

With a nod, Hammer tore out of the lot. Urgency breathed down his back. He wanted to press the accelerator to the floor, but his mind warred with him. If he got pulled over for speeding, that would give Bill even more opportunity to—

No. Don't fucking go there. You already failed and buried one woman you loved. You'll never make it back again if Bill goes too far and you lose Raine, too.

Hovering just above the posted speed limits, Hammer cursed. He couldn't get the visual out of his head of Raine's limp body slumped against Bill or the demented look of triumph on the bastard's face as he hoisted her into his arms and hurried away. The cowering black-and-blue state in which he'd found the girl in his alley years ago also haunted Hammer. The images blended, flashing through his head in a never-ending loop.

Guilt stung him. Why had he cut off Bill's stipend? Hammer didn't need the fucking money. He'd inherited a trust fund he couldn't possibly spend in three lifetimes. By comparison, the paltry amount he'd doled out to Bill was mere pennies. But the peace of mind had been priceless.

Right now, Hammer would gladly give every cent for that peace of mind again. But Bill confessing last week that he'd indeed attempted to rape Raine as a teenager had sent him off the deep end. If Hammer hadn't cut off the stipend he'd paid to keep the animal at bay, she would be safe and sound and happily baking at Shadows.

He gripped the steering wheel tighter. "I should never have lost my temper and stopped paying him. This is my fault."

* * *

"Don't blame yourself, Macen," Liam insisted. "I'm at fault. If I hadn't been comparing the love she gave me, Raine wouldn't have left the club."

"Comparing? What the hell are you talking about?" Hammer's brows slashed down in a scowl.

"When I came back from the hospital and lost the bloody plot, I accused Raine of loving you more than she does me," Liam confessed, banging a fist against the car door.

And didn't he wish he could take it all back now? That he hadn't let exhaustion and frustration get hold of his tongue? He should merely have asked Raine about her feelings. If something unspeakable happened to her because he'd demanded that she prove her love for him with everything from sex to scones, he'd never forgive himself.

Hammer's jaw dropped. "That's the reason for the jealousy?"

"She's loved you for years, Macen." Liam swallowed down his regret. "I didn't think she could ever…" He shook his head. "Then she proved me dead wrong earlier."

Beck leaned in and poked his head between the seats. "Raine loves you just as much as she does Hammer. She wouldn't have been so torn all this time if she didn't."

"I know that now, and I wish I'd never doubted her. She showed me everything in her heart." Liam hung his head, then turned to Hammer. "You saw her do it, too."

"I did, but do *you* believe her? No doubts?" Macen shot back.

"None," Liam replied. "I was convinced the half dozen years she'd spent with you meant more than the five weeks we've been together. I feared I'd always come second. I was wrong."

"It's not the quantity; it's the quality." Hammer gripped the wheel tighter. "Besides, I didn't tell her how I felt until you forced the issue—which you were right to do. You've given her so many things I didn't. You still give her things I can't. You see that, right?"

He nodded miserably. "I wish you'd smacked me sooner and

told me I was out of line, mate."

"Nothing I said would have convinced you. Raine had to open your eyes," Hammer gave Liam's shoulder a brotherly squeeze. "She did a fanfuckingtastic job of it, too."

"She's only whole when she's with you both," Beck interjected. "She'd never love one more than the other. At the lodge, she told you she would have both or neither of you because she'd rather live her life empty than half full."

Liam remembered. Beck had nearly as much insight into Raine's psyche as he and Hammer. The doctor was probably a damn sight more objective, too.

God, he'd wasted so much energy on jealousy he had no reason to feel. Liam didn't know if he could stand the regret.

In his pocket, his phone buzzed. He jerked it free, hoping Raine had managed to reach out to him or even that Seth called with good news. Instead, he saw Gwyneth's name pop up on his display. Why the devil would she be calling before six in the morning? Kyle might have taken a turn for the worse, Liam supposed, and he would be sorry if that were the case. But right now, he had to focus on finding Raine.

He shoved his phone back in his pocket.

The closer they drew to Bill's house, the sharper his memories of his last visit here. The more his skin crawled. The decay that permeated every inch of Raine's childhood home sent a shudder up Liam's spine. How could anyone live in such squalor? And what was the state of the room Bill had locked Raine in right now?

Fear pumped through Liam's veins like acid. He took little comfort in knowing that he and Hammer would ensure Bill was dead by sunrise. Instead, Liam couldn't stop wondering what depravity Raine would be forced to endure before they rescued her. Or if they would be too late.

"If Bill wants money, why hasn't he called for a ransom yet?" Beck pondered.

"Because he knows I'll come looking for him. I'm sure he wants a little time with Raine so he can finish what he started when she was a kid." Hammer looked ready to hit something again.

"He's going to rape her, isn't he?" Liam choked out the

question…but he already knew the answer. He and Hammer had been thinking the same thing, but speaking his fear aloud made it more real. His guts churned.

“Yeah, but she’s a survivor. I’m more afraid of what else he’ll do.” Hammer’s jaw clenched. “That drunk asshole has a violent streak. If he’s been hitting the booze this morning, he may do more than violate her. No telling what.”

The fear of never holding or touching Raine again made Liam feel as if he’d been swept up in a tornado and slammed to the ground. To have her loving, compassionate soul ripped away would be his worst nightmare. Dread, thick and scalding, filled him. The weight of the terror staggered him. Liam didn’t want to simply kill her sire; he wanted to make the bastard suffer interminably.

“Fuck the stoplights, Hammer. Go faster,” Liam growled.

“I can’t risk getting pulled over for a speeding ticket when we’re so damn close.”

Liam knew that, but the logic chafed. “I don’t understand why he had to use the fucking stun gun on her. She’s just a wisp of a girl.”

“Bill knew Raine wouldn’t go willingly. She fought him once and won. The scar she gave him is a daily reminder.” Hammer cursed. “I can’t stop thinking about the way she dropped like a stone into that son of a bitch’s arms.”

As they rounded the corner onto Kendall’s street, Liam tried to hold himself together because panic didn’t do her any good.

Beck handed both men a pair of latex gloves, then donned his own. Hammer drove slowly past the house as Liam craned his neck. He didn’t see a single light on, inside or out.

Pulling to the curb near the middle of the block, Hammer cut the engine. After slipping on their gloves, the three men exited the vehicle, carefully closing the doors with nothing more than a snick of sound. As they made their way down the sidewalk, a dog barked from somewhere behind them. Another followed suit, but neither animal was close enough to attract unwanted attention.

Hammer darted down the driveway, drawing out his gun when he stepped into the shadow between Bill’s house and the neighbor’s. Liam and Beck followed, both stopping to peer through the dirty windows. Liam couldn't see a thing except darkness. Not one sound came from inside. The place felt dead. An icy ripple slithered down his spine.

Pulling a penlight out of his pocket, Liam made his way to the attached garage. Shining the tiny beam of light through one of the grimy windows along the face of the door, he saw no sign of Raine. Even Bill's truck was gone.

"Anything?" Hammer whispered.

"No," Liam responded in the same furtive tone.

Quiet as a cat, Beck crept to the back door. Gripping the doorknob with a steady hand, he twisted it slowly. Giving a short, low whistle to get his and Hammer's attention, Beck flashed a triumphant smile and opened the door.

It hadn't been locked. They'd just been handed a gift—or walked into a trap.

Hammer hurried inside first, gun drawn. Liam followed in close behind as Beck quietly closed the door, then trailed them.

The stench of rotting garbage, sour gin, and stale cigarettes hit Liam's senses like a prizefighter's right hook.

"Jesus," Beck muttered under his breath, then pressed a palm over his nose.

Liam wanted to retch but forced himself to breathe through his mouth instead. Shielding the beam from the penlight, Macen raised his hand, and the three men froze like statues, straining to listen for the slightest sound.

Silence.

As Hammer moved through the room again, he looked both furious and frustrated.

"Fuck this. I'm not afraid of that cocksucker." Macen flipped on the kitchen light. "Kendall, you motherfucking coward, come out and face me!"

Cockroaches scattered in every direction. Stacks of moldy food stuck to mismatched dishes that littered the counters. Liam stared at the black streaks of grime on the yellowed linoleum floor as his eyes adjusted to the harsh light.

Beck cursed again. Repugnance crawled all over his face.

"Raine!" Liam called out, then cocked his head to listen intently.

Hammer and Beck paused, too. No answer.

"C'mon, you miserable piece of shit," Hammer provoked. "You want your money? I've got it right here."

Quiet enveloped them once again.

"Give Raine to us, and you can live out the rest of your days in style," Liam offered. "All five fucking seconds of it," he murmured, his voice low and deadly.

"Raine!" Hammer screamed again. "Make a noise for us. Kick. Scream. Anything."

Not even a creak stirred from the miserable house. The oppressive silence wrapped around them. Hammer's expression fell desolate.

Beck opened a drawer near the sink and withdrew two long knives, then handed one to Liam. "Let's check out the rest of the house, just to be sure."

"If you find Bill first, cut off his balls and shove them down his throat for me, will you?" Liam sneered.

"Then I'll finish him off with a round to the head…eventually." Hammer's icy glower left no doubt he meant to make the prick suffer.

Liam couldn't agree more with that plan.

"I want to hurt him, too," Beck drawled cynically. "I've got that shit down to an art form."

Making their way through the house, Liam found it remarkably more revolting than the first time he'd been there. The gut-churning odor of rotting garbage and fetid decay clung like an oily black film. Beer cans and cheap gin bottles littered the floor as they made their way down the hall, searching for Raine.

Exploring every closet and cubby, they called out to her, pausing to listen for the tiniest scrape or moan. With each room that turned out empty, the glimmer of hope Liam had been clinging to faded darker until the red he'd been seeing turned black.

Standing outside Raine's old room, Liam felt his hand tremble on the doorknob. He didn't want to see the posters of her teen idols on the walls again or be reminded that his raven-haired lass had once lain on the bed only to have her innocent dreams stripped away by the monster she'd called Dad.

Beck seemed to read his mind. "Go ahead. I'll check this

room."

Hammer's brows furrowed with concern as he stepped in behind Beck. A snarl rumbled from Macen's throat as he darted back out and raced down the hall toward Bill's room.

Beck emerged less than a minute later, pale and visibly shaken. He shook his head bleakly.

"Son of a bitch!" Hammer bellowed.

Liam and Beck ran down the hall, then bolted into the master bedroom to find Hammer pacing and cursing. Empty dresser drawers gaped open. Macen ripped several hangers from the barren closet before heaving them across the room in a violent rage.

Bill had left, and Liam had little hope the bastard had any intention of returning. The gravity of Raine's peril slammed into him anew. Finding her now would be difficult, if not impossible. A needle in a fucking haystack.

"I'll call Seth and have him contact the police," Beck said in a dismal tone.

"Goddamn it, I thought she'd be here." Hammer sounded stunned, shaken. "That he just wanted money and the chance to yank my chain. Where the fuck is he?"

Liam wondered the same thing. And what if they'd wasted time on this wild goose chase instead of calling the police, and it cost Raine her life?

"Come on," Beck urged. "We need to get out of here."

Hammer nodded, then he and Beck hurried outside. Liam followed, closing the door behind them. The snick of the knob left him feeling as if he'd abandoned Raine.

Liam swallowed the fear in his throat and followed the other men across the yard. A new level of panic trampled him. Time was running out if they wanted to find her alive. He could almost hear the mocking *tick-tock* in his head.

Once in the car, Beck rang Seth. Hearing the doctor say that they'd failed to find Raine choked Liam with hopelessness. But he'd bloody well keep fighting to get her back…unless he knew for certain he had nothing left to fight for.

"Before we head to the club, the private eye I hired to check in on Bill periodically sent me the names of a couple of the asshole's haunts. Let's check them out," Hammer suggested.

"What kind of places? You think he'll be at one of them?" Liam asked, almost hating his wretched hope but needing it so badly.

"Mostly restaurants and bars, so I doubt he'll be hanging out. I'm hoping someone will know where to find him or will have seen him recently." Hammer scrubbed a hand through his hair. "I don't know what else to do."

"Let's go," Liam urged.

Hammer pulled from the curb and sped down the street. Liam noticed his friend wasn't concerned about getting pulled over any longer.

As they darted onto the highway, he remembered the photos Hammer had shown him of the last beating Raine had suffered at Bill's hands before running away. Liam tried to clear his mind, not fixate on the horrors Raine could be experiencing as they broadened their desperate search.

The first bar Hammer stopped at was closed. The second, though open, had only two patrons inside, eating eggs. No one had seen Bill lately. Ditto with the third.

Liam felt the despair rolling off Hammer's body. It echoed inside him.

"Where next?" he asked, his frustration spiking.

"That was the last place on my list. Fuck!" Hammer snapped, anxiety taking its toll. "I'd convinced myself she'd be at Bill's, just waiting for his cash. Now I don't have a goddamn clue."

"We should head back to the club," Beck suggested. "I'm sure the place is swarming with cops. Maybe we can help them somehow."

Liam wanted to believe that. Unfortunately, he didn't. He had to pray that his strong, wily girl, who had escaped her sire before, could somehow do it again.

If not, he and Hammer would lose another woman they shared, only this one had been a blissful surprise who'd stolen his heart as well. The sick irony was, they'd be sharing the debilitating pain of losing Raine together, as they should have after Juliet's death. Jesus, how had Macen lived through this devastation alone?

Damn Bill Kendall to hell and back. The bastard had forced

him and Hammer to play by another set of rules, and having the control ripped from his hands filled Liam with a sense of despair. Still, he'd do, give, or say anything to have Raine back.

Chapter Eighteen

Dawn broke over the San Gabriel Mountains in the distance as Hammer pulled into Shadows' parking lot, now choked with police cars. Plainclothes officers gathered evidence. The camera's constant flash reflected off Raine's little compact like strobes. The driver's side door still hung open—a stark reminder that he'd failed to protect her from Bill after all these years.

Hammer remembered the day he'd given her the keys. He could still hear her squeal of excitement, see delight twinkle in her blue eyes. The memory only deepened his guilt. Desperation tore his heart from his chest. Fear made every anxious second feel like a century because he knew if Bill wasn't waiting around for his money, he'd chosen to end their cat-and-mouse game. He'd want maximum pleasure out of the pain he inflicted—on both Hammer and Raine.

Bill would probably torture her unspeakably and kill her.

Hammer dragged in a shuddering breath, trying to hold himself together and hang on to hope that somehow, some way he'd find Raine alive.

"Bloody hell," Liam complained. "The car park is a circus. We don't have time for this."

Beck snorted. "Just wait until the reporters show up."

With a curse, Hammer stopped the car and killed the engine.

"Reporters don't give a shit about anonymity. If you need to get out of here, go."

Beck shrugged. "I'm done caring about being outed. If my vanilla patients don't want a kink doctor, fuck them. I'm not leaving until we find Raine."

"I thought you were supposed to be in surgery. Isn't that why we left the lodge?" Liam asked with a puzzled expression.

Hammer hadn't thought to ask. He'd been too busy worrying about Raine.

"After I left you at the emergency room, I got a call from the head of the harvesting team. The donor died, but when they retrieved the heart, it was wasted. So my patient is back on the waiting list again," Beck explained. "I sure as fuck wasn't staying in my condo with your ex. Shadows was closer than my house, so I crashed here."

A hard tap at the window made Hammer jerk in his seat. An officer wearing a scowl bent to peer into the car. "You'll have to leave. This is a crime scene."

Hammer wasn't in the mood to deal with bureaucracy. Opening the door, he stepped out. Instinctively, the cop snapped back and put a palm on his revolver.

"Easy," Hammer soothed. "I'm the owner of this club. These men are with me."

Liam and Beck climbed out of the car and flanked him.

As they stood shoulder to shoulder, the officer eyed them. "I need to see some ID from all of you. Where have you been?"

I can't afford to placate you, fucker.

"Breakfast meeting," he replied curtly, digging into his wallet.

"Mr. Hammerman," a familiar voice in a uniform called out as he approached the group. Macen bit back a smile when he spotted Dean Gorman, a fellow Dom and member of Shadows. "Hey, I haven't seen you since the Policeman's Ball."

Dean extended his hand, and Hammer shook it, feeling a bit of relief. "Glad you're here, Sergeant. I was just explaining to your cohort that I own this club."

"I've got this," Dean dismissed the other officer, who grunted and walked away.

The sergeant turned to make sure his fellow cop was out of

earshot. "I'm sorry to hear about Raine. Bill Kendall is her dad?"

"'Fraid so," Hammer answered. "Do you have any leads on him?"

"No." Dean sighed. "A couple of units left Kendall's house a few minutes ago. They said the place was a pigsty and should be condemned."

He knew that but played dumb so he didn't put Dean in the awkward position of keeping his B and E a secret. "And they didn't find anyone?"

"Kendall's clothes are gone, so the assumption is he's skipped town and taken Raine with him."

"Maybe, but that monster has been itching to get his hands on her for years. I don't think he'd put off whatever he had planned to flee the city. My guess is, he'll stash her somewhere close but isolated where he can hurt her or…" *Fuck.* Saying the words stabbed Hammer with terror. "Maybe even kill her. Then he'll leave."

Dean winced. "I told the detectives that Raine is a family friend. They issued a BOLO for Kendall, his truck, the van, and Raine. Since everyone in my precinct now knows this is personal for me, they're not wasting a moment."

Hammer knew with every second that ticked by, the odds of finding a kidnap victim alive dropped exponentially. A thick lump of panic lodged in his throat. He couldn't speak. All he could do was nod in appreciation for Dean's help.

"Thank you." Liam gripped the officer's shoulder with a grateful squeeze.

"No worries." Dean glanced between Hammer and Liam as if he wondered which one of them she belonged to now. "She's irreplaceable to a lot of us. Shadows isn't our kinky home without her. Hang in there. We're doing all we can."

Please let her be alive. I can't lose her now.

Struggling to maintain his composure, Hammer stared at the cops still examining the crime scene. He wanted to rail at them to find Raine faster.

Then Macen saw two big television vans pull to the curb and clenched his jaw. "The vultures have landed. Let's get inside."

When they entered the club, the few members who'd been sleeping in the new rooms on the other side of the club were awake and looking shell-shocked as they gave statements to a pair of detectives. Hammer made a mental note to stress the importance of guarding his members' identities.

Scrubbing a hand through his hair, he spotted Seth at the bar, nursing a bottle of water and looking desolate. Before Hammer headed over, Dean and one of the detectives intercepted him.

Hammer directed them to his office, then spent the next thirty minutes answering questions about Raine and Bill. He tiptoed around the fact that he'd bribed Kendall to stay away from her. To prove the urgency of the case, Hammer showed the man pictures of a beaten and bruised Raine as a teenager. After that, the detective radiated fury.

Then Hammer joined Liam, Beck, and Seth at the bar, hoping to God something broke soon.

"How did the inquisition go?" Liam asked, nervously tapping his fingers.

"It was tedious but necessary." Hammer took a seat next to him.

Liam gave him a sympathetic stare. "What did you tell him?"

"Everything I could without explaining the 'contact' Bill and I have had over the years," Hammer replied bitterly. "I didn't want to give them any reason to look at me as a suspect. It would only waste time."

On his right, a couple who had joined the club after moving to Los Angeles a few months ago stepped up beside him. Submissive Vivian placed several steaming mugs of coffee on the bar under her Dominant's watchful eye.

"Our hearts are breaking for what's happened to Raine, Sirs," Vivian offered. "If there's anything Master Donald and I can do for you, please don't hesitate to ask."

Hammer forced a tender smile for the older couple. They were a genuinely warm-hearted pair whose children were grown and gone. Donald often took on the role of DM when Hammer found himself shorthanded, and Vivian watched over the unattached subs like a mother hen.

"Thank you. We appreciate that," Liam replied.

"If you guys want to look for Raine, I can hold down the fort here," Donald offered.

"Thanks, man." Hammer slapped the older Dom on the shoulder. "Honestly, if I had a fucking clue where to look, I'd take you up on that."

Hammer sucked in a deep breath, then took a sip of coffee. It tasted good…but it definitely wasn't Raine's. At the thought, he fought another wave of hopelessness that threatened to swallow him whole.

Suddenly, Dean poked his head around the corner. "O'Neill, your wife is here?"

Hammer heard more than a little steel in that question, as if the Dom wondered how Liam could be married but pursuing Raine.

Beside him, Liam groaned at Dean. "Ex-wife. I don't want her here."

But it was too late. Gwyneth struggled through the portal, rolling her suitcase and balancing the playpen on top with one hand. She schlepped Kyle awkwardly in the car seat with the other. A diaper bag weighed down her left shoulder, her purse the right. Hammer was fairly certain the bitch had never carried her own luggage in her life.

"Bloody fucking hell," Liam groused as he stood.

Hammer also stood, narrowing his eyes on the viper as Liam took the car seat from her and made his way toward his stool, propping the baby up beside him. Gwyneth scurried over, looking flushed and anxious.

Instantly, Vivian smiled and began cooing at Kyle. The little tyke responded, kicking his feet as a wide, drooling grin spread across his cherubic face.

Gwyneth dropped the playpen, purse, and diaper bag on the floor, then leaned over her suitcase with a weary sigh. Liam gripped her elbow and hauled her to a quiet corner at the back of the bar. Hammer followed, his temper rising with each step.

"I don't have time for you, Gwyneth," Liam insisted. "As you can see, we've got a situation here…"

"I-I need to talk to you." She darted a nervous glance at Hammer, then focused on Liam again. "It's urgent. About Raine."

She whispered as if trying to keep Hammer from hearing.

"What about Raine?" Liam sounded at the end of his rope.

Macen's gut tightened. The concern she'd voiced before they'd passed out in Liam's bed a few hours ago screamed through Hammer's head. *So she was just going to give up? She hijacked a baby, falsified birth records, came up with a whopper of a lie, and... I don't see her quitting. It's a huge fortune.*

If Raine had been right, then it was possible Gwyneth had come to the club to play her last, desperate card. Since he couldn't think of any active way to help Raine right now, Hammer had every intention of making Liam's ex-wife tip her hand.

"Spill it," Macen hissed.

"This is between Liam and me." Gwyneth glared at him. "And I'm not speaking to you. I haven't forgiven you for what you did to me earlier."

"You mean what I *didn't* do to you," Hammer sneered.

"Can we talk somewhere privately?" Her haughty tone made Macen want to punch something, preferably her face. Ignoring him altogether, Gwyneth sent her ex-husband a pleading stare.

"Hammer's office," Liam barked.

Without waiting for her to reply, he turned and dragged her through the bar and down the hallway.

"Vivian." Hammer glanced over his shoulder. "Would you please keep an eye on the baby? His name is Kyle." *At least I think it is.*

"Really, Sir? Oh, I'd be happy to. I *love* babies." She smiled before turning her attention back to the squealing boy, making ridiculous noises at him.

Too bad you weren't in town when Pike was pulling out his hair.

Hammer watched Liam drag Gwyneth into the office. Stepping in behind them, Macen closed the door, blocking her only exit as he crossed his arms over his chest.

"Tell me what you have to say," Liam spat. "And be quick. I won't tolerate any more of your games." When she slanted Hammer a sideways glance, Liam added, "Anything you say to me about Raine, you can tell Hammer."

Macen didn't think he could feel much joy today, but if Liam put Gwyneth in her place, he'd sure try.

Her mouth opened, then closed like a landed trout. "I came

to tell you something dreadful."

"You're pregnant with twins this time?" Hammer asked wryly.

Gwyneth shot him an icy glare, then pinned Liam with a look of anguish. "My father died just after lunchtime in London. I received the call shortly after we left the hospital this morning."

"I'm sorry for your loss," Liam replied without an ounce of emotion.

"Thank you, but that's not the reason I came to see you. I've made a mistake."

Liam sighed loudly, then drilled her with an angry gaze. "You've made many."

Hammer nearly seized her and shook the words from her throat. "What does this have to do with Raine?"

"Bill Kendall has her," she blurted out.

As soon as Gwyneth's words registered in his brain, Hammer knew the bitch was involved. The ice freezing his veins since he'd discovered Raine missing now blazed like lava.

He pushed off the door and lunged at Gwyneth, but Liam already had her pinned against the wall. His face burned with rage, but his eyes looked absolutely arctic. "How do you know that? Did you have something to do with Raine's disappearance?"

Hammer stormed closer, glaring hard. "You'd better start talking. Do you know where Bill has taken her?"

Gwyneth gave a little cry of fear. "I didn't plan for things to turn out the way they have. You must believe me."

Liam waved away her pleas. "Where is she?"

"After you humiliated me, I was outraged that you could me treat me so callously. I was your wife." She swallowed. "So I tracked the man down and offered him money."

"I hurt your feelings so you wanted Raine dead?" Liam looked shocked, as if he'd never hated anyone more in his life.

Hammer seconded that emotion. "Tell us where to find her!"

She gaped at Liam. "Dead? I merely asked him to keep her away from you for a few days until we could fly to Vegas and get remarried. But now that my father is gone, it's all moot." She wrung her hands. "I didn't think Raine's own father would really hurt her."

"You heard me berating the man in the car park because he beat her as a child and tried to rape her," Liam spat with incredulous fury. "Did you think he meant to play cards with her? Take her to a fucking movie?"

"I was angry. It was impulsive. I'm sorry," she screamed. "I've spent all morning phoning Bill, trying to stop him. I left messages telling him to disregard the whole scheme."

"You stupid whore! A message isn't going to stop that motherfucker," Hammer thundered as he fought the urge to wrap his hands around Gwyneth's throat.

"Well, I reached him more than an hour ago and tried to convince him to release Raine. He slurred his words. I could barely understand him."

"Because he's a violent drunk," Hammer snarled. "Did you catch anything he said?"

Remorse tightened Gwyneth's face. "I came to you because I didn't know how what else to do. I've already paid Kendall fifty thousand dollars. He threatened bodily harm if I didn't pay him the other fifty, which he wasn't supposed to get until we came back from Vegas."

"Raine would have been dead before we even left L.A.," Liam hissed. "There's a good chance he's already killed her."

"I offered him double to let her go," she cried. "But he said that since he had her now, he planned on having himself quite the party." Gwyneth looked at him with pleading green eyes. "I tried to call you earlier and tell you, Liam. You didn't answer. I left a message and rushed over here… I never meant any harm."

Hammer roared, then punched a hole through the drywall. Powder and plaster rained down to the floor as he thrust his fist in Gwyneth's hair, squeezing until she let out a cry. "Tell us where Raine is. Now."

At his deadly tone, more tears spilled down Gwyneth's cheeks. "I believe at a warehouse near the airport. He had me meet him there early yesterday evening." She trembled in fear. "I'm sorry, Liam, I—"

"Shut up," he commanded, his tone ice cold. "The address?"

"I-I wrote it on a scrap of paper. It's in my purse by the bar."

Hammer released her, then plucked out his cell phone. He fired off a text to Beck, instructing him and Seth to be ready to roll.

"I want it now." Liam grabbed her by the arm and hauled her out of the office. "And if Bill has harmed one hair on Raine's head, the fucking universe won't be big enough for you to hide from me."

Gwyneth sobbed with each step. Hammer didn't feel an ounce of sympathy for her, only seething rage.

When they reached the bar, Vivian and Donald had taken Kyle out of his car seat and were playing happily with him at the far end. Beck and Seth stood, waiting and tense. No one spared more than a glance for Gwyneth, who quietly fell apart as she dug through her purse.

The second she handed the paper to him, Liam punched the address into his phone. "Less than ten minutes away, maybe more with traffic."

Still, they had a lead. Fresh hope rolled through Hammer. He leaned closer to Beck and Seth, careful to keep his voice down. "Gwyneth might know where to find Raine. If she's there, let's rescue her. You ready?"

"Y-you're not going to tell the police?" Gwyneth asked.

"Not yet." Liam knew he and Hammer both intended to silence Bill, once and for all. "And you're coming along to show us exactly where he's hiding Raine."

"But it sounds dangerous." She shuddered.

Beck sent her a mocking brow. "Oh, boo hoo."

Seth held up his hands. "We need to leave someone behind to coordinate with the police in case they have questions or find anything."

Hammer and Liam exchanged a glance, then looked Seth's way. "Will you do it? And ask Vivian to watch the baby while we're gone?"

"On it." Seth nodded. "Go."

"But…Kitty and George are expecting Kyle and me to meet them at the airport in two hours," Gwyneth protested.

Hammer snatched paper and pen off the bar, then shoved them at Gwyneth. "Write down your sister's cell number. Seth can call Kitty and tell her where to pick up the boy. *You* are coming with us. That's nonnegotiable."

Hammer watched her fingers tremble as she wrote. Every

second they spent at Shadows left Raine at Bill's nonexistent mercy.

When Gwyneth finished, she set the pad and paper down.

Hammer shoved the number at Seth. "We're out."

"What will you do about Bill if you find him?" Seth arched a brow.

"You know the answer to that," Hammer snarled.

Seth sent him a long stare. "Liam, why don't you and Beck take Gwyneth to the car?"

"We'll load up in my SUV." Liam dragged his ex-wife toward the door. "Come on. No more theatrics, do you understand me? Or I'll turn you over to the police now. You'll go to jail."

"And you'll be forced to eat pussy instead of cock for the rest of your life," Beck snarked.

Gwyneth's nostrils flared as she pressed her lips together.

Hammer tossed Beck his car keys. "Get your medical bag from my trunk and bring it."

"You got it," Beck assured, helping Liam shepherd Gwyneth out of the club.

Once alone again, Seth stared Hammer down. "Listen, I've been thinking about this. What you're suggesting is called premeditated murder. When it comes time for sentencing, it'll be labeled first-degree, and that puts all of you on death row. Or merely life in prison, if you're lucky."

"Only if witnesses talk." Hammer gritted his teeth. "And if Raine is gone, I don't care."

Seth cursed. "Call me when it's over. If you need a cover story, I'll help you with one since I've been a cop. If possible, we need everyone to be copacetic with the final version before you call 911."

Hammer clapped him on the shoulder. "Thanks."

Inhaling a deep breath, he ran down the hall and toward the exit, slipping past the detective who had interrogated him earlier. He jogged to Liam's SUV, then climbed into the passenger's seat. In the back, Beck glared at Gwyneth, who looked pale and chastened.

The reporters swarmed the vehicle as they tried to leave the club's lot. Thankfully, the cops waved them on. Liam hit the gas.

As they pulled away, Hammer closed his eyes. An image of Juliet, lifeless and limp, flashed through his head. Her face morphed into Raine's, and Hammer clenched his jaw to hold in his despair. She couldn't be dead, too. He prayed they would reach the warehouse in time to save their precious Raine. If they didn't…Hammer would be grateful to have Liam at his side this time. But he wasn't sure he could get through the rest of this life without her.

* * *

"Wake up, slut."

The voice penetrated Raine's haze, but she couldn't place it. A sharp pain to her ribs shot her up through layers of consciousness. Gasping to absorb the agony, she tried to roll away, protect her side.

Instead, Raine found herself pinned and unable to move.

Exhaustion weighed down every muscle. She groaned and forced her eyes open. A corrugated metal ceiling hung high above her, dark with rust. The dim lighting, strung from the iron crossbeams, cast an anemic beam over the yellowing walls. She shivered. Where was she? Why was it so cold? Why couldn't she move?

"About time you came around," slurred a voice Raine had hoped never to hear again.

She managed to turn her head and found Bill standing over her, clutching a bottle of gin. He drew his foot back menacingly as if he anticipated the chance to strike her ribs with his boot again.

When Raine saw his face, her blood ran cold. She struggled to sit up, get up—anything to flee him.

Her father took a swig from his bottle. "You're not going anywhere. I've got you all spread out and ready. I even tied you down properly, just like Master Pervert. I've waited a long time for this."

Glancing down her body, Raine took in her dirty clothes, the heavy metal-framed cot on which she lay a few inches from the ground, the thick, scratchy rope he'd used to bind her wrists and ankles to the corners.

Around her, the empty warehouse looked stark and lifeless. Past her feet, she could see Bill's red truck. Beyond the vehicle, she spotted two doors. No windows, just a pair of skylights that filtered in an orangey hue and told her that dawn was breaking.

A plane flew overhead, its engines screaming in a deafening roar, as if it had just taken off nearby.

Oh, god… Where was she? Why had Bill brought her here? To repay her for thwarting him, for running away, for punching him—and any other reason he thought she deserved his wrath. And she didn't have any illusions. He wouldn't leave her alive to tell the police.

She wanted to hope that someone could find her, but if she had no idea where Bill had brought her, how could anyone else? Besides, after the hellacious day Liam had been through, he was likely still fast asleep. Doubtful he'd had a chance to miss her yet. Hammer's hours had been long, too. He might be still be snoring.

More than likely, she was on her own.

Raine started to shiver and tried to force herself to breathe, to use her head. If she couldn't fight back physically, then she had to keep him talking. Not for a second did she think she could reason with him, but his bottle looked half-empty. If she could engage him, maybe he'd keep drinking and finally pass out. Clandestinely, she tugged at her wrists. Getting free of these bonds would be difficult. He'd bound her so tightly that her fingers felt a little numb.

"What is it you want?" she finally asked. "I have money. I'll give it to you."

Bill gave her a drunken scoff. "Money won't do it anymore. It's high time I paid you and Master Pervert back. See, he thought he could stop giving me that cushy monthly stipend, and I—"

"What do you mean?" Raine cut in. She'd known that Bill had figured out where she'd gone after she'd run away from home all those years ago. Being an absolute asshole, her father would, of course, look Hammer up and threaten him. But… "Stipend?"

"Why else do you think I didn't march over there and drag your scrawny ass back home years ago? Why else do you think I didn't call the police and tell them he was harboring a minor in a sex club? I lived off that two grand a month, tax free, for the last six years."

Hammer had never said a word. Never mentioned it, never hinted, never given her even the slightest indication that he and her father had come to this agreement. Math wasn't her best subject, but she did a quick calculation. The amount he'd paid to keep her safe staggered her.

"Didn't know that, did you?" Bill looked pleased that he'd thrown her for a loop before his expression darkened again. "But then you had to knock on my door and fuck it up, like you do everything else. Of course, you've had this punishment coming for a long time." He took another pull from the bottle, then traced the scar on his cheek with the neck and sent her a menacing glare. "I owe you for this, Raine. Your daddy means to collect his pound of flesh."

She tried not to recoil or cry or panic. In the past, she'd had weapons at her disposal, like the knife she'd attacked him with the night she'd run away, Beck and his gun the last time she'd knocked on his door and punched him in the face. Now, she only had her words.

Maybe an apology would make him go easy on her, but Raine couldn't bring herself to say she was sorry to the sick fuck.

"I'll make him pay you again," she offered desperately. "Call him, and I'll arrange it. He has a lot of money." She suspected. Hell, she'd never asked. "You want double? Triple? A million dollars? He'll give it to you."

"Is your pussy that sweet?" He looked dubious. "I can't think of a single slut worth that much." Then a big, evil grin stretched across his face. He took another gulp of the gin, then stumbled as he bent to set the bottle on the ground. When he straightened again, he had his hand at his waistband, his fingers working at the button. "But I'm ready to find out."

Raine tried to shrink away but had nowhere to retreat. His maniacal laughter filled her ears.

"Let's get this party started. Oh, I almost forgot…" He swerved alongside her cot, scooped up the bottle again, and disappeared above her head.

Raine craned her neck to see what Bill was up to. All she

saw were the legs of a table. He stopped in front of it and swayed, picking up and dropping things with a metallic clang that made her heart race. Dear god, what did he have planned?

"Doesn't Master Pervert call you 'precious'?"

Her heart stopped. "H-how did you…"

He laughed. "When I knew he had my baby girl, I followed you around to find out what he was doing to you. I overheard you at dinner a few weeks after you went to live with him. When you weren't looking, he stared like he wanted to strip off your clothes and fuck you. Were you giving him your pussy then?"

"No."

"Don't you lie to me, girl. He plucked that pretty cherry for himself, I know. That's why he calls you 'precious.' Does the Mick have a pet name for you? He should call you whore for giving it up to both of them. Which one of them gave you all the bite marks on your neck?"

"Hammer never laid a hand on me as a kid." *Unlike you. He would never rape anyone, much less an underage girl.*

Her father sneered, then turned back to the table. "Next you're going to tell me he's a fucking saint. Girl, he's just a man with a cock who wants to stick it somewhere. Your holes aren't so special. No slut's are." He scoffed. "Your sister's certainly weren't."

"You…violated Rowan?" she choked.

"Oh, I didn't violate her; I plucked her. I made sure she had a thirteenth birthday she never forgot."

Raine bit her lip to hold in her icy horror. He'd be far too amused. She was thankful another plane took off overhead, giving her a few moments to gather her thoughts. But nothing came to mind except that she had to be near LAX. She'd love to be on one of those planes—to anywhere. No, where she'd really like to be was back at Shadows, cuddled up between Liam and Hammer, safe in their arms.

"I had…" *No idea.* But maybe she had. Sometimes, late at night, she'd heard grunting and the slam of Rowan's headboard against the wall. She'd assumed her older sister had been sneaking in boyfriends. In hindsight, she realized Bill had been far too watchful to allow that.

Their mom had abandoned them two years before Bill had

started abusing Rowan. Her sister would have had no way to protect herself or stop their father. Her brother, River, though the eldest, had rarely been home.

In fact, now that she really thought about it, Bill had often taken Rowan shopping. They'd always come home with clothes just shy of indecent, especially nightgowns, bras, and panties.

"You had no idea?" Bill laughed. "She never told you how many 'favors' she did for me so that you didn't have a thirteenth birthday to remember, too? I enjoyed every moment she spent being my dirty whore." He rocked back on his heels. "Except when the dumb bitch got pregnant—twice."

Shock stole Raine's breath. She felt as if she'd been struck in the chest with a crowbar. Her sister had always been so quiet, kind… Bill had often remarked that she should be more compliant, like Rowan. What the gentle girl had endured made her blood curdle.

Her father was a sexual predator, a deviant void of a soul. But then she'd known that for years.

"Twice?" she finally choked out.

Somewhere in the back of her head, Raine realized that she wasn't saying anything that would persuade Bill to reconsider what he had planned or release her. But she was pretty sure no such words existed. She also feared if she said anything truly on her mind, she'd set off his violent streak sooner. Her head reeled; her terror surged.

"I had a hard time finding a doctor who'd perform an abortion on a girl not yet fourteen, but I found him. He came in handy two years later. After the first slipup, I put Rowan on the pill, but the stupid cunt took antibiotics for some fucking illness and wham. But I made sure she understood she couldn't be careless again."

Raine didn't even want to know what Bill had done then.

When she'd started fending off her father's leers and "accidental" touches after Rowan's departure for college, she'd sometimes resented her sister. Not a single text, letter, holiday at home. Nothing. Now Raine completely understood the girl's decision.

"So…" she breathed. "That's why Rowan never came back to see me?"

"Well, not exactly." Bill cackled like he was enjoying himself way too much.

Raine froze. Fear almost seized her tongue before she could ask her next question. "What do you mean?"

Bill didn't answer. He just began humming some vaguely familiar tune her father used to play. Rowan had always hated the song. Raine did, too.

"*Tonight's the night. It's gonna be all right. I'm gonna fuck you, girl. Ain't nobody gonna stop us now,*" Bill wailed, then snorted. "Rod Stewart had his way of singing the song, and I've got mine. You know, that was my special song with Rowan. I sang it to her the very first time. *Don't say a word, my virgin child...*"

The clues clicked. The truth slammed through Raine's head. Every time her father had played that record, Rowan would sob. Then Raine would hear moans and grunts coming from her sister's room that night.

Tears leaked from Raine's eyes. *Poor Rowan...*

"But then your sister got uppity, thought she was better than me. She applied to all those fucking universities and got accepted. She decided she was going to leave me."

Raine heard the booze in the bottle slosh, then he slammed it on the table. She started and bit back a gasp.

At least Rowan had gotten out. She'd had an unspeakably awful five years with her father, but Raine counted it as a victory that her sister had fled to make her life better.

"So I took care of her." Footsteps sounded, and Bill meandered back toward her, filling her line of vision as he crouched, holding a gleaming serrated knife in his hand. "Just like I'll take care of you."

Chapter Nineteen

Raine understood instantly what had befallen her sister. Rowan hadn't simply decided to leave her childhood behind and carve out a better life for herself. Their twisted father had ended it.

"She packed up for college, and you pulled out for the airport so she could fly to London and…"

A sneer curled his lip. "I drove her out to the desert. We had us a raunchy little good-bye. Then…I sent her on her way." He held up the knife with a shrug. Terrible delight shined in his eyes. He'd enjoyed every minute of that. "In fact, that same shovel is in the back of my truck."

More cold terror rolled through her. She'd known her father had no ability to feel love or compassion. She'd known he was a rapist and a pedophile who didn't care if he caused others agony. She hadn't known that he was a closet murderer.

"Because she planned to leave you? That's why?"

"No one leaves me. Not even you." He lowered the knife to her, pressing the tip against the hollow of her throat.

"Wait!" she cried, panicked. How would she talk him out of this? "I-I'll do whatever you want."

"I know you will. And you'll like it."

Raine's skin crawled, and before she could say anything

else, Bill cut through her T-shirt and bra with the big knife, making ribbons out of her shirt…and leaving a long scratch from her throat to her waist. Just a little deeper and he would have drawn blood.

The smile playing at his lips told Raine that he very much enjoyed screwing with her head. He'd scare her, lording his control of her mortality over her—before he finally lost interest in his latest toy and ended her, too. He'd killed Rowan when she'd decided she'd had enough abuse and chosen to walk away. What if her sister hadn't been the only one?

"What about River?"

"That stupid hell-raiser got in so much trouble it was either go to jail or go to the army. I was happy to see his ass out the other side of my door. He'd gotten too mouthy to tolerate and too big for me to beat."

"What about Mom? Did she leave you?" she asked in a low whisper.

Bill's lips curled in a proud smile. "She tried. I stopped her."

Raine failed to swallow back her gasp of horror. He'd killed her mother, too. *Oh, god. Oh, god. Oh, god.*

Raine's whole body went numb. All this time, she'd thought that her mom had simply left, walked away. The knowledge otherwise sucked the breath from Raine's lungs. All the warmth leached from her body. She bit her lip to hold in a whimper.

She'd never see her mom or tell her that she understood her determination to escape. Raine could never again express her love to the woman who had given her life. She hadn't seen her mom in almost fifteen years, but she'd always believed that someday…

Raine bit her lip to hold in a scream, and Bill kept on talking.

"Your mother was a whore. I'm convinced she'd been screwing my brother for years. She always smiled at him. She flaunted her body, too. Hell, it wouldn't surprise me if he'd knocked her up with all three of you kids." Bill sneered Raine's way. "By the time you came along, I almost had her under my thumb. Then she suddenly thought she'd grow a spine and take you kids with her. I showed her who was boss. I wasn't surprised when you and Rowan turned out to be whores, too. It was in your blood, after all."

With every word, Bill sounded angrier. His expression told Raine that she was to blame for every imagined slight her mother and sister had dealt him. She was sure he'd already tallied the sins she'd committed against him. One look in his glowing eyes and Raine knew that if she didn't do something fast, she wouldn't be long for this world. He'd end her, and he'd love every second.

Mentally, she began ticking off all the options. Bill didn't want money; he wanted *her*. He couldn't wait to punish her for being female and not desiring him. For leaving him. For ultimately hating him, just like Mom and Rowan. He'd either rape her multiple times, then carve her up, or he'd lose his temper and do it up big once before slashing her throat. Raine swore that neither scenario would come to pass—not without a hell of a fight. If she wanted to live, she had to take control.

She trembled. She had only one thing in her favor: Bill was more than a little drunk. He could hardly stand up straight, and he just kept drinking from that bottle. On the other hand, he was fucking insane. Somehow, she had to figure out what his unhinged mind wanted to hear and make herself say it. Then she had to do whatever it took.

She couldn't think about specifics now or she'd lose her nerve.

"Now, it's time to show Daddy what a good little fuck you are." He brandished the knife again and cut through her sleeves, reminding her with every swipe of the blade just who had the power. Then he yanked the garments from her torso and sat back, staring. A lewd little half smile twisted his face. "Well, look at all those bite marks and bruises. Hmm…" Bill adjusted his cock in his jeans. "I see those boys of yours have trained you to like it rough. Good. I can dig right in and enjoy myself. But this time, you'll have a *real* man."

Raine felt the bile rise in her throat. Forcing it down, she tried not to flinch as Bill leaned in and traced a thick finger over the marks dotting her breasts. The stench of gin stole her breath.

"Give Daddy a kiss, baby," he murmured as he forced his lips onto hers.

She pinched her mouth tight, willing herself not to vomit,

but Bill gripped her jaw and squeezed until she opened. His fetid breath filled her mouth as his tongue swept inside like a slippery eel. She whimpered in disgust and tried to turn away.

He jerked back, attempting to focus his bleary gaze onto her. “Let’s get those pants off you so you can show Daddy what he’s been missing all these years.”

Another airplane flew over the building as he shoved the knife beneath the waistband of her yoga pants. Raine groaned in terror. Her body stilled like stone.

Bill gave her a wink and started singing again. “*C’mon, angel. My dick’s on fire. Don’t deny your daddy’s desire. You’re going to enjoy it, so don’t play dumb. Spread your legs and let me fill you with come. Tonight’s the night...*” Bill snorted and chuckled, obviously pleased by his perceived talent. “I surprised your sister with those lyrics, too.”

God, this couldn’t be happening. Not that long ago, she’d been wrapped in Hammer’s and Liam’s arms. If she ever wanted to be safe and surrounded by them again, she had to find a way to survive this nightmare. The thought of them filled her with agony. She wanted her forever with the men she loved. She couldn’t leave them this way—not at the hands of this demented sociopath.

As Bill sliced the knife through the fabric of her pants, he made quick work of the spandex, shredding the material over both legs, then tossing her tattered pants over his shoulder.

The December cold bit into her skin. She shivered as she lay bound and exposed. Every cell in Raine’s body implored her to fight. But helpless and at Bill’s mercy, she had to play his game as fear and fury rolled through her.

He knelt beside the cot, his hungry stare roving her body. His eyes grew wide, and he swayed, licking his lips as he studied the marks on her bare pussy.

He whistled long and low. “Oh, they chewed you up nice and pretty. You liked it, too, didn’t you?”

When Bill pinned her with a gaze that warned her he expected an answer, she told him what he wanted to hear.

“Yes,” Raine whispered.

“I figured you were a kinky slut. But you’re going to like it a whole lot better with me. Aren’t you?” She tried not to cringe, especially when Bill stared at her mound again. "Aren't you?" he insisted, twirling the knife in his left hand.

Forcing her panic down, she sucked in a deep breath. Raine knew what she had to do, and she was running out of time. No matter how much she hated him or how sick it made her, she had to suck it up to survive.

Raine forced herself to give him a sympathetic look. "Mom and Rowan put you through so much torment. I didn't know. I'm so sorry."

Bill blinked, then narrowed his eyes. "No, you're not. You fucking left me, too."

"I was just afraid. I didn't know what you wanted. I was a scared little girl. But I'm not anymore, Daddy." Raine tried not to gag on her words. "I see now that you're all I could have ever wanted or needed."

She paused, watching as Bill's expression softened both with melancholy and booze.

"You do?" He sent her a searching expression and cupped her hip in one rough hand.

Raine didn't mean to flinch.

When she did, rage instantly filled his face. "You're fucking with me, aren't you, cunt? Well, I'm not having any of it."

He leaned over her and raised a menacing hand. Raine knew what was coming but had no way to stop him from slapping her face with all his might. Pain blasted in a white-hot fire across her cheek, spreading up her scalp and down her neck.

Raine clenched her jaw, refusing to scream. If she couldn't fight, she had to endure.

Dragging in a deep breath, she tried to slow her racing heart, her manic thoughts. Everything in her head nearly scrambled when he raised his hand again. She forced down the panic.

"No, Daddy. Please. I'll be good. I promise," Raine begged, as her cheek throbbed and her stomach pitched. "You surprised me when you touched me earlier. It felt so good, it shocked me. Until now, I never understood how good a man could feel. But I know now. All you've wanted to do is love me. Show me…"

Don't throw up. You can't throw up. You have to convince him you mean it.

Weaving a bit, Bill lowered his hand and smiled. "Now,

that's more like it."

"I'll do anything you want me to," Raine whispered, fighting the urge to close her eyes and shut him out.

"That's my girl. You've learned real fast who's boss. For your sake, I hope you suck cock better than Rowan. She was pitiful. Mind you, keep your teeth to yourself, or I'll kill you and finish up inside your cold, dead body."

Bill stood and released his zipper impatiently. His jeans fell to the floor, displaying his semi-erect penis beneath a pair of yellowed, threadbare underwear. Raine fought the urge to hurl. As he shoved the tattered fabric off his hips, she hid her revulsion at the sight of his shriveled cock.

With a grunt, Bill spit in his hand and grabbed the half-flaccid appendage, pumping it furiously in his fist. He swerved on his feet. His cock refused to come to life. The longer and harder he stroked, the more Raine knew he'd be unable to get it up.

Bill stomped and snarled, his frustration mounting. Then without warning, he dropped his cock and raised his hand. "What's wrong with you, girl?"

His fist crashed toward her face, his knuckles planting into the socket of her eye. Pain exploded through her head. The lights began to dim until nothing but white fireflies danced in her vision. Still, Raine held in a scream.

"This is all your fault, you fucking bitch," he spat. "You're not exciting enough for me."

"I'm sorry, Daddy," Raine cried. These were real tears, and if she didn't want to fall victim to his rage, she was going to have to do something drastic. "Let me help you. I can do it. Untie my hands. I'll make it all better. Please, Daddy…"

"I don't need your hands, slut. I need your mouth." Bill knelt next to the cot.

It took everything Raine had to keep her revulsion off her face. "But I want to touch you. Stroke you. Feel your big cock in my hand."

"You want to get free so you can give me another scar." He fingered the one on his cheek. "Don't fuck with my head, little girl."

"No. No." Raine shook her head. "You have the knife. You

have the power. But you can't tease me like this and not let me feel your skin against my palm, sliding up and down as I suck you deep."

A spark of desire danced into his glassy eyes. Raine wanted to close hers and wail, but she held his stare and tried like hell to send him a come-hither look.

Bill studied her for long moments. Finally, he leaned up and grabbed the bottle of gin off the table. He took a long gulp, then wiped his lips with the back of his hand. "You try anything, and I'll slit you from stem to stern. You got it?"

"Yes. Oh, yes." Her heart skittered, jumped in her chest. "I'll be good. I swear."

Good enough to get away.

Bill slowly untied the rope from her right hand. She forced a soft smile as he watched her suspiciously. When her arm fell free, she rolled her wrist, trying to get the blood flow back to her shoulders, her fingers.

He scooted in closer to the cot. "Touch me, baby girl. Put me in your mouth and suck me hard."

Raine tried to force herself to reach out and touch him, but she hesitated. Holding in a cry, she closed her eyes for a precious moment and focused on getting her shit together. All she had to do was wrap her fingers around his flesh and pretend she wasn't here—whatever it took to get her through.

Suddenly, Bill let out a savage roar, pounding his fist against her lips. More pain blindsided her. Blood filled her mouth. Raine tried not to cry or lose hope.

Liam and Hammer. She had to live for them and find some way to escape. If she let Bill waste her, Liam would be devastated. Hammer would blame himself for the rest of his life and shut down again. She couldn't let that happen to either of them.

"You tricked me, you fucking whore. I can see it in your eyes. You don't want me."

With a snarl, he dropped the knife. It clattered to the cement before he pounced on top of her, straddling her body with his much larger one, then gripped her throat tightly with both hands. As his face contorted in rage, he squeezed. His blue eyes blazed with murderous glee as he cut off her air.

Where's the knife? Find the fucking knife.

Struggling, she bucked and writhed, trying again to displace him off her body. Bill growled and gripped her neck with even more menace. She felt him crushing her windpipe and gurgled as she gasped for more air. Black spots danced in her vision. If she passed out…it was all over.

Adrenaline surged through her system as she felt around for the knife, her fingers scraping the cold cement. Then she brushed cool metal. Raine knew she had a handful of seconds before blackness took her when she fumbled with the weighted bottom of the blade. Finally, she managed to grip the smooth handle.

Using the last of her strength, she plunged the blade into his side. The sharp tip skidded over bone, so she kept searching. The serrated edges found the vulnerable flesh between his ribs. She shoved hard.

Hot blood exploded over her hand and gushed down her arm. The handle suddenly felt wet and hard to grip.

Instantly, Bill released her with an ear-piercing roar. Raine sucked in a deep, gasping breath, grateful to have blessed air again. Her vision sharpened. A fresh rush of adrenaline jetted through her bloodstream as Bill leaned away from her blow, staring at the knife sticking out of his side with bulging eyes.

"Bitch!" He lunged at her again.

Raine yanked the knife out, then stabbed it into his chest as he tried to reach for her throat again. She met the bone of his sternum, then wriggled the blade until the serrated edges cut through his flesh like butter, stopping at the hilt. Over his scream of agony, she jerked down.

More blood. His shout became a gurgle. Bill tried to stand but only managed to roll half onto the floor beside the cot, directly to her left. He stared up at her, his eyes widening with shock as he tried to suck in more air but only managed to sputter. Blood gushed everywhere.

He reached up and tangled his fist in her hair in a surprisingly strong grasp. He tugged hard, dragging her face to his. Raine screamed and tried to pull away. Bill was weakening, but the death grip he held on her still felt absolute.

With a sob, she did her best to twist in his direction, half rolling to her side. Still clutching her blade, Raine stabbed him again, this time in the heart.

She watched him jerk, his expression fade… But his terrible blue eyes kept staring back at her, so Raine didn't stop. She stabbed and stabbed as screams echoed in her ears. Finally, she realized Bill had gone—and the screams of terror were her own.

* * *

"Fucking move, damn it!" Liam hit the horn, slammed on the brakes, and checked his mirrors as he swerved around a slow-moving vehicle, then accelerated.

He refused to think about anything except reaching Raine. It was all too easy to visualize what horrific tortures that psycho, Bill, might be inflicting on their girl.

Liam berated himself for not doing something about Kendall when he'd had the chance. Instead, he'd made things worse yesterday by threatening the man. If anything happened to Raine, Liam knew he'd never forgive himself.

Stay focused. Concentrate on the traffic. Keep it together. Raine needs you.

"I'm sorry, Liam. Really, I didn't think he'd truly hurt her," Gwyneth offered.

Hammer grunted. "Bitch, please…"

Liam couldn't even look at her without wanting to do something he'd never done in anger to a woman in his life. "Because you didn't think things through and you don't care about anyone but yourself. You set up an innocent woman to die. You used your own nephew as a pawn in your scheme," Liam accused. "Is there nothing you wouldn't do to get your way?"

"I didn't hurt Kyle. I took him on an adventure." When he cast her an incredulous stare, she sighed. "My father's company was worth a billion pounds. I had to do *something*, but now it's going to Kitty and—"

Liam's phone rang. He pried it from his pocket, hoping for some news about Raine. He glanced at the number. Local. Unfamiliar. Heart racing, he pressed the button to answer the call and engage his Bluetooth.

"O'Neill," he answered.

"Hi. This is Tom from Accudata Labs at the hospital. Dr.

Beckman said you wanted the paternity test results back quickly. Just calling to let you know…you're not the father. I ran the test twice. You're not related at all."

That information would have been vastly welcome twenty-four hours ago. Now, it was hardly news. "Thanks, Tom."

"I owe you," Beck hollered from the backseat.

Having no patience for anything unrelated to rescuing Raine, Liam ended the call.

"Y-you had Kyle's DNA tested in barely twelve hours?" Gwyneth sounded shocked. Clearly, she'd thought she'd have more time.

He sent her a cynical stare in his rearview mirror. "I'm not as trusting as I once was. And after what you've pulled, I'll never believe a word you say again."

Beck grabbed Gwyneth by the back of her neck as he leaned in close to whisper in her ear. "You know, blondie, I'm a sadist. And for you, I'd forget my Hippocratic Oath."

At his deceptively polite threat, she moaned fearfully and tried to shake free. But Beck knew how to restrain a woman, and she was unable to elude his grasp.

"Do you know how many pain receptors there are in the human body?" he asked.

Her eyes flared wide. Her mouth slackened with a gasp. Liam watched Beck fuck with her head. Perverse satisfaction filled him.

"I do," the doctor went on. "In fact, I've made it my personal mission in life to study just how long I can perfectly balance someone on the razor's edge, keeping the sensations so intense nothing else registers. I can give utter agony."

Gwyneth began struggling anew. "Liam, call this lunatic off me." When he didn't acknowledge her demand, she continued in a panicked tone. "Surely you can't hold me responsible for whatever Raine's father does to her? I didn't deliver her to the maniac."

"You're very responsible, Gwyneth," Hammer snarled. "If Kendall kills her, I suggest you find a cop and beg him to take you to jail. You'll fare better. And before you appeal to Liam to save you again…stop wasting your breath. He won't."

"I hope you like wearing orange," Beck quipped.

"I tried to get Kendall to stop," she protested. "I even came to you with everything I know. It's not my fault."

"The hell it isn't, you calculating, mercenary bitch." Hammer's voice dripped menace. "None of *us* paid Kendall to kidnap Raine. On some level, you knew exactly what he was. That's why you hired him. Even the possibility of him raping or murdering her didn't stop you. So unless we ask you a pointed question, shut your mouth. Or I swear I'll fucking shut it for you."

Liam watched in the rearview mirror. Gwyneth reared back as if slapped, her face flushing crimson. Her lips pinched together in a tight line. She tried to wedge herself in a corner of the backseat as far from Hammer as possible, but Beck held her firm.

"Liam!" she cried.

"No one here gives a fuck about you, least of all me. You only told me about your involvement in Raine's abduction because your father died and Bill threatened you. If not for that, you would have hopped on a plane this morning and left, never caring what happened to her. You're like a bomb, exploding whenever you feel like it and hell-bent on mass destruction wherever you go. And worse, you're incapable of comprehending the misery you leave in your wake, much less caring," Liam growled.

She gaped. "But that's not true. How was I to—"

"Shut up," Liam snapped. "You know the difference between you and Raine? Why I love her? When I asked you to marry me, your first question was about the size of the diamond and whether it would sparkle enough on your finger." He scoffed. "The first time I asked Raine to be mine, she hesitated because she was concerned about my feelings and whether she could love me well enough to make me happy." He sent Gwyneth a rebuking shake of his head. "You and I were married for two years, and you never knew or cared how I felt. In five weeks, Raine has done her best to overcome a lifetime of abuse and heartache to be what I need because she cares that much."

"Liam, I cared about you. I still do."

"You don't know how to give a shit about anyone. You're not even good enough for Raine to wipe her feet on." Liam dragged in a shuddering breath. "I'm done with you."

Gwyneth seemed to wilt. They rode in absolute silence for a few tense, grating minutes, broken only by the robotic voice of the GPS.

As Liam turned onto Imperial Highway, a row of industrial buildings and warehouses appeared on their right.

"There. Over there!" Gwyneth called out. "Across that road. The building with the black doors. I think that's the one."

"You'd better hope you're right." Liam heard the menace in his own voice.

Gwyneth's eyes flared wide in horror as their stares connected in the rearview mirror. She finally looked as if she understood the deep shit she'd stepped in.

"Slow up a bit, Liam," Hammer interrupted. "It's too deserted here. If Bill hears a car approaching, it might spook him. That plane just taking off should pass overhead and provide us cover."

Liam turned onto the side street, then pulled the car to the curb, studying the warehouse in question. There were no windows. Liam was confident Bill wouldn't spot them.

Sliding double doors painted in a chipping black stretched across most of the front of the building, tall enough that, when opened, a truck could back into the facility. It looked older than most of the buildings around it, lacking a proper dock. Tufts of weeds grew through the cracks of the asphalt. Neglect hung in the air. It seemed as if it had been long ago abandoned…but looks could be deceiving. Gwyneth had taught him that.

"Beck, when we pull up to the building, keep my ex in the car with you, please? If you need to restrain or hurt her, feel free." At the man's wicked grin, Liam added, "We'll be back."

"My pleasure," Beck sneered. "Blondie and I have lots to talk about, right?"

She blinked at him. "What? No. You can't leave me with him."

Liam ignored her as the plane flew almost directly overhead. He punched the Escalade's accelerator, then pulled up beside the warehouse, getting a closer look at the entrance.

Urgency pumping through him, he parked the car in the wide, empty lot and killed the engine.

The instant the vehicle stopped, Hammer bolted out of the SUV, drawing his gun and holding it close against his leg. Liam followed. Together, they darted forward. Macen gave him a look clearly asking if he was ready. Liam nodded grimly. Hammer rounded the corner, stopping to examine the doors. They weren't locked. In fact, a small gap between them attested to the fact that Bill hadn't even closed them completely.

Hammer tried to peek through, then shook his head. "It'll make noise if I open it."

Which would alert Bill.

Liam looked at the rusting tracks. "It will. There's a smaller door to the left."

When he jerked his head in that direction, Macen followed. Liam reached it first and wrapped his hand around the knob, then gave it a little turn, praying for a break.

Thankfully, he got one. The door shimmied a crack.

He eased it open farther, hoping the hinges wouldn't squeak. He managed to push it wide enough to squeeze through. Hammer slipped in behind him.

The space inside was huge and ominous in the low light. Just beyond the doors sat Kendall's late-model red truck covered in grime. The van he'd abducted Raine in was nowhere to be seen, and Liam suspected he'd dumped it elsewhere.

Breath held, he crept around the vehicle, Hammer just behind him. Then they both spotted Raine.

Hammer froze. Liam's heart stopped.

Oh, dear god...

Chapter Twenty

Raine sat naked and crouched on the floor. In one hand, she clutched a knife dripping blood. The other she wrapped around her knees as she rocked back and forth, staring at Bill beside her, unmoving and lying in a puddle of his own fluids.

Her swollen right eye and the bleeding gash in her bottom lip told them that Bill had beaten her. As she gripped the serrated blade, crimson stained her fingers, her face, and her body. Liam felt his heart seize. His poor, wee lass had battled her demon again, and it had taken a toll on her.

But thank God she was alive.

Hammer approached Bill, gun pointed. Bending slowly, he pressed two fingers against the carotid artery. “He’s dead.”

Liam went limp with relief. Thank the fucking stars Bill Kendall could never, ever hurt their girl again. She had fought and won—for the final time.

“Raine,” Liam breathed, afraid to dart toward her too suddenly and risk scaring her more.

She didn’t respond, simply stared fixedly at the body lying near a metal-framed cot. Bill had once tied her to it, judging from the rope still hanging off the corners.

Hammer shoved his gun in his holster. Before Liam could call out to him, Macen ran toward Raine, kneeling beside her. He reached for her, then stopped and clenched his fingers into a fist as if afraid to startle the terrified girl. His gaze flittered between her face and the knife, still tightly gripped in her hand.

"Oh, baby. Sweet Raine. We're here, precious." Hammer's voice broke. "Can you hear me, sweetheart? Look at me. Drop the knife. You're safe. Bill can't hurt you ever again. He's dead."

At the sound of her father's name, Raine clasped the knife tighter, refusing to take her eyes off his prostrate body. Suddenly, she screamed, a blood-curdling sound that reverberated through the empty cavern of the warehouse, turning Liam's veins to ice. Gooseflesh prickled across his skin.

Hammer jerked back and stood. He flashed Liam a look of helpless horror.

"She's in shock, man," Liam murmured. "Don't raise your voice. It's freaking her out."

Hammer glowered. "Damn it—"

Liam laid a hand on his shoulder and swallowed down his own anxiety. "She's naked, armed, and non-responsive. She's covered in blood, which might be hiding wounds of her own. And it's freezing in here. She needs Beck. Go get him. I've got this."

"I can't leave her now," he shot back, his face contorted with devastation and shock, with remorse, guilt, and terror.

Liam couldn't help them both at once.

Fighting his own panic, he tamped down his urgency to rush to Raine. "Let me handle her."

Hammer swiped angrily at his face, struggling to gather his composure, clearly torn. Finally, he nodded. "Bring her back to us."

Liam remembered Hammer saying nearly those same words to Raine just before she'd made love to him a few hours ago. Now they sounded like an eerie echo. "Call 9-1-1 and get Beck. Tell him to bring his bag."

"I'm on it."

When Hammer ran for the entrance, Liam inched closer, visually examining her for other injuries. He couldn't tell with all the bloody streaks coating her skin.

"Raine, can you hear me?" He kept his voice deliberately low, not taking his eyes off her. He didn't want to see her shredded clothes littered around the metal cot or the instruments of torture—a heavy baseball bat, a power drill, screwdrivers, hammers, pliers—lined up on the makeshift table nearby. What had Bill done to her?

Fuck.

An empty gin bottle lay nearby. The air around them reeked with the stench of copper, along with the contents of his bladder and bowels, which he'd voided as he'd died. Based on the man's ashen skin, starkly white in the gloom, Liam guessed that Bill had bled out. He lay on his back, eyes staring wide in surprise, pupils dilated and fixed. At some point in Raine's ordeal, Bill had removed his pants. His flaccid cock lay exposed.

Liam wanted to kill the bastard all over again.

Raine's voice rose once more in an unnerving wail of distress.

Easing closer, avoiding the pool of blood surrounding Bill so he didn't contaminate evidence, Liam took off his coat while speaking softly to her. The distance between them chafed. "There, love. He can't hurt you now. Not ever again."

This time she moaned as if she heard him and broke apart inside. But she never tore her stare from Bill, as though she feared the animal would rise up and finish her off.

Liam crept closer still, crouching before her and putting himself between her and the body of her nemesis.

Finally, Raine blinked, then moaned thinly as she tried to stare around him, still gripping the bloody knife for dear life. Her pupils flared wide. Shock swam in her eyes. Liam hated how haunted she looked and tried not to think about what the mongrel might have done to send her off the deep end.

Focus. Fall apart all you want later, but don't you dare fucking lose it now.

"Oh, my sweet Raine," he crooned. "Hammer and I are here. Drop the knife for us." He couldn't startle her by snatching it from her when she felt threatened. And he couldn't risk tampering with the evidence by putting his fingerprints on the blade. "Come back to me, love…"

Instead of answering, she shivered and tried to peer around him. Her lips had gone blue, almost matching her troubled eyes.

Liam shifted to block Bill from her sight line again. He

heard the sound of the warehouse doors being thrown wide, footsteps running toward them. Without looking back, he shoved up a palm to stop their approach and focused on Raine. Since cajoling wasn't working, he needed to try something else.

"Drop the knife, sub," Liam demanded, hoping the familiar tone of his Dom voice might reach her instead.

At first, Raine didn't respond—except to blink. She hadn't even done that since he'd found her huddled and keening. Liam counted the slight change as a win.

"Don't make me feed you pickles," he warned sternly, then let his voice drop to a whisper-soft tone. "I'd rather love you. Drop the knife, and I'll make you feel safe again."

A frown tugged at the corners of her mouth before she dissolved into a silent sob. She drew in a shuddering breath, blinked again, then finally looked up at him. Slowly, she loosened her hold on the knife, and it slid free from her fingers to clatter on the concrete.

Relief slid through him in a drugging rush as he stood, avoiding the pool of blood. "Good girl. Such a wonderful, sweet love. Rise and come to me now. You're cold. Let me warm you."

Liam watched her face. The stupor lifted slowly, like a fog fading away. Raine focused on him, her face crumbling as recognition seeped in. The shell-shocked horror in her expression nearly floored him. She didn't move.

"Liam…"

"I'll help you, love." He reached a hand out to her, praying she'd take it and let him hold her. Every moment she held herself away from him felt like another eternity of death. "Come here."

"H-he hurt me."

Those tiny words wrenched everything inside him as he reached out to her. "I know. I'm so sorry. We're here, and nothing else will happen to you. Take my hand."

As she tried to rise on unsteady legs, she wobbled. When she would have fallen, Liam caught her, wrapping her in his coat, then swept her into his arms, away from Bill Kendall's remains.

Hammer and Beck rushed forward, meeting him halfway.

"Give her to me!" Hammer thrust out his arms and took her from Liam as Beck performed a cursory check for open wounds, broken bones, and head trauma.

"She's bruised and obviously in shock," Beck muttered in a soothing monotone, clearly trying not to upset Raine. "The bite marks?"

"Ours," Hammer admitted.

Beck just nodded. "I don't see any new wounds, but we won't know for sure what she's been through until we get her to the ER."

Sobbing now, she clutched Hammer, who fell to his knees with her and gripped her tightly in his embrace, pressing his forehead to hers and breathing fast.

"That's it, precious," Hammer whispered. "You're back with us now. Everything is going to be all right. We love you, Raine."

Liam knelt down beside them and wrapped his hand in hers. He could feel the dam within him cracking as the fear and anger he'd suppressed finally escaped. He pressed a fist smeared with blood to his chest, working to hold in tears. They were useless now. Their girl needed help.

Beck knelt next to Hammer, his expression compassionate but insistent. "Raine? Are you with me?"

She nodded before another sob broke her.

"Good. Listen to me, princess. This is important. Vital." Beck checked her pupils again, then cupped her face and drew her stare to his. "The cops are coming. They're going to ask you a lot of questions. So will the doctors. No matter what, you *must* tell them every mark on your body is one your father inflicted. Do you understand?"

"But Hammer and Liam gave me—"

"I know. But if you tell the police that, they could be arrested. Then they can't help you. Or comfort you. You have to do this. Okay?"

"Yeah," she managed to breathe out. "I will."

"Perfect," Beck praised. "When they ask, just tell them that Kendall gave you every bite, bruise, cut, scrape, rope burn… Don't forget."

As Beck released her face, Raine stared at the three of them, holding tight to Liam's hand while clinging to Hammer with the other. "I won't. I want to go home."

"I know, precious." Hammer cupped her chin. "Soon. I'm so

sorry he got to you."

"We'll need to get you checked out at the hospital first," Beck explained. "But before the paramedics show up, I need to get some more details from you. Are you allergic to anything?"

"Just sulphur-based antibiotics," Hammer supplied. "That's all I know of."

Raine nodded in agreement.

"Do you take regular meds for any condition?" Beck inquired.

"Only the occasional pain pill for her migraines," Liam replied.

Beck nodded. "You're on the pill, right?"

Raine shook her head, and Beck shot a disbelieving look toward Liam and Hammer.

"When were we supposed to find time for that between holidays, running away, and psychos?" Hammer growled.

"Understood," Beck answered in a calm voice. "These are questions the ER doc is going to need to know. If I can provide him the answers, it will expedite Raine's treatment."

"We can tell him," Liam insisted.

Beck shook his head. "You two won't be allowed back with her for the initial examination. This is a crime scene, and you're not family."

"Bullshit. We're all the family she's got." Hammer clearly struggled for composure.

"I'll help get you two back to see her as soon as possible. Just a few more questions before the cavalry shows up…" Beck focused his attention on Raine once more. "So I'm assuming you haven't voluntarily had unprotected sex recently?"

Liam heard the subtext and winced. *So the presence of any semen should be Bill's?*

"She and I made love earlier this morning," Liam breathed. "Bareback."

Christ, it felt like a lifetime since she'd surrounded him with her warm body.

Shock swept over Beck's face, one brow arching up sharply.

In the distance, the wail of sirens screamed closer. A movement near the door caught Liam's eye. *Gwyneth.* She stared at Raine trembling in Hammer's arms. Somehow, his ex managed to look completely shocked that Raine had truly been hurt.

Rage roared inside Liam. Battling his anger, he softly released Raine's hand and stood slowly. Once out of her sight, he tore off and headed straight for Gwyneth. When she saw him charging after her, she backed away, clearly deciding it might be a good idea to flee.

With a scream, she took off running. Liam pursued her. She didn't get far. Emergency vehicles poured into the car park. A patrol car skidded to a halt in front of her.

Jerking her hands into the air, she startled the emerging officers, including Sergeant Gorman, with her pleading. "Arrest me. Please!"

* * *

Hammer wore out the carpet in the emergency room. Thirteen paces. Back and forth. Over. And over. Since they'd arrived, forty-eight minutes had gone by according to the clock above the triage desk. It felt like forever. How fucking long until they had some information about Raine's condition? Until they found out what the hell she'd survived? How much longer before he and Liam could see her, touch her, assure themselves she'd be all right? Hell, his attorney had already been escorted to Raine's side and would see her even before he did. What a stupid injustice.

The image of her clutching the bloody knife, rocking and in shock, had seared itself in his brain. It would never fade. He would never forget. And he'd never stop reliving this terrible day.

Would it haunt Raine for the rest of her life, too?

He'd almost fucking lost her. He'd closed his eyes to sleep, and when he'd awakened, she had been gone. She'd nearly been taken—poof, in a blink, in an instant—forever.

Macen picked up the pace as he trekked across the room once more, as if he could escape that reality. He watched Liam parked on the edge of a chair, staring fixedly at the wall, somewhere between shocked and too furious for words. He'd said almost nothing since the ambulance had carted Raine away.

Dean Gorman had sent the detectives to take their statements, and Liam had given appropriate, if short, answers to all their questions. Since then? Nothing.

In a corner of the empty room, a small TV irritated him with canned talk show laughter. A breaking news story interrupted, and a perky newscaster appeared to say that Raine Kendall, a sex worker at a local BDSM club, had been abducted in the parking lot by her estranged father. She'd been found alive and was being treated at a local hospital. Her condition was uncertain. They also flashed Raine's picture all over the screen.

Liam's head snapped up. Hammer let out an ugly curse.

The anchor cut scene to a reporter, who stood just outside the ER door, posed in front of the camera, vomiting out the sketchy details of Raine's ordeal.

"I'm going to kill them all." Hammer charged at the door, ready to shove the mic up the young dude's ass and make sure it reached the station manager, too.

Liam leapt to his feet and grabbed Macen's arm. "And I'd like to help you. But we can't go charging out there now. We have to wait for news about Raine. What if she needs us? Besides, your attorney is with her so her rights are protected when the police question her. You can't get yourself arrested just now."

Hammer still struggled to breathe without thinking of murder, but Liam's logic finally penetrated. "She's not a fucking sex worker."

"I know." Liam tugged on his arm and shoved him into a chair. "But you've got to calm down. The important thing is that she's alive and—"

"Yes, but what the fuck else do we know?" He made a mental note to call the TV station and ream them out as soon as he'd seen Raine and assured himself she was well.

Liam sighed tiredly. "Too little, I grant you. But since I was just here last night with Kyle and cunt-face, I can tell you that nothing happens quickly. Beck is back there with our girl, expediting what he can and watching over her. When there's news, you know he'll tell us."

Vaguely, Hammer realized that, somewhere in the midst of all the shit they'd endured, Liam had learned to trust Beck. They hadn't exactly been buddies since meeting just over a month ago, but Liam finally had decided not to hate the guy anymore. A small but welcome victory.

Right now, Hammer would chuck it all just to see Raine.

He stood again, feeling ready to crawl out of his skin. "I can't stand this."

"Do you think I can?" Liam asked. "I'm every bit as worried as you, Macen. But you darting back and forth, wearing a path into the carpet, won't make anything happen faster."

God, he needed Liam's voice of reason…but sometimes he really despised it. At least he had his best friend at his side. That kept him from tearing up the place. Now if he could just crush the TV and kill the reporter…

"I feel like shit," he admitted.

"You look like shit," Liam returned with a little grin. "But I don't suppose I look any better."

Wearing yesterday's clothes and all covered in blood, no. Hammer glanced down at himself, then over at Liam. "Not so much."

His friend sank into the chair beside him. "I can hardly breathe, mate. While she was missing, I just kept asking myself how I was going to survive without her." Liam stared down at his hands, wincing at the remnants of blood in his cuticles, under his nails, despite the twenty times he'd washed them. "She's my life now. It was bad enough when I'd convinced myself she didn't love me. But a world without her at all is one I don't want to live in."

"Yeah. If we'd lost Raine…" He swallowed a lump in his throat. "I couldn't go through that shit again. It would be a billion times worse than what I went through with Juliet."

"I finally understand how you must have felt when she died. I can't change the past, and I'm more sorry than I can say that I wasn't there for you. But I'm here now."

He exhaled a rough breath. "That means more than you know."

The glass double doors whooshed open. Seth came striding in, plastic bag in hand, beside Dean Gorman.

"What's the news about Raine?" Seth asked.

Hammer shook his head. "Nothing. We don't have a fucking

clue."

"I can give you some news on the investigation," Dean offered, sweeping a coat from his broad shoulders. "Gwyneth has been arrested for conspiracy to commit a kidnapping, as well as aiding and abetting. The fact that she left the assailant a voice mail with a time stamp prior to Raine's actual abduction and recanted the scheme might persuade the judge to give a little leniency, but…" Dean rubbed at his neck. "Her sparkling personality will undo all that. I see the judge slapping her with contempt of court in the first five minutes. She had the nerve to complain about the smell in the squad car and insisted we find an air freshener."

Liam groaned. "That sounds about right. What's likely to happen to her?"

"She's already lawyered up, and she'll probably work out some deal. But with the voice mails on your phone, Liam, and the one she left on Bill Kendall's, I'd say she's going down for a long time."

"There *is* a God," Seth muttered.

"And He's smiling down on us for a change." Hammer clapped Liam on the back.

"As long as I don't have to look at the bitch's face again, I don't care," Liam said.

"On the flip side, the crime scene at the warehouse is being processed. I need pictures of your clothing." Dean held up a camera and snapped a few shots.

"Hell, you can have them," Liam swore. "I won't ever wear them again."

Hammer looked down at his own stained, grimy garments. "Me, either."

"I figured you'd want clean clothes." Seth handed them the bag in his hand. "There's a set for each of you."

Macen peeked inside, thrilled to find a complete change, down to the shoes. "Thanks, man. This will feel a whole lot better."

Liam nodded. "I'm grateful we won't be seeing Raine while still covered in blood. Thank you, Seth."

A sight like that would set her back, no doubt. Hammer grimaced.

"That's what I thought." Seth sent them a faint smile as his phone dinged. He pulled it from his pocket and scanned the screen. "Vivian just texted. She got off the phone with Gwyneth's sister a few minutes ago. Kitty and her husband are boarding a flight to L.A. as we speak. They'll be picking up Kyle as soon as they hit town this afternoon. Naturally, they're frantic. And shocked."

More remnants of Typhoon Gwyneth. Hammer couldn't be more thrilled that selfish, psycho hag was out of their lives forever.

"At least the boy will be back with his parents soon," Liam murmured.

Seth pocketed his phone. "And until then, Vivian is having a ball."

Dean cleared his throat. "I hope you guys have a damn good explanation for why you reached the warehouse before the police."

"I'll tell you what I told the other detective: Talk to my lawyer."

Gorman sighed, clearly realizing he'd hit a brick wall. "Fine. Then I need to prepare you for a few other things before you're called back to see Raine."

A terrible thought occurred to Hammer. "Does the DA want to charge her for Bill's murder? She acted purely in self-defense. Any fucking idiot—"

"Can see that? Yes," Dean cut in, his voice soothing and low, and Hammer realized he'd been shouting.

"Sorry."

Gorman just shook his head. "No apology necessary. It's been a terrible fucking morning for you guys. But you're right. I doubt the DA will file charges against Raine. It's obvious she did what she had to in order to fight for her life. Rest easy on that."

Hammer let out the breath he didn't realize he'd been holding. Beside him, Liam did the same.

"Thank God our lass will be coming home," he murmured.

Yes. But would she be the same lass who'd left their arms mere hours ago?

Hammer shoved the thought away. They had to get through today before they could worry about tomorrow.

"I need to fill you in on what will happen next," Dean went on, then dragged in a breath. "In cases like this, the victim will always be interviewed by a female detective. Seth provided me copies of the pictures you took of Raine after her father's beating, just before she first came to live with you. So Detective Bates, who will be questioning her, has already seen the images and knows the history."

That was a relief, but how had Seth known?

"I told him where to find the pictures, mate," Liam muttered. "After the police read Gwyneth her rights and cuffed her, I called Seth to update him and told him to find the pictures."

Again, Hammer felt blessed to have his best friend at his side. "Smart thinking. Hopefully, it will make her interrogation a bit smoother."

Dean hesitated. "I wish that were true. You need to be ready for the fact that, as a woman living and working in what some people see as a pornographic or abusive environment, Raine will be grilled." When Macen would have objected, Gorman cut in. "It's an uneducated perspective, and Bates is a bit of a hard ass. She'll want to be one hundred percent sure Raine isn't afraid of or being abused by anyone at home. Independent of the criminal investigation, which won't be easy, Bates will ask tough questions. They might rattle Raine."

Hammer gritted his teeth. Goddamn it, it was his job to protect her, and he felt so fucking helpless. Liam had to be fighting the same struggle. "Why the hell can't they wait until she's calmer?"

Dean shook his head. "As a Dom, I totally understand why you'd want that and why it's chafing you not to be there, holding her hand. As a cop, they need her unfiltered story as soon as possible, before the details go cold."

"We don't like it," Liam said, looking grim and exhausted. "But we understand."

"Mr. Hammerman? Mr. O'Neill?" a soft, female voice called from an open door that led to the depths of the ER.

Hammer turned to a painfully young blonde with her flaxen curls tucked into some wispy, complicated cross between a braid and a bun. When he and Liam both charged at her and pinned her with their attention, she bowed her head, her cheeks flushing.

"Yes," Macen barked when they stopped in front of her.

"Do you have news?" Liam asked.

She raised big blue eyes to them, full of gentle intelligence. "Dr. Beckman sent me to tell you that Ms. Kendall doesn't have any major injuries. She's alert and talking. He's been with her since she arrived. He's personally ensuring she's comfortable."

Liam let out a huge sigh of relief. "Our girl is okay?"

The nurse nodded. "She'll be fine."

"When can we see her?" Hammer demanded.

"Neither of you are family?" the little blonde asked.

"Technically, no but…" He gritted his teeth and looked at Liam. "Why hasn't one of us married her yet? That would have solved this."

"That's a good idea." Liam nodded as if testing the idea and liking it. Then he slanted Macen a wry stare. "We should do that. Are we going to arm wrestle for it?"

"Maybe you should flip a coin." Seth horned in beside him, staring at the little nurse like a starving man at a buffet. He stuck his hand out to her. "I'm Seth Cooper."

She sent him a confused frown as she placed her fingers in his palm. "I'm Heavenly."

Yes, you are. Hammer read Seth's unspoken reply all over his face.

"Are you the patient's family?" she asked.

"Just a friend," Seth assured.

"She has no one else. We're like her family," Hammer insisted.

"But you're not actually related or married?" she double-checked.

"One of us will marry her in the next ten minutes if we'll be allowed to see her. Hell, we both would if it was legal," Liam groused, sounding exasperated.

The innocent little submissive in uniform bit her lip, looking as if she'd never heard of, much less considered, a ménage.

Heavenly shook her head. "I'm sorry. I don't make the rules."

Hammer elbowed Seth. "What else can you tell us about Raine's condition?"

"I'm just a nursing student. I've only been in to give her

water and blankets."

"Do you know how much longer before we'll be able to see her?" Liam asked.

Heavenly shook her head regretfully. "The police haven't even finished with her, so I suspect it will be a while. In the meantime, Dr. Beckman asked me to escort you to a nearby lounge. You'll be able to shower there. Just let me know when you're ready."

After exchanging a glance with Liam, Hammer knew they were on the same page. "Let's do it now, just in case we're able to see her sooner, rather than later."

"Follow me." She let the ER door close behind her and led them to another closed door, accessible only with her electronic ID badge.

"Thank you, Heavenly," Seth called to her.

She turned to him with a shy smile, not quite meeting his gaze. "You're welcome."

In fifteen minutes, he and Liam had both showered and changed clothes. The hot spray had done a world of good in reviving him. Liam looked a bit more alive, too.

When they emerged, Heavenly stood there with two hot plates of food. "Seth found you some breakfast at the cafeteria. There's a little break room around the corner with coffee."

Heavenly pointed to her left. They smiled, thanked her, grabbed hot cups, then returned to the waiting room to juggle their plates in their laps, shove down food, and wait for news about Raine.

By then, Seth was speaking to various members of the club who'd stopped by, updating them on what little they knew of Raine's status. Hammer was grateful for their caring. He wiped his mouth with a napkin, finished the last swig of his coffee, and greeted the members, thanking them. Liam joined him.

In the corner, they spotted a young man behind a magazine with wide shoulders, big hands, and piercing eyes. He didn't look familiar, but as far as Hammer knew, the ER wasn't clogged up with other cases at the moment.

He frowned. If the asshole was a reporter looking for a scoop…

Another Dom approached him before he could finish that

thought and accost the stranger. Hammer and Liam talked to that club member and the others, managing to pass the next twenty minutes in only mild agony. The waiting still rubbed him raw, but being surrounded by concerned friends was definitely a balm. Raine would be touched by the number of people who had come to express their support.

Finally, the door to the back of the ER snapped open, and Beck walked toward them.

Hammer and Liam both cut their conversations short and rushed over.

"What can you tell us?" Liam insisted, as if he couldn't say the words fast enough.

"Anything?" Hammer added.

"Calm down. She's shaken. Tearful. Afraid. But mostly fine. We cleaned her up, stitched her lip, and checked out the rest of her trauma."

"What do you mean by that?" Hammer barked.

Beck held up a hand. "Kendall punched her in the eye. We've managed to reduce the swelling. The eye socket wasn't broken, thankfully. But she's bruised. There will be more contusions around her neck where he tried to strangle her."

Hammer's blood iced over. A chill settled into his bones as he buried his face in his hands. Why the fuck hadn't he been able to protect her? Yes, he knew the news was mostly good. He could be standing in the emergency room again hearing the speech about how they'd tried but there had been nothing the doctors could do to save her… He refused to fall down that mental black hole now.

"Strangle her?" Liam breathed the words in shock. "Oh, Raine must have been terrified."

"But she's a survivor." Macen kept reminding himself of that over and over. If he didn't, he'd go fucking insane.

"We didn't do a rape exam. Raine swears Bill didn't penetrate her. Apparently, he couldn't get it up."

Besides finding Raine alive, that was some of the best news he'd had all day.

"What a relief," Liam said, again mirroring his thoughts.

"She's talking to a female detective now. As soon as the woman is done, you can see Raine. But you should know, the police treated Raine's body like a crime scene because it is. It's… Honestly, it's been nothing short of a nightmare for her. She's fragile and she'll need you."

"We're ready. Just lead us to her." Hammer wanted to barge past Beck.

"Please. We can't do anything for her out here." Liam sounded at the end of his patience.

"As soon as she's done with the questioning, I'll have Heavenly escort you back. But during this interview, no one is allowed to be with Raine except her attorney. We just have to wait until the interrogation is over."

Hammer knew that. Some distant part of his mind accepted that fact. The man in him railed. The Dom in him roared. Why the fuck was it taking them so long to let him and Liam see their woman? How fucking crazy would he go before they could?

Beck returned to Raine's side. Macen took up pacing again. Liam couldn't seem to decide whether to stand or sit. The club members milling around talked. The man with the magazine said nothing.

After what seemed like an eternity, Heavenly appeared again with a smile. "You can see Raine now."

Neither one of them could move fast enough. He and Liam bounded through the door and followed her down a hall.

A few paces away, Macen ran into his attorney, a fifty-something grandfather who wielded the law like a shark. They shook hands.

"I'll call you later so you can fill me in," he said, dashing for Raine's room.

"Give me a ring." The man in the pristine suit waved. "But she did great. She's a tough cookie. You shouldn't have any worries legally."

Absorbing that relief, Hammer jogged back to Liam's side, then rounded the corner. There, they found Raine cradled in Beck's arms. The doctor stroked her hair as her shoulders shook in silent sobs. The sight ripped out Hammer's soul. The look on Liam's face told Macen he felt the same.

"I've been asking for Liam and Hammer," Raine cried. "I've done everything the police and the doctors needed. Why can't I see them?"

"We're here, love." Liam rushed into the room.

Macen followed, dying to hold her in his arms now—and until the end of time. "We came to see you as soon as we were allowed, precious."

Beck eased back and turned to them. Finally, Hammer and Liam got a good look at their girl.

Hammer's chest tightened. Though she was no longer covered in blood, the brutality Bill had inflicted on Raine enraged him and broke his heart. But under the stitches and bruises lay a strong, resilient woman. *Their* woman. And she'd never looked more beautiful.

"Liam…Hammer." Raine opened her arms to them, despite the IV and a few assorted bandages. Tears streamed down her cheeks.

Beck stepped back as Hammer rushed toward her. Liam did the same, flanking the other side of her bed. Hammer bent and nuzzled his face into her neck, inhaling her familiar scent deep with weak-kneed gratitude. He brushed gentle kisses over her cheek. Tears stung the backs of his eyes as he drank her in. Slowly, he lifted his head. She took his hand.

Liam had her other hand tucked in his as he leaned in and brushed a reverent kiss on her forehead, closing his eyes to savor the sweet moment.

Heavenly hurried in, carrying a white blanket over her arm—and stopped short at the sight of them both giving Raine affection. The pretty nurse blushed furiously and darted Beck a curious stare before dropping her gaze again. The doctor tensed and stared a hole into the girl. Couldn't the damn sadist step out of his fucking door without attracting subs like a damn magnet?

"I have a warmer blanket for you, Ms. Kendall."

"Please don't call me that," Raine snapped at the other woman, then frowned. "I-I'm sorry. Just call me Raine, okay?"

"Of course." Heavenly quickly tucked the blanket around Raine before scurrying out of the room.

Beck's eyes narrowed on the sway of the woman's ass as she walked away.

Raine tried to smile but winced as the stitches in her lip pulled. "Honestly, Beck. You've been mentally undressing that poor nurse since we got here. You can't be serious. She's like

Little Red Riding Hood to your Big, Bad Wolf. The instant you finish sucking the flesh off her bones, you'll be picking your teeth with them."

Hammer was relieved to hear the sassy Raine he knew, but she clearly forced the levity.

Beck frowned. "I'm not going to hurt her."

"Said the sadist," Hammer grumbled under his breath.

The frown creasing Beck's face became a scowl.

"What are you waiting for?" Liam asked him. "She's getting away, mate."

"I can take a hint." Beck grinned. "I'll give you all some privacy. Back in a few."

"Try to leave her in one piece," Hammer called after him.

After shooting him a dirty glare, the doctor hustled out the door, taking the levity of the moment with him. The guilt and pain that had wracked Hammer the instant he'd discovered Raine missing returned.

Finally alone with the two people he loved most, Hammer wrapped his arms around Raine, thankful that Liam was on the same page, embracing her as if she was his everything. "Let it out, precious. Give your pain to us."

Their reassurance seemed to break the dam holding in Raine's emotions. She sobbed for endless moments. Neither he nor Liam let go. Instead, they whispered how glad they were that she was safe, that she'd found a way to survive, that they loved her.

Long minutes later, Hammer kissed the tears from her cheeks, then Liam placed a tissue beneath her nose. She stared up at his partner with those beautiful blue eyes.

"Blow, Raine," Liam instructed.

She didn't protest or argue that she could do it herself. She simply let Liam pamper her—no questions asked—because they both needed it. Hammer sent her an approving smile.

"How are you feeling, love? Is there anything we can get you?" Liam asked in that tender voice that always made Raine glow.

"I'm fine."

She put on a brave face, but Hammer saw through it.

"Tell him the truth," he pressed.

Raine laced her fingers through his. "Right. Honesty. Communication." She blew out a breath. "I'm sore everywhere. But the pain tells me I'm alive. And I'm so thankful to be out of that horrible place and away from that monster forever."

Hammer clenched his teeth as he inhaled a deep breath. "So are we."

"God, yes," Liam seconded. "Would you like to talk to us about it, love? Or is it too soon?"

"We'll help you through this no matter what," Hammer assured. "Lean on us. I swear to god we won't let you down again."

"Neither of you let me down. I went running out of the club instead of waking you up. I didn't think anything so terrible would…" Raine's chin quivered.

"Shh." Hammer leaned in and gingerly touched his lips to hers, careful not to disrupt her stitches. "It's all right. Tell us how to help you."

Raine blinked as if unsure what she needed, then swallowed. "I don't know where to start. Every minute seemed more and more horrific. I was so scared." Her voice cracked but she continued. "H-he told me he'd been raping my older sister for years, and she let him to protect me."

Hammer silently thanked the woman for her tragic sacrifice. But he couldn't say he was at all surprised to find out that Raine's sister had suffered under Bill's hand.

"Oh, love," Liam moaned. "It must have been awful."

"Then, instead of taking her to the airport to leave for college, he k-killed her. He just took a knife and…" Raine sobbed out in a gut-wrenching wail. "He couldn't wait to tell me that he'd killed my m-m-mom, too."

Shoving down his wrath and wishing he could kill the dead man all over again, Hammer perched on the bed beside her. Liam did the same. Together, they wrapped their arms around her and held her until she slowly regained enough composure to carry on.

"I don't even know where their bodies are." She sniffed. "The only one who truly escaped was my brother, but I don't know where River is or what's happened to him." Then what little self-possession she'd managed dissolved. "I thought once you two found me that all the bad stuff was over, but god, the

EMTs came and…"

Raine pushed against them as if suffocating. He and Liam both eased back, exchanging a worried glance. Hammer suddenly realized Raine didn't need their physical comfort as much as she needed to vent the torment bottled up inside her.

"They bagged my hands. I couldn't touch anything until the police came. They took the bags off but scraped under my fingernails to 'preserve evidence.' Then they examined all my bruises and bite marks with so much pity in their eyes I wanted to scream. They took pictures of every single inch of my body, poking at me and making me pose for them as if I were some kind of freak. When they finished scrutinizing every crack and crevice, I felt as if all the loving marks you two had left on me were tainted and disgusting. I couldn't even say one word in our defense to make them understand."

Hammer took her hand as the words spilled off her lips. He had to clench his jaw so he didn't lash out in rage. Liam's expression bled self-reproach and anger as he skimmed his fingers up and down her arm. Neither of them knew what to do, except listen and offer comfort.

"But I remembered what Beck said at the…" Her breath shuddered. "What I had to do. So I told the female detective and your attorney that Bill did everything to me. God, the questions she asked… They never seemed to stop. The police wouldn't let Beck stay with me while she interrogated me. That woman kept asking if I was afraid or being abused because I live in a sex club. I tried to explain that Shadows wasn't simply a club for folks who wanted to randomly get it on, but she didn't acknowledge anything I said, just kept asking questions."

More tears spilled down her cheeks. Hammer couldn't fucking stand that he was unable to erase the injustice she'd had to endure after the atrocities at the warehouse.

"I had to tell a total stranger everything about my family, starting as far back as I could remember. But she didn't stop there. She also wanted to know all the hateful, degrading, vile things my father had said to me my whole life. I wanted so badly to tell her that when I stuck that knife into Bill and watched him die, I didn't feel a damn thing except relief because he fucking deserved it."

Raine hung her head and burst into tears. Low, long sobs filled the room and tore at his heart. Hammer and Liam surrounded her once again, holding her, encouraging her to release her grief and anger, repeating that they loved her, assuring her everything would be all right.

Macen had no way of knowing whether he could keep that last promise because he no longer had to wonder if the day's events would haunt her for the rest of her life. He knew they would. Instead, he had to help her find a way to move forward.

Something he'd never been particularly good at himself.

"We're proud of you for being so brave, love," Liam cooed.

"You're alive, Raine. You have so many tomorrows to look forward to," Hammer murmured. "If you'd like, we'll move into the new house before Christmas. Just the three of us…together."

"That's right," Liam added. "There's no stopping us now, love. It's you, Hammer, and me from now on. You'll have your hands full making that house into our home. Start your new life with us. We'll fill it with so much love you won't be able to drink it all in."

Raine sucked in a quivering breath before she raised her chin and wiped her eyes. There she was, their Raine—bold and beautiful and determined to fight back the darkness, at least for this one priceless moment.

"I'm beyond ready," she vowed.

Hammer couldn't help the tears of pride that filled his eyes. If he and Liam nurtured and coaxed this brave girl, she could conquer the world.

Suddenly, Seth and Beck entered the room. Seth sent a gentle smile her way. Just as he opened his mouth to say something, Heavenly scurried in with a fresh cup of ice chips.

"Well, hello again." Seth smiled at the sweet-faced blonde.

She couldn't quite meet his gaze. "Hi."

Both Beck and Seth homed in, watching the woman's every move as she set the plastic cup on the hospital tray near Raine's bed, then hurried toward the door with a nervous smile at the pair.

Beck stopped her with a hand on her arm, and Hammer didn't think he'd ever seen the doctor touch any submissive so tenderly. "Thank you for your help."

"My pleasure. I enjoy helping others."

No doubt, the innocent girl had no idea how much her words fired up Beck's Dominant loins. Instead, she darted out of the room. When Beck realized Seth stared at the sway of her hips as she walked away, he growled in warning.

"What?" Seth asked, arching a brow.

Hammer smirked as the beginnings of a plan hatched in his head. He and Liam had endured a shitload of ballbusting from these two. Finally, the opportunity for some payback looked promising.

"Not you, too?" Raine shot Seth a suspicious look.

"I didn't do a thing," he insisted way too innocently.

"Make sure you keep it that way." Beck sounded more than annoyed.

Seth rolled his eyes, then sidled up to the bed next to Liam and gently caressed Raine's inky hair. "You doing okay, little one?"

"Yeah." She did her best to send him a smile. "Thanks."

Before they could say more, the ER doctor strolled into the room, glaring at the sudden crowd.

Beck gave Seth a shove and nodded toward the door. "Let's give them some privacy, Captain America." He waved at Raine. "We'll be back shortly."

"Thank you, guys. For everything."

After they'd gone, the doctor introduced himself to Liam and Hammer, then turned all his attention on Raine.

"We're going to keep you overnight so we can keep an eye on you and give you some IV antibiotics for the bite marks, just in case. I don't think you'll need to stay longer than that."

Raine sighed. "Can't I just go home?"

"If he wants you to stay, you'll stay," Hammer ordered.

"But don't worry, love. We'll be with you, too," Liam assured.

"How are you feeling now?" the doctor inquired, pen and chart in hand.

"Much better now." The look she sent him and Liam told Hammer how relieved and grateful she was to have them at her side.

Macen's heart opened even wider to her. How had he ever

denied a moment of her love?

"Good." The balding, thirty-something doctor smiled. "I've got your test results back. Would you like to go over them privately?"

"Whatever you have to say to me, you can say to the three of us." She reached out and clasped both their hands.

"Okay." He took their unusual relationship in stride, like a medical professional who'd seen and done it all. Then he glanced again at her chart. "Most everything came out normal. I've just got a few questions. Are you having any tingling or numbness in your feet or hands?"

"No, they feel fine," she replied as she held up her hands and wiggled her toes.

The ligature marks around her wrists from Bill's ropes were red and chapped. Hammer couldn't wait for the day they disappeared—as well as the wounds on her face—so he'd never have to be visually reminded of Bill Kendall or his brutality again.

"Good." The doctor nodded. "Any floaters or sparks of light in your eyes?"

Raine shook her head.

"Do you have any discomfort in your jaw when you talk?"

"A little, but it's going away," she assured.

"Are you having other pain? Anything hurting more than a Tylenol can relieve?" The doctor darted a glance at the bite marks on her neck but didn't mention them.

"My shoulders are stiff from being tied… In fact, I'm getting a little sore all over."

The doctor nodded. "Then I'll get you a couple of acetaminophen. I see your last period started November twenty-second, is that right?"

"Yes."

"Was it normal?"

"Not really. It was late and a bit short, but I was under a lot of stress."

She sent Liam an apologetic frown. He merely squeezed her hand.

The doctor nodded. "That sometimes happens, but it's nothing to worry about. But I don't foresee any problems from today's ordeal. Even so, I recommend you follow up with your OB/GYN in a week or so and have him check you out thoroughly."

"Why?" Liam asked with an alarm that reflected Hammer's own.

Had fucking Bill raped her after all?

The doctor ignored Liam and cocked his head at Raine. "Didn't you know? You're pregnant."

** Doms of Her Life will return with book 4, The Edge of Dominance, and will contain both a conclusion and new beginnings for our beloved characters. **

His To Take

A Wicked Lovers Novel
By Shayla Black
Coming March 3, 2015

Racing against time, NSA Agent Joaquin Muñoz is searching for a little girl who vanished twenty years ago with a dangerous secret. Since Bailey Benson fits the profile, Joaquin abducts the beauty and whisks her to the safety of Club Dominion—before anyone can silence her for good.

At first, Bailey is terrified, but when her captor demands information about her past, she's stunned. Are her horrific visions actually distant memories that imperil all she holds dear? Confined with Joaquin in a place that echoes with moans and breathes passion, he proves himself a fierce protector, as well as a sensual Master who's slowly crawling deeper in her head…and heart. But giving in to him might be the most delicious danger of all.

Because Bailey soon learns that her past isn't the only mystery. Joaquin has a secret of his own—a burning vengeance in his soul. The exposed truth leaves her vulnerable and wondering how much about the man she loves is a lie, how much more is at risk than her heart. And if she can trust him to protect her long enough to learn the truth.

* * * *

"…What about you? You're with another government agency, so you're here to . . . what? Be my lover? Does Uncle Sam think you need to crawl between my legs in order to watch over me?"

Joaquin ground his jaw. She was hitting low, and the logical part of him understood that she was hurt, so she was lashing out at the messenger because she didn't have anyone else. But that didn't stop his temper from getting swept up in her cyclone of emotion. "I'm not here on anyone's orders. In fact, I'll probably be fired for pursuing this case because Tatiana Aslanov isn't on my boss's radar. When it became obvious the agency intended to do nothing, I couldn't leave you to that horrific death. So here we are. But let me clue you in, baby girl. Uncle Sam doesn't tell me who to fuck. I can't fake an erection, even for the sake of God and country. That kiss we almost shared? That was me wanting you because just being in the same room with you makes me want to strip off everything you're wearing and impale you with every inch I've got."

When he eased closer to Bailey, she squared her shoulders and raised her chin. "Don't come near me."

That defiance made him wish again that he was a spanking kind of guy. He'd really like to melt that starch in her spine. If she wasn't going to let him comfort her, he'd be more than happy to adjust her attitude with a good smack or ten on her ass, then follow it up with a thorough fucking. A nice handful of orgasms would do them both a world of good.

"I am so done with people lying to me," she ground out.

That pissed him off. "You think I'm lying to you? About which part? Your parents being agents? That I'm sorry? Or that my cock is aching to fill your sweet little pussy until you dig your nails into my back and wail out in pleasure?"

Her face turned pink. "You're not sorry about any of this. I'm also not buying your sudden desire bullshit."

"I will be more than happy to prove you wrong right now." He reached for the button of his jeans. "I'm ready if you are."

In some distant corner of his brain, Joaquin realized that combating her hurt with challenge wasn't going over well. On the other hand, something about arguing with her while he'd been imagining her underneath him hadn't just gotten his blood flowing, but boiling. If fucking her would, in any way, prove to her that he wasn't lying, he was beyond down with getting busy. If she let him, he'd give it to her hard and wicked—and repeatedly.

"No!" She managed to look indignant, but her cheeks had gone rosy. The pulse at her neck was pounding. Her nipples poked at her borrowed shirt angrily.

He put his hands on his hips. If she looked down, she'd see his straining zipper. "Do you still think I'm lying?"

"I'm done with this conversation."

“If you’re telling yourself you don’t want me at all, then you’re the one lying.”

“Pfft. You might know facts about me on paper, but you don’t know me.”

“So if I touched your pussy right now, you wouldn’t be wet?”

He’d always liked a good challenge. It was probably one of the reasons he loved his job. But facing off with her this way made his blood sing, too.

“No.” She shook her head a bit too emphatically. “And you’re not touching me to find out. Leave me alone.” “You’re worried that I’d find you juicy.

You’re afraid to admit that I turn you on.” He stalked closer, his footfalls heavy, his eyes narrowing in on her.

“Stay back,” she warned—but her eyes said something else entirely.

“Tell me you’re not attracted to me.” He reached out, his strike fast as a snake’s, and gripped her arms. He dragged her closer, fitting her lithe little body against him and holding in a groan when she brushed over his cock. “Tell me you want me to stop. Remember, you don’t like liars. I don’t, either.”

She didn’t say a word, struggled a bit for show. Mostly, she parted her lips and panted. Her cheeks heated an even deeper rose. Her chest heaved. Never once did she look away from him. “I’m involved with someone else.”

“If you think whatever you’ve got going with Blane is going to stop me . . .” He didn’t bother to finish his sentence; he just laughed.

“So you’re not listening to me say ‘no’? You’re not respecting my feelings for another guy?”

“Let’s just say I’m proving my sincerity to you.” He tightened his grip. When she gasped and her stare fell to his lips, triumph raced through his veins. “I’m also testing you. That pretty mouth of yours might lie to me, but your kisses won’t.”

Joaquin didn’t give her a chance to protest again. Normally, he would have. Women 101 was never to proceed without express consent, but this thick air of tension electrifying his blood and seizing his lungs was something entirely new and intoxicating. Their fight seemed to be helping Bailey forget her shock and sadness, not to mention the fact that it revved her, too. She wasn't immune to him—not by a long shot. Thank fuck.

Thrusting a fist in her hair, he pinned her in place and lowered his head.

About Shayla Black

Shayla Black (aka Shelley Bradley) is the New York Times and USA Today bestselling author of over 40 sizzling contemporary, erotic, paranormal, and historical romances produced via traditional, small press, independent, and audio publishing. She lives in Texas with her husband, munchkin, and one very spoiled cat. In her "free" time, she enjoys reality TV, reading and listening to an eclectic blend of music.

Shayla's books have been translated in about a dozen languages. RT Bookclub has nominated her for a Career Achievement award in erotic romance, twice nominated her for Best Erotic Romance of the year, as well as awarded her several Top Picks, and a KISS Hero Award. She has also received or been nominated for The Passionate Plume, The Holt Medallion, Colorado Romance Writers Award of Excellence, and the National Reader's Choice Awards.

A writing risk-taker, Shayla enjoys tackling writing challenges with every new book.

Connect with her online:

Shayla Black:
Facebook: www.facebook.com/ShaylaBlackAuthor
Twitter: www.twitter.com/@shayla_black
Website: www.shaylablack.com

Also from Shayla Black/Shelley Bradley

EROTIC ROMANCE

The Wicked Lovers
Wicked Ties
Decadent
Delicious
Surrender To Me
Belong To Me
"Wicked to Love" (e-novella)
Mine To Hold
"Wicked All The Way" (e-novella)
Ours To Love
Wicked and Dangerous
"Forever Wicked" (e-novella)
Theirs To Cherish
Wicked All Night
Coming Soon:
His to Take (March 2015)
Pure Wicked (e-novella, September 2015)

Sexy Capers
Bound And Determined
Strip Search
"Arresting Desire" – Hot In Handcuffs Anthology

Masters Of Ménage (by Shayla Black and Lexi Blake)
Their Virgin Captive
Their Virgin's Secret
Their Virgin Concubine
Their Virgin Princess
Their Virgin Hostage
Their Virgin Secretary
Coming Soon:
Their Virgin Mistress

Doms Of Her Life (by Shayla Black, Jenna Jacob, and Isabella LaPearl)
One Dom To Love
The Young And The Submissive
The Bold and The Dominant
Coming Soon:
The Edge of Dominance

Stand Alone Titles
Naughty Little Secret (as Shelley Bradley)
Watch Me (as Shelley Bradley)
Dangerous Boys And Their Toy
"Her Fantasy Men" – Four Play Anthology

PARANORMAL ROMANCE

The Doomsday Brethren
Tempt Me With Darkness
"Fated" (e-novella)
Seduce Me In Shadow
Possess Me At Midnight
"Mated" – Haunted By Your Touch Anthology
Entice Me At Twilight
Embrace Me At Dawn

HISTORICAL ROMANCE (as Shelley Bradley)

The Lady And The Dragon
One Wicked Night
Strictly Seduction
Strictly Forbidden

Brothers in Arms
His Lady Bride, Brothers in Arms (Book 1)
His Stolen Bride, Brothers in Arms (Book 2)
His Rebel Bride, Brothers in Arms (Book 3)

CONTEMPORARY ROMANCE (as Shelley Bradley)
A Perfect Match

SEDUCED BY MY DOMS

The Doms Of Genesis – Book Five
By Jenna Jacob
Coming early 2015!

EXCERPT

"Is there a full moon tonight, or what? This is beyond crazy," I mumbled, sidling up next to Cindy—best friend and supervisor—at the nurses' station.

She didn't take her dark eyes off the patient chart she studied, but nodded in agreement. "It's balls to the wall, that's for sure. Oh, and Dr. Reynolds just informed me, EMS is en route again. E.T.A. is six minutes."

The Emergency Room of Highland Park Hospital, where Cindy and I worked, had been filled to capacity since my shift began at noon. The entire unit had been hopping with patients suffering minor ailments to filled trauma bays after a six-car pile up on the Interstate. We'd barely had time to utter more than a few words to one another all night. The waiting room was still packed with no end in sight.

"Somebody needs to take away the baton from whoever's leading this parade." I grumbled, waiting for the printer to spit out discharge papers for a six year old with tonsillitis.

"They will, in two more hours when it's time for shift change." Cindy laughed then quickly sobered. "Hey, if you'll keep an eye on my patients in two, six, seven, and fourteen, I'll take the guy that's coming in."

Though Cindy's offer seemed benign, my suspicion spiked. She never passed off her patients and the concern lining her face, made me even more wary. She wasn't telling me something, but what?

"Who are they bringing in, the Pope?" I joked, hoping she'd spill the truth.

"No. A bunch of drunk frat boys decided to beat the shit out of some guy."

"Piece of cake. Let me drop these papers off to my patient in twelve and prep the trauma room," I offered. "My guy in three is being admitted, and my woman from eight is down in x-ray.

They're so swamped, she won't be back for another hour or so."

"I said I'd take care of the new guy."

Cindy's tone was unusually short, and I shot her my best, '*bitch, please*' look.

"I'm sorry," she amended with a heavy sigh. "Just cover my patients for a bit, okay? I'll take them back as soon as I can."

"What is it about this patient coming in that you think I'm not qualified to handle?" My voice held a bitter edge as I scowled at my bestie. "An hour ago I was sopping up blood from a dude who nearly cut his leg off with a chain saw. I think I can handle a guy who's been in a fight. Unless you're suddenly questioning my abilities, in which case, I find your lack of confidence in me insulting"

"It's not that you can't handle it, Liz. It's that I don't *want* you to."

"Why not?" I countered.

Cindy wrapped a soft hand around my elbow. Her dark eyes swam in a pool of apology and compassion. "Liz, you're an amazing trauma nurse. I've never once questioned your skills. They're impeccable. This isn't about the job. It's about *you.* I love you, and I don't want you dealing with what's coming through that door. Can't we just leave it at that?"

"No, we can't. What is it you think you have to protect me from? Christ I'm thirty-one years old. I've been a nurse longer than most of the doctors doing rotation here."

She exhaled a heavy sigh as a look of resignation settled over the delicate bones of her pretty face. "The guy they're bringing in is gay. He told the cops that a bunch of homophobic assholes beat him up. From what I hear, he's in bad shape."

My heart lurched to my throat. Swallowing tightly I tried to detach my personal emotions from my professional duties. Digging deep, I squared my shoulders. "I appreciate your concern, but you don't need to coddle me. Just let me do my job, okay?"

As I turned on my heel to walk away, Cindy gripped my arm tighter. "Liz, you've been through hell and back, after Dayne…" She closed her eyes and let out a heavy sigh.

"Killed himself? Yes, I know." Simply saying the words brought a rush of anguish so bitter and hot, I clenched my jaw to keep from howling.

"Take my patients. Please. Let me deal with the beating victim."

I shook my head. "No. I need to do it. I *have* to. For Dayne's sake as well as my own."

Cindy frowned and nodded defeat. "If the ghosts get too real, come get me. I'll take over for you. Understood?"

With a weak smile, I nodded. "Don't worry. They won't."

The double doors swung wide as the paramedics wheeled in a thin, young man covered in blood.

"Bay one," Cindy called out. We both raced into the room followed by other members of the trauma team.

Racing into the room, other members of the trauma team poured in behind us. In a familiar and well-choreographed ballet, we moved around each other seamlessly, easing the patient from the gurney to the bed. While other nurses cut off the young man's clothes, Dr. Reynolds and I started assessing the man's injuries. A paramedic's read from the run sheet while Cindy frantically took down the information. Listening, I made a mental note of the victims vitals while trying not to notice the patches of blonde hair—not covered in blood—was the same color of sun-bleached wheat as Dayne's had been. So were the young man's aqua blue eyes.

Don't go there. Focus. This isn't the time or place to mourn Dayne.

Running an IV, I took a new set of vitals, watching as Reynolds's poked and prodded checking for internal injuries. The patient's face was swollen and bloodied. He had a large contusion on his forehead and a deep laceration over his right eyebrow. Blood oozed from his nose and lips, and he had a gash above his ear that looked to be about eight centimeters long. The chicken-shit bastards had worked the poor guy over well.

Doctor Reynolds pressed under the young man's rib cage. The victim screamed in agony.

"Hang in there, sweetheart," I assured in a calm voice. "We're going to get you fixed up. Tell me your name."

"Ever," he murmured.

I gently lifted his split top lip to find both front teeth missing. His gums were bleeding badly. So was the deep laceration on the side of his tongue.

"Evan?" I asked, leaning in close.

"Trevor," he sobbed. "I want Dadddyyy."

About Jenna Jacob

Bestselling Author Jenna Jacob's erotic romance comes from the heart of submission. With over twenty years experience in the dynamics of the BDSM lifestyle, Jenna strives to portray Dominance and submission with a passionate and comprehensive voice. Her stories will make you laugh, cry, and may leave you with a better understanding of the fulfillment found in the BDSM power exchange.

A married mom of four grown children, Jenna and her husband lives in Kansas. Her passions include her family, reading, camping, cooking, music, and riding Harleys. She loves to make people laugh with her outgoing and warped sense of humor. If you're looking for hot romance with a kinky twist, pick up one of Jenna's books.

Connect with me online:
Website: www.jennajacob.com
E Mail: jenna@jennajacob.com
Facebook Fan Page:
https://www.facebook.com/authorjennajacob
Twitter: @jennajacob3
Newsletter: http://bit.ly/1Cj4ZyY

Also from Jenna Jacob:

The Doms Of Genesis
Embracing My Submission
Masters Of My Desire
Master Of My Mind
Saving My Submission
Coming Soon:
Seduced By My Doms

Doms Of Her Life (by Shayla Black, Jenna Jacob, and Isabella LaPearl)
One Dom To Love
The Young And The Submissive
The Bold And The Dominant
Coming Soon:
The Edge Of Dominance

The Diva And The Dom

By Isabella LaPearl
Coming Soon!

"Do you really believe that I can just walk away from you?" His fingers trailed softly up the length of her spine sending a shiver of need pulsing through her again.

"You'll just have to. I haven't anything else to offer you." Cristina shifted to glance back at him over her shoulder, taking in the hard muscled length of his body and wished helplessly for a different outcome. She turned away with a sigh and made to get up. His warm palm in the center of her back stopped her, yet the languid pool of ecstasy from his lovemaking that had drugged her limbs and evaporated her senses had dissipated. The spell of intimacy between them was irrevocably broken.

"I won't allow what we have to end like this, Cristina. Dammit, listen to me. I need to see you again."

David's harsh tone gave way to gentle coaxing. Seven little bites of temptation that tugged at her aching heart, willing her to heed him, as she had his every command of her body.

She concentrated instead on the surf beyond the open doorway, listened as it pounded rhythmically against the shore. Drew deeply of the salty air, savoring the clean fresh scents of the sea and turned her head toward the faint cries of the gulls.

It was so peaceful here.

Even as every part of her insisted that somehow, in some way, this magic between them didn't truly have to end—another part of her already mourned its passing. The timing was wrong, that was all. Somehow their souls had miscalculated, and they'd missed their divine opportunity. Despite that, this meeting of mind, body, and spirit had been inevitable, no matter their wants, they'd both already chosen their respective paths and now they had to follow them.

Prolonging the agony was pointless. Sighing regretfully, Cristina rose from the bed and silently dressed. His accusing stare did nothing to change her mind.

And yet despite the years that would pass between this

moment and next, a part of her she never gave to another remained with him and the stolen hours they'd shared in that little shack by the sea.

About Isabella LaPearl

Isabella LaPearl is a New Zealand-American author of erotic romance. She loves to spin a good yarn and word paint a picture into life. One Dom To Love, The Young And The Submissive and The Bold and The Dominant are her first full-length novels.

Connect with me online:
Website: http://www.isabellalapearl.com
Facebook Fan Page:
https://www.facebook.com/isabellalapearlpage

You Only Love Twice

Masters and Mercenaries, Book 8
By Lexi Blake
Coming February 17, 2015

A woman on a mission

Phoebe Graham is a specialist in deep cover espionage, infiltrating the enemy, observing their practices, and when necessary eliminating the threat. Her latest assignment is McKay-Taggart Security Services, staffed with former military and intelligence operatives. They routinely perform clandestine operations all over the world but it isn't until Jesse Murdoch joins the team that her radar starts spinning. Unfortunately so does her head. He's gorgeous and sweet and her instincts tell her to trust him but she's been burned before, so he'll stay where he belongs—squarely in her sights.

A man on the run

Since the moment his Army unit was captured by jihadists, Jesse's life has been a nightmare. Forced to watch as those monsters tortured and killed his friends, something inside him snapped. When he's finally rescued, everyone has the same question—why did he alone survive? Clouded in accusations and haunted by the faces of those he failed, Jesse struggles in civilian life until McKay-Taggart takes him in. Spending time with Phoebe, the shy and beautiful accountant, makes him feel human for the first time in forever. If someone so innocent and sweet could accept him, maybe he could truly be redeemed.

A love they never expected

When Phoebe receives the order to eliminate Jesse, she must choose between the job she's dedicated her life to and the man who's stolen her heart. Choosing Jesse would mean abandoning everything she believes in, and it might mean sharing his fate because a shadowy killer is dedicated to finishing the job started in Iraq.

* * *

Jesse pushed through the double doors, his whole being surprisingly calm. This was what he needed. He'd been sitting in his office waiting for her to wake up, thinking about how he would handle this interrogation with some modicum of civility.

It was so good to know civility wasn't going to be required.

It wasn't so good to realize that the minute she'd opened that bratty mouth, he'd gotten hard as hell and he wanted to fuck her more than he wanted to figure her out. There was a little voice playing in his head that told him to just get inside her and all those secrets would open for him. All he had to do was thrust inside her tight body and the mysteries of the universe would reveal themselves.

Yeah, he wasn't going to do that. He was going to do his job and find out who she worked for and then he would walk away from her. He wasn't going to hold her tenderly or hope she could love him. No. It was time to grow the fuck up. How was it being through what he'd been through in Iraq hadn't managed to teach him what this one woman had? He needed to shut down and do his job.

But that didn't mean parts of his job couldn't be very pleasurable.

"Uhm, Jesse, don't you think you should handle this in the conference room? It's where Ian planned on keeping her." Adam Miles's voice was an unwelcome intrusion.

"No." He knew the old Jesse would have stopped, but this was between him and Phoebe.

"Adam, I can really explain. This is all one huge misunderstanding." Phoebe tried to bring her head up.

That was an easy move to counter. He brought his hand down on that sweet, sweet ass. Phoebe had the damn prettiest ass he'd ever watched for hours and drooled over, and now he had zero reason to not spank that gorgeous flesh. He heard that sound, that smack as his hand hit her, and he felt her shiver. She didn't scream. Nope. He'd thought if he smacked her good, she would call him a fucking pervert, but he'd been a dumbass idiot and this Phoebe just moaned a little as the slap went through her.

It wasn't the type of moan that would cause him to stop spanking a sub at Sanctum.

Motherfucker. He knew he hadn't been wrong about her. He'd thought there was a submissive streak buried under her "I'm a good girl so don't fuck my sweet little asshole" exterior.

"The only explanation is I'm a dirty little spy and I need to tell my captor everything in order to keep him from slapping my ass silly." He couldn't be professional with her. It wouldn't work. It would only serve to put distance between them, and now he could see that distance was what she'd worked for the whole time. She hadn't let him do more than hold her hand and give her an awkward peck. She'd had him convinced he just wasn't her type, but he could smell her now. Yeah, that wasn't sweet or gentlemanly, but then that obviously didn't work for her. "She likes me slapping her ass. Take a deep whiff, Adam, and you'll be able to tell she's aroused."

She gasped and her whole torso came up off his. "Jesse!"

Yeah, she sounded like a pissed off girlfriend, but she wasn't his girlfriend. She was the woman who had played him and then nearly painted her initials on his chest. And he was the idiot who had stood there and almost begged her to do it.

He cringed at the thought of how stupid he'd been about her. He knew he was ping-ponging, caught between wanting to understand her and wanting to throttle her, but most of all, he wanted to get his hands on her.

He wanted to see just how much she'd lied about.

"You might want to think this thing through, Jesse," Adam began.

He was just about to tell Adam where he could shove his thought process when Big Tag strode out of his office. A thunderous look clouded his boss's face, but Jesse was ready to throw down with whoever he needed to. This was his op and his…fuck, he didn't even know what to call her, but Phoebe was his.

Ian stopped in front of them. "Take her to your office. Do what you need to do but keep it down. Apparently we're still having a baby shower and I have to attend or risk having my balls ripped off my body. I like my balls, Murdoch. Keep her quiet. Charlie's serious about this party thing. When did I fucking lose control? She's not even an employee here."

"No. I'm part owner," Charlotte said, her voice a sharp instrument. She was a beautiful woman with strawberry blonde hair. She rested her hand on the bump on her belly that seemed to get bigger every day. "Eve and I own half this company, you know. And we have all the boobs so try getting around us. Phoebe, I swear to god if I find out you've done one thing to put this company and our people in danger I will take you apart myself. Is that understood? You better hope you can prove you weren't going to hurt Jesse. He's one of my men and I will deal with you."

Phoebe's head came up again. "Your men? That's a little presumptuous, isn't it? You treat him like a puppy you can pat on his head and send away. He isn't yours and if you think you can take me, you're wrong."

Charlotte's lips curled up and Jesse realized Phoebe had just fallen into a trap. "She doesn't like the fact that I said you're mine, Jesse."

Big Tag was frowning at her. "I didn't either."

She waved him off. "I meant as a friend and employee, but Phoebe's brain goes straight for the sexual. I wonder why. Li's right. You're going to owe him a hundred bucks at the end of this thing. She's all Stockholmed out. Who wants cake?"

Into His Dark

The Cimarron Series, Book 1

New…from *USA Today* Bestseller Angel Payne

The Cimarrons:

They're the mysterious, magnetic ruling family of the most secretive kingdom on earth: The Island of Arcadia. No westerners have ever been allowed inside Arcadia's borders…until now.

A new adventure…

Camellia "Cam" Saxon struggles not to pinch herself. Is she really here, as a guest in the castle of the world's most mysterious royal family, working on the only western film crew allowed on the island of Arcadia? A year ago, she was the girl who finished college with a sigh instead of a bang, moving on to a safe job and a steady suburban routine without a blink…

Until she gets the call from a film graduate buddy that will change everything.

A dangerous desire…

Cam's excitement turns to dread in an instant—as soon as she lays eyes on Evrest Cimarron. Beautiful, commanding, and regal, he turns her logic to ash and her blood to fire…making it damn hard to remember the crown on his head.

As an Arcadian alone, Evrest must be thrust into Cam's don't-even-go-there column. As the leader of the kingdom, he's now the face on her delete key, too. A fantasy never to be fed…ever

A journey to the forbidden…

A mishap lands Cam in Evrest's most secret chambers, surrounded by luxury beyond imagination—and seduced by a creature who is no longer charming host and alluring king but powerful, passionate man. In Evrest's arms, Cam learns she has new identities, too. The sensible girl is abandoned for a woman of illicit needs and sinful desires.

It's the most incredible night of her life. The most perfect man she's known. The most flawless fit for her soul.

A mistake she can never make again.

Sneak Preview Excerpt

"Hello."

I watched every mesmerizing inch of his lips move with the word, though the sound seemed to resonate through my heart, not my ears. On the other hand, nothing in the room moved again, so it was easy for me to hear both the velvety syllables.

"Hi." I didn't push it above a rasp. I didn't want to restart the world yet—though somewhere far away, a classical guitar and a harp blended in one of the most beautiful pieces of music I'd ever heard. It helped carry my soul's plea to heaven.

Please don't let this end.

Never.

Ever.

Please.

He reached. Slipped both his hands around mine.

And the certainty encompassed my heart.

I'd been waiting for this moment. For a very long time. Perhaps forever. The air in my lungs knew it. The very marrow of my bones knew it. The reaches of my soul knew it.

Why? How?

I didn't know the questions had fallen out aloud—maybe they hadn't—but as he branded his gaze deeper into mine, I knew he'd somehow heard. The corners of his mouth turn up a little, just enough to sluice all my nerve endings with high-octane awareness. Everything became him. Only him.

"Thank you for coming." The words, seeming rote and protocol, evoked much more. There was a meaning beyond his meaning, but I couldn't grasp it. *What are you trying to say?*

I hoped my eyes conveyed the question because I couldn't speak the words. Tiny crinkles formed at the corners of his eyes, as if assuring me there was an answer to that, and he couldn't wait to share it with me.

"I'm happy to be here."

Nope. *Please try your connection again.* "Happy" was for free hot fudge sundaes on my birthday or a freak heat wave in January. This was something past happy. Something that didn't have a word. Something twined to the completion of my hands inside his, my nearness to him, the electricity of my whole body in his presence.

"Are you certain of that?" His thumbs caressed the insides of my wrists, shooting rockets through my belly and fireworks through my brain.

Fireworks? Seriously, Cam?

But it made sense. Weirdly, insanely, suddenly, everything just…made sense.

"It's just hard to believe this is happening." I'd caught the double meaning virus, too—and it felt pretty nice. Until now, the whole living-in-a-dream thing was confined to excitement about the movie and simply being here in Arcadia. That was before this. Before him. Before the bubble that lowered over the two of us, this strange and wonderful cocoon sealed by the bridge of our touch, the embrace of our stares, the lock of our spirits…

Not just meeting each other. Recognizing each other.

"I am Evrest." He dipped toward me, an edge of bashfulness in his voice. So beautiful. I treasured every note, gluing the sound to my memory like a precious flower in a scrapbook.

"I'm…Cam."

"Cam." He extended the last note, almost turning the word into a silken song. My lips parted as I imagined how it would feel if he did that against my bare skin, though I didn't dare venture on what body part. Did it matter? His smile, parting wider, provided that definitive answer. Didn't matter one damn bit.

22650969R00235

Made in the USA
Middletown, DE
05 August 2015